RaeAnne THAYNE
CARO CARSON

Orchard Bay

ISBN-13: 978-1-335-92662-3

Orchard Bay

Copyright © 2018 by Harlequin Books S.A.

The publisher acknowledges the copyright holders
of the individual works as follows:

Saving Grace © 2000 by RaeAnne Thayne

Her Texas Rescue Doctor © 2016 by Caro Carson

Recycling programs
for this product may
not exist in your area.

This edition published by arrangement with Harlequin Books S.A.

For questions and comments about the quality of this book, please contact us at
CustomerService@Harlequin.com.

® and TM are trademarks of the publisher. Trademarks indicated with ® are registered
in the United States Patent and Trademark Office, the Canadian Intellectual Property
Office and in other countries.

Printed in U.S.A.

HARLEQUIN®
TM www.Harlequin.com

CONTENTS

Saving Grace

RaeAnne THAYNE

To Donald and Janice Thayne, for sharing the beauty of the Islands, and for raising such a wonderful son.

Special thanks to Cissy Serrao of Poakalani Hawaiian Quilt Designs in Honolulu for her vast knowledge of this exquisite art form.

CHAPTER ONE

IF SHE WAS GOING TO DO THIS, IT WOULD HAVE to be soon.

Grace Solarez crouched in the dirt and watched cars move in an endless rhythm past the orchards that marched along this desolate stretch of interstate.

Three-hundred-sixty-five days ago she would have savored the sensory assault around her: the sweetness of the apples just a few weeks away from harvest, the tweet-tweet-tweet of the crickets; the cool, moist night breeze kissing her face.

Now, she could only watch the headlights slice through the night and wonder which pair she would see right before she died.

A mosquito sunk its teeth into her right biceps, honed and toughened by the last few months of hard labor on the docks. She glanced down briefly at the first sharp needle prick of pain, then ignored it. What was the point in swatting it away?

She had blood to spare.

Her eyes felt gritty, as if she'd grabbed a handful of dirt

and rubbed it across her face. And she was tired. So tired. For a year she had gone through the motions of living, functioning on only the most basic of levels. Breathing, eating, sleeping. She couldn't bear it another day, another hour, another minute.

This grief was too huge, too constant. Nothing slipped through it, not even the smallest shadow of respite. She couldn't survive it anymore. The grief and the guilt had become burdens too heavy for her to carry.

She pulled the snapshot from the pocket of her T-shirt one last time. Moonlight filtered across the image, washing out the colors to a grayish blue, but she could still see the mischief glimmering in her daughter's eyes. She traced Marisa's smile with her fingertip.

"I'm sorry, Marisita," she whispered. "So sorry. I tried—I swear, I tried—but I'm not strong enough. I just can't do it anymore."

Looking at the picture—at the image of a laughing, beautiful child frozen forever in time—was too excruciating to endure for long. After a few moments she carefully slipped it back into her pocket. Her right hand lingered over her heart protectively while she watched the mesmerizing parade of oncoming headlights, trying not to wonder if she would feel the impact of the collision before she died.

What she was about to do was a mortal sin, she knew. If Padre Luis—the bitter old priest at Tia Sofia's church—could be believed, she would be damned for eternity, consigned forever to a special kind of hell reserved for those who defied God's will.

But what did she care? She'd already been damned in this life, why not the next one, too? Besides, she had no problem pissing off a God vengeful enough to take away the only thing that had ever mattered to her.

Now, a few minutes past midnight on the anniversary of the day her life had effectively ended, she might as well make it official.

Muscles tensed and ready, she scanned the traffic, trying to pick her moment. From the orchard elevated six feet or so above the roadway, she had a good view of traffic in both directions.

Headlights a mile or so in the distance caught her attention. Even in the dark—and even absorbed, as she was, in the unchangeable past—she could tell it was moving much faster than the other vehicles, weaving and darting crazily from lane to lane.

From this distance, it looked like some fancy foreign make. A Porsche, judging by the sleek, curvy lines. Probably some spoiled rich kid coming home drunk after a night of clubbing.

As it approached her spot in the orchard, she watched the little sports car come dangerously close to hitting the fender of a pickup truck. The pickup driver apparently didn't like being tailgated and she saw the angry red glare of brake lights suddenly light up the night.

The sports car driver apparently saw them, too, but just an instant too late. He slammed on the brakes and yanked the wheel to the left, sending the car hurtling toward the wide barrow pit in the median.

Just before he would have slammed into a reflector post, the driver jerked on the wheel again, overcorrecting the car and sending it screeching back across the lanes of traffic.

At such a high rate of speed, the driver couldn't possibly regain control of the vehicle. Just as it passed her, the Porsche rolled, flipping side over side until it came to rest upside down in the empty drainage ditch a few hundred yards ahead of her.

For an instant, she stood stunned, disoriented by the abrupt, jarring shift in her emotions, from weary despair to adrenaline-laced shock in a matter of seconds.

Smoke began to pour from the mangled carcass of the car and she could smell that scent peculiar to accidents: a combination of gasoline, scorched rubber and hot metal.

What were the chances of the drunk walking away from such a crash? It was hard to gauge. When she'd still been on the job, she had worked accidents she would have sworn no one could possibly survive where the victims came out completely unscathed. And she had worked simple, no-frills fender-benders that resulted in fatalities. Every situation was a crapshoot, like so much of police work.

She looked through the filter of leaves but couldn't see any activity around the car. Her stomach churned suddenly, unexpectedly, as she fought the urge to check out the scene, to make at least some effort to help the idiot driver.

She didn't want to get involved, couldn't *handle* getting involved. She could hardly think past her own agonizing grief. But she had been a cop for almost a decade and it was hard to ignore those powerful instincts.

The battle with indecision lasted for only a few seconds. With a defeated sigh, Grace scrambled down the small slope toward the accident scene.

A few other motorists had already stopped and a small crowd had gathered around the periphery of the accident scene. They all looked stunned, with the kind of dazed disbelief civilians share during traumatic incidents.

Nobody seemed inclined to move closer, which was just as well. A shower of sparks rained down beneath the sports car's hood and she was afraid it was only a matter of time before those sparks ignited the fuel line and the whole thing exploded.

Just as she reached the edge of the crowd, a man pulled

himself out of the car, his face a bloody mass of cuts and his arm cradled against his side. He looked scruffy and ill-kempt, with dark, shaggy hair and a long, droopy mustache. Through a rip in his T-shirt, she could see a twisted tattoo, some kind of snake peeking through.

Not exactly what she would have expected from the driver of such an expensive car. Most likely it was hot.

Regardless, he would walk away, like so many drunk drivers, she thought with disgust. He weaved a bit and started to topple over, but righted himself just before she reached him. Grace grabbed his arm—the one with the tattoo—and helped him the rest of the way to safety.

"Anybody else in there?" Grace had to yell to be heard over the traffic still speeding past.

The man didn't answer, just gave her a bleary-eyed stare, so she tried again. "I said, is anybody in there? Was there anybody else in the car with you?"

The question finally seemed to sink in. The man looked back at the car and she could swear there was perfect clarity in his red-rimmed eyes, then a strange, furtive look slunk across his battered features.

"No," he said hoarsely. She could see a ruby earring glint through the shaggy dark locks when he shook his head. "Nobody else. Just me."

A plump woman with teased blond hair and wearing surgical scrubs rushed over to them. "I'm a nurse," she said, and quickly, efficiently, led the drunk farther from the wreckage.

Grace watched them for a moment then turned to give the vehicle one last look. The police would be here soon. She could already see the faint flicker of flashing lights off in the distance. Somebody in the crowd must have a cell phone to summon them so quickly.

She wondered if the patrol would be someone she knew,

then discarded the thought. Not this far east. She doubted if she was even in King County anymore, although she didn't quite know where she was, exactly. She'd been driving all evening trying to outrun her ghosts and it was only by chance that they had caught up with her here, on this isolated stretch of road. She knew she'd come some distance, though.

Wherever she was, she knew she didn't want to be here when the police arrived. She turned and would have slipped back into the safety and solitude of the orchard when she thought she heard a tiny cry.

Marisa.

Her daughter's voice called to her, haunted her. It seemed to float across the noise of vehicles whizzing by, past the crowd's excited hum, above the scream of approaching sirens.

Was she the only one who could hear it? She must be—no one else in the crowd reacted at all.

Her head buzzed from the fumes and the noise and the emotional trauma of the last few hours. Maybe she was hearing things.

"Daddy! Help me!" she heard. Louder this time, but still faint. She frowned and shook her head in confusion. Why would Marisa be calling for a father she never knew, for a seventeen-year-old boy who had refused to take responsibility for the child he'd helped create in a brief, forbidden moment of passion.

It made no sense. Still, she had to find out.

"What are you, crazy, lady? That thing's going to blow any second now." A burly trucker tried to bar her way but she shoved past, barely aware of him, and slipped away from the crowd toward the wreckage, toward the beckoning call of her dead daughter.

She ignored the shouts of alarm behind her, focused only

on following that tiny voice. Her daughter needed her and this time—dear God, this time—she would be there to help her.

The instant she reached the overturned car and knelt in the gravel of the shoulder to look through the window, reality hit her with a cold, mean slap.

It wasn't Marisa calling her at all. It was a small blond-haired girl, several years younger than her daughter would have been, strapped into her seatbelt and suspended upside down in the passenger seat of the smashed sports car.

Smoke poured from the hood, obscuring her vision and burning her eyes and throat. Grace coughed and tried to wave it away so she could see into the vehicle.

"I want my daddy!" the girl cried, her voice wobbly with fear.

A cold fury swept through Grace. The driver had *known* the little girl was in there, Grace was sure of it. That moment of clarity had been unmistakable. Yet he had lied and said he was alone in the car, consigning his daughter to a fiery, gruesome death.

Not if she could help it.

"There's a kid in here!" she shouted with a quick look over her shoulder. "I need help!"

The other motorists just stared at her, not one of them willing to risk death for a stranger. The flames licked the side of the car now, and the roar of the fire seemed louder. She was going to have to move fast. Conscious that with every passing second her chances of rescuing the girl—and of escaping the inevitable blast herself—diminished, Grace sank to her stomach and pulled herself in through the driver's-side window. The rollover had smashed the other door and she could see no other way in or out.

She dragged herself along the overturned roof of the car, heedless of the scrapes and cuts she earned along the way.

When Grace reached her, the girl appeared to be on the verge of hysteria. Who wouldn't be, strapped upside down in a burning car?

The first order of business was calming her down, she decided, although she knew she had precious seconds to spare.

"Hi. I'm Grace."

"Are you an angel?"

The soft question nearly destroyed her. "Nope," she answered. The understatement of the decade. "Just somebody who's going to help you. What's your name, honey?"

"Emma. My daddy calls me Little Em."

If we make it through this, Little Em, I hope your daddy rots in prison for the rest of his life for child endangerment. She let her fury give her strength while she battled to unhook the stubborn safety belt latch from this awkward angle.

Despite her efforts, the belt refused to give. She yanked and pulled for several more seconds, then knew she couldn't afford to mess with it any longer.

"Okay, Emma, this isn't working. Let's see if we can slip you out of there." Her heart pounding with exertion, she pulled the shoulder strap behind the girl's back and supported her weight while Emma tried to wriggle out of the lap belt.

"Almost there," she encouraged. "Just a little more. That's it."

With a small cry, Emma toppled free and into her arms. Grace cradled her with one arm and tried to slither back out to the window. Both of them wouldn't fit through the opening at the same time, but when she tried to push the little girl through ahead of her, Emma's little arms clung tightly around her neck.

"Honey, you have to let go. I'm right behind you, I promise."

The girl must have finally understood because she let Grace

push her through the window frame. She crawled out after her and scrambled to her feet.

Fueled only by adrenaline now, Grace lifted Emma into her arms and cradled the girl's head against her shoulder as she raced away from the car. She made it only a few feet before she heard a hissing rumble behind her and knew with sick certainty that she wouldn't be able to reach safety before the car blew up.

She wasn't ready to die.

In that instant, her whole world seemed to shift, to spin crazily, and she discovered a fierce survival instinct lurking somewhere deep inside her.

She wasn't ready to die.

It was the ultimate irony. She'd come so close to killing herself and now—when that bastard Fate finally decided to cooperate—leave it to her to change her mind.

Be careful what you wish for, Gracie.

With one last, tremendous burst of energy, she dropped to the pavement, her body curled protectively around the little girl, an instant before the explosion rocked through the night, shaking the pavement and rippling the leaves of the apple trees.

She cried out as something sharp and scorching hot ripped across the flesh of her back. For a moment, she could only concentrate on breathing past the pain.

After several seconds, when it faded somewhat and she could think again, she straightened. She must have been hit by flying debris. It hurt like hell but she was alive and so was the child she held.

"Wow. That was exciting." Her voice sounded hoarse, not her own. "Are you okay, sweetie?"

She felt the little girl's hair brush against her cheek as Emma nodded. "I think so."

Grace hugged her, dizzied by the pain from her back and the waves of grief crashing over her at the feel of the warm, small weight in her arms, against her chest.

Oh Marisa, Marisa.

"There are people who can help you now," she creaked out. She could see three highway patrol vehicles on the scene, as well as a fire engine and paramedics. Already, rescue workers were heading toward them carrying a stretcher for the child.

It was suddenly vitally important that she get away before they arrived. She didn't want to face the inevitable questions, couldn't bear to have anybody poking and fussing over her.

She pulled her arms away from Emma and climbed to her feet, ignoring the razor blades of pain slicing across her back where the blast had scorched through her clothing.

"Don't leave me! Please don't leave me!" the little girl begged.

Grace summoned the last of her energy and managed a facsimile of a smile. "You don't need me now, sweetie. You'll be just fine. I promise."

The paramedics were almost upon them. In the bustle and confusion, it was easy for Grace to slip through the crowd. No one even tried to stop her as she made her way carefully, slowly, back to the cool refuge of the orchard.

The place was a dump.

Jack Dugan double-checked the slip of paper he held with the address on it. It was a shipping invoice, but it had been the only piece of paper he could find when Mike called an hour ago to give him the information they'd been seeking for a week now.

The numbers hanging crookedly against the cinderblock walls of the apartment building matched the numbers on the paper, but he found it hard to believe anybody actually lived here.

The place was falling apart. Weeds thrust through the cracked sidewalk and choked what likely had been a flower garden once. The peeling aquamarine paint of the roof and shutters had probably been cheerful—trendy, even—thirty years ago but now it made the building look just like the rest of the neighborhood: worn-out, tired, an area sagging into itself with a kind of quiet despair.

Grace Solarez lived here alone, according to Mike and the rest of the team of private investigators he'd paid a hefty amount to locate her. She had no husband, no kids, no pets. Just a failed career as a Seattle cop and a dead-end job hauling freight on the docks.

He shoved the Jaguar into Park and studied the building. Inside those walls could be the answers to the tangled quest he'd embarked upon a week ago. Inside, he would find either an amazingly heroic stranger who had faced almost certain death to rescue his daughter—an angel, Emma called her—or he would find the truth about Emma's kidnapping.

Anticipation curled through him. Since that terrible night, he had tried to be patient while the investigators—both the police and his own—followed various leads to determine the identity of the mysterious stranger who had come out of nowhere to pluck his daughter from the wreckage of the stolen car her kidnapper had used to take her from him.

They'd had precious little to go on—just a few eyewitness descriptions of a slim, wild-eyed Hispanic woman and a well-handled snapshot that had been left at the scene, a photograph of a little girl in two thick dark braids giving a mischievous smile to the camera.

It hadn't been much, but it had been enough. He now had a name to put with the woman. Grace Solarez. And it was only a matter of time until he could find out more, until he could learn whether she had helped the "bad man" Emma described as her kidnapper escape in the noise and confusion after the accident.

No one remembered seeing her drive up before the accident or drive away after it. It was as if she appeared out of thin air then disappeared into it again. What had she been doing there? How had she managed to slip through the crowd? And had she taken the kidnapper with her?

One way or another, he would get to the bottom of it.

A cool September wind, heavy with impending rain, rattled the rusty chains of an old metal swingset in what passed for a play area as he made his way across the uneven pavement to apartment 14-B.

Did the little girl in the snapshot play there? he wondered. It hardly looked safe, with two swings barely hanging on and the bare bones of a glider with no seats swaying drunkenly in the wind.

If Grace Solarez turned out to be just as she appeared—a brave stranger who had risked her own life to save his daughter's—he planned to do whatever it took to ensure she wouldn't have to live in this bleak place anymore.

If not—if it turned out she had a role in his daughter's ordeal—he would see that she paid, and paid dearly.

As he climbed the rickety ironwork stairway to the second level of the building, he thought he saw a curtain twitch in the apartment next to 14-B. Other than that, the place seemed eerily deserted.

He rang the doorbell and heard its buzz echo inside the apartment, then waited impatiently for her to answer. She had to be here. He'd called McManus Freight, her employer, as soon as he hung up from talking to Mike and had learned

Grace Solarez hadn't reported to work since the night of the kidnapping, eight days ago.

Besides that, Mike said she had one vehicle registered in her name, an old junkheap he could plainly see decomposing over in the parking lot.

He rang the buzzer again and added several sharp knocks for good measure. The curtains fluttered next door again and he was just about to see if the nosy neighbor might be able to tell him anything about his quarry's whereabouts when he heard a faint, muted rustling behind the door inside her apartment.

It swung open, barely wide enough for the safety chain to pull taut. Through the narrow slit, he could make out little more than tangled brown hair and a pair of huge dark eyes, very much like the pair belonging to the girl in the snapshot he held.

"Grace Solarez?"

The eyes narrowed suspiciously. "Yes?"

Now that he was here, he hadn't the faintest idea where to start. He cleared his throat. "Hello. My name is Jack Dugan. I need to speak with you, please."

"About what?" Her voice sounded thready, strange, as if she'd just taken a hit of straight oxygen in one of those hip bars downtown.

Maybe she was a junkie. Maybe that's why she hadn't waited around long enough to give a statement to the police and maybe that's why she was no longer with the Seattle PD.

Would a junkie have stuck around the scene long enough to rescue a terrified little girl?

So many damn questions and she held the key to all of them.

He pushed them away for now. "I've had investigators working around the clock for the past week, trying to locate you." He watched carefully for some reaction in those eyes: curiosity, guilt, anything, but they held no expression, as deep and fathomless as a desert canyon.

The nosy neighbor was at it again. He could see movement in the window and fought down annoyance. He didn't care for an audience and somehow he doubted she would either. "May I come in?" He tried a friendly, casual smile he was far from feeling. "I swear, I left my ax-murdering kit at home."

Those eyes studied him for a moment longer, then she pushed up the safety latch and opened the door.

The inside of the apartment was as depressing as the exterior. It had the unlived-in air of a seedy motel room, the kind where they charge you extra for sheets.

A particularly ugly gold-and-blue couch ran the length of one wall and a matching chair faced it, but they were the only pieces of furniture in the room. The only *anything* in the room. He frowned. There were no pictures on the wall, no books, no knickknacks. None of the little personal items people liked to scatter around the corners of their lives.

So Grace Solarez wasn't much of an interior decorator. There was no law against that.

He shifted his attention from her home and looked at her—really looked at her—for the first time. She appeared as tired and worn-out as her surroundings, with sallow skin and huge purple shadows under her eyes.

And she was younger than he would have expected. Late-twenties, maybe. Certainly too young to have that look of fragile despair haunting those big dark eyes.

She wore a thin T-shirt, faded gray from many washings, a pair of worn cutoffs and nothing else. His gaze was drawn to her long, slim legs, to the soft curve of her breasts under the threadbare cotton, and Jack was astonished—and disgusted—at himself for the little kick of awareness in his gut.

Maybe Piper McCall was right. His business partner was always telling him he'd been too long without a woman. There might be some truth to that, especially if he could get all worked up about one who looked like she'd been on the wrong end of a runaway bus.

She had left the door open, so she could call for help if he decided to attack, he imagined, and now she clutched the frame as if she couldn't stand without it.

"Why did you say you've been looking for me?" Her voice again sounded thin, disoriented.

"I don't believe I said." He decided to put his suspicions away for now. Whatever her reasons for being there, whatever her involvement, she had plucked Emma from that burning car where the man who took her would have been willing to let her burn.

"I've come to thank you," he finally said.

"For?"

"For saving my daughter's life," he said quietly.

She frowned and he noticed her knuckles were bony and white on the doorframe. "Wh-what?"

"Oh, and to give you this." He thrust out the picture.

At the sight of it in his hands, those huge dark eyes widened even farther and what little color he could see in her face leached away like sheets left hanging too long in the sun.

With a soft, almost apologetic moan, Grace Solarez collapsed in a tangled heap on her gold shag carpet.

CHAPTER TWO

FOR AN INSTANT AFTER SHE FELL, JACK JUST stared in shock at the tangle of dark hair hiding her face. Maybe she *was* a junkie coming off a bad trip. Maybe that's why she risked almost certain death to save Emma—because she was too high to know any better, so whacked out she had lost all sense of self-preservation.

The reminder of how very much he owed Grace Solarez—junkie or not—spurred him to quick action and he knelt by her side. "Ma'am? Ms. Solarez?"

She didn't answer. He pushed back a thick hank of hair to find her eyes closed, her face the color of faded newsprint. Her skin felt hot, and up close she looked even more haggard than she had at first, with those dark circles ringing her eyes and cracked, swollen lips.

If not for the slight rise and fall of her chest under the thin shirt, he would have thought she was dead. He started to roll her over but a tiny cry of pain slipped from her dry lips, stopping him cold.

He sat back on his haunches. What could be wrong with her?

How the hell was he supposed to know? he answered his own question. He was a pilot, not a damn doctor.

Should he slap her, see if that would rouse her? He started to, then stopped before his hand could complete the movement. It seemed highly presumptuous to strike a woman he had just met.

Cold water might do the trick. That's how they did it in Hollywood, anyway. He stepped gingerly over her prone form to reach the sink in the small kitchen area and found a clean drinking glass in the dish drainer next to it. After filling it quickly with rusty-looking water from the tap, he turned back toward her.

And caught his first sight of her back.

He growled a raw expletive, the water glass nearly slipping from his hand. What the hell had she done to herself? The cotton of her shirt was soaked with what looked like fresh blood and it seemed to stick to her back in spots. If that was as painful as it looked, no wonder she had passed out. She needed medical attention and she needed it now.

Before he could find the phone to dial the emergency number, she stirred again. This time she started to roll to her back. The pain must have stopped her because she moaned and froze at an awkward angle.

"Easy now," he murmured. "Let's just roll you to your stomach."

Grace Solarez whipped her head around at his voice, her eyes wide with disoriented panic. "Who..." The single word seemed to sap her energy because her eyes closed and for a moment he thought she had passed out again until they fluttered open again. "Who are you?" she finally asked.

"Jack Dugan. Remember? Right before you decided to take a header on me, I was trying to explain why I was here."

The confusion faded a bit from her dark eyes. "You have my picture," she whispered. "What have you done with it?"

She tried to prop herself up but he laid a hand on the hot skin of her forearm to stop her. "Easy. I don't think you ought to be moving around too much right now. Here's your picture. I haven't done anything with it. It's just like you left it."

He pulled the photograph from his shirt pocket and handed it to her. She gazed at it for a moment, then clutched it to her as if he had just handed her a briefcase full of diamonds.

"Thank you." Her voice was even huskier than before. "I have others, but this...this is my favorite."

The raw emotion on her face made him shift uncomfortably. "No need to thank me. I'm just returning what belongs to you. Now why don't you tell me what you did to yourself. Is it a cut?"

Her cheek rubbed against the ugly carpet in what he took for denial. "Burn," she murmured. "Tried to put something on it but I couldn't reach the whole thing. Think it's infected."

"How did it happen?"

She closed her eyes again. "Car exploded. Couldn't run fast enough."

His heart seemed to stutter in his chest as he stared at her. She did this to herself pulling his Emma out of the crash? He reached blindly for her hand and squeezed it tightly. "We need to get you to a hospital."

Grace lifted her head, the panic back in the flaring of her pupils. Her hand fluttered in his like a tiny butterfly trapped in a net. "No! No hospital!"

"You're hurt. You need medical attention."

"No hospital. Promise!"

She seemed so agitated, he didn't know what else to do but agree. "Fine. Whatever you say. Settle down now, ma'am, or you're going to make that thing start bleeding again."

But he was speaking to the walls of her dingy little apartment, he realized. Grace Solarez had headed back into the ozone.

He bit out the kind of oath that would have earned him a sharp rap on the knuckles with a wooden spoon if Lily had heard it. What was he supposed to do now? He had an unconscious woman on his hands with God knows what kind of injury. And not just any woman, either, but the one who appeared to have risked her life—who had sustained an incredibly painful injury—to rescue his daughter from a burning vehicle.

He couldn't possibly leave her in this dump of an apartment by herself, not when she was in this kind of pain. And he had just given his word he wouldn't take her to the hospital.

Lily. Lily Kihualani could take care of her. He seized on the idea with vast relief. She was always looking for somebody else to mother and with her nursing background, she would know just how to treat a burn like this one.

And if she didn't, he'd make her find out.

It was only after he had carried Grace Solarez out of her apartment, laid her carefully in the back seat of the Jaguar and pulled out onto the highway back toward the ferry and home that he realized, with a grimace, that he hadn't been able to answer a single damn question about Grace Solarez.

She awoke to agonizing pain.

"Shhh little *keiki,*" a voice as comforting as the sea murmured in her ear. "Hush now. Stay still."

Someone was taking a hot poker to her back and she was supposed to just lie here and take it? Yeah, right. Forget it, sister. She tried to rise but strong arms held her in place.

"How much longer is this going to take, Lily?" A deep male voice asked. It sounded familiar but she couldn't see anything past the floodlights of pain exploding behind her eyelids.

Her head throbbed at the effort but still she tried to place the voice. She had a fleeting, strangely comforting memory of a sun-bronzed stranger with a sweet smile and eyes the pure, vivid green of new leaves.

He'd given her back Marisa. She frowned. That was impossible, wasn't it? Marisa was dead, had been gone for a year. No one could bring her back. No one.

"It'll take as long as it takes," the sea-voice answered. "No more, no less."

"I think she's coming back to us. She's going to hurt like hell when she wakes up."

"You think I don't know that? That there's one nasty burn."

"Can't you give her something to take away the pain?"

"What do you think I am, some kind of miracle worker?"

The other voice was like waves crashing against the rocks now. Listening to it made her head ache as if she were stuck in a room full of pounding hammers.

"I'm not a doctor," it went on. "I said take her to the hospital. Would you listen to me? No! She stays here, you said. She don't want no hospital. Okay then. You want me to fix up the *wahine,* I fix up the *wahine.* But I don't need you yappin' at me."

"Sorry."

"You better be. Now hold her still while I put the ointment on."

Fire streaked down her back again as cruel hands rubbed the raw skin of her back. Grace fought to hold on to consciousness but the pain was too great, screaming and clawing at her. In a desperate bid to escape it, she finally surrendered to the quiet, peaceful place inside her.

The next time she opened her eyes, it was to find two huge

green eyes and a head full of blond curls peeking over the side of the bed. Emma, she remembered. The child she had pulled from that wreck, what seemed a lifetime ago. What was she doing in the middle of her nightmare?

"Hi," Emma chirped.

Grace tried to answer but her throat was thick, gritty, like she'd swallowed a quart jar full of sand. Her back felt as if the skin had been flayed open and scoured with the same stuff.

The burn she had suffered from the flying debris of the explosion, she remembered.

She had tried to care for her injuries on her own but hadn't been able to reach the center of her back well enough to apply salve to the burn or even to bandage it.

She had done her best, but by the third day after the accident she had become shaky, feverish, disoriented. She remembered weird, nightmarish visions of whirling cars and demons with orange eyes and men who would leave little girls to burn to death.

The blistering skin must have become infected. That explained the fever, the dizziness, the hallucinations. So how did she get from curling up in her single bed with its thin, lumpy mattress—afraid to move for the pain that would claw across her skin if she did—to this strange room with its cool linen sheets and a curly-haired little elf-spy?

"Are you gonna die like my mama?"

Startled, Grace blinked at the girl watching her with a forehead furrowed by concern. She cleared her throat and tried to speak but couldn't force the words past the sand.

A crystal pitcher of ice and water and a clean glass waited tantalizingly close, on the table next to the bed. She fumbled her fingers out to reach it but came up about six inches short. After several tries, she let her arm flop to the side of the bed in frustration.

Emma must have understood. "You want a drink?" she asked eagerly. "I'll get it. I can even pour it all by myself."

With two hands around the pitcher and her tongue caught carefully between her teeth with fierce concentration, she filled the glass then carefully set the pitcher back on the table.

"Lily said you prob'ly wouldn't be able to drink right from a cup at first because you can't turn over, so I said you could use my bendy straws. See?" she said, with a proud grin that revealed a gap in her upper row of teeth.

She helped Grace find the straw then held the cup steady while she sipped. In all her life, she didn't think she'd ever tasted anything as absolutely heavenly as that ice water. It washed away the sand, leaving only a scratchy ache in her throat.

"Thank you," she murmured when she'd had enough. Her voice sounded rough and gravely, as if it hadn't been used for a long while.

"You're welcome," the little girl said. "Lily and my daddy said I'm not supposed to bother you but I'm not, am I? I'm helping."

Something didn't make sense. It took her several seconds before she realized what had been nagging at her subconscious. *I've come to thank you for saving my daughter's life,* the golden-haired stranger had said. His daughter.

If he was Emma's father, who was the man who had been driving the car that night, the scruffy-looking drunk with the dark hair and tattoo who had been willing to let the little girl die?

Somehow it didn't seem appropriate to ask the child. "Where am I?" she asked instead.

"My house. My daddy brought you here yesterday." The little girl's forehead crinkled again. "Or maybe it was the day before. I forget."

Grace tried to remember coming here but couldn't summon anything but fragmented images after opening the door to the stranger Emma claimed was her father. "Why am I here?"

"Daddy said you were sick and we needed to take care of you for a while. Lily put some gunk on your back. It stinks." The girl bent down until her face was only inches away from hers, until she could feel the moist, milk-scented warmth of her breath on her cheek.

"Are you gonna die?" Emma asked again.

She had wanted to, hadn't she? She remembered headlights and the sharp bite of a mosquito and a dark night of despair, and then that survival instinct bubbling up inside her out of nowhere when she thought the car would explode.

Did she still want to die? She didn't want to think about it right now.

"My mama died when I was only two," Emma confided. "She was in an airplane crash. She didn't live with us but I still cried a lot."

"I'm sure you did."

"Who's that?"

Grace's gaze followed the direction of Emma's finger. She was completely unprepared for the agonizing pain that clutched her stomach at the sight of Marisa's picture propped against a lamp on the bedside table. She must have been so focused on the pitcher of water she hadn't noticed it before.

She absorbed those little gamine features—as familiar to her as her own. The big dark eyes, the dimpled smile, the long glossy braids. The grief welled up inside her, completely blocking the physical pain of the burn.

"Is that your little girl?"

Grace nodded. "I...yes," she whispered.

"Where is she?"

31

A cemetery, a cold grave marked by a plain, unadorned headstone, all she had been able to afford after the funeral expenses.

"She died." The words were wrenched from her. They sounded harsh and mean but the little girl didn't seem to notice.

"Just like my mama." Emma's face softened with concern and she patted Grace's arm. "Did you cry a lot, too?"

Buckets of tears. Oceans of them. Her heart hadn't stopped weeping for a year.

Before she could form her thoughts into an answer appropriate for a five-year-old girl, the door opened and the man who had come to her apartment, who had brought her Marisa's picture, entered the room.

He wore tan khakis and an icy blue polo shirt. With his slightly long, sun-streaked hair and tan, he looked like the kind of man who had nothing more pressing to worry about than whether he'd remembered to wax his surfboard.

When she looked closer, though, she recognized an indefinable air of danger about him. He reminded her of a tawny cougar, coiled and ready to pounce.

What had he said his name was? She sorted through the jumbled-up memories until she came up with it: Jack, wasn't it? Jack Dugan.

"Emma!" Jack Dugan said in a loud whisper. "You know you're not supposed to be in here. What do you think you're doing, young lady?"

"I helped Grace get a drink, Daddy. She was thirsty so I poured her some water all by myself."

He turned his head quickly from his daughter toward Grace. "You're awake."

She suddenly felt vulnerable, off-kilter, lying facedown in a strange bed, in an unfamiliar room, watching the world from this odd, sideways angle. Her stomach fluttered like it used to in the old days before she went out on an unknown disturbance call.

She blinked at him but said nothing.

"She waked up and I helped her get a drink all by myself," Emma announced again.

He gave his daughter a smile of such amazing sweetness it completely transformed him, gentled those lean, rugged features. His eyes warmed, darkened. Instead of a cougar, now he looked like a sleek, satisfied tomcat letting a kitten crawl all over him.

The little girl dimpled back and Grace's chest felt tight and achy at the obvious bond between the two of them.

"What a good nurse you are, Little Em," Jack said.

"Just like Lily, yeah?"

He chuckled and tweaked her chin. "Just like Lily but not so bossy."

Lily was the one who had put the "gunk" on her back, Emma had said. She gathered Lily was the sea-voice.

From her sideways perspective, Grace watched him pull a chair to the side of the bed and tug Emma onto his lap. Those vivid green eyes studied her intensely, like a boy watching a bug trying to scurry along the sidewalk, and she again felt exposed, stripped bare before him, even with the soft quilt covering her.

"How are you feeling this afternoon?"

"Peachy," she muttered.

"I could probably round up some aspirin for you but that's the best I can do. If you would let me take you to a hospital, you could probably get your hands on some kind of serious pain medication. I imagine something like that would hit the spot right about now."

No hospitals. Hospitals were anguish and death. Doctors

who told you, without any emotion at all, that your world had just ended. "I don't need a hospital."

"That's a matter of debate, Ms. Solarez."

"What is there to debate, Mr. Dugan? I don't want to go to the hospital and you can't admit me without my permission." She knew she sounded petulant, childish, but she couldn't help herself. *I don't want to and you can't make me.* Exhausted suddenly, as if her brief spurt of defiance had drained her last ounce of energy, Grace rolled to her side, wincing as pain scorched along her nerve endings. "I appreciate what you've done for me but I—I just want to go home."

It was a lie. She hated that apartment, hated the gray desolation of the neighborhood. But it was as far as she could get from the cheerful little two-bedroom cottage near the university, with its white shutters and the basketball hoop over the garage and the wooden swingset in the backyard she and Marisa had built together.

She had lived there for a month after her daughter's death and then couldn't bear it any longer. She had wanted to sell it but Beau had talked her out of it, so now she was renting to a married couple. Schoolteachers, both of them, with a son about Emma's age.

The hovel she lived in now was her penance, her punishment for the sin of not protecting her daughter.

"You wouldn't be able to take care of yourself for one day if I took you back to your apartment," Jack said. "Sorry, but you're stuck with us. At least until you regain your strength."

She could hardly think past the fatigue and pain battling for the upper hand but she knew she couldn't stay in this house where there was such love. "You can't keep me here."

"Don't you like us?" Emma asked, her face drooping.

What was she supposed to say to that? How did she explain to a five-year-old that being here—seeing this warm, loving relationship between father and child—was like having not just her back flayed open but her whole soul.

She was spared having to answer by the return of the sea-voice.

"What do you two think you're doing in here?"

"Uh-oh. Busted." Jack sent a guilty look towards his daughter, then together they turned to face the woman glaring at them from doorway. Grace could see immediately why he looked so intimidated. Though an inch or two shorter than her own five-foot five-inch height, the woman had to weigh at least two-hundred pounds.

She had the brown skin and wavy dark hair of a Pacific Islander, probably Hawaiian, and right now she looked as if she wanted Jack Dugan served up at her next luau with an apple in his mouth.

"Uh, your patient's awake, Lily."

"Didn't I say she needed to rest? Didn't I say leave her be?"

"Well, yes—"

"I go for ten minutes and what do you two do? Come in here and start pestering her. You even wait 'til Tiny and me pulled out of the driveway before you came barging in here?"

"Yes," he said defensively, then gave a rueful grin. "Almost."

She rolled her eyes at him. "Next time you want dinner, maybe I'll 'almost' fix it, then."

Despite her annoyance, she looked at both of them with exasperated affection. It was obvious to Grace that the woman doted on Jack and his daughter. Again she felt excluded, more isolated than before.

Emma seemed impervious to the big Hawaiian's temper. She hopped down from her father's lap and skipped across the room. With a winsome, dimply smile, she grabbed the woman's big brown hand in hers.

"Guess what, Lily? I gave Grace a drink of water all by

myself and Daddy said I'm a good nurse just like you." She giggled and tugged on the hand. "But not so bossy."

The housekeeper lifted an eyebrow. "Bossy, hmm?"

"Someone better be careful," Jack said with a pointed look at Emma, "or a bee will fly into that big mouth of hers."

The little girl just giggled and even the housekeeper looked like she was fighting a smile. Still, she aimed a stern look at the pair. "Well, I'm gonna boss you both right out of here so my patient can get some sleep."

"We're going, we're going." Jack stood and, in one clean motion, scooped Emma up and over his shoulder. She shrieked with glee as he headed toward the door. At the last minute, he turned and met Grace's gaze.

"Oh, I almost forgot to ask you. Would you like us to make any calls for you?"

"Why?"

He looked startled. "To let somebody know where they can reach you. You know. Family. Friends. Anybody who might worry about you if they couldn't find you for a while? I can do it for you or bring the cordless phone in when you're feeling better."

She shook her head, her cheek rubbing against the sheet. She had no family, at least none that cared where she was. And in the last year she had distanced herself from all of her friends in the Seattle PD, unable to bear their sympathy.

All except Beau, her former partner and best friend. He refused to let himself be distanced, wouldn't let her push him away.

"No," she whispered. "I don't need to contact anyone."

"Are you sure?" Jack asked. "Someone is probably worried sick about you."

She had just enough energy left to glare at him. "I said I didn't have anyone I need to contact." To her horror, her voice broke on the last word and unexpected tears choked in her throat, behind her eyes. She must be more exhausted than she thought.

Lily must have seen it, too. With a flip of her wrists, she shooed the father and daughter out the door then glided to the bed despite her girth.

"You just rest now, *keiki*." The housekeeper skimmed a gentle hand down Grace's hair. "You had a bad burn and now your body needs time to heal. Don't let that *huki'ino* bother you."

With fluid movements, she checked Grace's bandage, fluffed the pillows, smoothed the blanket.

And then, comforted in a way she hadn't felt in longer than she could remember, Grace slept.

CHAPTER THREE

"YOU KEEP THOSE DIRTY PAWS OF YOURS OUT of my strawberries or I'll chop 'em off."

Used to her threats, Jack just grinned at his housekeeper brandishing a paring knife dangerously close to his fingers, and popped a slice of fruit into his mouth. For all her bluster, he knew Lily loved him nearly as much as he loved her. Even though neither of them spoke of it, both understood and accepted that she was the closest thing to a mother he or his daughter had ever had.

"If you chopped off my hands, I wouldn't be able to do this." Heedless of the knife in her hand, he grabbed her around her ample waist and scooped her off the ground in a hearty embrace.

She shrieked and slapped at him with her free hand. "You think I got time for this kind of crazy stuff? Put me down. I just get that girl of yours down for a nap and try to get some work done and you have to come in with your nonsense."

He set her back on her feet, snitched another strawberry

and leaned back against the counter to watch her finish making a fruit salad. "You work too hard, Lily. You need to relax."

She snorted. "Food doesn't just show up on your table like magic. Your clothes don't wash themselves. Somebody's got to do all that. Now I have to take care of the *wahine*, too. Just when am I supposed to relax?"

Her diatribe was as familiar as her threat to chop his fingers off for picking at food between meals and he treated it the same way—with a grin. Despite his frequent offers to hire someone to help her, Lily refused assistance from anyone.

Only once had he dared to go behind her back and had hired a maid through a temp service. Lily had been nothing short of livid and the woman had ultimately left in tears after only a few hours trying to meet her unreasonable expectations. Since then, he just let his housekeeper complain and tried not to give her too much extra work.

Until this week, and Grace Solarez. With a mental note to give Lily a hefty bonus, whether she wanted it or not, he reached into the refrigerator for a juice. "How is your patient, anyway?"

Lily shrugged. "She don't say much. She seems to be getting better—the burn, anyway. Her heart, now, that's different."

He glanced up from twisting the top off the bottle. "What do you mean by that? What did she say to you?"

"Not much. I told you, she don't talk much to me. I don't need the words for me to see she's got pain, though. You just have to look in her eyes to see she's hurting big. Maybe too big even for words."

He sipped the juice and thought of the report on his desk, outlining in stark detail the reason why Grace Solarez grieved. He pictured the child in the photograph, all big eyes and toothy grin. Her daughter, Marisa, he had learned. The innocent victim of a drive-by shooting while waiting outside her school for her mother to pick her up.

She had been killed a year to the date from the night her mother had given Emma back to him.

He grimaced at the bottle and set it down. The police had no leads into Emma's kidnapping, and despite the lengthy report from his private investigators, he was no closer to unearthing the truth about Grace Solarez.

She had been staying in his house for five days and her presence on the highway that night—the anniversary of her daughter's death—was still a mystery.

"How long you gonna keep her here?" Lily asked.

"She's not a prisoner."

"Does she know that?"

"Of course."

Lily went on as if she didn't hear him. "Because last I heard, you were telling her you wouldn't let her leave."

"I had to tell her that. If you had seen that apartment of hers, you wouldn't want her going back there either. At least not until she builds up her strength."

"Why don't you take her dinner to her and tell her that yourself. You can save my old legs a few steps." She held a tray out for him, brimming with food.

"I think you have a few good hulas left in those old legs." He grinned, but took the tray from her, not willing to admit even to himself that he was eager for an excuse to talk to his guest again.

The door to the guest room had been left open and he found Grace sitting on a curvy old rocking chair and gazing out at the Sound. She made a stunning picture, swallowed up by what had to be one of Lily's massive muumuus, with her dark hair curling around her face and her feet tucked under her.

She should have looked ridiculous in the oversize garment, but it just seemed to make her look delicate, ethereal. A lighter-than-feathers little sprite who could float away wherever the breeze took her, like a character in one of Emma's favorite storybooks.

She seemed unaware of his presence so he rested a hip against the doorframe and studied her profile, wishing he could read in her features some clue to the mystery woman who had invaded their lives.

After five days of Lily's mothering, she definitely appeared healthier, he could say that much for her. Her skin had lost that sallow tinge it had worn when he first brought her here and those plum circles had faded from beneath her eyes.

No shadows remained *under* those mocha-colored eyes, but there were definitely still shadows *in* them, a sadness that looked as if it had been there for a long time.

He thought about what Lily had said, about her hurting too big for words. How would he bear it if he lost Emma the way she had lost her daughter?

If he hadn't been holding the tray of food, he would have rubbed his chest at the sudden ache there. The startling depth of his compassion made his voice more curt than normal. "Are you supposed to be out of bed?"

She glanced up and those too-serious dark eyes blinked at him. "Beautiful view you've got here, Dugan," she said, instead of answering his question.

He looked over her shoulder at the garden with its colorful late blossoms, framed by the vast blue of the sky and the water. It was one of those perfect, unusually clear fall days in the Northwest, and it looked like everyone on the Sound had decided to take advantage of the great weather. Dozens of pleasure boats—everything from sailboats to yachts to sea kayaks—dotted the water.

He had fallen in love with the view the first time he'd seen it, from the back of a motorcycle on the other side of the Sound. He'd been a badass seventeen-year-old, angry at the world and at himself. And most of all, hurting and furious over his father's betrayal.

Trying to go as far and as fast as he could from the chaos left in the wake of his father's, William Dugan, suicide, he had spent six days on the back of the bike. He remembered stopping on the water's edge and staring out at Puget Sound, knowing he couldn't go any farther, that he would have to stop here or go back the way he had come.

Suddenly, it was as if the anger and the grief fueling him through the trip had kept right on going without him, had slid into the ocean and washed away with the tide.

His father had left him with nothing but obligations, debts he had spent years paying off. But he had done it. And when it looked like the shipping company he had created out of the wreckage his father had left behind would survive, the first thing Jack had purchased had been this strip of land on the shore of Bainbridge Island.

"I like it," he finally murmured to Grace Solarez. It was a vast understatement and couldn't even begin to describe the tie he felt to this place.

He held out the tray to her. "I come bearing food." He scanned the contents of the tray, pulling lids off of containers to snoop underneath. "What do we have here? Looks like soup, homemade bread, a fruit salad and some juice."

She drew her bare toes even farther under the edge of the muumuu until they disappeared. "Please tell Lily thank you, but I'm not very hungry right now."

He set the tray down on the bed. "You need to eat to get your strength back."

"If I eat all that, will you let me go home?"

"Why are you in such a big hurry?"

"I don't belong here. We both know that. While I certainly appreciate all you've done for me, I'm feeling much better now and would like to leave. I'm not used to having all this time to…to do nothing. Besides, I have a life to get back to in the city."

Not much of one. A slum of an apartment, a job on the docks. No friends, no family who would worry about her. She couldn't possibly be happy in that bleak existence.

"Can't you just look at this as a well-deserved vacation?"

Her mouth pursed into a frown. "Why are you so insistent I stay here?"

"I just want you to be comfortable, for you to have someone to look after you while you heal."

"Why?"

"You earned those burns saving my daughter's life. I can never repay you for what you did for her. For me. The least I can do is make sure you have people to look after you while you recover."

Her short laugh sounded harsh, caustic. "You don't owe me a thing, Dugan."

"I owe you *everything*," he corrected softly.

She studied him for a moment, those big dark eyes murky, then she shrugged. "Fine. You've repaid me by giving me the royal treatment for a few days. It's been a real blast, believe me, but we're square now. Why don't you just give me a lift to the ferry and we can call it even."

They weren't even close to being even. Besides that, he didn't want to let her out of his sight until he could be absolutely sure she wasn't involved in the kidnapping, until they had a suspect in custody.

Jack couldn't shake the gut instinct someone else besides the man Emma described had been involved in her kidnapping. He didn't want that person to be Grace Solarez, but he couldn't let what he wanted interfere with the investigation.

He sat on the bed, careful not to tip the tray. "I understand you used to be a cop in the city."

The gentle movement of the rocking chair ceased and her expression became closed. "Used to be. A long time ago."

"Not so long. You resigned about a year ago, didn't you?"

"Your snoops were efficient."

"It wasn't exactly a state secret."

She was silent for a moment, then turned curious eyes to him. "How did you find me, anyway?"

"The picture."

She stared at him. "What?"

He gestured to the photograph still propped against the lamp by the side of the bed. "Your snapshot. You dropped it at the scene. We were able to identify the park in the background of the photo and then hit all the film processing places in the general area. I thought we had hit a dead end but it turned out a photo technician at the QuikPic where you developed the film knew you."

"Pham Leung."

He nodded. His private investigator told him the clerk hadn't wanted to talk at first. He had been fiercely protective of Grace—to the point of rudeness—but had cooperated after Mike told him she had saved a little girl's life, that the girl's father only wanted to thank her.

"Once we had a name," Jack continued, "the rest was easy."

"You had no right asking questions about me."

"Maybe not. But I had to find you."

"Fine. You've found me, you've patched me up. Now let me leave."

"Why are you so uncomfortable with my gratitude?"

"Why can't you clue in that I don't want it?"

At an impasse, they gazed at each other across the length of the room. Anger sent a flush of appealing color to her cheeks, turning her eyes almost black. Now that she was on the road to recovery, she looked much less the injured waif and much more a lush, soft woman.

There were curves somewhere in that voluminous robe, he remembered. They had been hard to miss when he carried her to his car that day. Now, with her spine stiff and her chin at an angle, he could see the high, firm outline of her breasts beneath the bright Hawaiian print.

To his shock, his body began to stir, to sizzle to life. He felt his blood begin to thicken, begin to churn through his veins like golden honey through a straw.

Where the hell did that come from? She wasn't at all the kind of woman that usually attracted him. If he had a type, it was tall, willowy blondes, not scrawny ex-cops with wild dark hair and big, wounded eyes.

The situation between them was complicated enough. The last thing he needed to do was toss his suddenly unruly libido into the mix. With fierce determination, he clamped down on the burgeoning awareness.

His gaze found the photo by the bed, the one that had brought him to her. "I didn't have the chance to tell you this before," he murmured, "but I am very sorry about your daughter."

At his words, the defiance seemed to drain away from her features. Hell, the whole life seemed to drain out of her, leaving only a cold, stark grief. He instantly regretted mentioning Marisa Solarez. If Grace had wanted to talk about her child, she would have brought the subject up herself.

She slowly sank back into the chair as if her bones couldn't support the weight of her pain. "How did you...? Oh. Pham."

He nodded. "Is that the reason you quit the police force?"

For a moment, he didn't think she would answer him. She sent him one quick, unreadable look, then gazed out at the relentless water beating away at the shore, her fingers twisting restlessly amid the flowery folds of Lily's colorful dress.

After several moments, she looked back at him. "I couldn't do it anymore. I had too much rage, too much hate built up inside me. The department psychiatrist thought I would be a danger to myself and others." She said the words with bitter self-mockery.

"Have you ever thought about doing any private security consulting work?"

"Excuse me?" She stared at him as if he'd just asked her to climb on the bureau and yodel.

"With your background in police work, I think you would be exceptional at it."

This wasn't the first time the idea of hiring her had occurred to him. Since he had brought her here, the idea had percolated in the back of his mind. It was the perfect solution on several levels. It would get her out of that dismal apartment, for one thing. And he would have a better chance of proving whether she participated in the kidnapping—and, if so, of finding the other kidnapper—if she stayed close enough for him to keep a watchful eye on her.

"I suppose you've heard by now about my daughter's kidnapping." He watched her intently for any sign of guilt—a nervous twitch, a flicker in her eyes—but she returned his gaze without emotion. She was either as cold as an iceberg or she was innocent.

He was almost positive it was the latter. Almost.

"Yes," she replied. "Your housekeeper mentioned it. I imagine you both must have been terrified."

His gut clutched in memory. The ransom note had arrived at the office: *500,000. Not much for a little girl's life.*

At first he'd put it down to some kind of sick joke and then his phone had rung with that panicked call from the director of Emma's preschool saying she hadn't come in from outside play time and had he somehow come to pick her up without checking in at the office?

Terrified didn't even begin to describe how he had felt then—that cold, sick, paralyzing fear.

Would he ever be able to let her out of his sight again or hear the phone ring without that jolt of panic?

"How is your daughter handling it?" Grace asked. "It must have been a terrible ordeal for her."

He uncoiled the lingering tendrils of fear that wrapped around his insides whenever he thought of that day and rested a hip on the edge of the bed, crossing his legs out in front of him at the ankles. "She's seems to have emerged relatively unscathed."

"That must be a relief."

He nodded. Odd how he hadn't been able to talk about this with anyone else—not even Piper or Lily—but he found himself wanting to confide in this slight, quiet woman.

"I would hate for her to live her life afraid," he admitted, "but I hope she has gained at least a little healthy suspicion for strangers. She still treats everybody like her best friend, from the garbage man to the bag boys at the supermarket. She probably jumped right in the car with the guy who took her."

He realized his hand had fisted in the quilt covering the bed and forced his fingers to relax. "If it can happen once, it can happen again," he went on, "and I want to do everything I can to prevent that. I want to hire *you* to do everything you can to prevent it from happening again."

"Is that your gratitude offering me a job, Mr. Dugan?"

"In part. I also hear you were one hell of a cop, that you

made detective after just four years on patrol. It seems a shame to waste that hauling dead fish around."

"My career choices are really none of your business." That frosty, screw-you tone was back.

"You're absolutely right. But protecting my daughter *is* my business."

"You can't keep your daughter in a bubble," she said quietly. "No matter how good your security system is, how many people you hire to protect her, there would still be risks."

"I know. But I want to do everything I can to minimize them, both here and at my business."

"Global Shipping Incorporated. Specializing in Far East imports and exports."

He lifted an eyebrow. "You must have a few snoops of your own."

"Just Lily. She's full of information. In fact, if you're looking for a security leak you might want to start there."

He grinned at the idea. People didn't come any more loyal than Lily and Tiny Kihualani. "She must really like you. Usually she keeps her lips sealed up tighter than an oil tanker."

Instead of returning his grin, Grace just continued regarding him solemnly, and he found himself wondering what it would take to make that lush, kiss-me mouth break into a smile.

He indulged in the possibilities for only a moment then returned to the business at hand. "I'm prepared to pay you well if you take the job." He named a figure and had the satisfaction of seeing her eyes widen. "That would, of course, include room and board, since the most logical thing would be for you to stay here."

She shook her head. "That's certainly a very generous offer, Mr. Dugan, but I'm not interested."

"Why not?"

She tilted her chin defiantly. "Does it matter?"

"Yeah," he replied. "It matters to me."

Her eyes were as cool as her voice now. "I was a police detective, not a security guard. I don't know the first thing about what you're asking me to do."

"You solved crimes, right? I just want you to take it a step further and try to prevent this crime from happening again."

"I'm not interested," she repeated.

He studied her, noting the implacable thrust of her jaw, the stubborn light in her eyes. Finally he straightened from the bed. "Don't give me an answer now. Just think about it for a while. Overnight, maybe. Then, if you're still not interested in the morning, I'll have Tiny take you home."

For long moments after he left the room, Grace stared after him. The room felt colder, somehow, emptier without his presence.

Something about Jack Dugan appealed to her, in a way she hadn't been attracted to a man in longer than she could remember. It startled her—frightened her, even—the way her heart seemed to catch in her chest and her pulse fluttered wildly when he grinned, when he looked at her out of those green eyes.

Another reason why she absolutely could not take the job, as if she needed more.

Despite what she had told him, she knew she was capable of handling the assignment. Like he had said, she had spent enough time solving crime to have picked up plenty of knowledge about how to prevent it and she had worked enough VIP security detail to give her some idea of how she could make life safer for Jack Dugan and his daughter.

Still, capable was a far cry from expert.

Not that it mattered. No way could she even consider taking

the job, not if it involved staying here in this house where there was such love, filled with toys and hugs and laughter.

She couldn't bear it.

No, the smartest thing for her to do would be to catch a lift in the morning and ride away from Jack Dugan and his little blond daughter without a backward glance.

A knock interrupted her thoughts and she grimaced, not wanting another run-in with him. To her relief, it was Lily, the loquacious housekeeper.

"You've got a phone call."

She straightened from the rocking chair. "There must be some mistake. No one knows I'm here."

Lily shrugged. "It's some man. Want me to tell him you don't want to talk?"

"No. No, I'll take it."

Lily handed her a cordless phone and then slipped from the room, respecting her privacy. Still thinking the house-keeper had erred, she spoke hesitantly into the phone. "Yes?"

"Dammit, Grace. Where the hell have you been?"

She relaxed at the familiar voice. "Nice to talk to you, too, Riley."

Her former partner bit out a curse. She could just picture him, clothes slightly rumpled, dark hair characteristically messy, hawk-like features twisted with irritation as he glared at the phone he hated.

Beau Riley was the closest she had to family. Six years of being partners, first on patrol and then as detectives, had made them closer than blood. Brain clones, Riley called them. They knew how the other thought, felt. They even finished each other's sentences half the time, which was exactly why there could never be anything romantic between them.

In the hell of the last twelve months, he had been the only

person she had stayed in contact with, although even that had been as sporadic as Seattle sunshine.

"You got any idea how worried I've been?" he snapped now.

"No." Suddenly, unaccountably, famished, she speared a strawberry with a fork. "But I'm guessing you're about to enlighten me."

"You don't answer your phone for a week. I go by your apartment and you're not there. I go to that crummy job of yours on the docks. You're not there. I go back and forth between the two until I feel like a stinkin' yo-yo. Finally, I get one of your stupid neighbors to answer the door, only to learn some guy carried you out the door and into some fancy car a week ago. A stranger hauls an unconscious woman into his car and not once did the idiot think to call the police. What the hell is this city coming to?"

She settled back into the rocking chair and nibbled at the fruit salad while she listened to his familiar rant about the pitiful state of society.

When it finally sounded like Beau was beginning to wind down, she interrupted him. "How did you find me?" That seemed to be the question of the hour.

"The idiot neighbor at least had the brains to remember part of a license plate and the make of the car, although why he didn't contact the police before is a complete mystery to me. Took me two days but I finally traced it to Dugan. What the hell are you doing there, Grace?"

Good question, one she'd love to answer if she only knew. "It's a long story," she finally said. "Why were you looking for me?"

The silence stretched thin between them, a few beats longer than was comfortable. When he finally spoke, he sounded almost sheepish. As sheepish as macho-man Beau Riley could sound, at any rate. "I was worried about you." He cleared his throat. "What with the anniversary and all. Afraid you'd do something crazy."

Crazy like taking a little stroll into traffic on the interstate. He didn't say it, but she knew exactly how his mind worked. Hers had worked the same way, which is probably why he'd been worried about her.

Sitting here in Jack Dugan's sleek, elegant guest room with a bowl of luscious food in her hands—with the waves licking at the shore and gulls crying out overhead—the desperation and despair of that night seemed as far away as the moon.

She felt a deep guilt at her weakness, that she had even considered ending her life. That she had almost succumbed to the pain.

"You okay?"

She blinked away the shame, knowing there would be plenty of time for it later. "I'm fine," she lied. "You?"

Beau cleared his throat again. "Yeah."

She heard the raw emotion in the single word and drew a shaky breath. She should have known the anniversary would hit him hard, should have tried to reach out to him.

Beau had loved her daughter, too, and had relished his role of honorary uncle. She thought of birthday parties and piggyback rides and lazy Sunday picnics in the park.

Before she could answer, though, to offer whatever kind of meager comfort she could, he changed the subject.

"So tell me what you're doing with Jack Dugan, of all people." His tone shifted suddenly, edged with a suspicion that hadn't been there at the beginning of their conversation. "What are you up to? Dammit, Grace. Don't you dare tell me you're playing Lone Ranger on this one."

She frowned, puzzled by his anger. "What are you talking about?"

"Don't try to con me. I know you better than that. There's no way I'll believe it's purely a coincidence you're staying with the owner of Global Shipping Incorporated."

The first glimmer of unease began to stir within her and, suddenly restless, she rose to return the empty bowl to the tray on the bed. "Should that mean something to me?"

There was a long silence on the other end of the phone line, then Riley swore softly. "You don't know, do you?"

"Know what? I'm too tired to play games with you. Spit it out."

"Global Shipping, Inc., and your friend Jack Dugan are smack dab in the middle of a multi-jurisdictional investigation for smuggling."

The lingering taste of the fruit turned to ashes in her mouth and the glimmer of unease became a riot of foreboding. "Drugs?"

"No, big, bad nasty assault weapons. Name a kind of illegal weapon and he's suspected of bringing it in."

Somehow this had something to do with her, otherwise he wouldn't have been so suspicious of her reasons for staying with Dugan. She frowned. She must still be woozy from her illness because, try as she might, she couldn't figure it out. "It's been a year since I turned in my badge. Why would you think I'd suddenly develop an interest in some petty smuggling ring?"

When he spoke, Beau's voice was as sharp as a switchblade. "You need me to spell it out for you? Weapons, Grace. GSI and Jack Dugan are suspected of bringing in most of the assault weapons on the street today, including the AK-47 favored by our mutual friend Spooky Lawrence. The same Spooky Lawrence currently serving fifteen-to-life for killing an eleven-year-old girl named Marisa Solarez in a drive-by shooting outside her school."

CHAPTER FOUR

GRACE COULDN'T SPEAK FOR SEVERAL SECONDS after Beau's announcement, couldn't think straight, could only stand there, an empty bowl in her hand, while an awful, cold numbness began in her stomach and spread out through the rest of her body

Weapons smuggling.

The man with the sweet smile and the green, green eyes and the gentle way with his five-year-old daughter was a weapons smuggler.

She thought she would be sick suddenly. Totally and violently ill all over Jack Dugan's glossy, elegant guest room.

"Grace? You okay?"

She blinked several times, then set the bowl down gingerly on the table, fearful it might shatter into a million pieces if she wasn't careful. "I… Yes," she whispered. "Fine."

But she wasn't. Her thoughts had turned black and horrific, to blood and sirens and a child's shattered body.

Most of the time, she tried not to think about that day—

just living without Marisa was torture enough—but with Riley's words, everything she tried to block from her mind came rushing back.

She hated most that the last words between them hadn't been spoken out of love but out of exasperated anger. Marisa had called her at work to tell her she'd missed the bus for the third time in two weeks.

"Can you come get me?" she had begged, and Grace—with a dozen cases open on her desk and two interviews scheduled within the hour—had snapped at her about being responsible and trustworthy.

In the end, she had reluctantly agreed to pick her up, but she had been too late.

Five minutes.

That's all it took for her world to shatter.

If she had been five minutes earlier—if she hadn't stopped to buy a Coke from the vending machine at the station house or to exchange jibes with the desk sergeant on her way out the door—her daughter would have been just fine.

They would have been at the little house they'd worked so hard to fix up, catching up on long division homework or watching TV or taking a bike ride through the park.

But she *had* stopped for a Coke. She *had* stopped to ride the desk sergeant about his pot belly and his junk food habit.

And she had arrived at the school five minutes too late to protect her eleven-year-old daughter from being caught in the crossfire of rival punks fighting over drug territory.

Her stomach pitched and rolled as she relived driving up to the school and seeing the two squad cars already on the scene, their flashing lights piercing the long afternoon shadows. Already a crowd had gathered on the playground. She'd picked out the principal of the school, the gym teacher and the lanky, tow-headed boy Marisa had a crush on, the one probably responsible for her missing the bus.

Their faces had been taut with shock, and she had known. Somehow she had known.

She remembered stumbling out of her car and rushing toward the crowd, then the horror—the devastating horror—of seeing Marisa there, covered in blood and completely, terribly still.

"You still there?" Beau asked in her ear.

She couldn't answer him, lost in the nightmare she couldn't seem to wake from.

"Say something, Gracie," he demanded, and she could hear the concern roughening Beau's voice.

She cleared her throat and felt the pain of the action through vocal cords suddenly thick with emotion. "What... what do you want me to say?"

"Hell, I don't know. Anything. Just don't freeze up on me like that. I hate it when you do that."

"I didn't know any of this. About Dugan, I mean. You shocked me. I'm sorry."

He swore viciously. "You've got nothing to be sorry about. It's Dugan who should be sorry. And he will be. Trust me, Gracie, if he's dealing in illegal weapons—if he played the slightest part in providing the assault weapons Spooky and his crew got their hands on for their little turf war—Jack Dugan is going to be very, very sorry."

With monumental effort, she managed to gather the memories and shove them back into the corner of her mind where they usually lurked. They wouldn't stay long, she knew, would soon be scratching and clawing their way out. But for now she forced herself to tune them out, to become detached and clinical. The hard-nosed cop sniffing out a lead.

"How strong is the case against him? Who's working it?" she asked.

She could almost see the shrug of his broad shoulders. "Who's not? Customs, ATF, FBI. Five of us from the Seattle PD. Everybody wants a piece of it."

"So do I." She stared out at the water. "I want in."

He snorted. "Absolutely not. No friggin' way."

"I'm part of this, Beau. I want in."

"You're too close."

"And you're not?"

He swore again. "Dammit, Gracie. You turned in your badge."

For the first time in a year, she felt the loss of it, of the gold detective shield she had worked so hard to earn. She had been so proud of it once, amazed that she was finally doing the job she'd dreamed of since she was younger than Marisa.

Her father had worn his own uniform with such dignity. Manny Solarez had loved being a cop, the honor and the integrity and the ceremony of it. In the end, he had given his life for the job.

Her own passion for becoming a peace officer had been born that day when she was eight years old, after her father's partner and best friend had come to the house bearing the news of Manny's death in the line of duty.

Her job and her daughter had been the only things that mattered to Grace. Without one, though, the other had seemed pointless and she had surrendered her badge without protest.

Now she wanted it back, if only to make Jack Dugan pay.

"I don't have to be official," she said now. Excitement clicked through her, the almost forgotten buzz of bringing a criminal to justice. "I'm in the perfect position. I'm staying at his house, Beau. You can't get any closer than that."

"Which brings me to my original question. What the hell are you doing there?"

She debated how much to tell him, then shrugged. "I told you, it's a long story, but he thinks he owes me right now. What do you know about his daughter's kidnapping?"

"Holy cow! That was you?"

She frowned into the phone. "I was in the wrong place at the wrong time. That's all."

"*That's all?* You're a damn hero, Gracie!"

"Drop it, Riley," she snapped. She wasn't a hero. She was a weak, pathetic coward.

To keep him from making the inevitable leap and start asking her what she was doing there in the first place on the anniversary of her daughter's death, she changed the subject. "How does the kidnapping play into the whole thing?"

Beau immediately changed gears, and she sat back, with a minor congratulatory pat on the back for still knowing exactly how to work him. "We're still trying to figure it all out at this point," he said. "One theory is that a deal might have gone sour or he might have pissed off one of his customers somehow."

"So they took the kid as payback? Nice. Dugan must run with a real swell crowd."

"That's one of the screwiest things about the case. As far as we can tell, he doesn't hang with any known criminal elements. He comes from East Coast money, but built GSI from the ground up after a well-decorated stint as an air force pilot. Other than a few problems with the law when he was a juvie and one disturbing the peace citation for hosting a loud party when he was in the military, the man is so clean he squeaks."

"Or at least he manages to put on a good show."

"Right."

"I can find out, Beau. I can dig deeper than anyone on the task force. You *know* I can."

"Grace—"

"I'm staying in his house. Not only that but he just asked me to handle his personal security. I told him no, but I can go to him and tell him I changed my mind. Think about it. I can work it so I have complete access to everything—where he goes, who he sees. What kind of damn breakfast cereal he prefers. Everything."

His silence dragged on so long she was afraid she had lost the connection. "I don't like it," he finally said, reluctance clear in his voice. "My butt would be toast if anybody else on the task force found out what's going on."

"So don't tell them. Just think of me as any other informant."

He snorted. "Right."

"Come on, Beau. Take a chance. You want Dugan and you know I'm the one to help you get him."

"Yeah," he finally said. "Yeah, I do. Okay. You can feed me whatever information you come up with. But for Pete's sake, Gracie, be careful, would you?"

She tried not to let her grim anticipation filter through her voice. "I always am, Beau. I always am."

Jack sliced through the water of his swimming pool with strong, steady strokes. Ten laps. Eleven. Twelve. With each turn, he felt his stress level drop a notch.

He had left the lights off in the indoor spa, preferring the glow from only the pool's green underwater lights reflecting off black tile and the occasional moonbeam that thrust its way through the thick storm clouds to pour in through the wide row of skylights overhead.

Including an indoor pool in the house design had been purely an indulgence—and an expensive one at that. But he didn't regret a penny of the money he'd spent. In stress reduction alone, the thing had more than paid for itself.

At the end of the day, with his work finally done and Emma tucked into bed, all storied-out, he retreated here to unwind.

He needed it today. He had more kinks in his shoulders and neck than the cord of the damn telephone he sometimes felt was permanently attached to his ear.

He had spent the morning going over contracts, then had been on the phone in teleconference negotiations most of the afternoon. He had haggled and bartered and wrangled until he was bleary-eyed and hoarse-voiced, but he'd been successful. He had managed to swing a multimillion dollar deal for GSI.

Now, though, he wanted nothing more than to lose himself in hard, mindless physical activity.

After twenty laps, he paused to catch his breath and floated on his back for a few minutes, trying to see if he could find any stars in the murky night sky.

He ached to be up there. He hated sitting behind a desk—even when that desk was at his home office where he worked two days a week, instead of GSI's hangar at the airport where he spent the rest of the week.

Desk work—even very lucrative desk work—made him feel trapped and edgy and out of sorts.

He wanted to be flying. If he had his choice, he'd leave all the negotiations and paperwork to Syd—hell, she was better at it than he was anyway—then he could do nothing else but fly.

But he *didn't* have a choice. He had Emma to think about.

Even though Lily was wonderful with her, he hated leaving her overnight more than once or twice a month. She was only five years old and she needed her daddy right now more than he needed the thrilling rush of being behind the controls of a jet airplane.

Maybe it wouldn't be so hard to leave her if he didn't know exactly what it was like to be on the other side of the equation. He had a whole childhood full of memories of yearning for his parents to remember he was alive. He knew firsthand the loneliness of another night spent in the company of only a surly housekeeper, of waking up alone after a bad dream and knowing he would have to comfort himself.

During those long nights after Camille took off, when he had been the only one there to get up with a baby crying out for a mother who wanted nothing to do with her, he had made a promise to himself and to his little girl. Even though her mother had jumped at the first chance to abandon her, he had vowed that Emma would always know she came first with him.

In a few more years, she'd be old enough that he could leave her without this guilt, without worrying about whether the pizza she had for dinner would give her a stomachache or if she had her favorite stuffed poodle tucked into her bed or if she remembered to brush her teeth.

Until then, he would work out his frustration at what amounted to a self-imposed standdown here in the water.

He curled over to his stomach again and started to free-style toward the shallow end of the pool when a flash of color caught his attention.

He glanced up and found his houseguest standing in the doorway to the spa wearing that same robe of Lily's, with vibrant red hibiscus and fronds of greenery splashed over it.

Her hair was tousled and her feet bare. From his vantage point in the water, he could see them clearly—slim and brown and somehow unbearably sexy.

Man, he needed a woman if he could get all fired up over a pair of bare feet.

"I'm sorry," she said when he stopped swimming, in a voice

as cool as a January wind blowing off the Sound. "I didn't mean to disturb you."

He frowned, wondering just what he'd done to earn such dislike, or if she treated everybody with the same chilly detachment.

"You didn't disturb me. I was just about done anyway."

With three quick strokes, he finished the lap and hoisted himself out of the pool then grabbed a thick towel hanging from the back of a koa wood chaise cushioned in bright tropical colors and wrapped the towel loosely around his hips.

"It's after midnight—if you're still determined to head over to the ferry in the morning, shouldn't you be tucked in your bed, saving up your strength?"

She buried her fingers in the fold of the robe. "I was too restless to sleep. It feels like I've done nothing else for a month."

"You push yourself too hard and you're going to regret it."

"I hardly think taking a few steps to the kitchen for a glass of warm milk is pushing myself too hard."

Despite her words, pale lines bracketed her mouth and she looked more than a little shaky. Stubborn woman. From what he had come to know of Grace Solarez, he had a feeling she wouldn't give in to her weakness until it knocked her over.

"Sit down," he ordered. "It won't kill you to take a little rest."

She opened her mouth as if to argue with him, then reluctantly sat down on the closest chair.

He crossed the room and sat next to her. Through the skylight, he could see the clouds had begun to unleash more raindrops to click against the glass, much heavier than the soft mist of earlier in the evening.

"Nice place you've got here," she murmured.

"Now, why do I detect just a hint of disdain in your voice? You prefer that lovely place of yours?"

"There's no place like home."

He barked a laugh. "No offense, but I don't think even one of Dorothy's Kansas tornadoes could make that apartment any worse."

"Not all of us need swimming pools and a couple dozen acres of wood floors inside our houses."

"People said the same thing about indoor plumbing, and just look how that caught on."

She glanced at him and he thought he saw just the tiniest shadow of a smile playing around that lush mouth before she seemed to catch herself. Instantly, her lips hardened into a thin, tight line and she gazed back at the lights flickering green on the water.

"I hear you had a phone call today."

She shot him a quick glance and he tried to figure out why there would be a trace of unease in her eyes. "Yes. My partner, Beau Riley. Former partner," she corrected herself. "From my days with the Seattle PD."

"Everything okay?"

"Why wouldn't it be?"

He shrugged. "Lily said you seemed upset after your phone call."

She met his questioning gaze with a cool one of her own. "Checking up on me again, Dugan?"

"I just asked Lily how your back was healing. She said it was fine until you started pacing in your room all evening."

"I'm fine. It was nothing." She paused and fidgeted a little on the seat as if her back were bothering her again. "Actually, I'm glad I ran into you tonight."

"Yeah?"

Her fingers played in the folds of her robe again. She did

that when she was nervous about something, he'd discovered. "I've had some time to reconsider what we talked about today. Your job offer. If it's still open, I'd like to take it."

He narrowed his eyes at her. Where did this sudden change of heart come from? And did it have anything to do with her phone call?

When he left her in her room earlier, he was under the impression she wouldn't work for him under any circumstances, and all afternoon he'd been trying to figure out how he might be able to convince her to stay. Now it looked like he wouldn't have to.

Still, with her fingers nervously kneading the folds of her dress and her shoulders set in tight, stiff lines, she didn't exactly look thrilled at the prospect of being employed by him.

"Are you sure this is what you want to do?" he asked.

"Of course I'm sure," she snapped. "I wouldn't have said anything if I wasn't."

"Don't let me twist your arm or anything."

Her chin lifted. "Look, you want me to take the job or don't you?"

He nearly laughed at her in-your-face belligerence. Not what most people would be dishing out to a prospective employer. Then again, Grace Solarez wasn't like most people.

"I want you to take it. But I've got to tell you, I've seen people work up more enthusiasm for a wart removal."

Her mouth tightened again. "Excuse me if I'm not quite up to cartwheels and baton twirling yet. Give me a few more days."

He grinned and decided he could really grow to like this woman. And not just because he had developed this sudden hankering to touch that soft skin and taste that prim mouth. "The job is yours. You can start whenever you feel up to it."

"What exactly do you want from me?"

Now there was a loaded question if he'd ever heard one. He

reined in his unruly thoughts and focused on a job description. "Anything you think it would take to keep Emma safe."

"That's pretty vague, don't you think?"

"I really don't know what to tell you, since I have no idea what needs to be fixed."

"I suppose the logical place to start would be your security system. From there, we can examine your day-to-day practices to see if there are areas that might need improvement."

"Sounds good." He paused, wondering again about the mystery of Grace Solarez. If not for the dim intimacy, he might have held his tongue, but he was still puzzled by so many things about her. "You mind if I ask you a question?" he finally asked.

That familiar wariness crept into her dark eyes again. "Depends. What's your question?"

"What were you doing there that night? At the accident?"

She instantly tensed. He could see it in the sudden clenching of her jaw and the way her body seemed to freeze in place. "Just driving. What else would I be doing?"

"It was pretty isolated for a pleasure trip. Not much to see out there but orchards and fields."

"Maybe I like orchards and fields."

"In the middle of the night?"

"I was just driving, Dugan. Last time I checked, there was no law against that. Unless one has been put on the books since I was a cop, it's nobody's business but my own. If you've got a problem with it, maybe we ought to just forget this whole job thing."

She was obviously hiding something. The signs couldn't be more clear if they were painted on her forehead in fluorescent colors. But he had the sudden conviction that whatever she was doing out there that night had more to do with her daughter than with his.

It was the first anniversary of her daughter's death and she had the right to grieve in her own way. If that included driving along an isolated stretch of freeway in the middle of the night, she was absolutely right, it was none of his business.

He thought of the raw pain in her eyes whenever she looked at the photograph of that bright, laughing little girl and decided to let the matter rest.

For now, anyway.

"You ought to be in bed. Why don't you head in that direction and I'll swing by the kitchen and heat up that milk for you? Or I could make you some herbal tea, if you'd prefer."

"You don't need to wait on me. I can take care of myself."

He smiled softly, amused by her stubborn independence. "I don't doubt that for a moment. But for once, why don't you let somebody else help you? It won't kill you."

She looked as if she wanted to argue but clamped her mouth shut and shrugged. "Fine. It's your house. I'll have tea, then, if it's not too much trouble."

He waited to see that she made it to her room, then stopped on his way to the kitchen long enough to change out of his wet surfer trunks and throw on jeans and a T-shirt.

When he returned to her room with the tea on the same tray he'd brought her at lunchtime, he found her in the rocking chair again, staring out at the night. The curtains were open and the lights of the city glistened on the water, despite the clouds.

He gestured to the tray. "Haven't we done this before?"

She nodded. "I'm going to forget how to tie my own shoes, the way you and Lily have been spoiling me."

"I doubt that." He set the tray on the bed again. "You strike me as a woman who treasures her independence. I doubt you'd surrender it that easily."

She looked surprised at the observation but didn't comment. "Well, thank you for the tea," she said after a pause. Her voice sounded on the far edge of exhaustion. "You make a passable waiter."

He grinned. "Whoa. All these compliments are going to turn my head. Now drink your tea like a good girl and hop into bed, where you should have been hours ago."

"Yes sir." She stopped just short of saluting him, and *he* stopped just short of giving in to the overwhelming urge to kiss that lush smart mouth of hers.

"I'm very glad you changed your mind about the job," he said instead.

"When did you want me to start?"

"Not until you can walk to the kitchen and back without having to stop to rest along the way."

She summoned the energy to glare at him over the lip of her teacup. "I was doing fine. You were the one who ordered me to sit down."

He smiled again. "Seriously, there's no hurry. We can work out the details when you're feeling better. And when you're not so tired."

"I'm not tired," she grumbled, then ruined her protest with a huge, ear-popping yawn.

"Okay. Whatever you say." *And I'm not attracted to you in the slightest.* "Now get some rest and we'll talk about the whole job thing later."

Layer after layer of mystery surrounded Grace Solarez, he thought as he left her to her tea. But with each layer he uncovered, the woman he found was beginning to intrigue him more and more.

CHAPTER FIVE

SHE HAD TO GET OUT OF HERE.

Staying at this beautiful house on the water, she felt as if she were slowly suffocating, as if someone had locked her in a trunk with just enough air to keep her gasping for more.

In the four days since she had stumbled on a half-naked Jack Dugan swimming in his indoor pool, she had been poked at and fussed over and scolded by her unrelenting Hawaiian nursemaid.

Lily had stuffed so much food into her, she thought she must have gained at least five pounds. Not that any of it showed, since she was still trapped in these voluminous clothes, but she still found herself resenting being coddled this way.

She wanted to return to the way things were before she came here, when the world was a bleak, colorless place, where she could feel and taste and see nothing but her own emptiness.

It sounded crazy, but she felt guilty every time she caught herself savoring something new Lily produced. As if somehow, the slow, subtle reawakening of her taste buds demonstrated a lessening of her grief.

Not only that, but the woman never stopped talking. Every time she saw her, Grace was subjected to a continuous stream of conversation, about cooking and current events and the latest romance novel Lily had just finished.

For a year, she had lived in silence and isolation. She had wanted it that way, had *needed* it that way. But now Jack Dugan and his gabby housekeeper were forcing her out of that desolate place and into a world overflowing with life and laughter.

And she hated it.

This, though. This was the worst. Fifteen minutes earlier, Emma had invaded the guest room. Cute, bubbly little Emma with the green eyes and the curls and the sweet giggle, who didn't seem to understand that Grace couldn't stand the sight of her.

"...and this is my dog, Betty." From the armful of stuffed animals she'd piled onto Grace's bed, the little girl plucked out a raggedy-looking stuffed white poodle with a wilted purple bow and a matted ruff of fur circling its neck and the tip of its tail.

She held it up proudly. "I got her from Santa Claus last year. I wanted a real puppy but Santa wrote me a note and said maybe I could practice taking care of Betty for a while so he could see if I would be 'sponsible for a real dog. I been real 'sponsible," she said solemnly. "I feed her and give her water and even a bath, 'cept Daddy said I was gonna ruin her if I took her in the tub again."

Grace wanted to shove Emma and her stuffed dog Betty and the rest of her toys out the door and lock it against them all.

This is why she had hidden in solitude, why she had tried to avoid everyone for the last year, especially children. Listening to this little girl's cheerful chatter, she felt as if her skin had been flayed open and her insides exposed.

No matter how hard she tried, she couldn't stop thinking about her daughter at this age, with missing teeth and that same infectious giggle and a tattered stuffed dog of her own named Petey.

Emma cocked her head and frowned at her, forehead furrowed and her mouth pursed as if she were pondering some deep, existential mystery. "Do you think Santa Claus might bring me a real dog this year if I don't take Betty into the bathtub again?"

She hated this.

"I wouldn't know," she said, instead of what she wanted to say. *Go away. Please go away and leave me alone.*

"I think he will. He promised. And if he does, know what I'm gonna name it?"

She shook her head, afraid to trust her voice.

"Grace." Emma beamed. "Even if it's a boy. 'Cause you're my bestest friend in the whole wide world, that's why."

She drew in a ragged breath, but Emma didn't seem to notice she was dying.

"If Santa Claus brings me a dog, you could help me take care of him and teach him tricks, like how to shake and how to roll over and how to bring my daddy his slippers."

She frowned again. "Only Daddy doesn't wear slippers. But maybe we could teach Grace-my-dog how to bring my daddy's tennis shoes or his flip-flops."

She couldn't do this. She thought she was strong enough to stay here, that she could somehow bury her feelings if she focused only on doing the job, on bringing Jack Dugan to justice. But looking at his daughter with her pink corduroy overalls and her sweet-as-an-angel face, Grace had serious doubts about whether she had the guts to go through this.

She had only seen Emma a few times in the four days since Beau had told her about the investigation. But with each encounter, the child seemed to slip through her meager defenses, to poke and prod at the raw, seeping wound around her heart.

"...and this is George." Emma dropped Betty on the bed and turned her attention to a tie-dyed plush reptile of some sort that looked about two feet long. "Know what he is?"

Grace thought about just ignoring her. If she did, maybe the little girl would eventually give up and wander away again. But she knew she couldn't. None of this was Emma's fault—she was an innocent child who couldn't be blamed for random schoolyard violence or for the fact that her father was an amoral jerk who put profit above all else.

Grace couldn't vent either her grief or her anger by being cruel to a little girl.

She cleared her throat and studied the toy. "Uh, is it a lizard?"

"Kind of." Emma giggled. "It's a gecko. We have geckos at our house in Hawaii. Little tiny ones that climb on the screens. I try to catch them whenever we go there but I never can. They're way too fast!"

A house in Hawaii in addition to this sleek estate with its indoor swimming pool and incredible view of the city across the Sound. Crime apparently *was* paying for Jack Dugan, and paying very, very well.

"Did you ever catch a gecko?" Emma asked her.

"No. I don't believe I've ever even seen a gecko," she answered. "Except for George, here."

"Maybe you could come to Hawaii with us next time and help me catch one. I want to bring it home and put it in my room."

"Maybe," she said, in what she hoped was a noncommittal tone.

"I have a book about a gecko. I'll go get it and you can read it to me." With all the confidence of a princess making a royal decree, Emma hopped from the bed and skipped out of the room, leaving an overpowering silence behind her.

Grace again fought the urge to lock the door against the little girl. Or even better, to find some way to completely disappear, to go somewhere safe and warm where nothing could touch her, nothing could hurt her.

That place didn't exist. If she had learned anything in the last year, it was that she had nowhere to hide.

She crossed to the window. Although it was still early afternoon, the Sound was choppy and dark through the rain streaking down the window. Only a few boats were out on such a bleak day, under gunmetal gray clouds that scudded across the sky.

The sight of the water only made her feel more like a prisoner here, even though she knew that was ridiculous. The ferry left every hour to the city and she could leave any time she wanted.

She stretched a hand out to trace a raindrop's crooked journey down the glass just as Emma returned, a book tucked under her arm.

"Here," she said and held it out proudly.

With a deep, fortifying breath, Grace took it and sat on the rocking chair. Before she could protest, Emma climbed onto her lap, wiggling around for a few moments until she was comfortable.

If she closed her eyes, she could almost pretend this small, warm weight was Marisa as she'd been at this age, snuggling onto her lap at bedtime smelling of baby shampoo and talcum powder, with her hair damp from the tub and her favorite Dr. Seuss book in her hands....

"Aren't you going to read it?" Emma asked impatiently.

"Sorry." Grace forced her attention back to the present and began stiffly reading the colorful legend of a gecko who saved his family's honor through his cleverness and bravery.

She read the words automatically while her mind pondered her conundrum. The only way she could do this, could stay in this house, was to stay as far as possible from Emma. She would just have to make it clear to Jack and Lily that she would prefer not to have anything to do with the girl.

Either that or she would have to completely lock her memories away so she wouldn't have to suffer any more of these comparisons.

If she couldn't do that, she would have to leave. Illegal weapons be damned.

"And the geckos all laughed," she mumbled. "The end."

Emma wore that puzzled, solemn face of hers again. "I think the gecko's family shouldn't have been so mean to him at first. He was only trying to help. Don't you think they should have been nicer to him?"

Before Grace had a chance to ponder this literary critique, she saw a flicker of movement out of the corner of her gaze. She turned to find Jack leaning against the doorjamb watching them, his golden hair slightly messed and those green, green eyes gleaming with tenderness as they lit on his daughter.

How long had he been standing there? Long enough to see the emotions she knew she couldn't conceal?

"Daddy!" Emma shrieked. Her "bestest friend in the whole wide world" forgotten like yesterday's soup du jour, she jumped from Grace's lap and leaped into her father's arms.

Jack picked her up effortlessly and she threw her arms around his neck and planted a huge, sloppy kiss on the afternoon shadow stubbling his cheek. He nuzzled her neck, earning squeals of glee as he tickled her with his whiskers in what was obviously a ritual between the two.

No matter what his crimes might be, it was obvious Jack Dugan loved his daughter.

At the thought, she stiffened in the rocking chair. She couldn't afford to let any soft emotion interfere with this investigation. It was too important to all the innocents who had suffered because of the deadly weapons he was suspected of dealing.

"What have you been up to, Little Em?"

"Grace and me were just reading my story about the gecko."

"Grace and I."

"Right. Grace and I. Daddy, can she come with us next time we go to our other house so she can help me catch a real gecko?"

He glanced at her over the girl's blond head and Grace felt her face heat up, as if she'd been angling for an invitation to his vacation home. The reaction annoyed her and she returned his inquisitive look with a cool one of her own.

"We'll have to see." He set Emma back to her feet. "Lily's making some of her macadamia nut brownies. Why don't you go see if she'll let you lick the spoon while I talk to Grace for a few minutes?"

"Okay. I'll take Betty with me. She loves brownies, too." She grabbed the stuffed poodle from the bed and scampered out.

Immediately, the room seemed to shrink. She didn't quite know how he did it, especially given the sheer size of the room and the wide wall of windows that made it appear even larger, but somehow he seemed to fill up every available inch with his presence.

With his slow, easy gait, he ambled inside and sat on the edge of the bed, stretching his long legs out in front of him as if he planned to stay awhile, whether she wanted him to or not.

"Sorry I've been a little scarce the last few days. I haven't been a very good host, I'm afraid, but things have been a little crazy."

The last thing she wanted to do was sit here and chitchat with him, especially when she was wearing nothing but one of Lily's muumuus. She had been in too much pain at first while she was still recovering from her burns to let it bother her. Now that she suffered only the occasional twinge from her wounds, though, she felt awkward and exposed in the robe, despite the fact that the thing completely swallowed her up.

On the other hand, she needed to remember the investigation. Any chance she had to learn more about what he did and who he associated with could lead to the information that would help bring him down.

She inched back in the rocker and covered her bare feet with the hem of the robe, feeling about as far from a hard-nosed police detective as she possibly could.

She tried to ignore her discomfort and forced her features into an expression of casual inquiry. "Are you having problems at the company?" she asked.

"Just the usual hassles. A shipment of circuit boards from Korea got stalled in Customs because of some lost paperwork, so I've spent the last four days trying go-between an angry customer and a frantic supplier and convince the feds to bend the rules a bit."

Did he have any idea at all that he was under investigation? she wondered. And just how far was he willing to bend the rules? Far enough until they shattered?

"Do you have many problems with Customs?" she asked.

He laughed. "Show me anybody in the business who doesn't have problems with Customs and I'll show you somebody who's slipping some serious money under the table.

Yeah, I've had problems with Customs before. It goes with the territory."

"How big is GSI?"

"Big enough to be a major headache most of the time. But not as big as I'd like it to be." He grinned. "We're the second largest private shipping company in the Northwest. I expect to take over the top spot within the next year. From there, who knows?"

"Nobody would say you're not ambitious, would they, Dugan?"

"I don't think I am. I started out with one tiny single-engine plane I bought when I left the air force. I never intended things to work out like this, I just wanted to fly."

"So why didn't you stay in the military?"

She heard the hard, accusatory note in her voice and gave an inward wince. Good grief, she was rusty at this. She used to be pretty good at undercover work. There was a time the guys in the squad used to *beg* her to run stings with them.

But sitting here with Jack Dugan in her bare feet and a borrowed muumuu, she was afraid she had completely lost her touch. Instead of skillfully weaving her questions into the conversation, instead of subtly leading her prey in the direction she wanted him to go, she sounded exactly like she was grilling a suspect under hot lights in one of those airless little interview rooms at the station house.

Jack didn't seem to notice, though. He just shrugged. "It took me a few years but I discovered I'm not crazy about following orders."

Oh, big surprise there. "So you quit and went off on your own, naming your company Global Shipping Incorporated, even though you had no ambitions whatsoever."

He grinned again at her sardonic tone. "The name started out as a joke. For the first six months we only had one account, a restaurant in Utah who wanted to be able to claim they had fresh seafood flown in daily. They didn't seem to care that it was flown in on a rickety old plane with no seat belts and duct tape on the windshield. We were barely able to afford fuel with what they paid us, but for some strange reason we made the brilliant business decision to incorporate. Piper and I came up with the name. I'm pretty sure at least one of us was drunk at the time."

"Piper?"

"Piper McCall. My partner. I'm sure you'll meet him eventually. He's always in and out."

She filed the name away to ask Beau about as Jack went on. "Anyway, I guess you could say the name turned out to be some kind of self-fulfilling prophecy. We picked up a few more accounts, eventually leased a 727, and found our niche in the market; delivering computer components to start-up companies here in Seattle who needed a faster turnaround than they could get by boat. Now we have over a hundred-fifty employees, fly into thirty-five different countries and—" he broke off and she was fascinated to see a ruddy tinge climb his cheeks.

"I'm sorry. I didn't mean to bore you. I tend to ramble on when I'm talking about the company."

Keep rambling, she thought. *Tell me all your secrets.*

But he seemed to think he'd said enough because he cleared his throat and abruptly changed the subject. "How's your back?" he asked.

She swallowed her disappointment. "Fine."

"Lily says it seems like it's healing."

Why did he bother even asking her when he'd probably been getting daily progress reports all along? She barely refrained from glaring at him. "It is, so I would appreciate it if you would stop treating me like some kind of invalid now and let me do the job you hired me for."

"I just don't want you to overdo it."

"I'm perfectly fine," she repeated. *And anxious to start digging into all the dirty corners of your life, Dugan.*

"If you're sure you're up to it, you can officially start tomorrow, then. As you said the other night, I think the alarm system here at the house is the logical place to start. After you've made whatever improvements you think are needed here, you can take a look at the company's system."

She would have preferred it the other way around but knew she couldn't protest without sounding suspicious. "Great," she replied. "I only have one problem."

"What's that?"

Although she hated drawing more attention to it than she absolutely had to, she pointed to the tropical tent she wore. "I don't have anything to wear. Everything I own is at my apartment, except for the clothes I was wearing when you brought me here. And as much as I appreciate your housekeeper's generosity in lending me some clothes, I believe I would feel more comfortable in something a little less, um, roomy."

He cocked his head and examined her. As his gaze traveled from the loose neckline—with its tendency to slip off her shoulder, since it had been made for someone more of Lily's ample proportions than her own—to her toes that insisted on peeking out from under the hem, something hot and glittering sparked in his eyes.

Definite male interest. She could read it in those sea-green depths as clearly as a blinking neon sign.

And even though her mind had built up plenty of blockades to protect her from Jack Dugan's appeal, her body apparently didn't give a damn. She felt an answering heat flash through her like lightning arcing across Puget Sound. Her stomach fluttered and the room seemed a great deal smaller suddenly.

"I don't know," he murmured, a small, intimate smile dancing at the corners of his firm mouth. "There's something to be said for roomy and what it leaves to the imagination."

A slow, sensuous shiver rippled down her spine at his low words. She felt it and frowned. Where was this coming from? She didn't want it, couldn't handle it. She never wanted to feel anything like this again, especially for a man who could very likely be a criminal.

She sternly ordered her hormones to behave and decided the best way to handle this attraction between them would be to completely ignore it. Maybe, if she was really, really lucky, it would go away.

"What about my clothes?" she asked.

He studied her for a moment longer, then nodded. "I should have thought about this before and had Lily pick something up for you."

"I have plenty of clothes. Just not here."

"I'll drive you to your apartment after dinner and you can pick up what you need."

"You don't have to do that," she said quickly. "I could ask Lily or her husband to take me. Or I can just catch a cab."

"It's no problem at all." He grinned. "Em loves any chance to ride the ferry and she'll be thrilled to come with us to your apartment. Just let me know when you're ready."

She wouldn't *ever* be ready, she thought as he walked out of the room. Emma might be thrilled to come with him, but she definitely couldn't say the same to have the girl tag along. Hadn't she just told herself the only way she could handle this job would be if she could manage to avoid his daughter? How was she supposed to do that when Jack Dugan insisted on shoving them together?

CHAPTER SIX

THE RAIN HAD STOPPED BY THE TIME JACK drove his car onto the ferry heading for Seattle and Grace's apartment. Although it was still cloudy, the sun was beginning to set in a fiery blaze of color.

He started to point it out to Grace, then decided against it. She probably wouldn't care. The woman who had carried on such a lengthy, interested conversation with him back at the house had disappeared like the fog.

Now she sat silent as a ghost beside him in a pale blue sweater and a pair of too-big jeans of his she had borrowed, her face set in stiff lines.

"Daddy, can we go watch for mermaids?"

He glanced in the back seat where Emma practically jitterbugged with anticipation.

Mermaid-watching from the ferry was one of their little rituals, like Eskimo kisses at bedtime and piggyback rides around the pool.

"Can we, Daddy? Can we?"

"We'll have to see what Grace wants to do," he answered. "She's our guest."

Right now their guest looked as if she would rather be having her toenails plucked out one by one than find herself sitting on the Bainbridge-to-Seattle ferry with the two of them.

She had barely spoken the entire ten minutes from the house to the ferry, had kept that delectable mouth in a tight, tense line nearly the entire drive.

He wasn't sure what, exactly, was responsible for this abrupt change in her, but he was afraid it had something to do with Emma and her constant chattering.

Being around his cheerful little girl couldn't be easy for her. He hadn't missed the awkward way Grace had held her back at the house while she read the gecko story or the pain she had been unable to conceal that darkened those huge mocha eyes.

He ached whenever he thought of all she had lost, but her distance unquestionably put him in protective-father mode.

Emma was a sweet, joyful little girl who was happiest when she had somebody new to love. He wasn't willing to sit idly by and watch her new favorite person break her heart into little pieces.

Em's own mother hadn't wanted the inconvenience of raising her and had only consented to marry him and go through with the pregnancy if he would agree to pay her an obscenely large divorce settlement.

He couldn't completely blame Camille—her pregnancy had been a mistake, something neither one of them had expected.

By all rights, theirs should have been a short-lived, if passionate, relationship. That was all both of them had wanted at the time. He had been overwhelmed as GSI started to become more successful and Camille had been a wild, thrill-seeking pilot—even more thrill-seeking than he had been before Emma was born. She had been much too reckless and ambitious to be content as a corporate wife and dutiful mother.

Things hadn't worked out that way. Even though Emma had only been three days old when Camille left—much too young to know rejection from her mother's desertion—*he* had known.

And he had done the hurting for her.

He'd be damned if he'd let another woman treat her the same way, even if Grace did have reason for her coolness.

Because he was worried over his daughter's feelings, his words sounded harsh, curt. "Would you prefer staying with the car or walking around on deck with us?"

Grace stared straight ahead at the gleaming rows of cars. "It doesn't matter to me."

Emma seized on the answer. "See, Daddy? She said it doesn't matter. Let's go! I just know we're going to see Ariel and her sisters today."

How could he refuse, in light of such absolute faith? He glanced across the length of the car at Grace again. "You're welcome to come along if you'd like."

He fully expected her to stay with the car. When she opened the door of the car and climbed out, he had a feeling it surprised her as much as it did him.

She stood by the passenger door looking a little lost for a moment, until Emma opened her own door and slipped her little hand into Grace's larger one. "We always watch for Ariel when we ride the ferry, don't we, Daddy? Have you seen *The Little Mermaid*? It's me and my daddy's favorite movie. We've seen it a billion times."

Confronted with such relentless cheer, Grace seemed to soften. Instead of pulling away from Emma's hand, she just raised an eyebrow at him, over the top of his daughter's blond head. "*The Little Mermaid,* Dugan? Hmm. Somehow I would have figured you more for a knock-'em-down, shoot-'em-up kind of guy."

He laughed because he basically *was* a knock-'em-down, shoot-'em-up kind of guy. "Not me," he lied. "Give me a good animated feature and a big bowl of buttered popcorn and I'm happy as a flea on a dog."

He almost got a smile out of her with that one. Almost. The corners of her mouth tilted up just a bit, as if the muscles were trying to remember how to work right.

Before a smile could break free, though, her lips slipped back into that tight, uncompromising line.

He sighed his disappointment. It was rapidly becoming an obsession, this desire to see what it might take for her to forget herself long enough to smile at him or, heaven forbid, actually laugh.

Looks like he had a long, long way to go.

With Emma tugging them along, they climbed the metal stairs to the deck. The sun had slipped a few more inches behind the pines on the island, enough to send brilliant peach rays peeking beneath the clouds to shimmer across the water. Ahead were the lights of the city, beginning to gleam in the twilight.

There weren't many others on the ferry. Most of the ferry business this time of evening consisted of commuters coming in the other direction, from jobs in Seattle back to their homes on the island, so they had the deck to themselves except for a group of teenagers on the other side.

Grace seemed to relax even more as the ferry lifted anchor. Elbows on the railing, she leaned into the brisk fall wind while it caught strands of her dark hair and twirled them around.

A couple of sea kayakers glided by out of range of the ferry's wake, their paddles barely rippling the surface, and she watched their progress until they were out of sight on the other side of the vessel.

To his amusement, Emma copied Grace's pose exactly, right down to the chin lifted defiantly to the elements. Her little elbows couldn't quite reach the railing, but that didn't seem to bother her. "Can you see any mermaids yet?" she asked him.

He shaded his eyes and scanned the horizon in all directions with exaggerated movements. "Not yet. You?"

She mimicked his actions, peeking through the bars of the railing. "Nope. Not yet. I wonder where they are?"

"Maybe they're having a party down there. Watch for party hats sticking out of the water."

Emma giggled. "I don't see any. Grace, what about you? Can you see any mermaids yet?"

He held his breath, expecting her to pull away. To his surprise, she played along. "Nothing here." She paused, then focused hard on a spot to starboard. "Wait…is that one? Nope. Just a piece of driftwood. I'll keep looking, though."

As he expected, Emma soon tired of mermaid-watching. Her attention span could just about stretch across a paper cup. "Can I get a treat, Daddy?" She pointed to the row of vending machines lining the inside wall.

He fished some change from the pocket of his jacket and handed it over. "One, that's all, or Lily will cook me for breakfast."

Emma snickered. "She will not. You won't fit in any of her pans."

He tweaked her nose. "You're too smart for your own britches, aren't you?"

"Yep." She put the change into the front pocket of her overalls and hopped on one foot over to the vending machines.

"Do you really think that's wise?"

He turned back to Grace. "What?"

She craned her neck to watch Emma gazing up at her treat choices. "Letting her go alone like that."

"It's just a dozen feet or so. She's not even out of sight."

"Not now, but what if the ferry were crowded with people?"

"Then I would probably go with her."

"Do you have any idea how easy it would be for you to lose sight of her, for someone to just grab her and walk away?"

"And go where? In case it's escaped your attention, we're surrounded by water here."

"We won't be for long. If somebody wanted to, he or she could hide her in the trunk of a car or under a pile of blankets. Before you figured out that she hadn't simply wandered away, they could drive off the ferry once it reached the city, with no one the wiser."

His stomach lurched sharply as he contemplated the possibilities. He had tried to convince himself that her kidnapping had just been a fluke. A random criminal act.

He made a comfortable income with GSI, but there were plenty of others in the Seattle area with a whole hell of a lot more money than he had.

So why had Emma been a target? And if it happened once, what were the chances of it happening again?

The police were no closer to answers and neither were his private detectives. The frustration over having no one to blame but some nameless, faceless stranger willing to let his daughter burn to death only added to his anger.

"What do you suggest I do to keep her safe?" he asked, with his gaze now fixed on Emma.

"You could hire a bodyguard, I suppose, but even that's not completely foolproof. If she could slip away from you, she could probably slip away from a bodyguard."

"For the rest of her life?"

"Or at least until the kidnappers are caught, I suppose."

"I don't want her to have to live with some hired goon constantly shadowing her. What the hell kind of life is that for a little girl?" His knuckles whitened on the railing. He hated this. It wasn't right that his daughter should have to live this way, as a prisoner to other people's greed.

"She didn't do anything wrong," he snapped. "She ought to be able to walk to a damn candy machine without always having somebody looking over her shoulder."

"The other alternative is to change your routines. When I was a cop, we advised people who had been victimized to never take the same way home twice. You're at a disadvantage because you live on an island with only one route on or off, but if you took a few basic precautions with Emma, you could go a long way toward protecting her."

"What kind of precautions?"

"Vary the times you leave and the routes you take. Keep her away from large groups of people. Stay close to her at all times."

"Basically smother her, you mean."

"I'm sorry there are no easy answers, Dugan. You hired me to keep her safe and I'm just trying to do my job."

"You could be her bodyguard," he said suddenly. "Just until this is over and the creeps who took her are behind bars. She likes you and it wouldn't be the same as having some stranger tailing her all the time."

She looked out at the water, appalled at the very idea. "No," she said emphatically. "That's not part of my job description."

"But you could do it."

"I could. But I won't."

She prayed he wouldn't push her on this. Mercifully, after one long, searching look, he said nothing more about it and she breathed a tremendous sigh of relief.

How could she explain to him that being with his daughter

even occasionally was difficult enough. Having to shadow her day and night would be torture.

Dear God, she missed Marisa. She filled her lungs with salt-soaked air, hating herself for the melancholy that was a physical ache, but unable to prevent it.

Marisa seemed so close to her here on the water and yet so terribly out of reach.

She had loved the water. Beau used to take them out on his junk heap of a fishing boat whenever the weather was good and the three of them would spend the day watching for dolphins and whales just as Emma watched for mermaids.

She would give anything—*anything*—for one more day like that.

Instead, she was stuck here with a man she despised and a little girl who broke her heart every time she looked at her.

As if on cue, Emma returned, hands held behind her back.

"What are you hiding?" Jack asked her.

"You have to guess."

"Is it…an elephant?"

She rolled her eyes. "No."

"Is it…a new car?"

"Daddy, you're being silly."

"I give up, then. What did you buy."

"It's a present. For Grace."

Grace turned warily.

"You gave me four quarters so I bought two of the very same things, one for her and one for me." In Emma's chubby little hands were two identical cheap bracelets, braided from colorful string. She thrust one out to Grace. "See, they're friendship bracelets."

"I don't…" Her voice broke off and she just stared at the loop of string. She wanted to push her away, to refuse the gift, but how could she without sounding cruel?

The harder she tried to keep Emma Dugan and her father at arm's-length, the harder they tried to sneak through her defenses.

"Thank you very much," she finally said solemnly, taking the offering from the little girl. "Pink and purple are my favorite colors."

Emma grinned her gap-toothed little grin. "Mine, too! Daddy, will you put them on us?"

She opened her mouth, ready to protest that she could take care of it herself, but the words caught in her throat when she found him watching her intently. His green eyes had lost the coolness she'd seen in the car—now they had warmed to the lush color of maple leaves in July.

An answering heat revved to life in her chest and began to spread outward. Before she could close her hand around it to keep him from taking her gift, the rough pads of his fingers brushed her skin as he pulled the bracelet away from her.

He slipped Emma's bracelet on her wrist with all the ceremony of a court attendant fitting Cinderella for a glass slipper.

She was so fascinated by the sight of those broad, strong fingers performing the delicate task that she forgot to think of some way to keep him from putting her own bracelet on. All too soon, he turned to her, the entwined strings dangling from his fingers.

"Your turn. Give me your hand."

Her heart began to pump harder, faster. She didn't want him touching her again. She *didn't*. His touch made her feel too much, and she hated it. "I can do it. Really."

"No, you can't."

She blinked as the full force of his smile hit her straight on, sweet and tantalizing and unbelievably potent. "I can't?"

"We've bought these before, in fact I have a green one just like it on my desk at home. It's a clever little thing, actually.

You have to have someone else adjust it on your wrist, you just can't do it one-handed. That's why it's called a friend-ship bracelet, since you need a friend to help you put it on. Come on, give me your hand."

She chewed her lip for a moment then thrust her arm out, knowing she had no choice. Not with both of them watching her so expectantly.

He lifted the sleeve of her borrowed sweater that smelled like him, and took her hand. The bracelet had been made for a child so it took some effort to get it past her fingers, although with all the weight she had lost in the last year, it hung on her bony wrist with room to spare.

Was she imagining things or did his hand linger on hers a bit longer than strictly necessary? He was warm, much warmer than she was. She could feel the heat of him against her skin, and despite her efforts at self-preservation, it lured her like a woodstove on a cold day.

With his head bent over her hand, his scent drifted to her on the sea breeze. Masculine and alluring, with a hint of sandal-wood and perhaps a dose of pine, like the towering trees that surrounded his house there on the water.

His neck was tanned and strong, corded with muscle, but she could see where the tan line ended above his hairline. Would that hair be as soft as it looked, like fine suede?

Just before she would have reached her fingers to find out, the ferry horn sounded, deep and loud.

She snatched both hands away from him as if he had just poured hot ash on them and thrust them into the pockets of her borrowed jeans. Even through the layers of cloth she could feel her fingers trembling.

Good heavens. What had she nearly done? Touched him, caressed him. *Wanted* him.

He might be the enemy. She had to remember that, that

this man with the green eyes and the ready smile could be one more cog in the vast criminal wheel that had taken her daughter's life.

She had to remember the reason she was here with him. And even more important, she had to completely forget that for the first time in a year, she felt alive again.

Her apartment building was just as grim as he remembered. The same peeling paint, the same rusty swings hanging forlornly from the cracked playground, the same stench of desperation.

"It shouldn't take me long to pack a suitcase," Grace said in a low voice so she didn't disturb Emma, who had conked out the moment they drove off the ferry.

"Take all the time you need."

Pack up everything, he wanted to say, *because I'm sure as hell not letting you come back here.*

"Do you think she'll wake up?"

He glanced in the back seat again. Emma's head lolled to the side and she was sleeping with her mouth open. It didn't look the least bit comfortable, but she'd been known to sleep all the way to Oregon like that.

"Once she falls asleep in the car, it takes a foghorn to wake her up again. I can carry her into the house, change her into her pajamas and put her into her bed without her even stirring."

Grace's features softened, and her mouth curved up in the barest shadow of a smile. "Marisa…" her voice faltered and she cleared her throat before continuing. "My daughter used to be the same way. She could sleep through anything."

It was the first time she had voluntarily brought up her daughter's name with him. Maybe she was finally ready to let him inside those high walls she'd built around herself.

Before he could pursue it, though, and ask her more about her child, she slipped from the car and hurried up the rickety iron steps without a backward glance.

Dammit. The woman was more skittish than a whole blasted herd of wild horses. The minute he started to believe he might be making some small degree of progress gaining her trust, she hightailed it away from him.

Not this time, he decided. He wasn't going to let her run away this time. He scooped Emma out of the back seat and hefted her over his shoulder, hoping she wouldn't suddenly decide to turn into a light sleeper tonight of all nights. She stirred a bit, then nestled into the curve of his neck while he climbed the steps to Grace's apartment.

He didn't bother to knock, just tried the knob. Ms. Former Cop must have been more overwrought than she was letting on—she hadn't bothered to lock it behind her, a caution he felt sure was as instinctive to her as breathing.

He pushed the door open and cocked his head, listening. The place was just as depressing as he remembered from before, only this time it had the stale, closed-up air that came from being empty for over a week.

He could hear the soft rustle of movement in the rear of the apartment, in what he assumed was a bedroom, so he gingerly laid Emma on the ugly gold couch, checked to make sure she didn't awaken, then followed the sound.

He found Grace in the bedroom, with a suitcase already gaping open on the bed. Her back was to him as she sorted through her things inside a drawer of the chipped old bureau.

He started to knock on the doorframe to alert her to his presence, then he froze, his fist hanging in mid-air, as he caught sight of her reflection in the wavy mirror above the dresser.

While she went about the ordinary task of packing up the

pieces of her life—the socks and jeans and hairbrushes she would need during her stay in his house—silent tears coursed down her cheeks like slow summer rain.

CHAPTER SEVEN

PANIC SPURTED THROUGH HIM AT THE SIGHT of her tears.

He was no different from the next man. He would rather bring down a 747 with no landing gear and only one engine in the middle of a frigging ice storm than have to deal with a crying woman.

Before he could take the coward's way out and figure out how to back away from the room without giving himself away, she sensed his presence. Her head lifted sharply and their eyes met in the mirror, his concerned and edgy and hers suddenly wary.

She whirled to face him and he had a feeling she wasn't even aware of the tears trickling down her cheeks. It was so incongruous—the glare peeking through the tears—that he would have smiled if not for this heavy ache in his chest.

"What are you doing in here?"

He paused, unsure how to answer her. If he told her he had

been worried about her, that he could see how just the mention of her daughter upset her, she probably would deny it.

She definitely wouldn't welcome the comfort he was all too willing to offer. Grace Solarez struck him as a woman who preferred to do her grieving alone, who didn't like to show this raw, vulnerable side to anyone, no matter how compassionate that person might be.

He thrust his hands in his pockets. "I thought you might need a little help carrying your things out to the car," he finally said.

"I suppose it never occurred to you to do something normal for once like, oh, I don't know, maybe *knock* first?"

He gave a half-smile. "It occurred to me." He left it at that.

"And you just as quickly decided to ignore the impulse."

He shrugged. "I had my arms full. It just seemed easier to come on in."

"Full of what?"

"Emma. She's on the couch, sound asleep."

With the reminder of his daughter, she seemed to finally realize she continued to weep even as she confronted him. Those dark eyes widened with horror and she tried to surreptitiously wipe her tear-stained cheeks against the shoulder of her borrowed sweater, as if she thought he wouldn't notice them.

Her movements became brisk. "I'm almost done here. You can wait in the other room with your...with Emma."

She had a hard time even saying the word. *Daughter. Your daughter.* The life that had been taken so cruelly from her.

"Grace," he began, then fumbled for words, not sure what he could say. He was no good at this stuff.

Excessive emotion of any sort had been frowned upon in the Dugan household. William Dugan allowed no loud laughter, no raised voices, and—God forbid—no tears.

He'd learned young to conceal everything, that any outward show would only result in his father's stiff, silent disapproval.

Only as an adult had he realized how unhealthy it was. His mother drank herself to a slow, painful death. And his father…

Jack blew out a breath at the image that was scored into his mind like a brand, even after all this time.

Rather than cope with his financial failures and the death of his wife, William Dugan chose the coward's way out. Escape. He sat behind his antique oak desk, shoved a gun in his mouth and put a bullet through his brain at a place and time where he had to know his only son would be the one to stumble onto him.

He wasn't that boy anymore, Jack reminded himself. He was a grown man who had learned the bitter lesson that covering up a wound sometimes only prevented the healing touch of air from reaching it.

"Would you like to talk about her?" he finally asked.

Grace gave him a deliberately obtuse look. "About Emma? She's a sweet little girl. Just a little warning, though. She thinks Santa Claus is going to bring her a puppy this year if she doesn't take her stuffed dog into the bathtub with her anymore. You might want to be prepared for that."

"No. Not about Emma. About Marisa. About how you can't even ride the ferry without thinking about her, without grieving for her."

Dammit. He'd blown it. At his words, her face grew stony and cold, her body even more tense. "No, I don't want to talk about her. And if I did, it wouldn't be with you." She slammed the lid of the suitcase down so hard it bounced up again.

"Why not?" he asked, stung somehow even though he knew damn well he shouldn't be.

She closed the lid more carefully this time and thumbed the snaps without looking at him. "Because it doesn't concern you. Stay out of that part of my life, Jack. It's my business, something you know absolutely nothing about."

"It might help. To talk about her, I mean."

"Drop it, Dugan."

He should. She was right, it wasn't any of his business. But he wanted fiercely to help her find a little peace. She had done so much for him—had given him back his daughter—he owed her that much, at least.

"I don't know anything about what you've gone through during the last year," he said, choosing his words carefully. "I can't even imagine it. But I do know something about grief and anger, about how closing yourself up with it will eventually suffocate you."

She glanced at him, that wariness back in her eyes.

He again debated what to say and felt like a hypocrite. Despite his grand advice, it was still difficult for him to talk about the summer he'd lost his family.

"My parents died when I was eighteen," he said abruptly. "My mother was an alcoholic and died of advanced liver disease. A few months later my dad killed himself. Chewed on one of the handguns he collected."

She stared at him, shocked. For some reason she pictured him as having a pampered, idyllic childhood, private schools and riding lessons and trips to Europe.

"For a long time," he went on, "I refused to talk about it with anyone. I was exactly like you and thought it wasn't anybody's business but my own."

He paused and met her gaze. "Eventually it started to eat away at me until I thought I was going crazy. Even though I knew alcohol had killed my mother, I started drinking all the time. It was the only way I knew how to deal with it all. I'd still be lost in that dark, ugly world if I hadn't met Piper in a bar one day, if he hadn't taken me under his wing, excuse the pun, and decided to teach me how to fly. In the air, I found I could talk about all the things that had been bottled up inside me."

She studied him, at the rare vulnerability in his green eyes, and almost gave in to the powerful urge to do as he said and talk about Marisa. But she had shut herself off from everyone for so long she didn't know how or where to begin. "Well, we're not flying, are we?" she finally said.

She heard the bitchiness in her voice and hated it but couldn't seem to stop the brittle words from bursting out. "I'm sorry about your parents, Dugan, but this isn't 'True Confessions' where you bare your soul, then I bare mine. It doesn't work that way."

She picked up the suitcase and started for the door, intent only on escape. Just as she started to brush past him, he reached a hand to stop her and grabbed her arm.

With her mind still seething and churning, her nerves completely on edge, she didn't stop to think. She just relied on the self-defense instincts she'd developed over ten years as a cop. In one motion, she dropped the suitcase and grabbed his wrist in a twist lock. She would have toppled him to his knees if he hadn't turned into her, making the hold useless.

As soon as he parried the move, she snapped back to her senses. Jack Dugan posed no threat to her. No physical one, anyway. She had drastically overreacted to what was a completely innocent touch.

Mortified heat soaked her skin and she closed her eyes, wanting to sink through her ugly gold carpet.

"I'm sorry. I don't... I wasn't thinking."

"I upset you and pushed you too hard. I don't blame you for wanting to knock me to the floor."

"It wasn't that."

"You didn't want to knock me to the floor?"

Incredibly, unbelievably, she felt a small laugh bubble up in her chest. "I never said that."

He laughed, too, a low, raspy sound in the hush of her cramped bedroom, and she tilted her head to take in the full impact of his smile. Too late, she realized their bodies were in intimate contact, chest to chest, knee to knee. Only a shadow of a breath hovered between them.

She should back away. *Now.*

Before her body could translate the thought into action, though, he sighed out a breath, then bent his head and brushed his lips over hers with aching gentleness.

For a few seconds, she was too stunned to withdraw from his soft assault. Then, before she could marshal her defenses, a slow, insidious heat uncurled in her stomach, poured through her limbs like smoke.

Inch by agonizing inch, her body began a long, painful thaw.

How long had it been since she'd felt the sizzle of a man's kiss? Since she'd been made to feel so…wanted?

She couldn't even begin to remember. After the illicit liaison that had ended in pregnancy when she was sixteen—after she had finally given in to weeks of persuasion and surrendered her innocence to Alex Rosales—her serious relationships had been few and far between.

She'd had more important things to worry about, juggling career and home and Marisa as a young single mother, with little time for romantic entanglements.

Even if she had wanted them, she'd also never had that many opportunities. Cops generally associated with three classes of people: perpetrators, victims and other cops. She'd had no desire to become involved with someone from any of those demographics.

That inexperience must be why Dugan's touch affected her

so powerfully. Why the hardness of his muscles against her, around her, muddled her thoughts and tangled up her breath.

She fought it for a moment, then realized she was losing ground. He had such warmth, such life, and she wanted nothing more than to stay right here and steal some of it for herself.

She closed her eyes and decided to give in to his kiss. Just for a moment, she promised herself. Just long enough to get it out of her system so she could concentrate on the case against him.

His mouth was warm and fluid on hers and tasted like cinnamon candy. He feathered soft kisses at the corners of her mouth and she couldn't prevent her lips from parting just enough to let him in.

The heat of his breath, the slick feel of his mouth on hers, took away the remaining fragments of reason. Everything faded away, leaving only this: his taste, his scent, his touch.

He pulled her even closer and she felt surrounded by him, engulfed by him. Without even being aware of it, she sagged against him with a soft, aroused moan.

The sound was just enough to sink through her subconscious. Her eyes flew open as she realized what she was doing, that their mouths were deeply entangled, that her body was wrapped around him and crying out for more.

Horrified, she scrambled away, backing up until her legs hit the bed, and sucked in a ragged breath.

What was she thinking? *She was kissing Jack Dugan!* And not just kissing him, but *enjoying* it. Savoring it. She had been oblivious to the world, lost in the hot mystery of his mouth, of his touch.

She seriously needed to have her head examined.

She swiped at her mouth with the back of her hand, as if she could rub away the feel and taste of him that still lingered there, while fury and, worse, sick humiliation burned in her chest.

What kind of woman was she to burn in the arms of a man who might be a heartless criminal?

"What the hell was that all about?" She wanted to snap at him, but it came out sounding more like a croak.

He leaned against the doorframe and crossed his arms, looking as relaxed as if he'd just stepped out of a sauna. "About two people who share a powerful attraction to each other seizing the moment when it comes along."

"I'm not attracted to you," she lied. "Not in the slightest. Not one teeny tiny iota. In fact, I couldn't be any less attracted to you."

Grace, shut up! She snapped her teeth together when she realized she was protesting much too vehemently.

He raised an eyebrow. "My mistake, then."

"It was. A mistake, I mean." She drew in another ragged breath. "A mistake we can't allow to happen again."

"Can't we?"

"No. Absolutely not." She rubbed her hands on the thick cotton of her borrowed jeans. "Look, I'm serious about this, Dugan. I'm not interested in any kind of…of fling with you. I mean it. If you can't keep yourself from 'seizing the moment,' as you called it, I won't be able to work for you."

He studied her out of those mesmerizing green eyes for a moment, then to her surprise, he nodded. "You're right. I was out of line. I hope this won't affect our working relationship."

She almost laughed. How could it *not* affect their working relationship? She had tasted his mouth, tangled her fingers in his hair, absorbed the strength of his body against her.

She had a feeling things would never be the same again.

She hid from him successfully for three days.

No. Not hid from him. She frowned, disliking the implications of the word. That somehow she was afraid to face him and what had happened back at her apartment. It wasn't like that. She *avoided* him, that's all.

When he wasn't in the city at his office, she stayed in her room, taking her meals there and spending the evenings reading or watching inane television shows.

She even managed to keep her mind from dwelling on the hard strength of his mouth on hers back at her apartment, on that wild rush of feeling that had threatened to overwhelm her.

Most of the time, anyway.

So she spent every night alternating between tossing and turning in that big oak and wrought-iron bed or standing at the window with her arms wrapped around herself, looking out at the city lights reflected across the water of the Sound. So what?

It had nothing to do with Jack Dugan or his seductive touch. Or the life and heat that had flowed back through her for the first time in a year when she had been in his arms.

She pushed the memory away along with the elaborate breakfast Lily delivered a few minutes earlier. She wasn't going to dwell on it anymore. She had spent enough time obsessing, trying to figure out what would compel her to let him kiss her.

And, she admitted to herself, to return his kiss with an eagerness that still stunned her.

There were a million reasons why their kiss had been a colossal mistake. She was staying at his house to spy on him, for heaven's sake. That was certainly reason enough.

But even if he wasn't the key suspect in an arms dealing ring, she could never consider becoming involved with him. Yes, she was attracted to him, with a ferocity that alarmed her. But not enough to forget the little five-year-old reason she could never let herself care about Jack Dugan, even if the situation had been different.

Emma, his sweet little girl, whose very presence stabbed a knife into her heart again and again and again.

To her relief, after two days his daughter seemed to finally tire of Grace's repeated refusals to play with her. The morning before, she had given her one last mournful look when Grace told her she would be too busy all day, and then the little girl left her in blessed, Emma-free peace.

She knew she would have to face both of them, and soon. She wasn't helping Beau's investigation at all while she was holed up here in her room, and Jack was probably beginning to wonder exactly what she was doing to earn her paycheck.

Besides, it wasn't in her nature to hide out. Well, okay, it might have been once, she conceded, but she had buried that meek, dutiful girl a long time ago. Since the moment she had found herself pregnant and alone at sixteen, with no home and no family left after Aunt Tia kicked her out of the house, she had determined that she would never again be that docile, submissive girl.

Where had it gotten her, after all? She had tried hard to do everything right for eight years, had been just the kind of pious little saint her aunt had demanded as the price for taking in a frightened orphan. An orphan who had no memory of the mother who had died when she was an infant and who had lost her father suddenly and violently.

She had sat through hour after hour of prayers with Tia, had gone to confession every single day because her aunt required it, had buried every impulsive, emotional impulse in a vain effort to earn the woman's approval.

It had all been for nothing. Because of one slip in judgment—she refused to call Marisa a mistake—she realized all of it had been for nothing.

No, she wouldn't hide out here simply because Jack Dugan had kissed her with such devastating thoroughness.

She would start now, she decided. She would march out there and act as if nothing had happened three days ago. She would concentrate only on the case, on doing what she could to bring him to justice.

She needed to see GSI, she decided, to get a feel for the layout of the place and the people who worked there. He had asked her to examine security at the company as well as his home, so she knew he wouldn't find it unusual when she asked to go with him.

She would tell him about what she'd been doing the last three days with his security system, then tell him she was ready to turn her attentions to GSI to help her see the whole picture.

But before she could do anything, she would have to find him. And when she did, she was going to purge from her mind any lingering, haunting memory of their heated embrace.

Completely.

With firm resolve, she opened the door and plowed head-first into a hard, muscled chest.

CHAPTER EIGHT

JACK'S HANDS AUTOMATICALLY WENT TO HER arms to help her maintain her balance when she came barreling out of her bedroom. Her skin was warm and soft under his fingers and he nearly forgot his vow to give her the space she so obviously needed.

For once she wasn't in borrowed clothes but wore tailored gabardine slacks and a silk short-sleeved sweater in pale yellow. She'd pulled that thick sable hair into a style she probably thought looked professional and competent. Instead, he briefly entertained several racy fantasies of pulling it loose to watch those dark curls pool around her naked shoulders.

She looked ice-cream cool and good enough to swallow whole.

He dropped his hands and curled them into fists to keep from reaching for her again. "Where are you off to in such a hurry this morning?"

She stepped back a pace. "Actually, I was on my way to find you."

"Me?"

She wiped her hands down her tailored slacks, making him wonder if she could possibly be as edgy around him as he was around her. The thought gave him an optimism he knew was probably totally unwarranted.

"I...yes. I've finished going through your security system here at the house. I have a few changes I'd like to see you implement."

"Yeah?"

"Well, a lot of changes, actually."

"Is it that bad?"

She twisted that delectable mouth into a frown and he found himself watching in fascination as the tiny little beauty mark at the corner of her lips moved.

"Worse," she said briskly, and he snapped his attention back to her words. "I'm surprised you don't have every crook in Seattle knocking down your door. You need much more than just that one paltry little intrusion alarm you have now."

"Do I?"

"At the very least you should set up video surveillance, both inside and outside. The security company you're already using probably can provide you with an updated system. I would also advise motion sensors around the perimeter of your property, especially on the waterfront. Anybody with an outboard motor can access the house that way."

What about armed guards and slavering Doberman pinschers? He shoved his hands in the pockets of his jeans, hating the idea of living in a damn prison but knowing it was necessary, at least until Emma's kidnappers were caught. "Feel free to change whatever you think is best. That's why I hired you."

"Of course, before I make any major changes, I'll run them past you."

"You don't have to do that. I trust you to do what you think is best."

She lifted those big dark eyes to his. "There's your first mistake, Dugan. You shouldn't trust anyone."

The cynicism in her eyes bothered him, for reasons he couldn't explain. Why should it, after all? For the most part, he shared that same attitude—that in general, he couldn't count on anyone but himself. He gave his trust to very few people. Lily and Tiny and Piper would just about fill the list.

But when he did decide to trust someone, he did it with absolute faith.

He couldn't imagine having no one at all.

"You're being a little melodramatic, don't you think?"

"You're a very wealthy man. Surely people have tried to take advantage of you before this kidnapping."

He thought of Camille and her selfishness. "Yeah," he murmured. "A few times. But that doesn't mean *everyone* has some hidden agenda."

She met his gaze coolly. "Take it from a cop, Dugan. Everyone has something to hide."

"Even you?"

Her brown eyes shifted away and focused on the bleached pine planks under their feet. "*Especially* me."

She didn't elaborate. He would have asked her what she meant but she interrupted him before he had a chance.

"Actually," she said, "I was thinking today would be a good chance to go into the city with you and have you show me around GSI. If you're not too busy, anyway."

He paged through his mental schedule. He had several appointments scheduled with a group of Korean computer manufacturers who wanted to give GSI exclusive rights to import their product to the U.S.

But he thought he could spare her a few hours first thing

in the morning. After he showed her around, he could give her free rein to talk to Piper or Sydney and they could fill her in on anything she needed to know.

"That could work," he said after a pause. "I'll be leaving in about fifteen minutes. Can you be ready by then?"

She nodded.

"Great. I'll meet you out front."

He wasn't sure spending even a few hours with Grace Solarez was the smartest of ideas, especially with this cool distance she seemed to want between them. But what could he say about it?

He *had* hired her to improve security here and at GSI and he couldn't very well prevent her from doing her job just because he was having one hell of a struggle keeping his hands to himself.

A little more than an hour later, Grace climbed out of the luxurious expanse of his sports car onto hard tarmac. She suddenly could relate to the way she imagined convicts must feel when they experienced freedom after years on the inside.

The morning had barely started but she was already exhausted after spending an hour alone with Jack Dugan in the close confines of his car, trying to keep this cool, professional attitude in place when all she could remember was the way his mouth had tasted of cinnamon and the life that had flowed through her while she was in his arms.

She forced her mind away from such dangerous territory and concentrated instead on the cluster of hangars, each bearing the distinctive company logo—an elegant line drawing of the world with "GSI" intertwined through the continents. The buildings gleamed in the sun, fresh-scrubbed and shiny and not at all the way she would have pictured the command center of a multi-national smuggling ring.

It might not be, she reminded herself. *Innocent until proven guilty.*

And that's exactly what she intended to do. Prove him guilty.

"Very impressive," she murmured when Dugan came around the length of the car and joined her.

"Thanks. I'm pretty proud of it. Come on and I'll introduce you around and then let you get to work on the security system."

She followed him into the hangar, which seemed much larger inside than out. It was a huge, cavernous warehouse-like area with metal walls and concrete floors, and she was immediately assaulted with the thick, not unpleasant smell of oiled machinery.

A row of glass and chrome offices marched down the length of one wall but the only people around seemed to consist of a crew of three men and one woman who climbed like monkeys over a huge black jet. A maintenance crew, she assumed.

As soon as they walked into the building, a well-dressed man in his late-fifties broke off his conversation with one of the crew members and hurried toward them.

Something about him reminded her of several of the detectives she'd worked with on the job who tried to look much younger than their age and clung desperately to a long-ago youth.

"Man, are you in trouble!" the man shook his head and his hair that had to owe its dark sheen to some artificial agent gleamed in the fluorescent overhead lights. "You were supposed to be here an hour ago. Syd's having a major cow looking for you."

Jack frowned and checked his watch. "I don't have anything scheduled until noon. That should give me at least another hour."

"All I know is she came in here hotter than you-know-what. Says the Koreans came early and they're all waiting in her office."

Jack winced and muttered an oath. After a moment, he turned to Grace, his expression apologetic. "I'm so sorry. I really can't get out of this. I'm afraid I'm going to have to abandon you for a while, but I'll do my best to hold the meeting to an hour or so."

"Don't cut things short on my account."

"If you don't want to wait around for me you're welcome to drive the car back across the ferry." He pulled his keys from his pocket and tossed them to her.

She caught them in midair. "I don't mind. I can take care of myself, Dugan. I've been doing it for a long time. This will give me a chance to look around on my own."

And do a little snooping while I'm at it.

"Great." With a distracted smile, he started walking away, then added over his shoulder, "Just ask Piper here for anything you need. Oh, Piper, this is Grace Solarez. Grace, Piper McCall, my partner. He knows as much about the company as I do."

Before either one of them could acknowledge the introduction, he walked away with long, purposeful strides.

She watched the lean-hipped gait for a moment, wondering just how he managed to make the simple act of walking across a room look unbelievably sexy, then realized what direction her mind was wandering into and gave herself a sharp, swift slap.

She was here to do a job and, dammit, she was going to do it.

Turning abruptly, she found Piper watching her, his eyes intense behind blue-tinted contact lenses.

"You're Grace? The Grace?"

She floundered. "I don't know. Am I?"

"You're the one! The lady who pulled our little Emma from that burning car, right?"

Great. More gratitude she neither wanted nor needed. "I just did what anyone else would have in the same situation," she mumbled, praying he would drop the issue.

Either the man didn't hear the vexation in her voice or he chose to ignore it. One minute he was simply standing there, the next he grabbed her and pulled her into a tight embrace.

She was immediately enveloped in an odd mixture of oil and cologne.

"Thank you so much for saving our little girl. When I think about what might have happened to her if you hadn't been there...." He shuddered and while he was busy pondering the grim possibilities, she managed to extricate herself.

His eyes had filled with raw emotion, she saw, and she found herself warming to the man. Even if he did seem to be trying to regain something that was forever lost to him, he apparently cared a great deal for Emma Dugan.

"Mr. McCall..."

"Piper. Everybody just calls me Piper."

"Piper. I really don't want to talk about this."

"That little girl means the world to us. She would have died in that crash if you hadn't come along, if you hadn't been so brave."

Bravery had nothing to do with it. She was about as far from a hero as a person could get, and she was really growing tired of trying to explain that to everyone.

If she were truly brave, she would have the courage to go on without Marisa. She wouldn't have these endless days when all she wanted to do was curl up in bed and wither away.

"I'm just glad I was there," she lied.

"We owe you the world. If you need anything—anything at all—just ask."

I need you to drop this, she thought, but swallowed the words. "Jack said something about a tour," she said pointedly.

"Sure. Right. I guess we can start in here."

What was she looking for? She didn't have the first clue. While Piper showed her around the four hangars that made up GSI, she tried to absorb everything around her, to be on the lookout for anything out of the ordinary. The problem was, she had no idea what was ordinary and what wasn't.

From her perspective, GSI seemed like a clean, well-run, organized company. But what did she know? Obviously something—and someone—in it was dirty or it wouldn't be the focus of scrutiny.

What she needed was a good briefing. She needed to talk to Beau and learn a little more about the progress of the investigation so she didn't waste her time covering old ground.

By the time they walked through the entire company, it was nearly noon. They returned to the main hangar and Piper showed her into a large office filled with dark, elegant furniture that seemed very uncharacteristic of Jack.

One wall was glass, offering a view of the work going on in the hangar, and the other was dominated by a huge oil painting of a tropical sunset. She could believe he picked out the painting, but the rest of it looked entirely too formal for him.

"I've got an appointment in a couple of minutes." Piper gave her an apologetic smile. "This is Jack's office. Do you mind waiting in here until his meeting gets out?"

She glanced around Dugan's territory with a small, private smile of anticipation that she quickly concealed and shook her head. "No problem. That would be fine."

With luck, she just might have time to make contact with

Beau and set up a little meeting of her own before diving into his files.

"Great," Piper said. With another apologetic smile, he walked out of the office, leaving her alone.

She waited several beats, checked to make sure no one was coming, then sat in the leather executive's chair behind the huge, gleaming desk and dialed the number of Beau's cellular phone.

He answered with his customary, grouchy-sounding, "What?"

"Guess where I'm calling from?" she asked, without any preliminaries.

"The 50-yard line in the Kingdome?"

She snorted. "Ha ha, very funny. Not even close. How does Jack Dugan's office hit you?"

"Like a runaway truck. You're yanking my chain, right?"

"Nope. I'm sitting in his great big throne behind a mahogany desk bigger than my car, staring at a row of mahogany file cabinets I'm just itching to let my fingers wander through."

"You're all by yourself?"

She rolled her eyes, even though she knew he couldn't see her. "No, Dugan's sitting right in front of me, hanging on my every word. What do you think?"

Riley said nothing for several seconds. When he spoke, his voice was low, intense. "I think it's good to hear that smart mouth of yours again. I've missed it, Gracie."

For a moment, she didn't know what to say. She realized suddenly that she'd missed it, too, their jokes and their banter and their comfortable, easy relationship. Even when they used to catch the most sordid and ugly of cases, Beau would always help her keep things in perspective.

She was suddenly profoundly sorry that she had put so much effort into trying to push him away for the last year.

He had tried to offer comfort, but she hadn't let him. She hadn't *wanted* to heal.

She cleared her throat, uncomfortable with the realization and the guilt pinching at her, and chose to change the subject. "So what's the status of the case on your end?"

"About the same," he answered. "What about you?"

"I'm still trying to find my bearings. I'd probably be able to make more headway if I was up to speed on your case. That's what I'm calling about, actually. I need to have you give me the bigger picture."

"Right now?"

"No. Dugan might be back any minute. I don't want to waste this chance to look around while I can. What about tonight?"

"You think you can get away from him without arousing too much suspicion? I can come out to Bainbridge and brief you while we grab a couple of burgers."

"He's my boss, not my keeper. I'll just tell him I need to do a little shopping tonight and I'll meet you in Winslow."

Riley snorted. "If you think he'll buy that excuse, he must not know you too well. You and shopping go together like peanut butter and anchovies."

She gave a small, rueful laugh. He was absolutely right. She'd never had the patience required to spend hour after hour wandering through the mall—maybe because she was too busy being a mother when she was a teenager to get much practice at it. "I'll tell him it's for girl stuff and he won't ask any questions. Guys hate that."

Beau paused for several seconds. When he spoke, his voice sounded wistful. "Seems almost like old times, doesn't it, Gracie? You and me, workin' a case."

A lump rose in her throat and she stared at Dugan's oil painting, concentrating until the striated yellows and oranges of the sunset merged into one color. "Yeah," she mumbled. "Yeah, it does."

She was so busy trying to force the lump down that she didn't hear the door open, didn't realize another person had entered the room until an outraged female voice rang through the office.

"Who are you and what do you think you're doing in here?"

CHAPTER NINE

GRACE SWIVELED AROUND IN THE PLUSH OFFICE chair to face a tall blond woman standing in the doorway wearing a power suit, killer heels and a militant glare.

She cleared her throat. "I've, uh, got to run," she said to Beau. "I'll see you at seven tonight at the ferry landing in Winslow."

She returned the receiver to the cradle and offered a cool smile to the blonde, who had walked into the room and now stood looming over her with an angry glare. "Hello. I don't believe we've met."

The woman's face tightened even more. "No. We certainly have not. I repeat, who are you and why are you sitting in that chair as if you owned the place?"

She was trying to come up with a suitable answer when she heard the low rumble of male voices in the hallway. A few seconds later, Jack and Piper walked into the office.

"Grace, I'm so sorry. I didn't mean to keep you waiting so long." Jack smiled at her and she was annoyed to feel her pulse kick up a notch. In the hour since she'd seen him, she had forgotten the impact of that smile. "I guess you met Sydney Benedict. Part bulldog, part financial wizard and the best damn secretary in the whole state of Washington."

The woman's perfectly made-up lips curved into a peeved kind of smile. "Executive assistant."

"Right. Executive assistant. Sorry." He grinned again and Grace had the distinct impression this was a battle the two of them had fought before. "She knows that whatever I call her, I'd be lost without her. She practically runs the place. Syd, this is Grace Solarez. You know, the one from Emma's car accident."

That flawless mouth stretched into a wider smile that still fell a few yards short of genuine. "I'm sorry. You should have told me who you were immediately. I was just surprised to find someone in Jack's private office, that's all."

Even the woman's apologies sounded like an accusation. Grace bared her teeth in an almost-genuine smile of her own. "No problem."

Now why would Sydney feel that she had to be so territorial of Jack? That was definitely the vibe she was getting from the other woman. Was it strictly the protectiveness of a secretary to a boss or did she have other, more intimate claims on him?

"How did it go?" Sydney asked. She turned her head and with her elegant upswept hairdo, discreet diamonds Grace would swear were real winked in her ears. Either Jack Dugan paid his personal assistants extraordinarily well or Sydney Benedict was independently wealthy.

Or she had another source of income. An illegal source. As Jack shrugged, Grace made a mental note to ask Beau about the woman's background and whether she might be part of the arms dealing.

"Hard to say," he answered. "They want to mull over our terms and meet again next week for another round of negotiations."

Surprise flitted across Sydney's coolly beautiful features. "They're staying in Seattle until next week?"

"No. Apparently this trip to the states is part business, part pleasure, at least for Mr. Kim and his sons. They're heading to Maui tonight for the pleasure part to play Kapalua. Big golfers, those Kims. They weren't planning a trip to Oahu but I offered to fly them over in the Learjet toward the end of the week so they could take in some of the Waikiki nightlife."

Grace blinked at his casual tone. She couldn't even begin to imagine what it must be like to have the kind of green to take a private jet to Hawaii on a whim, just to wine and dine a couple of clients.

Sydney frowned. "You can't do that. You've got a flight to Mexico City scheduled Thursday."

"Somebody else can take it. In fact—" his face broke out in a dazzling grin "—I just had a great idea. Why don't you cancel everything from Monday on. I told Em we would try to take Grace with us to help us try to catch geckos at the house in Hali'ewa and Lily's always eager for an excuse to go home and see her grandson for a few days. We can leave tomorrow."

Just like that, without so much as a "How about it, Grace?" he was ready to cart her off to Hawaii. She bristled, but before she could protest, his personal assistant did it for her.

The woman's mouth flattened into a tight line. "Jack, you can't just drop everything and take off like this."

"You can handle things, can't you?"

If she couldn't, she obviously wasn't going to admit it. "Of course. But still…"

Jack didn't wait for the rest of her arguments. "Piper, you

want to come along with us and co-pilot for me? You haven't been to Hawaii for a while, have you?"

If Grace hadn't been watching Sydney Benedict, she would have missed the way her mouth opened as if to protest, then a strange, sly light flitted through her blue eyes.

"Yes, Piper. Why don't you go along?" she said.

The older man sent her a swift, confused look and some silent message passed between them. What was the woman up to? Maybe she wanted the chance to be in complete control back on the homefront. She struck Grace as the power-hungry sort.

"Uh, sure," Piper said. "That'd be great. It'll give me a chance to look up that cocktail waitress from the Prince Kuhio I met last time we were there. What was her name? Kelly something-or-other?"

"How should I know? I can't keep track of your cocktail waitresses," Jack answered. "For that matter, *you* can't even keep track of your cocktail waitresses."

Sydney walked to the door. "I suppose I'd better begin rearranging your schedule then and handling your travel arrangements. Piper, shall I book a room for you on Waikiki?"

"Yeah. Sure. Try to get me in the Prince Kuhio, would you?"

"I'll see what I can do."

The older man followed Syd out of the office, giving alternative resorts he wanted to stay at if his first choice wasn't available—probably hotels of other cocktail waitresses he could look up, Jack thought with a grimace.

He would have thought Piper would start slowing down on the ladykiller front. But even as he neared sixty, he was clinging to his ways.

He was a damn good pilot—and he'd been loyal to Jack

when he had no one else—but the man went through women like other men used drugs or alcohol or gambling.

In the fifteen years Jack had known him, he'd been married and divorced twice—and had one more ex-wife from before Jack met him. Now he dated a different woman every week.

The pace had to be wearing on him.

He pushed his worries over Piper away and turned to Grace. He knew she wouldn't appreciate the observation, but she looked small and delicate in the huge leather chair Syd had ordered behind his back to replace the ratty old vinyl thing he hadn't wanted to part with.

Even overpowered as she was by the chair's dimensions, she took his breath away, with those huge dark eyes and that lush mouth.

Right now that mouth was drawn so tight against her teeth, they were probably leaving imprints on her lips, and those dark eyes had narrowed into thin slits.

It occurred to him that she seemed less than thrilled about the idea of going with him to Hawaii. Maybe he shouldn't have sprung it on her so abruptly.

"I'm sorry, Grace," he said warily, leaning a hip on the desk. "I didn't even ask if a day would give you enough time to pack."

"No. What you didn't ask is if I would even go. You just naturally assumed I would."

"You don't want to go?"

"No, I don't."

"It's Hawaii. You know, tropical paradise. White sand, blue water, gorgeous sunsets. Who would turn down a free trip to Hawaii?"

She glared at him. "Me."

"Why?"

"I'm not part of the family, Dugan. I'm your employee."

She enunciated the words slowly, carefully. "You hired me to oversee security for you."

"And so far you've been doing a hell of a job."

"How can I do that job if I'm loafing around on the beach in some skimpy bikini, watching those gorgeous sunsets?"

A picture of her doing exactly that flashed through his head. A hard rush of heat hit him first as his imagination fired into warp speed at just the thought.

On its heels, though, was a deeper image. Grace at peace, for once, relaxing on the sand while the sea rumbled a few yards away and trade winds rustled the fronds on the palms.

He had a feeling a change of scenery was just what she needed and wasn't about to let her wiggle out of it.

With the way her mind worked, he was afraid the more he argued with her, the more she would dig in her heels. He pondered his strategy for a few minutes, then straightened from the desk.

"Okay," he finally said. "If that's the way you feel, I understand. Emma will miss having you along to help her go gecko-hunting, but you're right. I hired you to overhaul security and that's exactly what you should do."

She frowned at him suspiciously, obviously geared up for a fight that wasn't going to happen.

"Of course," he added casually, "if somebody were really determined to harm me or my family, they wouldn't find a better place for it than Hawaii. You think the security system at the house here stinks, you ought to see the one in Hali'ewa. Hell, a chipmunk with a fingernail file could break in over there."

"Let's hope there aren't many chipmunks who've got it in for you, then," she answered coolly.

"Fine. Make jokes." He grinned, adoring this flippant side of her. "When I'm attacked in the night by a vicious ring of felonious squirrels, I'm going to hold you personally responsible."

"I know what you're trying to do and it won't work, Dugan."

"What?" he asked, the picture of innocence.

"You're trying to play me and it won't work. You're not going to be able to guilt me into coming with you."

"Who, me?"

"I'm your employee. You can't just pack me along on a week's vacation to Hawaii."

"Lily's my employee and she never complains about it."

"That's different. Lily is your...your... What exactly is she?"

He shrugged. "Housekeeper. Nanny. Surrogate grandma to Emma. Pick one."

"Whatever. It's just different."

"Would it make you feel any better if I told you I bought the house in Hawaii for my employees?"

She snorted in disbelief and he gave her an offended look. "I did! Lily and Tiny needed to have a place to stay when they go back to the islands to visit their family. Over the years, it's sort of turned into a corporate retreat. Nearly every single one of the people working for me have stayed there at one time or another. Just ask them."

"I don't care if you've taken the whole damn city of Seattle over there. Nothing you say will change my mind. I'm not going with you, and that's the end of it!"

"You're crazy. You *have* to go with him!"

"Not you, too." Grace glared at Riley across a table laden with every kind of fried food known to man.

She didn't need this from him right now. She really didn't. She'd been dealing with it all day and she was sick to death of it.

Jack had mercifully dropped the subject of her going with

him after her vehement proclamation in his office. But that hadn't stopped Lily and Emma from haranguing her about it from the moment she walked in the door of the house earlier in the afternoon until she'd managed to escape a half-hour ago to meet Beau at this hole-in-the-wall diner.

It was exactly his favorite kind of place—loud and rough, with sticky floors and greasy food. Just breathing the fumes from his plate was clogging her arteries.

Sitting in this vinyl booth across from him talking over a case—while a ceiling fan stirred around stale smoke and a honky-tonk song about no-good cheating women wailed from the jukebox—seemed so comfortably familiar that it brought a sting of tears to her eyes.

Or maybe she was just upset at Beau for coming down on the side of Jack Dugan and the rest of his household.

He usually agreed with her about everything. She had expected him to nod his head and agree with her that going with Jack Dugan to his vacation home in Hawaii would be a mistake. He was supposed to agree that she would be far better off using the time that Dugan was away to concentrate on the case against him.

Leave it to Beau to be contrary.

Didn't anybody care about what she wanted? She could imagine few things more miserable than spending a week hovering on the fringes of someone else's family vacation.

Knowing she was an outsider, that she didn't belong, that she had no right to be there.

Always conscious that she no longer had a family of her own.

It was hard enough keeping Jack and his daughter at a distance here. She could just imagine how tough it would be while in a tropical paradise together. At least here she could hide away in her room when things became too hard for her to handle, but she seriously doubted she'd be able to get away with that at his house in Hali'ewa.

Ice rattled as Beau took a swig of his jumbo cola. "Why are you so upset about going with them anyway? Seems to me you should be jumping at the chance."

"The man's a possible criminal, for heaven's sake. He could be facing indictment any day now. Why on earth would I possibly want to spend any more time than I have to with him? I can barely stand to be in the same room with him."

It was as blatant a lie as she had ever uttered, but she hoped Beau was too busy stuffing his face full of fried clams to figure it out.

"Besides," she added. "With him gone, I'd have a good chance to give a little closer scrutiny to GSI and its dealings, without having to worry about him always looking over my shoulder. Now that I have his security codes, I could even snoop through his office at the house and see what I can find there that might implicate him."

Beau looked up from his plate. "Searching his premises without his permission or a search warrant would be illegal. Nothing you found would hold up in court."

She sniffed. "Since when did that ever stop you, Riley? Besides, I'm just a lowly informer now. I don't have to play by the rules anymore since I'm no longer a cop."

"Yeah, but I still am. And I'd like to stay that way, thank you very much. I'm already walking the line letting you work the case on an unofficial basis. You want to get me fired?"

"What's with you?" she snapped. "Since when did you turn into such a wuss? Don't you want to bring down Dugan?"

"Yeah, *if* he's involved in the GSI smuggling ring, which we still don't know for sure."

She narrowed her gaze at him. "What do you mean, you don't know for sure?"

Those big blue puppy-dog eyes that could get most women to tell him anything he wanted to know—and to his eternal chagrin, plenty of things he *didn't* want to know—shifted away from her. He set down a french fry and wiped his fingers on a napkin.

It was a classic Beau stall maneuver, one she wasn't about to let him get away with this time. "What's going on, Detective Riley? What exactly aren't you telling me?"

He hemmed and hawed a few more minutes, then finally came clean. "The task force met for a strategy session after I talked to you today. The latest consensus is that there's a chance—a slim one—that Dugan might not actually be involved in the gun-running."

She stared at him. "What are you talking about? You're telling me I've been wasting my time staying at his house?"

"I didn't say that. There's no question the contraband is coming in with GSI shipments, but so far we can't find any evidence that Dugan has direct knowledge of it. That doesn't mean he's not involved, just that we haven't found proof of it yet."

So there was a tiny ray of hope that Jack Dugan might not be a scum-sucking sleazeball wrapped up in a pretty package after all. She didn't even want to *begin* to try figuring out why that thought should send such relief coursing through her.

Why should she care whether he was guilty or not? He meant nothing to her. Absolutely nothing. Right?

She took a sip of her water to hide the sudden flush she felt heating her cheeks. "So you haven't found proof. So what? All the more reason why I should stay right where I am and keep digging."

"No. All the more reason why you should go with him and his kid to Hawaii."

"How do you figure that?"

"Even if he's not involved, somebody else at GSI *is*. Some-body who would know exactly where to find Dugan and his kid and would know they'd be vulnerable while they're on vacation."

"If he's not part of it, what motive would somebody have to kidnap her in the first place, then?"

"Who knows? Money? Get Dugan out of the way so he doesn't interfere with a big shipment coming in? Whatever. But what better time to try again after they screwed up the first go at kidnapping the girl than when he's let his guard down?"

Dammit. He was right, as usual. If she were of a sinister mind, she would use exactly this chance to move in. She sat back in the vinyl booth and closed her eyes, hating what she knew she was going to have to do.

"It won't be that bad. Besides, what do you have to com-plain about? I'd kill for a chance like this."

She opened her eyes. "Then *you* go with him."

Beau grinned. "Yeah, but you look so much better in a bikini than I do."

She aimed a killer glare at him, but he just laughed. "Come on, Gracie. It'll be good for you. You look like you haven't seen the sun in months. Go get a little color in your cheeks."

"This is Seattle. *Nobody* has seen the sun in months."

He finished the rest of his meal without haranguing her about it. Both of them knew she was backed into a corner and didn't have a choice. That didn't mean she had to like it.

When they left the diner and reached the parking lot, he pulled her into a hug and planted a brotherly smack on her forehead. "It's good to see you, Gracie. It kills me to say this, but I think staying with Dugan has been good for you. You're looking a whole hell of a lot better than you did the last time I saw you."

"It's good to see you, too," she murmured.

He set her away from him. "You know, when this thing with GSI is over, you ought to think about coming back to the job. You know there's always a slot for you."

A month ago, she never would have considered it. But she was shocked to realize she didn't find the idea completely repugnant.

"I'll think about it," she murmured.

He gave her one more quick hug then climbed into his pride and joy, a jacked-up old pickup truck with splotches of gray primer and a top-of-the-line stereo system.

The truck rumbled to life but before he drove away, Riley rolled down the window.

"Have a good time with Dugan in paradise," he shouted above the snarling engine. "And bring me back a couple of them Aloha shirts, would you? Nothing too girly, just something that'll make me look like Magnum PI."

She laughed and blew him a kiss as he drove out of the parking lot.

Maybe he was right. Maybe it was time she returned to the job. Her stomach knotted as guilt swamped her with the thought. Returning to work meant returning to life. Feeling again. Caring again.

She wasn't sure she was ready for that.

She wasn't sure she would *ever* be ready.

CHAPTER TEN

"RELAX. I'VE DONE THIS THOUSANDS OF TIMES before." Jack took his gaze from the instrument panel just long enough to give Grace a reassuring smile.

"Well, I haven't. Forgive me if I'm a little edgy."

Edgy didn't even begin to describe it, he thought. With her face pale and set and her back ramrod straight, she gripped the edge of her seat behind him with bloodless fingers.

Everybody else in the sweet little Learjet he leased didn't even seem to notice they were preparing to taxi down the runway.

Emma and Tiny were in the middle of a heated game of Old Maid, Lily was engrossed in a magazine and Piper, in the co-pilot's seat, was trading jokes with a buddy in the control tower as they waited their turn for takeoff.

Grace, though, appeared to be doing enough worrying for all the rest of them.

He sent her another reassuring smile. "If I didn't know better, I might think you don't trust my flying ability."

"Don't flatter yourself, Dugan. This has nothing to do with you."

"What is it, then? You don't like to fly?"

"I don't know. Ask me when we land."

He stared at her. "You've never been on a plane?"

"No," she answered shortly.

"Ever?" He couldn't even conceive of someone living to the ripe old age of twenty-nine without flying in an airplane. To him, flying was like breathing—something so necessary to his existence that he didn't even think about it anymore.

"Never." Her mouth wobbled in a shaky smile. "Terrible, isn't it?"

He had seen her grieving and he had seen her angry but he had never seen her this nervous and off-balance. He found himself intrigued by it, while at the same time it touched a deep, tender place in him.

He was coming to care for her entirely too much and it scared him more than she could ever worry about flying.

He had to help her relax. Couldn't have his passengers spending the whole time white-knuckled and pale. "Man," he teased. "Talk about putting pressure on a guy. Now I'm obligated to give you a perfect ride or risk turning you off of it forever."

She rolled her eyes. "We're talking about flying here, not sex."

He grinned, relieved to hear her tart tone. If she could relax enough for that, she'd probably be okay. "Most pilots would tell you there's not much difference."

"If that's the case," she answered primly, "it seems to me they must not be doing one or the other right."

He laughed so hard he had a difficult time hearing the tower clear them for takeoff. "Hang on, sweetheart," he said after he had acknowledged the clearance. "I'll let you be the judge of at least one of my skills."

He didn't have time to check on her again until they were well out over the Pacific and he could put the Learjet at cruising altitude and turn the controls over to Piper.

When he sat in the plush chair across the aisle from her, Grace didn't even look up from gazing raptly at the glittering blue sea below.

"At the risk of damaging my frail male ego," he finally asked, "how was it for you?"

"Incredible!" She finally turned to face him and his heart gave a funny little bump at the sheer pleasure there. "Absolutely amazing! When we took off, at first I couldn't breathe and I thought we were all going to die, and then we lifted off and it was like nothing I've ever experienced. This astonishing rush of sensation, of power, as we took to the air. I can't explain it. I just know I want to do it all over again."

He grinned. "Stop. You're gonna make me blush."

She caught herself in midsentence as if she was finally remembering where she was, who she was talking with. To his delight, she was the one who blushed. A soft pink tinged her dusky cheekbones and she looked away. "Um, don't you have a plane to fly or something?"

"That's the beauty of having a co-pilot. I get to do the really exciting things like takeoffs and landings and Piper handles the boring parts, like holding steady at this altitude for the next five hours."

"Sounds like you've got a real tough life, Dugan. Snatch all the fun for yourself and leave the dirty work to somebody else."

"I'll go back and help him in a minute. Just thought I'd better check on my passengers."

"Guess what, Daddy?"

At Emma's high-pitched little lisp from the rear of the cabin, the animation in Grace's features shut off as abruptly as if someone had flipped a switch.

He felt a muscle in his jaw twitch as she looked away from him—or more accurately, away from his daughter—and gazed out the window again. How long would she continue to keep shutting Emma out?

He turned to Em with a distracted smile. "What, Em?"

"Tiny was the Old Maid three times in a row!" She laughed uproariously, as if beating a big burly Hawaiian at a child's card game was the funniest thing in the world. "And guess what else? He says he's not gonna play with me no more 'cause I cheat. Only I didn't, really. I beat him fair and square. He's just bein' a sore loser, aren't you, Tiny?"

Lily's husband gave Emma a fierce glare that had put the fear of God into many a man. "Am not. You tricked me. You got X-ray vision in those big green eyes, don't you? That's how you knew which card was the Old Maid so you could leave me with her."

Jack winked at her. "Em, have you been using your X-ray vision again? How many times do I have to tell you it's just not fair to use it against mortals?"

She giggled again. "I don't have X-ray vision, Daddy. You know I don't."

Before he could tease her more, to make up for the aloofness he knew she must sense from Grace, the plane began to shiver and jerk.

"What was that?" Grace reached out and dug her fingernails into his forearm.

Her eyes looked huge and terrified. For all her enthusiasm about the headrush of takeoff, she was still a novice when it came to flying, he reminded himself.

He covered her fingers with his other hand. Her skin was

warm and smooth and for one wild moment—even with her coolness toward Emma—he wanted to lift her hand to his lips, then pull her into his arms to devour that incredible mouth of hers.

In front of Tiny and Lily and Emma and anybody else in the damn world who might be watching.

He was still reeling from the fierceness of the impulse when the jet jumped again. Her nails tightened on his arm and he squeezed her fingers. "We just hit a pocket of turbulence. Happens all the time. It's nothing to worry about."

"I don't like it. Make it stop."

He gave a short laugh. "Wish I had that power, sweetheart. But I'll go see what I can do to smooth things out for you."

He returned to his seat in the cockpit with a hollow ache in his gut. He was coming to care about Grace Solarez entirely too much, despite all the reasons he shouldn't and despite the fact that he knew damn well nothing could ever come of it.

Jack's house in the North Shore surf town of Hali'ewa wasn't at all what she expected.

For some reason, she would have predicted his vacation home on the beach would be a modern showplace, with gleaming furniture and expensive artwork. Instead it was cozy and comfortable, with big plump sofas, sisal rugs and simple Hawaiian prints decorating the walls.

Everywhere in the house were windows, even here in the guest room Lily showed her to. The windows in her room overlooked a porch—a lanai—that opened out above the beach and offered breathtaking views of sand and coco palm trees.

And the sea, a deep, endless blue she couldn't seem to look away from.

"You like it?"

She turned to find Lily standing in the doorway to her room with an armload of linens. The lines on her round, weathered face seemed to have smoothed out here in her native land and she looked younger, happier. For all her bulk, Grace realized, Lily was a striking, majestic woman.

"It's beautiful." Grace answered. "The view, the house, the flowers. Everything."

"Yeah. Jack picked a good spot. Our house used to be about two miles windward."

"Oh? You lived near here?"

"Yeah." She set the linens on the cane chair near the window, pulled sheets from the pile, and flipped one out to make the bed.

"I can do this," Grace said. "You probably have a million other things to do."

Lily lowered thick dark eyebrows at her. "I'll do it. You're a guest here."

She wasn't truly a guest here anymore than Lily was but she couldn't seem to make the woman accept that.

"At least let me help," Grace insisted. She went to the other side of the bed and the two women worked in silence for a few moments.

They were alone in the house, she knew. Piper had stayed in Waikiki, over an hour's drive away, to begin hunting for his cocktail waitress. Tiny had gone after supplies to stock the kitchen, and Emma and Jack had headed right for the beach.

As soon as they arrived, Emma insisted on going to check for the mynah bird she had made friends with the last time they were here. She had named the bird Mr. Squawky and insisted he could say hello if he tried hard enough.

Lily was the first to break the silence now. "Did Jack tell you he bought this place for me and Tiny?"

"He mentioned it. I wasn't sure whether to believe him or not."

"He did. Mikia, our *kaikamahine,* or daughter, she got married and had a baby boy. Little Puakea. He's almost three now. After he was born, Jack knew how hard it was on us not seeing the *keiki* very often so he bought the house for us to stay in. We fly over all the time, maybe four, five times a year. He's a good man."

She would have thought him a better man if he had just given the couple a healthy pension and let them find their own home near their grandson. "Why didn't you just move back here permanently after your grandson was born?"

"And leave Jack and Emma?" Lily's shoulders shook with laughter inside her maroon-and-white muumuu. "What would he do without us?"

Pay someone else to do your job, Grace thought, then felt ashamed of herself. Even *she* had to admit Lily and Tiny were more to Jack than just employees. He treated them more like treasured members of the family.

"You know what *'ai'e* means?"

Grace shook her head.

"It means loyalty. It means we won't come back home for good until Jack and that little girl of his don't need us anymore."

"I'm sorry. I don't understand."

Lily tucked a pillow into its case and fluffed it before answering. "It's a long story. Want to hear?"

"Um, sure." She perched on the edge of the bed as the older woman moved the remaining linens aside so she could sit in the chair.

"Tiny used to work the sugar cane. Never made much money, but we always had enough. About ten years ago, the sugar cane market went bad. Now you won't find hardly a cane growing on any of the islands. Lots of people lost work."

"Tiny as well?"

Lily nodded. "He couldn't find nothing else around here. Nothing else he knew how to do, anyway. I was working as a nurse down at the hospital in Kahuku, so we had enough to get by, but it's hard on a man when he can't support his *ohana,* his family. He started to drink pretty good."

She paused and looked out to sea. "Then I had some hip trouble and lost my job, too. It was a bad time. Tiny went drinking more and more and one day decided maybe he could get easy money off some *haole.* Only he was too drunk to pick a good one."

"Let me guess. He tried to mug Jack?"

Lily nodded. "Stupid, huh? Jack was stationed at Hickam then with the air force. Instead of turning Tiny in to the police like he deserved, Jack bought him a coffee and a meal."

Grace felt a soft, warm tug at her heart, but as soon as she recognized it, she frowned. She couldn't afford this softening toward him. She shouldn't be sitting here and listening to the woman sing Jack's praises but she had no idea how to prevent it.

"And then the crazy man hired Tiny to do things around his apartment," Lily went on, oblivious to Grace's inner struggle. "Painting, fixing things. Stuff he didn't really need doing or could have done himself. And when Jack heard Tiny had a wife and daughter at home, he hired me to cook and clean for him. And we been taking care of each other ever since."

She couldn't say she was completely surprised by the story. When she thought about it, he seemed the kind of man to gather in strays, although she didn't think he would appreciate the observation.

But would a man who helped out a would-be attacker and his family be the kind of man willing to break the law for his own gain?

"He's a good man," Lily repeated. "I don't know what kind of mess we would have been in if he hadn't come along and helped us, even when he didn't have much money himself."

Before Grace had time to digest this new side of Jack Dugan, Lily slapped her hands on her thighs and rose from the chair. "Listen to me, sitting here talking story with all I got to do."

She stood to finish making the bed and unfurled the remaining linens in her lap, which turned out to be an exquisite Hawaiian quilt, a red-and-orange outline of chrysanthemums on a white background.

Grace ran a hand over the bright fabric, her fingertips skimming the raised edge of the design, appliqued with thousands of tiny, perfect stitches. "This is gorgeous!"

"It's a pattern called *Pua Pake*. Chinese Flower."

"Did you make it?" she asked.

Lily nodded. "Long time ago. When I was still a girl."

"I've never seen anything like it. It must have taken you a year of work, at least!"

Lily shrugged her massive shoulders. "It's not that hard. I can show you while you're here. You could make a panel to hang on the wall. It wouldn't take you that long."

"I'd like that," Grace said, and realized with a little jolt that she meant the words.

Now what on earth would have compelled her to say such a thing? She was definitely not the sort for handiwork projects.

She had tried to learn to knit when she was pregnant with Marisa, imagining cute little baby booties and tiny wool sweaters. With the typically minuscule attention span of teenage girls, though, she hadn't even been able to complete one yellow bootie before giving up, bored senseless with the whole thing.

This seemed different, somehow. The color and vibrancy of the native quilt called to her in some raw, elemental way.

It seemed to represent beauty and life, the polar opposite of the ugliness, the terrible emptiness of the past year.

To her shock, she discovered a fierce need to create something lovely, something good, as if in some small but tangible way she might begin to fill that emptiness.

"Good." Lily nodded her head, as if she'd expected no other answer. "I've got plenty of fabric here. I can help you come up with a pattern tonight and help get you started cutting it out."

Grace had the craziest feeling that she was teetering on the brink of something important. Momentous, even. Her stomach fluttered and spun, and she was suddenly not at all sure she was ready for whatever that something might be.

She forced a laugh that sounded small and hollow. "You don't waste time, do you? We're all tired after that long flight—why don't we wait until tomorrow before rushing into any grand projects?"

Lily studied her out of brown eyes that were entirely too perceptive. Grace squirmed under the scrutiny until the Hawaiian's features softened into a compassion that made her even more uncomfortable.

"Up to you," Lily said. "Tomorrow can be just as good as today. Sometimes even better."

She turned to leave just as Emma brushed past her into the bedroom, trailing sand across the floor and carrying a plastic toy bucket. Grace felt every muscle tense, as they always did in the little girl's presence.

"Hey, Grace, guess what?" Emma chirped. "My daddy and me found three hermit crabs. You can have one, if you want." She thrust the bucket out and Grace could see three tiny, bewildered-looking crabs trying to scale their pink plastic cage.

Mommy, look at the kitty I found at the park! Can I keep it?

The strand of old memory, sharp as coiled concertina wire, twined around and through her—Marisa's brown little face animated with excitement, her eyes eager and bright, as she held a scraggly gray-striped kitten in her skinny five-year-old arms.

The kitten had grown into a fat old tom Marisa named Gordo. He slept on her pillow, patiently endured being dressed up in doll clothes and lugged around by his armpits, and ate anything as long as Marisa had been the one to feed him.

Grace hadn't been able to stand having him around *after* and had finally made Beau take him away.

"Want one?" Emma asked now. "You could keep it in a bowl by your bed."

"No." Wrenched back into the present, her voice was cold, cruel. "Crabs don't make good pets."

Like a flower hit by frost, the excitement on the little girl's face shriveled and died. "Oh," she said softly.

Remorse over her harsh words swamped Grace and she wanted to gather Emma close and apologize. But she couldn't. She *couldn't*. Her emotions were too raw suddenly, too close to the surface and she didn't want to risk them blistering over.

"Grace is right, pumpkin."

She turned at the deep male voice and found Jack standing in the doorway. He gave her a swift frown then knelt to his daughter's level. "Remember what I told you? It's all right to study the crabs for a while, but they really belong on the beach. We'll go take them down and you can let them go."

"Okay." With the quicksilver mood swings typical of a five-year-old, she wriggled down and followed Lily down the hallway.

After another long, searching look, Jack left as well, leaving Grace alone with her guilt.

Alone. Always alone.

CHAPTER ELEVEN

THE MYTHICAL HAWAIIAN SUNSET HAD NOTHING on a tropical dawn, as far as Grace was concerned.

With her bare feet buried in damp sand, she sat on a straw mat she found in her room and watched the sky put on a dazzling display of color as the sun continued its climb above the horizon.

The ever-present trade winds stirred the feathery fronds of coco palm trees spearing into the sky and rattled the leaves on the other thick vegetation surrounding her.

There were no other houses on this part of the beach, only Jack's, and she felt as if she were the only person alive here in the pearly light of early morning.

The ocean dominated everything, overwhelming in its majestic beauty. It was a feast for every one of her senses; she inhaled the salty spray and tasted it on her tongue. The low musical murmur of the surf filled her ears with its ancient song.

And she couldn't look away from the endless, stunning blue.

She found it difficult to believe this was the same Pacific that battered against the Washington coastline. This sea was softer, somehow, gentler, despite the legendary North Shore waves so sought after by surfers.

It soothed her. Calmed her.

She felt a tickle and looked away from the water to find a tiny crab scuttling over her toe. It inevitably reminded her of the scene in her bedroom the night before with Emma.

The calm the ocean had given her receded and guilt washed over her like the sea licking at the sand. She had been cold and unkind and the memory of it pinched at her with claws sharper than any crab's.

As tired as she had been from the long flight, she spent most of the night staring at the clean, white-painted walls of the guest room, listening to the surf and feeling ashamed of herself.

All Emma wanted from her was friendship. Would that be so terribly hard to give? Was she going to spend the rest of her life avoiding any kind of association with children, being needlessly cruel because she couldn't find her way past remembering all she had lost?

She thought of the hurt in Emma's big green eyes when she had snapped at her, then the disapproval in Jack's identical pair, and again felt small and mean.

She couldn't do it anymore. It wasn't fair or right. She couldn't continue to blame an innocent child for simply living—for having skin and breath and substance.

Somehow she would have to find a way to break away from her memories and change her behavior toward the little girl.

She didn't have to open her heart to her, didn't have to let her in at all, really. She just had to be kind. She just had to force herself to deal with Emma as herself instead of projecting Marisa onto everything she did.

She could do it. She *would*. It was only for a few days, just while they were here. She could survive anything for a few days.

Above the sea's deep purr, she suddenly became aware that she was no longer alone on the wide stretch of beach, that her temporary sanctuary had been invaded.

She didn't know what alerted her to it—the snick of a sliding glass door, perhaps, or just a shift in the breeze—but she turned and looked through a break in the dense growth just in time to see Jack walking out onto the lanai of his beach house a hundred feet away.

So much for her solitary peace. She frowned in annoyance. She didn't want to talk to anyone, especially not him. And if she returned to the house now, she would have to pass him and be forced into conversation.

Maybe he wouldn't notice her. She was screened on all sides except the ocean by thick bushes. She backed against a tree with a trunk that looked like vertical strands of twined rope, hoping its large, oval-shaped leaves would conceal her.

A few moments later, he padded down to the beach wearing only baggy maroon surfer trunks and carrying a fluorescent blue boogie board under one arm.

To her relief, he didn't seem aware of her presence at all as he stopped at the water's edge and exchanged flip-flops for flippers.

He stood there for a moment silhouetted by the rising sun, looking out toward sea, and awareness bloomed in her like the plumeria and ginger surrounding her.

She thought about the first time she had seen him, all sun-bronzed and golden. It was funny how they had come full circle—she remembered thinking then that he looked like a surfer. She never would have imagined that one day she would be sitting on a Hawaiian beach, watching him prepare to challenge the waves.

It seemed as if a lifetime had passed since she had awakened in his home with her back on fire and her spirit as cold as death.

After lifting his face to the rising sun one last time, he waded into the surf. When the water was deep enough, he shoved the boogie board under his chest and began to swim toward the first line of breakers with clean, powerful strokes.

She watched, mesmerized by his strength and skill as he rode wave after wave. Jack embraced life, she thought as she watched him coil and twist on a swell. He challenged everything like he did those waves, with boldness and daring. Head-on, unafraid.

Everything she wasn't.

By the time he headed for shore, the sun was well above the horizon. She shrank back against the tree, hoping she could blend in enough that he wouldn't see her.

She might have made it undetected but a mischievous mynah bird—maybe even Mr. Squawky himself—called from the tree above her. Jack turned toward the sound and his features brightened when he saw her.

Water drops caught the sunlight and gleamed on his skin as he took off his flippers and headed toward her. Her mouth suddenly felt dry, her limbs heavy, ponderous.

"Morning. I didn't realize I had an audience."

"You put on quite a show."

He looked faintly embarrassed. "I haven't been on a board in a long time so I'm pretty rusty. Have you been out here long?"

She nodded and decided not to tell him she had already staked out the beach as her own before he arrived. "A while," she answered.

"I thought everybody would be sleeping off jet lag this morning."

"I couldn't sleep through such a glorious sunrise."

His teeth flashed as he smiled, sending her pulse churning through her like a riptide.

He didn't help matters when he sat next to her, entirely too close, with his elbows resting on his bent knees. "Dawn has always been my favorite time in the islands. I'm sorry I disturbed your view of it."

She *was* disturbed, but not in the way she was sure he meant.

"It's your house," she pointed out. "I'm the intruder here."

"You're not. I hope you know that. I wanted you to come."

"Why?" she muttered, thinking of her morose silences and her bad tempers.

Instead of answering, he gave her a long, searching look. As his gaze traveled over her, she became painfully aware of her bare feet in the sand and the faded yellow-flowered sundress with the ragged hem she pulled on before heading to the beach. She probably looked like a refugee from some forlorn country.

"How's your back feeling these days?" he asked, switching gears. Or maybe not, since the reason he probably claimed he wanted her here had more to do with that blasted sense of obligation he still seemed to feel over Emma's rescue than because he derived any pleasure from her less-than-cheerful company.

She looked out to sea. "Fine. It's just fine. Almost back to normal."

"Do you think you might be up to doing a little snorkeling today? I thought maybe we could go off Pupukea Beach, not very far from here. This time of year it starts to get a little rough, but I think we're still okay for a couple of weeks. It's one of Emma's favorite things to do and I know she'd like to share it with you."

"I don't know how to snorkel."

"You can swim, can't you?"

At her nod, his mouth twisted into a grin. "If you can swim, you can snorkel."

In the slanted morning light, he looked golden and beautiful—as breathtaking as the sunrise—and she couldn't look away.

His green eyes met hers. Something of her sudden sharp awareness must have shown on her face. A strange light kindled in his eyes, and she watched the expression there shift, take on a new intensity.

The ocean suddenly seemed to roar louder in her ears. Or maybe it was the slow, thick pounding of her pulse as his gaze fixed on her mouth, as the currents between them shifted and stirred like palms in the trade wind.

He murmured her name and then angled his tawny head, and she forgot to breathe, to think, as his mouth settled on hers.

His lips were cool and tasted faintly salty from the water. Hesitation held her motionless for a moment. She knew she shouldn't let him kiss her, that this was a dangerous game she was playing with herself. But it seemed so completely perfect to be sitting on this secluded beach in the early-morning light with him that she shoved her doubts down where she didn't have to look at them right now.

It was only a kiss, after all. A kiss couldn't hurt anything. Okay, so it made her toes tingle and her knees weak, but it was still just a kiss.

Her hands were trapped between them when he pulled her close, and now she pulled them free and slid them across the hard, smooth muscles of his chest to wrap around his neck.

He gave a low, hungry growl that mimicked the surf and deepened the kiss. When he pressed her back against the straw mat, she could feel the jut of his arousal through the loose trunks. It frightened her—she wasn't at all ready for anything like this—but at the same time she had to admit she found it unbearably exciting.

He couldn't get enough of her. With her light-brown skin and her dark curls dancing in the breeze, she was like some wild, exotic sea sprite and he wanted her with an aching urgency completely new to him.

It wasn't only a physical desire. He wanted to ease that sadness in her eyes, to watch that elusive smile appear and to hear her rare laughter. He wanted to take away her pain and help her heal.

He kissed her for a long time, until he lost track of everything around them, until he was shaking with need, consumed only by Grace.

She reacted so sweetly to him. He wondered if she realized how her arms tightened around him every time he tried to pull away and how she sighed his name when he trailed kisses down the long, elegant column of her neck, to the hollows and curves of her collarbone, to her shoulder, bared by her sleeveless sundress.

Her hands dipped into his damp hair, caressing, stroking. He trailed kisses along the scooped neckline of her dress and felt her fingers tighten when his mouth reached the slope of one high, firm breast.

Her breathing sounded ragged and harsh as he pressed his lips just beneath the neckline, where his hands ached to touch. Just before he would have given in to the need, before he would have filled his hands with her, the harsh call of their mischievous mynah friend rang through the secluded section of beach.

Forget it. Ignore it, he wanted to murmur, but he was too late. She stiffened in his arms as if the surf had doused them in icy water.

She opened her eyes, her pupils dazed and unfocused. When her gaze collided with his, he read shock and dismay there.

She rolled away and scrambled to her feet. She stared at him, her eyes huge and dark, and her fingers trembled slightly as she lifted them to her mouth, swollen from his kisses.

"Grace—" he began, not sure what he wanted to say, other than *don't leave.*

Stay, stay, stay.

"Don't," she mumbled around her fingers. "Don't say anything."

He stood, wishing for a good sturdy pair of jeans with pockets to shove his hands into, instead of these loose, baggy, entirely too revealing swimming trunks.

Wishing he knew what to say so they could return to the fragile peace they'd enjoyed before he had kissed her.

Wishing more than anything that she was still in his arms.

"It was just a kiss," she muttered. "That's all. Let's not make any more of it than that."

Just a kiss. Just a merging of lips and tongues and teeth in a cataclysmic explosion that rocked him to his soul. Hell, he was still feeling aftershocks from it.

He said nothing though, just continued watching her, until she finally looked away from him, down at her bare toes buried in the sand.

"When—" her voice broke and she tried again. "When did you want to go snorkeling?"

Surprised, he stared at her bent head, at the vulnerable, soft skin at the nape of her neck. Even though she wanted to treat it with such apparent nonchalance, he would have expected her to use the kiss as an excuse to avoid going with them, to make it yet another reason why she wanted nothing to do with him or his daughter.

"The surf can be a bit calmer in the afternoon. Would that work for you?"

She looked up, her high cheekbones dusted with color. "Fine. Sure."

Should he let it go, as she obviously wanted, or should he push her, insist she admit she had felt the raw impact of their embrace as well?

What would that accomplish, other than to appease his ego? Knowing Grace, she would react angrily and he would defeat his own purpose, to get her to relax and enjoy herself while they were in Hawaii.

He swallowed the instinct to poke and prod at her feelings. If she wanted to pretend nothing had happened, he could damn well pretend nothing had happened.

He forced his mouth to twist into a casual smile and unclenched his teeth so he could at least pretend to speak calmly. "Why don't we make a day of it? Emma and I can give you a quick tour of our favorite sights on the North Shore."

She looked away again, this time out to sea. "Why don't we?" she murmured, then gathered up her straw mat and walked away.

"What's that one, Daddy?"

Grace followed the direction of Emma's finger and found an odd-looking creature with a pointed mouth curving through the water.

"It's a trumpet fish," Jack answered. "See, isn't his mouth kind of like a trumpet?"

Emma—who looked absolutely endearing in a neon green swimsuit, orange life vest and bright pink mask—nodded solemnly. She clutched the foam noodle she was also using to stay afloat and stuck her face into the water again, as if she couldn't look away.

"Which one's your favorite, Em?" Jack asked her when she came up for air again.

Emma pulled her snorkel away to answer. "I can't pick. They're all too pretty."

Grace knew just what she meant. She felt as if she were swimming through some vast, exotic aquarium. The coral reef in the sheltered cove was home to every species of tropical fish imaginable. Jack seemed to know all their names— black-and-yellow striped tangs, funny-looking triggerfish, exotic-colored butterfly fish.

They pounded against the coral or darted through it alone or in vast schools, in an ever-changing kaleidoscope of color.

Marisa would have loved it here. She had always loved the ocean, had dreamed of being a marine biologist. As the thought drifted into her head—and with it, the endless, aching emptiness—Grace pushed it away.

She wasn't going to think about Marisa here. She had promised herself that she wouldn't ruin the day for Jack and Emma.

"I wish I could take them all home and put them in my room," Emma said, and Grace was surprised by the small laugh that escaped her at the speculative light suddenly flitting through the little girl's eyes that she could see even through her mask.

Jack must have seen, it too. He shoved his own mask back, shaking his head. "Get that look out of your eyes, young lady. No way are we carting any tropical fish home."

"But Daddy—"

He laughed and tweaked her nose. "Not a chance, pumpkin. The fish belong right here. Besides, where would you put them all?"

She frowned in concentration for a moment, then her face brightened. "Your swimming pool! Then we could watch them all the time, not just when we come here."

"You've got an answer for everything, don't you, Miss Smarty-Pants?"

She shook her head. "I don't have an answer for why I can't take some fish home. Just a couple? Please, Daddy?"

"No. But nice try." Jack's rugged, beautiful features twisted into a grin, and Grace stared at him, mesmerized.

Drops of water beaded his face and clung to the hard, sculpted muscles of his chest. She remembered the strength of those muscles against her, the salty-sweet taste of his mouth, the erotic coolness of his fingers against the swell of her breast.

She forced her gaze away and blew out a breath through her snorkel, grateful for the concealing mask she prayed hid the sizzling impact he had on her.

The heat they had shared on the beach that morning still simmered between them, bubbling and frothing like the edge of the waves breaking on the sand.

Just like the surf, it ebbed and flowed but it was always there.

Every once in a while he would slant her a look, his eyes turning a smoky green, and she knew without a doubt that he was also remembering their embrace, that he wanted to kiss her again—that he *would* kiss her again, given the chance.

Knowing he wouldn't try anything with Emma paddling happily nearby only seemed to add fuel to the slow fire coursing through her veins.

Not that she *wanted* him to try anything, she reminded herself. She absolutely did not. Kissing him this morning had been a huge mistake, one she didn't intend to let happen again.

What was she going to do about him? How could she convince him she didn't want him to touch her again when she wasn't at all convinced of that herself?

She couldn't let him, no matter how badly her body might yearn. He was getting too close. Sneaking under her guard, around the barriers she'd built so carefully. She couldn't afford to let him any closer.

This tropical paradise was a dangerous place. She already had a difficult time remembering why she was here, that she needed to keep an eye out for any suspicious activity, either by Jack or the people around him.

The idea of him as a cold-blooded gunrunner seemed ludicrous here on the islands. The man swapped elephant jokes with his five-year-old daughter, for heaven's sake.

She glanced at the two of them, heads bent to the water as a school of large gray parrotfish darted past.

Riley had to be wrong. The whole task force had to be wrong.

She had an easier time believing that trumpet fish back there might suddenly start playing Dixieland jazz than she could believe Jack Dugan was a weapons smuggler.

How had it happened, this total shift in her thinking? And what in the world was she going to do about it?

She drew another breath in through her snorkel, determined to forget about the case for a while. She headed in the opposite direction from the two of them and rode the waves for a while, letting her thoughts and her body drift on the current.

She lost track of time, suspended there in the peace of the water. Eventually she felt a soft feathery touch on her ankle. At first she thought it was just a curious fish, then the touch turned into distinct tap. She looked back to find Jack and Emma both there, beckoning to her.

She turned in the water to follow them. The coral dropped

off sharply here, to a pocket she estimated to be about fifteen feet deep, and there, gliding through the water with dignity and grace was an enormous sea turtle.

Faces close together in the water, they all stared, entranced, until it swam out of sight around another coral ridge.

"That was the biggest turtle I've ever seen!" Emma said when they all lifted their faces above the surface. Her eyes glowed with excitement, but Grace noticed her teeth were chattering and her lips were beginning to look a little blue around the edges.

While they'd been in the water, clouds had gathered, obscuring the late-afternoon sun and even she was beginning to feel cold.

"I think we better warm up for a while," Jack said firmly.

"Nooo," Emma complained. "I like it here and Grace does, too."

"I brought your sand stuff." Without warning, he reached out and snagged a hand around Grace's ponytail. His hand brushed her skin and she shivered—not at all from the cold. "You and I can build a sandcastle for this beautiful mermaid princess I just captured."

Emma giggled. "Mermaids don't live in sandcastles. They live in water castles. Besides, Grace isn't a mermaid. She's my friend."

A small, sweet warmth settled in her heart at the words. "I promise I won't escape," she told Jack. "You can let go now."

"What if I don't want to?" he murmured in her ear, and her body instantly reacted.

She sternly squelched the heat zinging through her. "Then Emma and I will just have to dunk you. Won't we, Em?"

The little girl giggled again. "Yeah. Watch out, Daddy. We're going to dunk you."

They swam to shore, twenty feet away, riding the baby

breakers. Once out of the water, the muggy heat not only warmed her quickly but also sapped her energy.

While Jack and Emma set to work building sand creations, she spread out on the blanket they'd brought along. It felt gloriously hedonistic to lie here on her stomach and do nothing, her head pillowed in her arms.

She barely summoned the energy to open her eyes when Jack joined her, stretching his long legs out beside her.

"So how was your first day in Hawaii?" he asked.

She smiled slightly. "Wonderful."

To her amazement, it was true. Once she concentrated on it hard enough she'd been able to wrap her memories in cotton and tuck them away. At least for the most part. And for the first time in a year, she had been shocked to find herself enjoying the sights and sounds around her.

They'd spent the morning wandering through the shops of Hali'ewa, looking at T-shirts and bright sarongs and row after row of vividly painted surfboards.

Since Lily was busy catching up with her family and friends, Jack took them to lunch at an Italian restaurant, of all places.

After lunch, they took a drive down the two-lane highway that nearly circled the island—past famous beaches with names like Sunset, Waimea and Pipeline—and bought fresh pineapple at a roadside stand.

Juice dripping down their chins, they ate it on the way back to the beach house before they grabbed snorkels and swimming suits for the short drive here.

"So how about we do it all again tomorrow?" he asked.

Right now, the very idea exhausted her. She laughed softly. "Ask me in the morning. If I can move again by then."

He didn't answer her for several moments. Finally she

opened her eyes and found him watching, his green eyes dark and intense. "I wish you'd do that more often," he murmured.

"What?"

"Laugh."

Her breath caught in her throat at his fierce expression, and she didn't know what to say.

She was spared from having to come up with an answer by Emma, who trudged over to them carrying pail and shovel. "You promised you'd help me build a tower," she complained. "You're not helping, Daddy!"

He sent Grace one more glittering look then climbed to his feet, brushing off the fine sand that clung to his tanned skin. He grabbed Emma around the waist and scooped her, giggling, up to his shoulder. "Sorry. Let's go build a tower. Then I'll put you in it for about thirty years and you'll have to let your hair grow long so the boys can climb in."

Long after the two of them walked away, Grace felt the impact of that look, of his words.

It took her a long time to relax again.

CHAPTER TWELVE

SHE DREAMED OF HER DAUGHTER.

They were at the ocean, a soft, breathtaking blue, and Marisa hung on a swim noodle much like Emma's, bobbing and floating on the waves like driftwood.

As she watched from the shore, her daughter began to float farther and farther away from her. Grace called to her to come back, told her she was drifting too far out to sea. She cried and screamed at her until her voice was hoarse, but Marisa didn't pay any attention. She just smiled and shook her head.

"I have to go," she mouthed. "Goodbye. I love you."

Then she blew kisses to her mother as the water carried her out of sight, and the sky began to weep.

Grace awoke with wet cheeks and familiar pain and loss choking her. For a moment, she just lay on the blanket with her eyes closed, disoriented by the abrupt shift from dream to reality, then she realized the sky's tears were rain and Jack was nudging her gently.

"Sorry to wake you up but we're going to be soaked in a minute if we don't hurry to the car," he said.

She sat up and rubbed a damp towel over her face, hoping to hide the traces of the grief that refused to leave her, even in sleep.

"You okay?"

She pulled the towel away and glanced briefly at him then away, unable to bear the concern in his eyes. "Fine. Just fine. Let me carry some of that."

She grabbed a blanket and Emma's sand bucket and walked to the Jeep without looking back to the ocean, to the water she knew would be empty of any trace of her child.

"Grace, will you read me a story and tuck me in?"

Jack swore under his breath. Emma was just supposed to knock on Grace's door, wish her good night and thank her for the good day they'd shared. This hadn't been part of the plan.

He studied her beautiful, fine-boned features, trying to gauge her reaction to the request, but he couldn't read anything there. She paused for several moments, then skimmed a hand over Emma's hair, still damp from the bath he'd just finished giving her.

"I'm not very good at stories, sweetheart. Wouldn't you rather have your father read to you? Or Lily?"

Emma shook her head with an obstinance he was all too familiar with. "No. You."

Grace sent him a helpless, "What-do-I-do-now?" look over his daughter's head and he prepared to step in. He knew damn well going through the traditional pre-sleep ritual for someone else's child would likely be agony for her and he refused to put her through it.

He reached out and grabbed Emma's little hand. "Come on. Let's go find the book about Max and the wild things."

"Okay. And then Grace can read it to me."

"Emma—"

"No. It's okay." Grace's voice was firm, suddenly, her eyes determined. "I can read to her."

"Are you sure you can do it?"

"Positive." Her mouth stretched into a wobbly smile. "I've been reading a long time, Dugan. You might have to help me on some of the big words, though."

A joke. She just made a joke. He stared at her, amazed. She met his gaze for an instant, then turned away to walk up the stairs toward Emma's room, down the hall from the guest room.

"You don't have to do this," he said in a low voice, when they reached the doorway.

She didn't look at him. "Yes. Yes, I do," she answered. With a shaky breath, she walked across the threshold like she was entering the fiery flames of hell.

He should leave them alone, he thought. But somehow he couldn't bring himself to walk away. He hovered in the doorway, feeling awkward and superfluous, while Emma made a huge, drawn-out ceremony of looking for the book.

Finally, when he was just about to tip the whole damn bookcase over and find it himself, she pulled it out with a triumphant flourish then climbed into her bed, straightened the covers just so, and waited for Grace to perch near her on the mattress.

"This is my most favorite-ist book. My daddy's, too," Emma confided.

"It's a good one," Grace agreed, and proceeded to read the story in a voice that didn't shake once.

By the time she finished, his chest ached as if he'd taken a hard punch. She set the book carefully on the bedside table then switched off the lamp there, leaving the room bathed only in the glow coming from a starfish night-light Emma insisted on.

"Okay. Now bedtime."

Emma obediently pulled the covers up to her chin. "Will you kiss me good-night?" she asked in a voice that already sounded half-asleep.

From the doorway, he watched Grace hesitate for several long seconds, then she bent down carefully and brushed her lips quickly over his daughter's forehead. "Sleep well, sweetheart," she whispered.

She rose, lingered by the bed for only a moment, then moved blindly towards the door, brushing past him as if she didn't even see him. Her dark eyes looked hollow, devastated, and the ache in his chest magnified a hundred-fold.

"Grace—" he began, but she ignored him, just walked swiftly down the stairs, across the living room and out the sliding glass doors to the lanai.

Should he follow her? He paused at the top of the stairs, knowing she wouldn't appreciate his interference, that she considered her grief her business and hers alone.

His indecision lasted only about three seconds before he took the stairs two at a time. Hell yes, he should follow her. She had handled this by herself for the past year. She had cut herself off from everyone, had lived like some kind of damn hermit.

Had done all her crying alone.

It couldn't be healthy and he wasn't going to stand for it anymore. Not when he could at least provide her with a willing shoulder.

He opened the door to go after her, then growled in frustration when he realized he couldn't leave the house without alerting Lily so she could listen in case Emma climbed out of bed.

By the time he found her and Tiny in the TV room watching reruns of their favorite detective show, explained to her where he was going, then walked out onto the lanai, Grace was nowhere to be seen.

She had no place else to go but the beach. The sand was cold and damp at night, he knew, so he grabbed a blanket from a chest on the lanai and headed toward the sea.

He found her under the spreading branches of the same ropy banyan tree they had kissed beneath that morning.

Almost invisible in the shadows, she was huddled into herself, arms wrapped around her knees and her face buried against the fabric of her sundress.

"I brought you a blanket," he said softly.

"Go away," she mumbled.

"No," he answered. He wanted nothing more than to gather her into his arms, but now that he was here he didn't know quite how to go about it. What could he say, after all, that would take away the hurt?

He did the only thing he could think of. He spread the blanket on the sand next to her, then shoved his hands into the back pockets of his jeans.

"Just leave me alone. Please, Jack."

For a moment he was silent as the leaves of the banyan tree chattered in the trade winds and the ocean murmured its eternal song.

Finally, he took a deep breath, hating himself but knowing she wouldn't welcome the comfort he wanted to offer. Maybe what she needed was to be shocked out of it.

"Leave you alone so you can have a pity party out here all by yourself?" he asked bluntly. "Sorry. I'm not willing to do that."

Her eyes widened at his cruelty, until they looked completely black in the night. "A pity party? Is that what you think this is about?"

"What else would you call it?"

"Grieving for my child! Aching for all the nights I'll never be able to read her a story or kiss her good-night."

His felt his heart crack apart at the raw pain in her voice. "What you've gone through is something no mother should ever have to face," he said, his voice low. "But you can't bring her back. All you can do survive. Give her life meaning by not allowing yours to end."

At his own words, he stared at her, suddenly struck by the unthinkable. She wouldn't. Would she? Yes, he realized with absolute certainty.

"*That's* what you were doing on the highway that night, wasn't it?"

She climbed to her feet and would have walked away from him but he grabbed her arm and held her in place. "Answer me. You were planning on taking a stroll into traffic that night. To put yourself out of your misery, weren't you?"

"None of your business," she snapped, and he knew with sick certainty that he was right.

He thought of his father, of a stupid eighteen-year-old kid walking into a horrific scene of death and waste, and gave her a hard, angry shake. "Dammit, Grace. How could you even *think* of doing something like that? Don't you know your life is worth so much more?"

"What?" She hurled the words at him. "What is it worth? I have nothing left. Don't you understand that? *I have nothing!* My daughter was everything to me. My whole world. From the moment she was born, from the moment I held her in my arms, she became the center of my life, the reason for everything I did. Without her I have nothing. I *am* nothing."

She pulled away from him and tucked her arms around her as if chilled, although the night was muggy for an October evening.

How could he even begin to ease such pain? He couldn't,

he realized grimly, helplessly, so he focused on the physical. "Here. I brought a blanket for you. Sit down."

He was afraid she would refuse, that she would wander farther down the beach, or worse. But finally she folded onto the blanket next to him.

They sat in silence for a long time, listening to the wind and the sea and the night. Finally, as if she'd been trying to draw the courage to begin, she spoke softly. "I was planning to give her up for adoption, can you believe that?"

He shook his head. "Tell me."

"I signed the papers a few weeks before she was born. There was this really wonderful couple from Bellingham. He was a doctor—an orthopedist, I think—and she was a preschool teacher who planned to quit and be a stay-at-home mother. They could have given her everything. Everything. What did I have to offer her? I was scared and alone, sixteen years old, with no home, no family, no job."

"What about Marisa's father?" He had wondered but never dared ask before. Somehow the night lent an intimacy that allowed the question.

She gave a short laugh. "Alex? He stopped taking my calls after the first trimester, when I refused to have an abortion. I tried to call him again after...after I finally found the courage to tell my aunt. After she kicked me out."

"What happened?"

"He told me it wasn't his problem anymore. If I wouldn't deal with it his way, he said, he didn't want to have anything to do with me. Or with our baby."

He was sorry he'd asked, and had a sudden violent wish he could find this Alex and make him pay for what he had done to her.

"So why didn't you give Marisa up for adoption?"

"I couldn't." She hugged her knees again. "It was completely selfish—the most selfish thing I've ever done in my life—but I couldn't give her away. One look at this little person I'd helped create, that I had carried inside my body, and I couldn't. For the first time since my father died, I had somebody to love. Somebody who loved me, unconditionally."

"How did you survive?"

"I found a job at a fast-food restaurant and lived in a group home for unwed teen mothers for a while until I could graduate from high school. I saved enough to get an apartment, enrolled in the local community college, and eventually was accepted into the Academy."

He imagined her simple, straightforward words concealed years of hardship. Hell, it was difficult enough being a single parent when he was financially secure and had Lily and Tiny to help him. Young and alone as she had been, it would have been so easy for her to give up, to just quietly slip into the welfare system. But she had clawed her way out and had built a happy, secure life for her and for her daughter.

Until a bullet had ripped it apart, had left her with nothing.

"What was she like?"

She blinked at the question. "What?"

"Tell me about Marisa. Was she funny? Shy? Athletic? What kind of books did she like? Who were her friends? What shows did she watch on TV? Anything you can think of."

For long moments, she could only stare at him, speechless. For more than a year everyone who knew her *before* avoided mentioning anything about Marisa—as if her death had erased any trace of her life, had wiped out her whole existence. Even Beau shied away from the subject as too painful for both of them.

And now here was Jack, who had not even known Marisa, who had no emotional investment in her whatsoever, asking Grace to share her daughter with him.

She didn't know when she had ever been so moved.

She settled against the trunk of the banyan, looked out to the ocean, and started to speak.

"She loved to tell jokes," she began.

Once she started, the words bubbled out of her like lava from Kilauea. While the palm trees swayed in the wind and the sea murmured softly and the night creatures peeped and cooed, she sat in the dark with Jack Dugan and brought her child back to life with words.

She didn't know long he sat beside her, patiently listening to her ramble on and on. When she finally stopped, her voice was hoarse, her cheeks wet. These tears were different, though, she realized. These were tears of joy, of celebration.

"Thank you," she whispered. "You were right. I... I needed to talk about her. You've made me remember her with a peace I haven't felt since she was killed."

"I'm glad." He reached out and covered her hand with his, then lifted it to his mouth and pressed a soft kiss against her palm, his warm breath stirring her skin.

"You must have been an amazing mother to raise such a beautiful child. I would have loved knowing her."

The impact of his words—of his touch—pierced her heart and crumbled the last of her defenses. What an extraordinary man he was. She tried to imagine any of the few men she had dated showing such patience, such forbearance, to sit quietly with a grieving mother for more than an hour while she rambled on about a child he would never meet.

None of them would have been able to do it. Yet with a few insightful questions, Jack Dugan had encouraged her to share her daughter with him and in the process she had found immeasurable comfort.

"I think she would have liked you, too," she said softly. Acting completely on impulse, she reached across the blanket and brushed her lips against his cheek, feeling the evening shadow she knew would be dark against his tan. "Thank you for listening to me," she whispered.

He turned his head and something bright and intense flickered in his green eyes, then he covered her mouth with his.

CHAPTER THIRTEEN

AS HIS MOUTH SETTLED OVER HERS—TASTING of mint and chocolate and the wine they'd had at dinner— a slow heat uncurled in her stomach and spread through the rest of her body.

The kiss was gentle at first, meant for comfort and solace, and she closed her eyes, welcoming both. He slipped one hand behind her to hold her against him and brought the other up to her face, his thumb skimming across her cheek with aching tenderness.

She leaned into the kiss, into him.

The warm trade winds eddied softly around them, caressing the sand as he caressed her skin. His touch seemed to breathe through her flesh, through her bones, blowing away all the icy numbness she had lived with for a year and leaving behind only need.

Wild, turbulent need.

After several moments of these long, drugging kisses, he started to pull away. She murmured a soft, wordless protest and slipped her arms around his neck to pull him closer.

For a moment, he remained motionless, his breath warm against her mouth, his breathing harsh and ragged. Finally, just as she began to think he would leave her, he deepened the kiss, and his mouth was urgent and fierce on hers.

She moaned and returned the kiss as a tidal wave of emotion crashed over her, leaving her gasping for air. Passion and yearning and need washed over her.

And fear.

Plenty of fear.

Whether he knew it or not, he was offering her a choice— she could remain in a past consumed with sorrow, frozen by her grief, or she could break free, could seize the promise he offered.

There was no choice. Not really.

Jack was life—fiery, scorching life—and even though it terrified her, she wanted to burn her fingers in him.

She parted her lips for him eagerly, tangling her mouth with his, welcoming the slick heat of his tongue.

He pressed her back onto the blanket and his body was warm and solid against her. The only solid thing in her world, suddenly. She clutched him to her, yearning to feel his strength against her, to steal some of it for a little while.

His mouth captivated her, mesmerized her, and she lost track of everything else around her. Her world condensed to only this, to the heated magic of his lips and tongue.

She was just remembering to breathe again when one hand found the curve of her breast through the fabric of her sundress and her breath left in a whoosh.

Wherever he touched, molten fire shot from his fingertips, scorching along her nerve endings.

Her nipple swelled, aching to be touched, and she arched against him, feeling his hardness through his jeans. She couldn't hold back her soft, aroused moan anymore than she could stop the tide.

At the sound, just a soft whisper in the night, really, he froze. With a growled curse, he rolled away from her and sat up, scrubbing his hands over his face.

For a long moment, he averted his gaze and said nothing. At his continuing silence, embarrassment began to replace the low, steady throb of desire and she could feel her face heat up.

Had she done something wrong? Okay, so she hadn't made love in a long time—and even then, her few previous relationships had been nothing to write home about. But surely she wasn't *that* bad at it.

He had wanted her, she knew that much. She was certainly inexperienced, but she wasn't stupid and she could definitely recognize a man's arousal when it jutted against her hip.

"I'm sorry, Grace," he said, his voice ragged. "I can't believe I let that happen."

"Did you notice me complaining?"

He didn't seem to hear her question. "I should never have let things get so out of control. It's just that there's this…this thing between us."

"Thing?"

"Attraction. Hunger. Whatever you want to call it. Whatever it is that makes it so I can't even look at you without wanting you."

She lifted her gaze to his and her pulse begin to drum loud and strong in her ears. "Really?"

He gave a harsh-sounding laugh. "I've been attracted to you since the moment I found you in that miserable apartment. Even when you were so out of it from the pain of your burns that you barely knew your own name, I wanted you. It's only grown more powerful since then. All you have to do is walk into the room and look at me out of those big, serious dark eyes and I'm hot and hard and ready to go."

At his words, her body gave an answering sigh. She gripped her hands tightly together to keep them from trembling. "And this is a problem for you because…?"

"Because you're too vulnerable, dammit. You're hurting and you want to forget your pain for a little while by tangling your body with mine." He snarled an oath. "I'd be the king of all sons of bitches if I took advantage of you like that right now."

He stopped kissing her, touching her because he didn't want to exploit her vulnerability? Because he thought she was too emotional to know what she was doing?

The irony of it nearly made her laugh.

For the first time in a year she felt as if she was choosing her own destiny—was charting her own course instead of being tossed around on the godforsaken route fate had picked for her.

She wanted this. Wanted him. And she wasn't about to let him talk her out of it.

She tried a smile that only came out a little bit wobbly. "When I think you're taking advantage of me, believe me, I'll let you know."

For a moment, the only sound came from the night, then he spoke in a voice that matched the sea's low rumble. "I care about you too much, Grace. If I didn't, I might just say to hell with my conscience and give us both what we're aching for. But I can't do that. You mean something to me. Something important. Something real."

The tenderness in his voice—in green eyes that she could just make out in the soft glow of the moonlight—destroyed her. She had to force herself to take several deep breaths before she dared speak.

"You're partly right, I suppose," she finally answered. "I *do* want to forget for a little while. But it's so much more than that."

He had talked about her vulnerability, yet she had never felt as exposed, as defenseless, as she did talking about this. Baring her soul to this man who had come to mean so much to her.

But he had been honest with her. She knew she owed the same to him.

"Jack, with you, I... I feel *alive*. I can't explain it. To tell you the truth, I don't know if I like it or not."

She stared out to sea, searching for the right words. "All I know," she finally said, in a voice barely above a whisper, "is that when you touch me, I feel my heart race and my pulse pound and blood rush through parts of me that have been frozen for what seems like forever and I don't want it to ever, ever stop."

"Grace—"

She glanced back at him and saw that her words had stunned him. His green eyes were wide, arrested.

She took a shaky breath, amazed at herself. She was practically begging Jack Dugan to make love to her here on this empty, moonlit beach, and she knew if she took the time to think it through she would never again find this kind of courage.

This was just not something shy little Grace Solarez would do. But she wasn't that frightened little orphan she had been through most of her childhood, any more than she was still the glib, tough cop she had worked so hard to become.

She was a woman. A woman who had spent the last year in hell—who, as Jack put it, had been through more than anyone should ever have to endure.

Because of him, she was beginning to think she just might make it through to the other side.

She wasn't going to take the time to analyze it right now. This was right. She knew it with complete conviction.

This was right, this was real, this was Jack—Jack, who made her smile and laugh and feel. Who showed such compassion to her and offered her such hope.

Her gaze met his and she knew all her emotions were right there in her eyes, stripped bare for him to see.

She spoke softly, fervently. "I've been dead for so long. Too long. Help me live again, Jack. Please."

He closed his eyes and swayed for a moment, feeling as if he'd been sucker punched. How the hell could he argue with that?

With a growled curse, he grabbed her and yanked her against him. She yielded to him so eagerly, so sweetly, it was all he could do not to shuck that damn flowing, sexy dress up around her hips and thrust inside her.

He forced himself to move slowly, deliberately, when what he wanted to do was pound into her like the ocean against the rocks. He lowered her to the blanket again, this time so they were on their sides facing each other.

With fingers that trembled slightly with the effort it took to hold the beast at bay, he traced her face—the curve of a cheekbone, the fragile line of her jaw, the lush, full bow of her lips.

She was so beautiful, she took his breath away.

"Ah, Grace," he murmured. "Sweet, sweet Grace."

Dark lashes fanned her dusky skin as she closed her eyes and leaned into his hand. She pressed her lips to his palm, stirring the fine hairs on his arm and he drew in a ragged breath and found her mouth with his own.

He would have gone slow. Dammit, he *wanted* to go slow. But her mouth opened for him so willingly and her body melted against him with such eager anticipation.

At her breathy sigh, at the feel of her softness cradling his hardness, he lost the battle to contain the wild, urgent need roaring through him.

His searching fingers found the small, sweet weight of a breast. He rubbed a thumb across her nipple and was rewarded with a sharp gasp.

Her head lolled back and he took that as an invitation to trail kisses down the long, slim length of her neck until he reached the neckline of her sundress.

Unlike this morning, this time he didn't stop there. Through the cotton of her dress, his lips followed the path of his fingers to the hard, aroused nub of her nipple and he drew her into his mouth while his fingers strayed to her other breast.

She dug her fingers into his hair and held him against her, offering her body to him willingly. He played with her, teased her, while raw need pulsed through her to pool and throb between her thighs.

She wanted more. So much more.

Withdrawing a few inches, she gathered her courage around her and pulled her dress over her head. He leaned back and gazed at her, washed by moonlight, then lifted hot, hungry eyes to hers.

Without looking away from her, with their gazes locked, he removed his own clothing. Finally, when there were no barriers left between them, she scanned his body as he had hers.

She was completely fascinated by the sight of him, by the tanned skin pulled tightly over firm muscles, by the hard angles and planes so different from hers.

It must have been a trick of the moonlight, but when she returned her gaze to his face, she was startled to find what looked like faint color climbing his cheeks.

He cleared his throat. "See anything you'd like?"

She gave a low laugh, amazed that she could be enjoying this so very much. "Everything. Wrap it up, I'll take it all. No, wait. Don't wrap it up. I think I prefer to take it home just the way it is."

"It's yours," he murmured, then reached for her again.

He kissed her until she couldn't think straight, until her thoughts were a senseless muddle, until all she wanted was to feel him inside her.

Then, when she didn't think she could handle anything more, his fingers found her. He touched her, the most sensitive part of her, and she felt as if she would incinerate, as if she would burn away into nothing but glowing embers that would dance up to join the stars.

He stroked her once, twice, and that was all it took. She was lost. Wave after wave of sensation crashed over her, more powerful than anything the Pacific could dish out.

And then he was there, kneeling between her thighs, asking permission to take her. She gave it with a murmur of his name and her hands clutching his shoulders.

He entered her slowly, inch by agonizing inch. Her body softened to accept him, to welcome him.

Long unused muscles stretched to accommodate him and then he was completely, deeply inside her, filling every part of her.

The sound of their ragged breathing drifted up to join the rustling, murmuring leaves of the banyan tree. His hands found hers and with their fingers as entwined as their mouths, he lifted their joined hands above her head and then thrust even more deeply.

She gasped his name as the heat began to blaze again, as flame after flame began to burn through her.

"I won't go anywhere without you," he promised, then drove into her in a rhythm as ancient as the sea.

The broad muscles of his chest rubbed against her breasts with each thrust. It was an overwhelming sensory assault, and that unbearably wonderful pressure began to build inside her again.

She arched her body to meet him thrust for thrust, her hands tightening on his. Finally, when she felt as if she would splinter apart if she had to endure another moment of this sweet torture, he reached a hand between their joined bodies, dancing his thumb across her aroused, aching flesh.

The night exploded instantly and her body convulsed around him. With a harsh groan, he withdrew slightly then buried himself inside her again and found his own release.

She slipped almost instantly into an exhausted sleep, her cheek tucked against his shoulder and her arms around him.

Moving carefully so he didn't awaken her, he pulled the blanket up and around them until they were wrapped in a warm, cozy cocoon. He knew they couldn't very well spend the night here on the beach, but he didn't have the heart to wake her yet.

Or maybe it was strength he didn't have enough of, courage to face what he had done.

Even with the blanket and with the warmth of her sleeping body against him, he still felt chilled. No, not chilled. He recognized it for what it was. Guilt. No matter what she said, no matter how powerful her arguments had been or how eagerly she had responded to his kiss or how much she had, amazingly enough, seemed to want his touch, he knew damn well he never should have let things go this far.

Sex—even earthshaking, pulse-pounding, incredible sex like they had just shared—was never enough to make the hurt disappear. It might mask it, might make you forget for a while. But he'd learned in those dark months after his father's suicide that making love with the wrong person would only intensify loneliness and pain.

And he was definitely the wrong person for Grace Solarez.

He risked a look at her lying against his shoulder, at long black lashes against dusky skin, at the straight line of her nose, at that full, generous mouth that melted so sweetly under his.

She was sweet and beautiful and brave, and she deserved so much more than he could give her.

She deserved someone whole and unbroken, a man who could open his heart and let her climb inside.

He wasn't that man and hadn't been for a long time.

He suddenly wished fiercely that things could be different. He had told the truth when he said he cared about her. He admired her strength and her courage and he would never be able to repay her for what she had done for Emma.

In any other man it wouldn't take much to slip headlong into love with her.

But somewhere between his father's suicide and Camille's selfish abandonment, a part of him had been smashed beyond repair—the part that could give the complete and unconditional trust so necessary for a healthy relationship.

He hadn't lived like a monk since Emma was born. He wasn't a diehard skirt-chaser like Piper but he liked women and spending time with them. He dated occasionally and had enjoyed a few healthy sexual relationships in the last five years with women who expected nothing more of him than that.

That's the way it had to be.

Early on, when Em had still been a toddler, he had started to regret his decision to raise her alone and had begun to think maybe she would be better off with a mother. It sounded cold-blooded in the abstract, but he had thought it through carefully and selected a woman he thought would fit the bill admirably. Kate had been sweet and kind and loving and she would have made Em a wonderful mother.

But every time their relationship started to feel too serious—when she would begin to talk about setting a wedding date—he would think of Camille and the bitter silence of his parents' marriage and would end up feeling like a coyote in a trap.

He had ended up hurting a very nice woman, something he still regretted deeply.

From that point on, he decided he would be better off if he limited his discreet entanglements to only those women who wouldn't expect anything from him, who wanted the same kinds of things he did at this stage in his life.

Grace wasn't that sort of woman.

And even if things were different, she didn't need this kind of complication right now. She was still trying to put her life together, and she needed someone solid, someone who could love her wholeheartedly, to help her through it.

Not that any of his angst mattered. He stared up at the moon and the scattering of stars, as regret pounded through him in time to the surf. Once she awoke and reality had time to settle in, he knew she would be quick to pull away from him.

And he would have to let her.

Somehow he would have to find the strength to stay away from her. It was the only option.

He blew out a frustrated breath, and immediately cursed himself when her eyes fluttered open at the sound.

"Hi there," she mumbled sleepily.

He felt a muscle in his jaw twitch as he fought the urge to kiss her again. To capture that mouth and again lose himself in the warm welcome of her body.

"Are you okay?" he asked instead.

"Wonderful." Her smile was soft, sexy. "And I thought *flying* with you was great."

He was surprised enough to laugh, but he instantly sobered as the inevitable guilt returned. "Seriously. Are you okay?"

She nodded.

"Jack, I'm fine. Better than fine."

She gave another of those soft smiles, and something inside him snarled and twisted painfully.

"Although if someone would have told me a few days ago I would be lying naked on a Hawaiian beach with you," she continued, "I probably would have decked them first, then had them committed."

"You always lead with your fists, don't you?" This fragile tenderness bubbling through him both astonished and terrified him.

She shrugged. "Most of the time. Beats getting hit first."

She felt his body tense beside her, around her, becoming as hard and implacable as the huge chunks of black lava scattered all around them.

"Who hit you first?" he asked.

She clamped her mouth shut, wishing she could call back her words. She never talked about those years with Tia Sofia, when her aunt would go off in sudden, zealous rages at nothing and everything that would sometimes last for days at a time.

She never, ever talked about it. Not even with Riley. It was simply a time she had survived, a time she rarely thought about anymore, other than the random, fleeting memory.

And the odd slip of the tongue.

"Nobody," she lied. "It was just a figure of speech."

In the moonlight, his eyes searched her face, trying to gauge the truth. She schooled her features not to give anything away, and he finally looked away. "It's late. We should probably go inside."

She heard the distance in his voice, felt the tension in his arms and a cold, heavy ache settled in her stomach. She rolled away from him and sat up, then felt around until she found her sundress. Even after she pulled it over her, she felt cold despite the balmy night air.

He couldn't have made it more plain that he wanted nothing more to do with her.

"Jack, I have no regrets," she said quietly.

He gave a short, harsh laugh. "That makes one of us."

"We're both grown-ups. We both knew what we were doing."

"You're my employee. A guest in my home. I didn't bring you to the islands for this. I hope you know that."

"I do."

"I never intended this. I only hoped that coming here would help you find peace."

"I did. Jack, tonight, with you, I found more peace than I ever believed I would have again."

But at what cost? she wondered later as they walked silently to the house. Now she had the added tumult of remembering exactly how it felt to hold him and kiss him and burn with him.

CHAPTER FOURTEEN

ON THE EVE OF THEIR DEPARTURE FROM HAWAII, Jack stood inside the house gazing through the screen toward the lanai, captivated by the scene in front of him.

The three females in his life were so busy with their own projects they didn't even notice him. Emma was repeatedly dunking her hapless doll into the birdbath, Lily's round face was content as she peeled potatoes for dinner and looked out to sea, and Grace frowned with concentration, her dark head bent over the Hawaiian quiltwork she always seemed to be working on.

They made quite a sight—the little blond cherub, the regal Hawaiian, and the exotic, exquisite Grace.

He had been afraid she would withdraw again after their night on the beach, that she would climb back into her distant, solitary world.

He was wrong. The lost, wounded Grace with the sorrowful eyes who had drifted through his house in Seattle like some kind of wraith had largely disappeared.

Although she reemerged at odd moments, for the most part Grace had become this bright, vital woman who took his breath away—who smiled more often and who even laughed occasionally, though rarely at him.

The change in her made it even harder for him to keep his vow to stay away from her.

An image of the day before flashed through his mind and he felt his blood begin a slow, thick churn at the memory. Emma had gone to a family party with Lily and Tiny, eager to play with their grandchildren.

Their departure left him in the house alone with Grace. After about five minutes of contemplating just how gloriously they could manage to fill those hours, he had jumped up and told her to put a swimsuit on under her shorts and grab her walking shoes.

He thought she would refuse—he had *wanted* her to refuse so he could put as much space between them as possible without feeling like a terrible host abandoning his guest.

To his surprise, she had frowned for a moment, put that damn handiwork aside, and done as he requested.

When she learned he wanted to take her to a remote waterfall he knew in the soaring, knife-sharp mountains that made up much of the interior of Oahu, she had protested that she wasn't much of a hiker.

But once she started up the jungle-like trail, he'd had to hurry to keep up with her.

Grace had been entranced by it all—the brilliant explosion of color and scent from the many species of tropical flowers, the lush, fern-like undergrowth, and especially the twenty-foot waterfall that cascaded down from a moss-covered cliff to a glistening pool.

She had been entranced by her surroundings. And he had been entranced by her.

He had wanted to kiss her—had ached with it—but had somehow found the strength to refrain. She hadn't made it easy on him. When she smiled at him, that soft, sweet smile, it had been all he could do not to take her there, against the bark of a hala tree.

He rubbed at his chest, at the sudden emotion clogging it. She was getting too close and it scared the hell out of him. For the last five days, he had been able to think of virtually nothing else but the silken welcome of her body.

He should probably let them know he was here, he thought now, and moved to open the door when Grace suddenly made a face. The breeze carried her mild curse to him.

"What's wrong?" Lily set down the potatoes she was peeling and tried to peer at the small wooden quilting frame in Grace's lap, covered in blue-and-white fabric.

"I can't do this. It's just too damn hard for me."

"You're doing fine." Lily's voice was calm, untroubled, like the Sound on a hot July day. "You just need to have more patience."

"I just need about four more hands to keep this blasted thing in place. I hate all these tiny stitches and having to turn the fabric after every darn one. I stink at this."

"You've made good progress. See? You're almost done with the dolphins. You just need to finish that and then do the outline of the shells around the edge."

"I'll never be able to finish it," she muttered. "I should never have let you talk me into starting it in the first place."

He felt like some kind of voyeur standing here listening to their private conversation, but couldn't make himself turn away. Instead, he leaned forward so he could hear them better.

The quilted wall hanging meant something significant to her, something greater than just the sum of thread and fabric. He didn't understand it, but he sensed that finishing it was more symbolic than anything else, and he was pretty sure it had to do with her daughter.

With healing and rebirth.

She worked on it all the time with an almost manic determination. He knew she even slipped out of bed in the early hours of the morning to work on it because he heard her moving around while he was in his own bed, tangled in his sheets.

Dying of frustration.

The wall hanging was another of those subjects they didn't talk about, just like what had happened on the beach the other night.

They also avoided mentioning the careful, subtle distance she maintained with Emma. She had been unfailingly kind to his daughter since the day they had gone snorkeling, but she hadn't read to her again and she went out of her way to avoid situations that might put her in close contact alone with Emma.

As if she knew he was thinking of her, Em suddenly lifted her attention from the birdbath. "Hey, Lily, can I have a banana Popsicle?" she asked.

"We're going to eat in a little while."

"Please? I promise I'll eat all my dinner. Long as it's not that yucky *poi* stuff again like we had last night at the party." She screwed up her face tightly and shuddered at the thought.

Jack couldn't help the soft laugh that escaped him. Unfortunately, it gave away his position and all three of them looked toward him, lurking here in the doorway.

"Daddy!" Emma shrieked. Without a backward look, she let her long-suffering doll drown and launched herself toward him.

He slid the door open and scooped her up, smiling in greeting to Lily and Grace as he did it.

"Hey, pumpkin. How was your day?"

"Good. We went to town again and had shave ice and I played with Pookie. He threw sand at me and it got in my hair."

He swallowed a grin at her disgusted tone. "Boys will sometimes do things like that. Better get used to it."

"I was going to throw sand back at him but Lily made me drop it. I don't think that's very fair."

Ah, the injustices of life. He smiled at her. "Did I hear somebody say something about a banana Popsicle?"

As always, she was easily diverted. She nodded her head. "I'm gonna have one. You want to share?"

Frozen banana sugar-sticks didn't rank very high on his list of favorite treats but how could he discourage such willing generosity? "Sure. You go get it and I'll break it in half for us."

He set her down and she hurried into the house. He loved her so much it caught his breath sometimes. How could Grace not adore such a sweet, loving, generous little girl?

He crossed the lanai and sat in the glider across from the two women, stretching his legs out in front of him.

"How was *your* day?" Lily asked.

Lucrative. Over eighteen holes at the Turtle Bay golf course in Kahuku, he'd cinched the multimillion dollar deal with the Koreans, snatching the account from his largest competitor.

It should have been a moment rich with professional satisfaction—but through the entire flight shuttling the Kims back to their hotel in Maui, he hadn't been able to think about anything but Grace and about this heat simmering between them.

He shrugged and snatched a potato chunk from Lily's bowl, barely escaping her customary knuckle-rap. "Did I ever tell you how boring I find the game of golf? What I want to know is, why aren't more business deals conducted over a good game of touch football?"

He was rewarded with a snicker—an actual snicker—out of Grace.

Lily—much harder to impress, apparently—just rolled her eyes. "I can just see you and Mr. Kim chasing each other around a football field while you negotiate terms, or whatever it is you hotshot business people do."

"It could work. Think about it. There's nothing like pitting the shirts against the skins to really condense issues down to bare bones."

Lily just shook her head at him. "Sometimes it amazes me that you have such a big, successful company. How do you even keep that business of yours running?"

"Charm and good looks." He grinned at Grace, who flashed him an amused smile, then quickly returned to the material on her lap.

Lily snorted. "Oh yeah, Mr. Charm-and-Good-Looks. I forgot to tell you. Sydney called while you were gone. I'm supposed to tell you to call her, no matter what time you get in."

He grimaced, hating the reminder of Seattle. He didn't want to leave. He wanted to stay right here and spend more time with this vibrant Grace, who laughed at his jokes and came alive in his arms.

He was afraid when they returned to Bainbridge Island, she would disappear back into her cold, lonely world.

And the realization of how badly he would miss her haunted him.

She was going to kill a certain Hawaiian.

It was two in the morning, her last night in paradise, and here she sat in her room with her eyes itching, her back aching and her fingers on fire. And for what? Because of this stupid quilted square Lily talked her into starting—a project she had no idea why she was wasting her time struggling with anyway, since she wasn't ever going to be able to finish it.

Despite five days of intense effort, she still had hours of work to do on the thing. She ought to just toss it in the rag bin, despite Lily's blasted calm assurance that she didn't have much more to do. Every time she was tempted to set it aside and try to forget about it, though, some compulsion would send her back to it.

If she was going to be frustrated, she'd certainly picked a beautiful place for it. She gazed out the big windows at the moonlight glistening on the water. A bamboo wind chime on the lanai clanked its low song in the ever present breeze that puffed the curtains and rustled the fronds of the palm trees outside her window.

She didn't want to go back to Seattle. She wanted to stay here and pretend all the ugliness of her life there was just a distant dream.

On the other hand, she didn't know how much more she could survive of this thick sexual tension between her and Jack.

Every time she was with him, it cranked up a notch, until now she felt as if her body was so tightly strung it would only take a touch to make it crack apart.

She wasn't sure what was more responsible for keeping her awake and edgy at night, the unfinished quilted square with its ring of leaping dolphins or this constant, restless craving to be in Jack's arms again.

She rotated her shoulders and stretched her neck from side to side. This was crazy. Absolutely crazy. She was going to be as stiff as one of those tiki statues they sold in all the tourist traps if she stayed in this position much longer.

She needed to get up and move a bit, she thought, and decided to sneak down to the kitchen for a glass of ice water from the refrigerator and a slice of Lily's heavenly banana bread.

She closed her door softly and padded in her bare feet down the stairs. The house was dark, as she expected, but the full moon provided enough light to help her make it down the stairs and through the house to the kitchen without stumbling over anything.

She turned on only the light above the stove, fixed her snack, then turned it off before starting back across the living room, munching banana bread as she went.

"Can't sleep?"

The low voice came out of nowhere, scaring her witless. She gasped, inhaling much too quickly for somebody with a mouthful of banana bread, and the glass of ice water slipped from her hands to shatter with a dainty crash on the sisal rug.

The gasp of surprise turned into a choking cough as a piece of banana bread lodged in her throat.

"Are you okay?" Jack's disembodied voice floated through the dark living room. She wanted to answer him but she was too busy trying to clear an airway.

The room suddenly lit up as bright as day when he flipped the switch and she finally managed to choke down the errant bite so she could breathe again.

The blessed oxygen in her lungs lasted only long enough for her to realize he had very little on, just a pair of surfer trunks even more disreputable than the pair she'd seen him in that first morning after their arrival.

A towel was slung around his neck, his hair was wet and beads of moisture clung to the sculpted muscles of his chest.

It only took her crack ex-detective brain about a minute of her gaping at him to figure out he'd been swimming.

She cleared away the last of the banana bread. "Good grief,

Jack. Are you trying to give me a heart attack? What are you still doing up?"

He shrugged his bare shoulders. "I couldn't sleep either and thought I'd work the edge off in the water."

"In the ocean? Is that safe in the middle of the night?"

"No. But the full moon tonight made it seem just like daylight out there. I didn't even go out to the first line of breakers. Just bodysurfed a little."

"I've always wanted to try that," she said, and was surprised at the wistful note in her voice.

"I'm sorry we're leaving before you had a chance. Maybe you can try it next time you come."

But there wouldn't be a next time, and both of them knew it. The thought filled her with an aching sadness.

She would never see this idyllic spot again, never feel the wonder of his touch. He would go on with his life and she would go on with hers and their paths would probably never cross again.

She gazed at the broken glass and the water spot spreading out across the rug. "I suppose I'd better clean up this mess."

"No, stay put. You don't have shoes on. I've at least got flip-flops to protect my feet. Sit down and I'll clean it up."

"It's my mess. I can take care of it."

"A mess you wouldn't have made if I hadn't scared you so badly. Sit down."

He hurried to the kitchen and quickly returned with a broom, dustpan and towel. While he went to work sweeping up the tiny shards of glass, she ignored his protests and took the towel to sop the water from the carpet.

When he finished, she followed him into the kitchen. He shook the tiny shards of glass from the dustpan into the trash—rubbish, they called it here—while she went to the sink to wring out the towel.

Everything would have been fine—they would have said their good-nights and parted to their respective bedrooms—if she hadn't turned to hang the towel on the stove just as he stepped away from the trash can.

Their paths collided, their bodies brushed. Both of them froze and the only sound in the kitchen besides the low hum of the refrigerator was her sudden intake of breath.

He was cool and damp from the water, and she was suddenly conscious of her flimsy nightgown, a simple white sleeveless cotton shift.

All her instincts shouted at her to step away, to put as much distance between them as she could. But then she made the mistake of lifting her eyes from the wide expanse of muscled chest, of letting her gaze meet his.

Her heartbeat seemed to stutter and catch in her chest. She knew that look shimmering in those brilliant green depths. She'd spent the last five days dreaming about that look.

He wanted her, and her body hummed an eager, enthusiastic response.

She should just ignore it. If she had a brain left in her head, she would just turn around and run as fast as she could to the safe haven of her room and lock the door against him.

Even as the thought flitted through her head, she heard herself murmur his name and felt her body lean into his.

CHAPTER FIFTEEN

SHE MELTED IN HIS ARMS LIKE HOT WAX IN THE sun.

He closed his eyes at the touch of her mouth, at her warm, lithe body in his arms again, and that ferocious need he had tried to contain for five days growled to life within him. It bayed and howled inside his skin.

He moved quickly to try to restrain it and took a step back, bumping up against the kitchen counter.

To his chagrin, she moved with him in a slow, sensuous dance. She gave a soft moan and wrapped her arms around his neck to pull him closer, and he was lost.

Completely lost.

All reason, all his arguments for staying away from her, disappeared in an instant, leaving only this raw, pulsing need inside his skin. He buried his hands in her hair and angled her head for his mouth. Her lips parted for him willingly, eagerly, and he groaned at the slick heat of her tongue on his.

She wore a thin white cotton nightgown, something she

must have brought from her apartment. It was plain and simple and shouldn't have been at all sexy, but it slid against his bare chest with every movement, creating an excruciating friction.

Her breasts pressed against his skin through the thin cotton, begging for his touch. How could he resist?

That soft, erotic moan escaped her throat again and he filled his hand with her, his thumb dancing across the hard, aroused peak that pushed against the cloth. Her head slid back and he kissed his way down the long column of her neck to the first tiny buttons on her nightgown.

His fingers fumbled on the buttons, but he finally found success and the material slid off one shoulder. He kissed the skin there, on the fine, elegant curve of her clavicle, then lifted her bottom to the counter so he could better reach the delights bared before him.

Her nipple pebbled to his touch and he drew it into his mouth. Her skin was hot—so hot—and smelled like plumeria.

She dug her hands in his hair, stroking, caressing, murmuring his name, and all he could think about was burying himself inside her.

It only took an instant for him to free himself from his swim trunks. Standing between her thighs, he lifted the hem of her nightgown and quickly yanked off her panties.

His fingers found her, slick and welcoming, and she arched against him, gasping his name. Just as he prepared to plunge inside her, she wrenched her mouth away and spoke in a low, breathy voice.

"Jack... Stop. We can't... Someone might come," she whispered.

He was so lost in the tight grip of desire that it took several seconds for her words to register. Damn. She was right. He was just about to take her against the kitchen cabinets, for heaven's sake, where anyone could walk in on them. What was he thinking?

Easy. He wasn't thinking anything but how wonderful—how completely perfect—she felt in his arms.

His body cried out a protest as he growled a harsh curse and stepped away.

"Wait. I didn't want you to stop. I *don't* want you to stop." Her voice trembled a little and she splayed a hand on his chest. He felt his muscles contract under the heat of her skin.

"That's not what I meant. I... I just thought maybe we ought to move this somewhere we are less likely to be interrupted. My room, maybe."

He knew he should put a stop to this. Dammit, he *knew* it. He could come up with a thousand reasons why it was wrong, starting with all the things he'd listed to himself the other night.

But all those reasons meant nothing compared to the need thundering through him and this soft, disconcerting tenderness.

He met her gaze and the dazed hunger in her dark eyes there nearly sent him to his knees. "Mine's closer," he muttered, and practically dragged her to his room at the top of the stairs.

He didn't even wait until they were inside the room before his mouth was on hers again. He pushed her inside the room, kicking the door shut and twisting the lock behind his back without severing the connection of their lips and tongues and teeth.

"You taste so incredibly good," he breathed. "Sweet and lush, like ripe bananas and heaven."

"And you taste like the sea," she murmured, and pulled her mouth away from his to press warm lips to the skin of his chest.

He survived only a few moments of the sweet torture before he pushed her toward the bed, pulling off her nightgown in one easy motion with a silent prayer of gratitude for the heat of the island that lent itself so well to loose, flowing clothing.

Just before he would have joined her, she took his hand. "Jack, no regrets this time. Promise me."

He gazed at her, at the tumble of sable hair in stark contrast to his white sheets, at those huge, luminous brown eyes watching him so seriously, at her exotic dusky skin.

How could he promise her that when he was already having regrets? They simmered at the back of his mind, just waiting for him to be able to think straight so they could break free.

He knew there was no going back this time, no withdrawing to the polite distance they'd maintained since that night on the beach.

"Grace, are you sure about this?"

"Positive. This is what I want. *You're* what I want."

He loved her. It was his last coherent thought before he pushed inside her. Despite all his efforts, despite all the reasons why he knew it was a mistake of phenomenal proportions, he had completely lost his heart to this beautiful, sexy, unbelievably brave woman.

And it scared the hell out of him.

The man had had no more than three hours of sleep. She knew it, since she had spent those three hours wrapped around him like a tangled vine. So how could he manage to look so competent, so completely self-assured, after five hours at the controls of the little jet?

She gazed at the back of his head, at the sunstreaked blond hair and the tanned skin of his neck.

He was speaking into his headset and checking the instrument panel in front of him with a seriousness in direct contrast to the relaxed playful man who built sand towers with his daughter and bodysurfed in the middle of the night under a full moon.

He was a multifaceted man—devoted father, aggressive businessman. Completely masculine, yet compassionate enough to hold a grieving mother while she wept.

What would she do without him in her life?

She shivered suddenly and reached above her head to turn off the forced air blowing on her.

She knew perfectly well that wasn't the real cause for her chills, but it helped her to focus on something external, something besides the jolt that rippled through her every time she realized how much she'd come to care about Jack Dugan.

What was she going to do?

She wrenched her gaze away from him and stared out the little round window at the hard blue of the Pacific beneath them. She had no choice. She had to leave his home, his life, before she did something completely stupid like fall in love with him.

If it wasn't already too late.

She shivered again. It wouldn't happen. She wouldn't *let* it happen.

She had nothing to offer him. Absolutely nothing but a whole damn cargo plane bursting at the seams with her emotional baggage.

He didn't need to be saddled with a woman whose heart was a barren, empty wasteland. He deserved someone who was unafraid to love him, someone who could feel joy again.

Besides that, she had to consider Emma. He and his daughter were a package deal—a matched set—and she knew she would never be able to love the little girl as she needed.

Although she had begun to heal, Grace knew that a portion of her heart—the maternal part that cherished silly jokes and crayon drawings and sticky, wet kisses—had been broken forever by Marisa's death.

It could never, ever mend enough for her to let Emma in.

She glanced across the length of the jet at the little girl with the blond curls and the mischievous dimples.

Emma had been restless and hyperactive the entire flight, racing up and down the aisle, laughing loudly at the same two videos they'd watched on the flight over, and pestering everyone with questions.

"Do whales swim in their sleep?"

"Who thought up mayonnaise?"

"When can I learn to fly an airplane?"

Now, all questioned-out apparently, she slept peacefully with her pillow wedged into the corner and a blanket tucked up to her chin.

She was a sweet little girl and Grace suddenly wished that she could love her. With a fierceness that brought an ache to her throat, she wished that she could be free to push those blond curls out of her eyes and kiss that forehead and gather her soft, sleeping weight against her.

She jerked her gaze away. It landed on Lily, across the aisle from Emma, who returned the look solemnly.

After a moment or two, Lily set down the magazine she'd been reading and pulled her bulk out of the seat and crossed the cabin to take the empty one next to Grace.

"We ought to be landing soon," she said. "It's been a pretty good flight, yeah? That Jack, he sure knows what he's doing."

"He does," Grace agreed.

"How are you doing with the quilting?"

The woman was worse than a damn slave driver when it came to this blasted thing. With a sigh, she pulled it from her lap and held it up for Lily's inspection.

"Wow! Look at this!" Pleasure lit up Lily's dark eyes and her plump cheeks rounded with her smile.

Even Grace had to admit it was beautiful. When she and Lily were going over patterns, this one had called to her in some inexplicable way—a ring of dolphins leaping and dancing joyously, surrounded by a border of intertwined conch and coral and starfish.

Marisa had loved the sea, and she would have adored this.

"You're just about done," Lily said. "A few more days and it'll be ready for framing. If you want, I can have Tiny make you a nice one out of koa. He's done a couple of pretty good ones for me."

Grace grabbed the square back, knowing she was more protective of it than she ought to be. "It's not ready for framing. Not even close. I still have a long way to go. And, you know, once we return to Seattle I won't be able to give it the time I did in the past few days."

Lily shrugged. "Doesn't matter. You'll finish it when you're ready to finish it. Then you can say good-bye."

She set her teeth against the arguments hovering there, knowing they would be useless against the Hawaiian, who could be as stubborn and immovable as the sharp, steep mountains near Hali'ewa.

For some bizarre reason, Lily seemed to think that once she finished the quilted square, she would be free of her sorrow. That while her fingers worked the cloth, her mind worked through her grief.

She wasn't buying it.

This past week had gone a long way toward helping her accept the finality of Marisa's death, but she knew she would never stop grieving, no matter how many blasted quilted squares she finished.

She would always feel that a part of her—the very best part—was gone and could never be regained.

"Everybody buckle your seat belts," Jack called suddenly from the cockpit. "We'll be heading down pretty soon. We're almost home."

Home. She stared out the window as they began their descent. The lights of Seattle glimmered through the clouds, but it looked as if the city would welcome them back with a cold, wet rain to match her mood.

She would tell him tonight she was going back to her own life. He would protest, she knew, would try to persuade her to stay, but she would have to stand firm.

Any debt between them for what had happened on that dark highway had more than been repaid. If he was still concerned about security, he could find someone else to protect his family.

She needed to protect herself.

She grimaced. How selfish was that? But there it was. The real reason she needed to leave, the real reason she was trying so hard to steel her heart against him.

She was afraid.

Terrified.

She had barely survived the endless pain of the last year and she couldn't bear the idea that she might be vulnerable again.

"Hey, sleepyhead."

The soft voice yanked her out of a dream of white sand beaches and the calming song of the sea and she awoke with her cheek pressed to the leather of Jack's family room sofa and his face just inches away from hers.

He crouched by the sofa, his face bathed in the unearthly blue light from the flickering television set and his green eyes gleaming with an emotion she couldn't place.

"Shouldn't you be in bed?" he asked

She blinked at him, still feeling disoriented. "What time is it?"

"A little after three."

She pulled herself up and stretched the kinks out of her back. It had been almost midnight when she, Emma, and the Kihualanis returned to the house on Bainbridge Island.

She had planned to stay up and talk to him when he finished his post-flight procedures at the airport. Even though she would have given anything to avoid it, she knew she had to tell him she was leaving in the morning.

She remembered turning on the television set and stretching out on the couch but nothing after that. She must have fallen asleep and now it nearly *was* morning.

She caught herself just before she asked what had taken him so long. It was none of her business. If he wanted to stay out all night, it had nothing to do with her.

"Why aren't you in bed?" he asked again.

"I wanted to wait for you."

That strange light in his eyes deepened and she finally realized what emotion she could read there. Tenderness. He watched her with a smile on his face and tenderness in his eyes.

He leaned forward. "I'm glad you did," he whispered, and tangled his mouth with hers, and she forgot all about the reason she had stayed up, about the grim knowledge that she would be leaving him in just a few hours.

"Ah, Grace," he murmured against her mouth. "I've missed you today."

"We just spent seven hours together on an airplane."

"Yeah, but I was too busy piloting the plane to do what I've been dying for all day."

"What's that?" She managed to hold on to her thoughts long enough to ask.

"This." He deepened the kiss and pulled her to him, molding his body to hers. The hardness of his arousal nudged against her hip and her body sighed in welcome.

She shouldn't do this. The thought flickered across her mind briefly, reluctantly. She chose to ignore it.

Just one more time. That's all she wanted. Just one more chance to savor the haven she found in his arms, to store up memories for the bleak, empty days ahead of her without his teasing grin and fiery touch.

Was that too much to ask?

CHAPTER SIXTEEN

SHE WAS PACKING WHEN BEAU CALLED.

Lily brought the cordless phone to her room. When Grace opened the door for her, the Hawaiian saw the pile of folded clothes in Grace's hand then looked past her to the suitcase on the bed.

She gazed back at her and said nothing, just frowned with a look of deep disappointment in her dark eyes.

Grace squirmed under the weight of that scowl. "Lily, I'm sorry. But I have to go."

The housekeeper's lips firmed into a tight line and she handed the phone to Grace. "Not my business if you run away."

"I'm not running away," she lied. "I just…"

"Not my business," Lily repeated more firmly.

"Look, I haven't had a chance to tell Jack yet." When she awoke in her bed, she'd been alone with just the scent of him, that pine and sandalwood fragrance that had imprinted itself on her synapses.

She would never again be able to walk through a forest without remembering him.

Besides his scent, the only other trace she could find that they had spent the night in each other's arms was a terse note on the bedside table: "Had to run to Seattle. Need to talk when I return. Jack."

Need to talk.

The words sounded ominous and she had a fleeting, cowardly wish that she could leave before he returned to avoid what she knew would probably be a ugly scene.

But how could he argue with a packed suitcase?

"You going to tell him?" Lily asked now.

"Yes!" Too late, she remembered the phone and covered the mouthpiece with her hand. "Yes," she repeated quietly. "I'll tell him as soon as he comes back. So don't say anything until I can talk to him, please?"

"What about the quilt?"

Didn't the woman ever think of anything else? She gritted her teeth. "I'll take it with me, okay? I know the stitches now and I can work on it anywhere. It's time for me to get back to my real life, anyway, and I probably won't be able to finish it for a long time."

Lily studied her for a moment out of eyes dark with disillusionment, then without another word she turned and walked down the hall with her colorful dress floating behind her.

She couldn't have made it more plain that Grace had let her down. Guilt and failure pulled at her. She felt them and she stiffened. It wasn't her fault if Lily was superstitious enough to believe she could somehow stitch all her emotions into a stupid piece of fabric.

She remembered the phone suddenly, that she had a call, and pulled her hand away from the mouthpiece.

"Hello?" she snapped.

"Jeez. About damn time. What took you so long?"

Beau's typical impatience grated on her already frayed nerves but she clamped down on her sharp retort. "What's up?"

The impatience changed to barely concealed jubilation. "We got him!"

"Who?" she asked, feeling not only dense but terribly ungrammatical.

"Dugan! Who did you think?"

Her face suddenly numbed and a deep, terrible chill settled into her bones. For an instant she forgot how to work the muscles of her mouth, as if they'd suddenly locked into place.

"What...what are you talking about?" she finally asked.

"Your little trip to Hawaii is going to be the last damn nail in Dugan's coffin. Word on the street is that it wasn't pineapples he brought back from the islands."

This couldn't be happening. It *couldn't* be. "What?" she asked urgently. "What was it?"

"We're still working on the search warrant. Damn judges." He paused, probably pondering on the vagaries of the legal system, one of his other favorite rants, until she wanted to scream at him.

She forced herself to speak calmly instead. As calmly as she could manage, anyway, when her heart felt as if it were going to explode into a million pieces. "What do your sources tell you he brought in?"

"Chinese-made AK-47s that took the roundabout way through Honolulu airport. Our guess is they slipped through Customs hidden under genuine computer parts."

She wouldn't believe it. He had to be wrong.

"Are you sure about this?"

"Pretty damn sure. Ninety-nine-point-nine percent sure. We got it from a reliable source."

So there was still some doubt. She had to cling to that doubt. She refused to contemplate the possibility that Jack might be involved in something this dark and sordid.

He *couldn't* be.

A man who treated an old Hawaiian woman with such teasing affection and whose day revolved around story-time with his five-year-old daughter couldn't possibly be capable of this kind of heartlessness.

The Jack Dugan she had come to know these last few weeks would never be willing to trade other people's lives for cold, hard cash.

Her complete conviction stunned her, but she couldn't deny it. She was absolutely certain he could not be involved, that he would never have the kind of callous indifference to both the law and to human life to perpetrate something like this.

Beau didn't know him as she did. He couldn't know. As far as he was concerned, Jack was just as she believed when she first came here, a crass opportunist without thought for anyone else but himself.

If she didn't do something, Jack would be arrested today. She blew out a shaky breath. This was all her fault. All of it. Instead of working the case like she should have been doing these last few weeks, she had been completely self-absorbed. She had let her own emotional uproar cloud her vision of anything but her own problems.

If she could have looked beyond herself, she might have found evidence by now that would clear Jack. She might have been able to figure out who at GSI had the guts to pull off a smuggling ring right under everyone's noses.

Maybe it wasn't too late. Maybe she could still do something.

She had to clear away the fear from her throat before she could speak. "So what happens next?"

"We should get the warrant by this afternoon, then we can move in and search GSI. I imagine we'll probably hit the house by early evening."

"That soon?"

"Yeah. The reason I called was to warn you so you can get out now. The sooner the better—I don't want you there any longer than you have to be. It might raise questions I'm not too crazy about having to answer right now. You think you can leave without tipping him off?"

No, no, no. She couldn't just run away. She had to stay and do what she could to help him. She looked at her suitcase on the bed, then out the window at the cold, gray water.

"I don't think so," she mumbled.

He was silent for a moment, then his voice sharpened. She had forgotten how well he knew her. "What's up? Jeez, Gracie. I thought you'd be happy about this."

"I'm just surprised things are moving so fast."

"Yeah, we're ready to bust the thing wide open and you don't want to be caught up in it. Get out while you can."

She was already caught up in it. So ensnared she didn't know how she would break free.

She murmured something noncommittal, then said goodbye to him and hung up. He sounded like an excited little boy, the way he always did when they used to be close to an arrest in a big case.

Dear God. Jack was going to be arrested. What was she going to do? She had to move fast if she had any hope of preventing it.

And then she would leave and return to the loneliness and solitude of her life without him.

So this is what it felt like to be in love.

It was the most terrifying thing that had ever happened to

him, including the time he'd had to bring down an F-15 on a bare stretch of tundra in the Yukon without landing gear.

There were definite similarities between the two experiences. His stomach was tied up in the same knots as it had been right before the belly of the F-15 scraped permafrost. His chest was just as achy, his palms just as sweaty, his nerves every bit as jumpy.

Actually, being in love was worse, when it came right down to it.

At least up in that plane, he had enough experience on his side to give him a rough idea what he would need to do to walk away from the impending disaster in one piece.

When it came to Grace and this vast, profound tenderness, he felt like the greenest of rookies soloing for the first time.

All he knew is that he had held her in his arms all night long as she slept and hadn't wanted to let her free. He didn't know what had happened to the anxiety he had always felt before at the idea of settling in to forever with a woman.

He just knew he wanted to hold her like this for the rest of their lives, to watch over her if she'd let him and do all he could to bring that soft, fleeting smile to her face.

He knew she cared about him. He could see the softness in her eyes when she looked at him, and the trust there humbled him.

She probably had no idea she did it, but when she slept, she clung to him as if he was the only thing standing between her and a turbulent, untamed ocean.

He loved it.

And he loved her.

He adored everything about her, from the little frown that furrowed her forehead whenever she worked on that quilted thingy to the strong core of courage inside her to that sly, quicksilver sense of humor that sometimes sneaked out, surprising both of them.

He loved her as he had believed he would never love a woman, and he couldn't imagine anything more perfect than spending the rest of his life watching for that sense of humor to erupt.

While he steered with one hand around the curving road toward home, he felt in the pocket of his leather jacket with the other to find the jeweler's box there.

The square, satiny package he'd driven over to Seattle to buy probably should have reassured him, but all he felt were these raw, cold nerves.

He was rushing things. He knew damn well he was moving faster than she would find comfortable. She still had issues to work through about her daughter's death, issues of guilt and accountability and grief.

And then there was Emma.

He frowned as he pulled the car into the driveway.

Emma.

What the hell did he think he was doing? Grace wouldn't let Emma close enough even to get to know her, forget about coming to care about her enough to take on mothering her.

The minute he pulled out the ring, she would take off faster than the Concorde. He knew damn well that's what she would do. His Grace had the most finely honed fight-or-flight instinct he'd ever seen, and in this case, he didn't have the slightest doubt which one she would chose.

So what was he doing with a glittering emerald ring in his pocket?

He didn't have to give it to her today, he reminded himself. Or tomorrow, or even next week.

That had been the final determining factor behind buying it. He could bide his time, wait and see how things shook out with her and Emma, give her the chance to grow more comfortable with her feelings for him.

When the time was right, he would be ready.

As he shoved the car into Park, nerves jumped in his gut. Was he crazy to do this? He thought he was ready for marriage and family when he proposed to Camille, and just look how dandy that all turned out.

But Camille and Grace were about as far apart on the humanity scale as any two people he could imagine.

He closed his fingers around the box again, suddenly fiercely glad he'd bought it, if only to demonstrate to himself that he was committed to a future with her. He would just put it in his office safe until she was ready to accept it—and she would. She had to. He didn't even want to contemplate the alternative.

No one seemed to be around when he entered the house. It took him a moment to remember today was Emma's play group, so she and Lily wouldn't be back for a while.

As for Grace, he would look for her as soon as he put the ring away.

He walked through the house to his office and was sorting through his chain of keys for the right one to unlock the door—kept latched since the day Em used a briefcase full of contracts for coloring paper—when he heard an odd rustling inside.

Puzzled, he tried the knob and found it unlocked.

The door swung open slowly, ominously, and he froze at the sight of Grace sitting in his chair, riffling through his private files.

He must have made some noise. He wasn't sure he could even speak through the shock clogging his throat, but he must have done something to alert her to his presence.

She glanced up and, under other circumstances, he might

have found it comical the way her face drained of all color, like a cartoon character left too long out in the cold.

He couldn't quite find it in himself to laugh.

He could only stare at her while his mind twisted and looped trying to find a logical explanation for her presence here.

"Jack! You're...you're back early."

He forced himself to fill his lungs with air. "Yeah. I just had a couple of errands to run. Was there something you needed in here?"

A pencil, some scissors, a three-hole punch. Anything. Say anything.

"I..." Her voice faltered and two high spots of color bloomed on her cheeks.

"You what?"

"I can explain."

He shut the door behind him and advanced on the desk. She edged back in her chair just enough to shatter his heart into jagged little pieces. She was afraid of him. After what they had been through together she was *afraid* of him.

This vast, devastating hurt turned his voice razor-sharp. "You can explain what you're doing in my office, the office I know damn well I locked this morning when I left it? How did you get in?"

"I picked the lock. It's pretty flimsy. You might want to look into upgrading it."

Anger was beginning to replace the hurt, and he welcomed the hot rush of feeling. At least it helped to fill the stunned, hollow ache. "What's going on, Grace? If you wanted something in here, all you had to do was ask me for it and I would have gladly given it. You didn't have to break in."

"Jack, we need to talk."

"Apparently." He sat down on the edge of the desk and she edged back even more in the seat. "So talk."

She bit her lip for a moment, rubbed her hands on her pants, blew out a breath. Finally she straightened her shoulders and met his gaze. "I shouldn't be telling you this. It breaks every code of conduct I once swore to follow. If Beau found out I'd tipped you, he'd never forgive me."

"Beau? Your former partner?"

She nodded.

"What does he have to do with the reason you're snooping through my office?"

Again she hesitated, looked away from him, then quickly back. "He's part of a multijurisdictional task force investigating you and GSI."

Her words startled a disbelieving laugh out of him. "For what?"

"Weapons smuggling."

He felt hot suddenly and then cold. Very, very cold. "You're kidding, right? This is some kind of sick joke."

She shook her head. "I wish it were a joke, Jack. I wish it were nothing more than a stupid, sick joke. But even as we speak, the task force is trying to obtain a warrant to search the company and your home. They will probably be here by this evening."

She had to be mistaken. She *had* to be.

He scraped a hand through his hair. "What the hell is this all about? I run a shipping company, completely on the level. We've never even had a damn safety violation."

"You've been under surveillance for several weeks now. It's a strong case, Jack."

Questions raced through his brain, one on top of the other. Several weeks? Before Emma's kidnapping? Could the kidnapping somehow be linked to this alleged smuggling ring?

And what about Grace? What was her involvement in this? She was no longer with the Seattle Police Department, he knew that for certain. And he had seen the anguish in her eyes when she talked about that night. She couldn't possibly have been lying about her reasons for being out on the highway, not unless she was the best damn actress in the world.

"Was Emma's kidnapping part of this? Did you know about the investigation the night you pulled her from the wreck?"

"No," she said, so emphatically he had to believe her.

"When did you find out? How long have you known I was under investigation?"

She fidgeted. "A few days after you found me and brought me here. Beau called me. It was the same day you asked me to work for you."

He thought back to that day, to her vehement refusal of his job offer then her abrupt about-face.

Suddenly everything made a grim, horrible sense.

"And that's why you took the job, right? What better way to help your friend investigate me than from inside my own house?" He nearly choked on his bitterness.

She nodded, looking miserable, and he felt as if he'd been kicked in the gut.

Betrayal upon betrayal.

He loved her, dammit. How could she do this?

"You're not a cop anymore, you haven't been for a year. How did he talk you into doing this?"

She studied her hands, folded tightly on the desk. "He didn't. I had to beg him to let me in on it."

He thought she couldn't wound him worse but he was wrong. Dead wrong. "You hate me that much?" His voice sounded ragged. "Why? What did I ever do to you?"

"Nothing. Not you."

"Why, then? Dammit, Grace. Why would you do this to me?"

She was quiet for a long time and when she finally lifted

her eyes to his, they glistened with unshed tears. "Revenge. It was all for revenge. I was hurting and I wanted you to hurt, too. I wanted you to slowly bleed to death like I have been for the last year, to know what it's like to lose every single thing that means anything to you."

His stomach pitched and churned at her vehemence. Before he could form his chaotic thoughts into words, she continued speaking, her voice now subdued.

"The task force believes nearly every illegal weapon to hit the streets of King County in the last three years is somehow tied to this smuggling ring." Her gaze met his again, locked there. "All of them, including the AK–47 used to kill my daughter."

"You think I'm responsible for that? You let me make love with you thinking I'm *responsible* for that?"

"No! I... I thought so at first, but not after I came to know you. It has to be someone else at your company—that's the only explanation I can come up with."

Someone else, probably one of his trusted employees. He didn't know which was worse, that he was suspected of this or that one of his employees might be behind it.

"Jack, you have to believe me. When Beau called me this morning to tell me the case would break open today, all I could think about was protecting you. I came in here looking for evidence to clear you."

"Find anything?" He didn't need to hear her answer. He could read the denial in the way she refused to meet his gaze and compressed her lips into a tight line.

The cellular phone in his pocket bleated suddenly, knifing through the thick tension in the room. He thought about ignoring it, just letting it go on bleating.

Considering he was apparently about to be arrested,

though, he decided he'd probably better answer it and then find himself a damn good lawyer.

"Yeah?" he said tersely.

It was Sydney. She sounded on the verge of hysteria as she told him a whole busload of law enforcement agents had descended on GSI like flies on roadkill. He listened to her babbling, perversely grateful he'd at least had some advance warning of what was happening.

"I'll be there as soon as I can. If I can catch the ferry, I should be there within the hour. And Syd, give them access to anything they want. I have nothing to hide."

He ended the call and slipped the phone back into his pocket, then turned to Grace. Her complexion had paled another notch. "They have the warrant?"

"Yeah. They're serving it right now."

"Jack, I'm so sorry."

He didn't want to hear this from her. He didn't want to hear anything. She had lied to him. She had wrapped her arms around him, had given herself to him, all the while knowing his world was about to be destroyed.

It took a Herculean effort but he managed to contain his fury just long enough to speak to her one last time. "I don't want you here when I get back," he said in a low voice, and didn't dare look at her again.

"Take one of the cars if you have to. I don't want you here when I get back."

She murmured a soft sound of assent, as if she had expected nothing less.

And then he turned and walked away without looking at her again.

CHAPTER SEVENTEEN

AT LEAST IT WOULDN'T TAKE HER LONG TO PACK.

Grace stood in the doorway to Jack's guest room, her eyes itchy with unshed tears and her heart aching. What a mess she'd made of things. She should never have gone to Hawaii with him. She should have stayed here and concentrated on the investigation.

But if she hadn't gone, she would have been just as willing as Beau to believe the worst of Jack, to see only what was on the surface. Only there, in the peace and beauty of his vacation home, had she come to know him and to recognize the strong vein of decency running through him.

If she had only concentrated on the investigation instead of herself, maybe she might have been able to convince Beau that Jack couldn't possibly be involved in this.

It was too late for that, though. The damage had been done and now he wanted nothing more to do with her. She couldn't blame him. She would have reacted the same way if their roles had been reversed.

She gazed across the room at the wide windows overlooking Puget Sound, gray and white-capped. Many of the flowers in the seaside garden had died while they were away, leaving bare, dried-up stalks. Still, the view of the city across the water was breathtaking.

She would miss this place. These people.

Lily, Emma, Tiny. All of them.

But especially Jack, who had dragged her from her monochromatic world into one of color and light and laughter.

She rubbed at her chest, as if she could take away the pain there, then walked inside the room to begin the process of excising herself completely from his life.

She hadn't brought much with her, and most of it was already packed. A few moments later, she had gathered the rest of her things and shoved them inside the suitcase.

The sound of the lid snapping shut echoed through the room. At the finality of it, she closed her eyes, helpless against the misery weighing down her shoulders, clogging her throat.

She didn't want to go back.

To that terrible apartment, to the bleak solitude of her life, to that dark, awful place she'd existed in for the past year.

Jack had showed her how to laugh and love and live again and she didn't know how she would survive without him.

"Hi, Grace. Whatcha doin'?"

Startled from her sorrow, she turned and found Emma in the doorway, holding that mangy stuffed poodle of hers.

Emma. Dear God, Emma.

The fist around her heart squeezed tighter. "Just looking out the window and thinking, sweetheart. What are *you* doing?"

"Playin' house."

"Where's Lily?"

"She said she needed a nap for a while. I think play group

tired her out. I'm supposed to take one, too, every time we come back, but I'm not a bit tired today, so Lily said I just had to be quiet in my room for a while. I'm playin' house," she repeated. "Betty is my little sister. You want to play, too?"

What would happen to Emma if Jack was arrested? Lily would take care of her, she knew, but she would still suffer trauma if she was forced to be without her father, even for a night or two.

It surely wouldn't help matters that Grace would be leaving her, too, just one more abandonment. She didn't have a choice, though. She had to go—Jack had made that perfectly clear.

She could at least stay with her for a few minutes, until Lily woke from her nap. "I guess I could play for a little while," she answered. "Not very long, though, okay?"

"Okay." Emma smiled happily and slipped her little hand into hers.

Grace paused for a moment, then let Jack's daughter tug her down the hall into her own bedroom, a little girl's wonderland of pink-and-white ruffles, filled with books and dolls and stuffed animals.

She had purposely avoided this room for most of her stay here, just as she had tried to steel her heart against Emma's dimpled smile.

"You be the mommy, okay? And Betty and me will be your little girls."

She could do this. She had discovered new reserves of strength these past few weeks. Surely they would be enough to carry her through a simple child's game.

All Emma seemed to require was for Grace to play at her miniature toy kitchen, pretending to make cookies while Emma read stories to her "little sister."

They played the game for ten minutes or so, then Emma

seemed to grow increasingly pensive and solemn. Finally she sat on her flouncy pink canopy bed and hugged her dog tightly, her green eyes shimmering as if on the verge of tears.

"What's the matter?" Grace asked. Maybe she was baking make-believe oatmeal cookies when Emma preferred chocolate chip.

"I don't want to play pretend anymore. I want you to be my mommy for real so you can make me real cookies."

At the words, raw emotion punched her in the chest and Grace hissed in a breath and felt her knees go weak. She could only stand there, speechless, for several moments. Finally, she forced herself to cross the room and sit next to the little girl on the bed.

She took it as a measure of how very far she had come these past few weeks that she was able to pull Emma into her arms without splintering apart.

"Honey," she murmured after she dared to trust her voice again. "Lily makes you cookies and cakes and brownies, too. Don't you like those?"

"It's not the same." Emma sniffled. "I want a mommy like my friend Brittany has. Why can't *you* be my mommy?"

"Oh, sweetheart." She rested her chin on Emma's head. "It doesn't work that way. Someday your daddy will find someone he loves. Someone you both love very much and who will love you both back, and then she and your daddy can get married so she can be your mommy."

"Don't you love us?"

The question echoed in her head. *Don't you love us? Don't you love us? Don't you love us?*

The answer came to her just as loudly—a complete, resounding *yes*.

Grace looked at Jack's daughter, with her curly blond hair and missing teeth, and felt her stomach pitch and roll as if she had just jumped from one of Jack's airplanes without a parachute.

How stupid she had been. How utterly, completely foolish. She thought she had done such a good job of protecting her heart, had been so very careful to keep them out. But Jack Dugan and his sweet little daughter had slipped inside anyway.

She loved them. *Both* of them.

All this time, she had actually believed she could lose herself in Jack's arms and remain completely untouched by it. But she must have fallen in love with him that night on the beach, when he had held her so sweetly while she grieved.

In the time since then, her love had only grown stronger, larger, until now it felt more immense than Mount Rainier.

And Emma.

When had Emma come to mean so very much to her? She thought she knew the answer. She had tried to deny it, but there had been a bond between the two of them since the accident that had brought them together, that had led her here.

She cleared her throat to answer the little girl's question, but before she could form the words, the door to Emma's bedroom swung open.

She expected Lily, and geared up for more of her quiet disapproval. When Piper McCall walked in, looking completely out of place in the cotton-candy bedroom, she was so surprised it took her several seconds to register the gun tucked snuggly in his waistband.

He looked about as thrilled to see her there as she was to see him. His jaw sagged and he rocked back on his heels, then raked a hand through his already-disheveled hair.

Adrenaline pumped through her as she took in his pallor and the tremors in his hands. She'd been on the job long enough to instantly recognize the signs of somebody running scared.

It didn't take her long to figure out what he was running from—she suddenly realized she was face-to-face with at least one of the GSI smugglers. He must have felt the net tightening around him and was probably trying to claw a way out.

Every cop knew that a cornered rat was the most dangerous creature alive. Piper still hadn't touched the gun and didn't even seem aware he had it, but she knew that particular state of serendipity wouldn't last long.

During her rookie year on the force, she'd been jumped by a crackhead in an alley. By all rights, she should have ended up with a knife to the gut but she'd somehow managed to keep a cool head and ended up talking the junkie down.

If she could do the same thing here—if she could keep her wits about her—maybe, just maybe, she could protect Emma.

"Hi, Uncle Piper," Emma chirped, oblivious to the sudden thick tension in the room. "Grace and me are playin' house. Wanna play? You could be the grandpa."

His gaze flickered to the little girl and there was clear affection there even in the midst of his obvious agitation. "Hi, sugar. I can't play right now. Maybe later."

Well, that was something, Grace thought. She didn't think he would hurt the little girl, not when he obviously cared about her. On the other hand, who knew what he might be capable of if he was desperate?

She forced her voice to be low, nonthreatening. "This is certainly a surprise, Piper. What can we do for you?"

He didn't answer for several seconds and seemed to be trying to organize his thoughts. He probably didn't even have a concrete plan, she realized, and the knowledge terrified her.

Desperate and disorganized weren't a good combination.

"I just came to…to get Emma," he finally said. "Jack asked me to take her to the hangar for him. He, uh, he wants to take her out to a fast-food joint for dinner."

She might have believed him if she didn't know that dozens of law enforcement officers had already descended on GSI. The last thing Jack probably wanted to deal with right now was his daughter.

Her mind roamed the angles. What would Piper hope to gain by taking Emma?

He probably had no idea the investigation was focusing on Jack as the mastermind behind the smuggling ring. Or if he did, he likely realized it was only a matter of time before the investigative spotlight would turn in his direction.

The logical thing for someone running scared from the law to do would be to leave the country, but wouldn't a five-year-old girl just be more likely to slow him down?

That must be it.

Her stomach churned as the implications sank in. Piper was a pilot. He would be looking for a plane to fly out of the country, probably to some country without an extradition treaty with the U.S., and he would have to realize he couldn't just hop into one of the GSI jets and take off. Not with cops from every possible jurisdiction swarming everywhere.

But how would the police stop him if he walked into the hangar with a hostage—particularly a five-year-old girl?

She blew out a breath. She had to stop him somehow. She wasn't about to let him use Emma as a bargaining chip. But what would be the best way to prevent it?

Should she tip him off that she knew exactly what was going on or would Emma be better off if she kept up this friendly pretense for now?

"McDonald's!" Emma chirped excitedly. "I'm gonna have a hamburger and a big order of french fries."

"Okay," Piper's mouth stretched into a sickly rictus of a smile. "Let's go, then."

No way in hell was she going to let him just walk out of

the house with Jack's daughter. She considered her options. The man was desperate and he had a gun and she had only her wits. Above everything else, she had to protect Emma and the best way to do that would be to go with them and wait for an opportunity to escape.

She gave Piper what she hoped was a friendly smile. "Let me just grab our jackets and I'll come with you."

That panicky look returned to his eyes. "No. Not you. Just Emma. Jack specifically said just Emma."

"They can't go without me. I love hamburgers."

She could almost see the wheels in his head spinning and she knew immediately when he reached the inevitable conclusion that two hostages just might be better than one.

"Fine," he muttered. "Get your jackets. But hurry up. We, uh, we don't want to keep Jack waiting, do we?"

The wait to board the ferry and then the trip across the Sound was a nightmare. Through the entire crossing, she tried to engage Piper in idle conversation. About the weather, about the basketball team, about anything she could think of to keep him calm.

She finally gave up after all her attempts met with that same blank, panicky stare, as if he'd forgotten she was even there.

Emma, in the back seat, seemed to sense something wrong with the situation. She, too, lapsed into an uncharacteristic silence and didn't even beg Grace to go with her to watch for mermaids.

Once off the ferry, Piper turned the car toward GSI and her adrenaline began to pump in a slow, steady rhythm. A quick glance in the back seat showed her that Emma had drifted off for that nap she had been fighting all afternoon.

Now was her chance. If she didn't move now, they would soon be at GSI and all hell would break loose.

"How far do you think you're going to be able to get?" she asked him quietly.

He didn't look at her, just concentrated on the road. "To GSI. So Emma can go to dinner with her dad. I told you that."

"You can drop the pretense, Piper. I know what's going on."

"What...what do you mean?"

"I'm a cop."

She said the words without thinking, then realized it was true. For a year now she had believed that part of her life was over forever, that she would never again carry a badge.

With three simple words—*I'm a cop*—she realized that even without the badge, she was still at heart the same little girl who used to watch her father don his dress uniform with awe, who had spent all her life dreaming of the time when she could follow in his footsteps.

Through their many years of working together, she and Riley had perfected the old Good-Cop/Bad-Cop routine. Although her real specialty was the latter, she sensed she'd have better luck with Piper if she tried to show him she was on his side.

Maybe she could manage to help Emma escape if she appealed to his vanity, could convince him he didn't need both of them and that he should let the girl go.

"I used to be a cop," she corrected herself. "I still have contacts on the force, though. I know about the weapons smuggling. I know GSI has been under investigation for months."

She forced a small, admiring laugh. "But you've been too slippery for them, haven't you? You've fooled everyone."

He glanced over at her and gave a modest little shrug, but she could see him preen a little. "It hasn't been easy."

"You've been outfoxing a half-dozen different agencies. I imagine you're trying to leave the country. Smart move."

"You think so?" He seemed desperately eager for validation.

"Yeah. It's exactly what I would do in your shoes." She paused. "There's something that puzzles me, though. Emma's kidnapping last month. How does that fit into the whole picture? I can't figure it out, and I know the police can't either."

A muscle in his jaw twitched beneath his pale complexion and he clamped his lips together. She thought she'd blown it for a minute, then he puffed out a breath.

"Wasn't my idea," he muttered. "I never wanted to use her like that but we needed cash in a hurry. Had a Chinese *tang* on our backs wanting to see some green upfront before they'd deal. You don't mess around with the *tangs*. I thought taking Emma was way too risky, but the others went through with it anyway. Said they knew Jack would pay in a heartbeat to get back his little girl."

Others? How many others? Two? Four? A dozen?

She didn't get a chance to ask before he continued. "Didn't do us any good. That damn Vasquez screwed up the whole thing. Stole a car, then the idiot crashed the stupid thing and took off."

"Took off where?"

He checked the rearview mirror as if he thought he might find this Vasquez person lurking there. "Beats the hell out of me. Anywhere *certain people* couldn't find him, I guess. Can't blame him for getting out while he could, but he left us scrambling to find the cash somewhere else or risk blowing the whole deal with the Chinese."

"So this is all about money?"

He gave her a hard look. "Isn't everything?"

"But you're a partner in GSI. The company is doing well, right? You can't be hurting for cash."

"Listen, I got three ex-wives, each one of them greedier than the one before. Every penny I make at GSI goes to pay their damn bloodsucking lawyers. I'm sixty years old next month and don't have a single thing to show for it. This was supposed to be my big chance."

He looked suddenly older—much, much older—and she was afraid for a minute he would cry. An instant's sympathy fluttered through her but she quickly suppressed it. He had let his greed cloud his judgment and his morals and he would probably spend what was left of his life paying for it.

They were beginning to pass landmarks she recognized from her trip to GSI with Jack and she knew they were close to the company's hangars. Her anxiety level escalated.

She had to get Emma out of this, and fast.

"We're almost there, Piper. Think about what you're doing now." She forced her voice to stay calm and unruffled despite the nerves twitching through her. "I don't really think you need Emma, do you? She's only going to slow you down, make things more messy than they have to be. Why don't we find some place we can drop her off, some place she'll be safe. You can use me for your hostage."

For a moment, she thought she had won. Doubt began to creep into his eyes and he seemed to be considering her words. At the last minute, though, that panic took over and his hands clenched on the steering wheel. "No. Nobody's going to stop me from taking that jet when they see I have her. They can't."

He sent her a quick look. "But don't worry. I'll try to make sure neither one of you gets hurt unless it's absolutely necessary."

Now why didn't that shaky declaration reassure her?

Jack stood in the doorway of his office surveying the carnage left by the team of investigators who had just finished methodically searching the room. The place was in a shambles, just like the rest of his life.

He couldn't manage to summon much more than mild indignation at them, though. All of his seething, writhing emotions were directed toward Grace, toward this vast, endless betrayal.

How could he have been so wrong about her? How stupid could he be? Didn't he ever learn his lesson? He had let her big sad eyes and her soft, lying mouth completely sucker him, completely blind him to her motives.

No wonder she had seemed so cool, so remote. She had been busy planning her revenge.

He heard movement behind him suddenly and found her former partner approaching.

Most of the investigators had left a few moments ago, after they found what they were apparently looking for—five wooden boxes hidden beneath piles of tools in an unused corner of the maintenance hangar. The boxes were filled with row after row of fully automatic assault weapons.

Jack was sick thinking that this company he had worked to build, given his heart and soul to, had been part of this.

But he was even more sick thinking about Grace.

"You all about done?" Jack asked him.

Riley nodded. "Yeah. Most of the team is on its way to your place."

He closed his eyes. What would Lily and Emma think when a horde of cops descended? He should have called earlier to warn them but he'd been too consumed by what was happening here to think of it.

He reached now for the phone under a pile of overturned files, but Riley held out a hand to stop him.

"You'll have to come with me now, Dugan. Looks like we're going to have plenty to talk about."

He tried to summon anger for the man but couldn't. None of this was his fault. He was doing a job, that's all. Just a job. Grace was the one who had turned the whole thing into a mission of vengeance, who had wormed her way into his home, into his heart, through her lies and her subterfuge.

Just because he bore no anger toward Riley didn't mean he had to like the man, though. Something about the big dark-haired cop set his teeth on edge. Maybe it was that too-handsome face or his rumpled clothes or that cynicism in his eyes.

Who was he kidding?

What really ticked him off was knowing that Beau Riley had held a place in Grace's life he could never hope to share. Even knowing her betrayal, he couldn't help resenting Riley for it.

"Am I under arrest?" he asked tersely.

The detective scowled. "Not yet, but it's only a matter of time."

"Then we both know I don't have to go anywhere with you, don't we? At least not until I talk to my lawyer."

"Look, Dugan," Riley growled, "we can do this hard or we can do this easy. Up to you."

He scowled back. "I'm not refusing to answer any of your questions. I have nothing to hide from you. But I'd rather do it here and with my lawyer present."

Riley opened his mouth to respond, but a sudden buzz of activity out in the hangar interrupted whatever he was going to say. He cocked his head, a puzzled frown on his pretty-boy face. They could hear muffled shouting out in the hangar, but Jack couldn't make out the words.

Both men headed at the same time for the windows that overlooked the work bay. The detective reached them first and separated the blind. He growled a short, pithy obscenity, whirled around and headed for the door at a full run.

Jack, just a few beats behind, felt grim foreboding flash in his gut. The sight that met him through the windows was worse—much, much worse—than anything he could have imagined.

Piper McCall stood near the steps of the jet, his face pale, his eyes wild and frenzied. He carried Emma hefted in one arm and the other hand held a sleek chrome handgun jammed into Grace's ear.

CHAPTER EIGHTEEN

STAY CALM, GRACE ORDERED HERSELF. HE'S not really going to hurt us. He's just looking for a way out.

She forced herself to detach, to disengage, to clinically record the scene like she used to do on the job.

The sharp, kerosene smell of jet fuel and other mechanical things hung heavy in the huge warehouse-like hangar. The fluorescent lights overhead burned too brightly, sending a glare off the same small, sleek jet they had taken to Hawaii, which was the only plane in the building.

The only sounds were Piper's harsh breathing, her own pulse ringing loudly in her ears and the staticky whisper of the uniform cop who had tried to bar their way speaking into his radio.

So much for the cops crawling everywhere that Piper had expected. The uniform was the only one who seemed to be around, and she prayed he wasn't some trigger-happy rookie without the expertise needed to handle a hostage situation.

She couldn't count on it, though. She couldn't count on

anyone but herself to save Emma, which didn't fill her with a lot of faith right now. Nothing she had come up with so far had managed to convince Piper to let them go, and her mind raced frantically as she tried to come up with another plan.

"Come on. Let's go." Piper nudged her toward the half-dozen or so steps up into the jet. Hoping to stall, to delay what appeared to be the inevitable, she tried to move slowly.

She had only ascended one step when she heard the clatter of footsteps in the doorway to the section of the building that housed the GSI corporate offices.

Piper whirled. Since the gun was still jammed in her ear and she didn't want to make any sudden moves that might startle him, she forced herself to hold perfectly still and shifted only her gaze toward the sound.

Relief poured through her when she saw Jack in the doorway about twenty feet away, looking strong and dangerous and comforting all at once. She was vaguely aware that Beau was there, too, with his big service revolver in his hand, but she could only focus on Jack.

She loved him. It poured over her, through her, and she thought it must radiate off of her like heat waves off a July sidewalk. She loved this man, with his sweet smile and his green eyes and his joy for life.

Not that it mattered. Even if she and Emma made it through this—no, not if, *when,* she scolded herself—she knew he would not welcome her feelings.

He had made it abundantly clear he had nothing but contempt for her now. Because she had been consumed by a past she couldn't change, she had destroyed her chance for a future filled with joy and light.

She wrenched her mind back to the present. The uniform was gone, she noted, probably on Beau's orders to keep Piper from doing anything rash.

"Don't come any closer," the pilot called to the two men. His echo sounded distorted as it bounced off the walls in the huge hangar. "All I want to do is get on the plane and take a little trip. As long as nobody messes with me, I'll let both of the girls go wherever I land."

"This is crazy," Beau barked out. "You're not going anywhere."

Emma—who had been half-asleep since Piper pulled her out of the back seat—started to cry as the shouts whirled around her.

"I want my daddy," she wailed and Grace saw Jack's face pale beneath his rugged tan. He took a step forward but Riley held an arm out to restrain him.

Piper hugged the little girl more tightly. "Shh, baby. It's okay," he murmured, then shoved the gun harder into Grace's ear. She could feel the barrel shaking with his tremors.

"I don't want to have to hurt either one of them, but I will. Don't think I won't!"

Jack shook off Riley's arm and stepped forward. "Piper, think about this, about what you're doing. Whatever you've done in the past, this is only going to make it worse."

Her gaze flickered back to Piper. The lines on his face had deepened and he looked completely miserable—guilty and ashamed. "You don't know, Jack. You don't know what I've done."

"I think I have a pretty good idea."

"I'm sorry," he called out above Emma's wails. "I'm so sorry. I never meant for things to go this far."

Grace held her breath. Piper again sounded on the brink of tears. Not a good sign. He was losing his flimsy hold on control, becoming more desperate and probably more reckless.

Her gaze flickered to Beau and she saw he had the same realization.

"I know you're sorry," Jack answered, his voice low and calm. He made a perfect hostage negotiator, she thought, with just the right touch of understanding in his expression. "I know you are. Look, drop the gun and let them go and I'll do what I can to find you the best lawyer around. We can try to work this all out, but not unless you let them go."

Piper didn't even seem to register his words. "I didn't mean for things to go this far," he repeated. She sensed he was trying to justify his actions not only to Jack but to himself. "I just needed a little extra cash. You know how I am with money, don't you Jack?"

"Sure. Sure I do."

"It just trickles through my fingers like sand. I can't help it. They made it sound so easy. Just slip a few extra crates in the load, they said, and nobody will suspect a thing."

"Who?" Beau asked urgently. "Who said that?"

The gun slipped a notch in Piper's sweaty hands and her nerves clutched in panic. "I can't tell you. They'll... She'll kill me."

"McCall, this could be your way out," Beau called. "Slow down and just think about this for a minute. If you were just a low man in the whole thing, just a soldier, and have dirt on somebody bigger than you, we might be able to cut a deal."

Piper tucked his face into his shoulder for a moment to rub the sweat off his upper lip on the fabric of his shirt. He took another shaky breath and the gun slipped another centimeter, until she felt it, cool and deadly, against her earlobe.

"What...what kind of deal?"

"That depends on how much you can give us," Beau answered.

"I'm almost sixty years old. I don't want to go to prison."

"We might be able to work something out. If you release the girls and don't go any further with this, I'll do what I can for you. I can't do anything unless you work with me here, though, and let them go."

She held her breath while Piper blinked several times. His agonized gaze flew first to Jack and then to Emma, whose wails had grown louder.

"Piper," Jack called softly, "He's giving you a chance to do what you can to make things right. Don't blow it."

Just like that, all the energy seemed to leave Piper and his shoulders slumped. With hands that trembled, he pulled the weapon away from her ear and handed her Emma.

Sweet relief flooded through her as she hugged the little girl's warm body to her. Her gaze met Jack's and the raw emotion there had her blinking away tears.

She had a sudden, fierce wish that some small portion of that emotion could be aimed toward her, but she knew it wasn't.

It was all for Emma.

"Drop the weapon and put your hands in the air," Beau commanded.

His face suddenly gray and haggard, Piper obeyed and the handgun hit the concrete floor with a clatter.

Beau met her gaze and he asked her without words how she was holding up. She tilted her mouth into a reassuring half-smile in answer. She was fine. A little shaky, maybe, but fine. More important, she had a little girl who needed her father.

Emma whimpered against her and Grace hugged her tightly.

"Everything's okay, sweetheart. See, there's your daddy." With a silent prayer that her wobbly knees would sustain her, she started to carry Emma toward Jack.

"I'm too old for this," Piper muttered behind her. "I should have known I'm too old to risk everything like this. I'm sorry, Jack. I was desperate and didn't know what else to do."

"You're doing the right thing now," Jack answered, although his eyes were only on Grace and Emma. "Cooperate and things will go much easier on you."

"I'll tell you everything. Names, dates, shipments, whatever you want to know. Serves that bitch right—"

The rest of his sentence was cut off as the world exploded into chaos. A sharp, thunderous gunshot blasted through the huge hangar and Piper screamed, a high-pitched, terrible sound. She heard him go down behind her, heard the sickening crack as his head hit concrete.

Grace didn't even think about it, she immediately dropped to the ground, her body shielding Emma's, just in time to hear another shot echo through the hangar. Over the little girl's head, she tried to see what was going on.

To her horror, Beau was on the ground about ten feet from the jet, blood soaking the front of his shirt. The second shot must have hit him. She thought she could see the slight rise and fall of his chest but other than that, he didn't move at all.

It was so much like before, like that terrible day at Marisa's school. For an instant, her vision dimmed and she felt the air leave her lungs, the blood rush from her face.

Beau. Dear God, not Beau. He was annoying and abrasive but he was all she had left and she loved him.

Agonized fury exploded within her and she jerked her head around, trying to identify the shooter's location. She didn't know why she was shocked when Sydney Benedict stepped out from behind the jet.

Jack's assistant looked perfectly composed, her typical cool, sophisticated self in a designer suit and high heels. The only jarring notes were the wild rage in her blue eyes and the sleek gun she held, aimed directly at Grace and Emma.

Jack, still standing near the doorway to the offices, looked as stunned as Grace felt but he didn't back away from the woman. "Syd, what the hell is going on?" he asked.

"Figure it out." Her voice dripped venom. "I had a great thing going until that stupid idiot over there on the floor had to go and ruin it all. If he had just stayed calm like I told him and kept his big mouth shut, nothing would have happened. All the signs would have pointed right at you, just like I planned it. You would have gone down and he and I would have been able to take over GSI and do what we wanted with it."

"I can't believe you would do this."

"I'm sure you can't. To you, I'm just your efficient little secretary, making your phone calls and typing your stupid letters. You have no idea how much I've done for this company. If it weren't for me, there wouldn't be a GSI. You're nothing without me."

"What is it you want?" he asked.

"Same thing Einstein over there had in mind. I want a free ride out of the country. I think I'd enjoy St. Croix, don't you? Jack, darling, care to give me a lift?"

He growled an oath. "Forget it."

The arm holding the gun swung back toward Grace and Emma. "Which one would you like me to take out first to show you I'm serious? The kid or your lovely new girlfriend?"

From her vantage point on the floor with a sobbing child underneath her, she could see panic flare in his green eyes. He quickly contained it and stepped forward. "Neither. I'll take you wherever you want to go. Just leave them alone."

"Ah, Jack. So noble. On second thought, why don't we just take them both along with us. I'm sure they'd love to see the Caribbean and they'll be my little insurance policy to prevent you from pulling anything stupid on the trip over."

Their lives would be worthless the moment they stepped on

the plane, Grace realized. If the woman was willing to shoot a Seattle cop in cold blood, she would have no qualms about finishing the job the moment she reached her destination.

She had to get them out of this. But how? There were a thousand things she would try if this were any other stand-off, if she were just a cop taking on a street criminal. But this wasn't any other standoff. The stakes were higher than anything she could have imagined.

If she failed, if she wasn't able to disarm Sydney Benedict, Jack and Emma would pay the price.

She had to protect them, above all else.

She bent her head low to whisper to Emma. "When I say so, jump up and run as fast as you can to your daddy, okay, sweetheart? You have to do just what I say."

She would just have to count on Jack to take advantage of the distraction she was about to provide and take his daughter to a safe place where Sydney Benedict couldn't reach them.

Emma nodded her head, her eyes frightened. Grace waited until Syd was almost upon them, then, with one last hug for courage, she murmured "Now," in the little girl's ear.

In one motion, she rolled off Emma and sprang to her feet, aiming an elbow into Sydney's face as she went.

Not expecting the move or the blow, the woman didn't have time to react other than to stumble back. Before she could fire, Grace was on her, grappling for control of the weapon and trying desperately not to think about the consequences if she failed.

The last thing Jack expected was for Emma to leap up and come charging at him. One minute he was watching in stunned disbelief, his blood pumping sluggishly through his veins as he realized Grace was making a crazy, suicidal move for the gun, the next, he had a tiny torpedo in his arms.

Emma threw her arms around him and hugged tightly and

he returned the embrace, consumed with relief. She was okay. He couldn't believe it, but she was really okay.

Somehow, Grace must have told her to run to safety.

He wanted to bury his face in her curly blond hair and hold her like this for the rest of his life, but the danger wasn't over yet, he realized. Sydney still held the handgun, although Grace's tight grip on her arm kept it extended above her head where she couldn't use it.

He pushed Emma behind him, into the first office. "Stay here, sweetheart. Whatever you do, stay here. I'll be right back for you, I promise."

Without waiting for her answer, he shut the door and stepped back into the hangar, to find Grace and Syd still locked in a deadly struggle for control of the weapon, the two of them edging ever closer to the jet.

Grace looked small and delicate next to Syd's height and he had no idea how she could even be holding her own.

Muscles straining with exertion, Grace focused all her energy on forcing the woman to let go of the gun. Jack's secretary was several inches taller than her and in better physical shape.

Before the car explosion, Grace could have taken her easily, especially with the upper body strength she built up working on the docks. She'd regained much of her tone since then but it wasn't quite enough to overpower the taller woman.

She could feel herself wavering, feel her energy reserves dwindle. Just before her muscles would have given out, before Syd would have won, she glanced over and saw Beau on the ground, terribly pale and still.

It was all the impetus she needed. With a last furious heave, she pushed Syd against the side of the Learjet and slammed her wrist against the metal skin of the airplane.

She heard the crunch of bone and Syd's screech of pain as

the gun flew through the air to land harmlessly several feet away. Syd hissed, like a feral cat, then sagged to the ground, holding her wrist.

A weight bigger than the jet next to her seemed to lift from Grace's chest and she bent at the waist, panting from the exertion.

This time, she had done it.

For Beau, for Marisa, for Emma.

And for Jack. For the man who had given her back her life. Who had helped her begin to heal.

She closed her eyes and murmured a prayer of gratitude to a God she thought had forsaken her. But her prayer came a moment too soon.

With her eyes closed, she didn't see Syd move until she felt her legs being swept out from under her. The breath oomphed out of her as her shoulder hit the concrete. Before she could catch it and climb up again, Syd scrambled for the gun.

No, no, *no!* Not now, not when she finally realized she wanted so very much to live.

"Syd, no! Drop it!" Jack yelled.

"Shut up, Jack!" Sydney snarled. "She's ruined everything!"

The world seemed to move in slow motion, then. Sydney lifted her arm to shoot, and Grace was mesmerized by the deadly black mouth of the gun. She didn't want that to be the last thing she saw before she died, she thought suddenly, so she shifted her gaze to the one person who meant more to her than anything else.

Jack's expression was frozen with shock. *I love you,* she thought. *Oh, Jack. I love you.*

It was all she had time to think before the hangar suddenly shook with the boom of a gunshot that seemed to go on and on and on.

Grace closed her eyes and waited for the pain to explode

in her. Nothing happened. Absolutely nothing. No impact, no blood, no searing pain.

After a few seconds, she blinked her eyes open.

Syd was sprawled on the ground with her designer skirt up above her knees, her outstretched arm still holding the gun, and an angry red bloodstain blossoming on the silk of her blouse.

What just happened here?

Grace turned her face just enough to see Piper McCall propped up against the landing gear of the jet. He gave her a ghost of a grin and dropped his own gun back to the cement. "Told you I'd try to make sure you didn't get hurt," he wheezed.

Suddenly the hangar buzzed with activity—police, paramedics, even the airport fire department, although she wasn't exactly sure why they had been called.

She looked for Jack but couldn't find him through the people. He had probably gone to gather Emma from where he had stowed her, she thought. Just as he ought to do.

She drew in a ragged breath and forced her muscles to move again, then hurried through the crowd of rescue workers to reach Beau's side. He was ashen, his mouth twisted in pain, but at least he was conscious.

She grabbed his hand tightly and he gave it a weak squeeze. "How are you?" she asked.

"I've had better days," he muttered. "I knew Dugan was going to be trouble."

She gave a watery laugh as relief cascaded over her. If he could rouse himself enough to complain, he would be okay. "I was so scared for you."

"How do you think I felt when I came to and found you wrestling with a gun-toting Amazon? What in the hell were you thinking, Gracie?"

About protecting the people she loved. About making sure that this time they would be safe. But she knew she couldn't explain it to him.

"I didn't know what else to do," she answered.

One of the paramedics tapped her arm. "Ma'am, I'm afraid you'll have to give us some room now. We need to get him on a gurney."

She nodded and gave Beau's hand another squeeze. "I'll see you at the hospital," she murmured.

As soon as she stepped away from the crowd gathered around him, her gaze immediately collided with Jack's. He stood in the doorway to the GSI offices, Emma snuggled tight in his arms, and he watched her over his daughter's curls.

She couldn't read the fierce expression there. All she knew was that the two of them were a family. A tight, loving unit where she could never hope to belong.

Standing there in the cavernous hangar amid the noise and bustle of a hundred people all talking at once, she had never felt so alone.

CHAPTER NINETEEN

JACK CHECKED THE SLIP OF PAPER IN HIS HAND and compared it to the numbers hanging on the neat little bungalow.

They matched, but he still had a difficult time envisioning the shaggy-haired Beau Riley living in a house with a yard perfectly mowed, without a blade out of place.

This was definitely it, though, the address he'd finally coerced out of Riley from his hospital bed, after he had begged and pleaded and finally humbled himself a hell of a lot more than he had wanted to.

The address where he could find Grace.

He drummed his fingers on the steering wheel and watched rain trickle down the windshield while he tried to figure out what the hell he was doing here.

He had tried to stay away from her. She had made it painfully obvious she didn't want anything more to do with him. Every time he came within a few feet of her that last time he had seen her—between answering questions for the police and handing Emma over to Lily's capable arms and seeing Piper and Riley off in their respective ambulances, she turned away and suddenly became busy with something else.

Syd no longer had need of an ambulance. She was beyond anyone's help. He couldn't be sorry for it. She had threatened everything he cared about. The only thing he regretted was how blind he had been to her greed and ambition, and that she had ensnared Piper in her scheme.

By the time he was done talking to the police, Grace had vanished. The woman was getting pretty damn good at that little disappearing act of hers.

He had waited for her to collect her belongings from his house, but he finally realized this morning—four days after he'd ordered her to leave—that she wouldn't be coming back.

If he wanted to talk to her, he was just going to have to rout her out.

He puffed out a breath and gazed at the little bungalow, with its white painted shutters and a climbing rosebush around the door that glistened in the rain.

It didn't escape his attention that—except for the vast improvement in setting—this scene was remarkably reminiscent of the day he had gone looking for her at that miserable apartment.

He supposed he ought to be relieved she hadn't gone back there, but he couldn't quite find it in him to be grateful she was staying at Riley's house. Even if the detective *was* still in the hospital recovering from the gunshot wound that narrowly missed his heart, Jack didn't like the idea of Grace in his house, sleeping in his bed.

It shouldn't matter to him, he knew it shouldn't. But for some reason it did. No, not just *some reason,* he corrected himself. The truth was, he was jealous. Plain and simple. It was stupid and selfish but he was fiercely jealous of Detective Riley for the easy affection he shared with Grace.

He had seen the devastated shock in her eyes when she realized Riley had been shot, a look that conveyed a deep, lasting bond between her and her former partner. Grace had rushed to the cop's side as soon as she realized the danger was past and hadn't left it until he had been loaded into that ambulance.

And not once, after that long, glittering moment when their eyes had met had she looked at him again.

She wouldn't welcome him here. He had no doubt about that. He couldn't blame her. When he found out about the investigation, he had lashed out at her like an injured dog and he had no doubt his angry words had hurt her. But he had to talk to her. Too many things had been left unsaid between them.

Screwing up his nerve, he finally reached across the passenger seat for the canvas bag there and climbed out of the car. Rain sifted down in fine sheets, coating him immediately. He should have brought an umbrella, he thought, but he hadn't been thinking of anything but seeing her again.

He tucked the bag under his coat and walked to the front door, then stood on the porch and rang the doorbell.

Unlike that first time at her apartment, she answered the door after only a moment or two. As soon as she saw him, surprise and wariness and something else he couldn't quite recognize flickered in her gaze.

Had it only been four days since he had seen her? It seemed like longer. Much, much longer. He had forgotten the stunning impact of those huge dark eyes, the delicate structure of her features, the way her skin stretched so perfectly over her bones.

They stood and stared at each other for several seconds.

She was the first to speak. "Jack. This is a surprise. How did you know I was staying here?"

"Riley gave you up."

Her mouth flattened in disgust. "That big rat. If you can't trust a cop to keep his big mouth shut, who can you trust?"

"Yeah, well, it wasn't easy to get it out of him, believe me." He shifted, uncomfortable remembering his encounter with the detective. Riley had flat-out refused to surrender any information to him at first, until Jack had swallowed his pride and told him exactly why he needed to see her.

Riley had finally given him the address, along with a snake-eyed glare and an ominous, warning about knowing exactly where Jack lived if he hurt her.

He jerked his mind from the memory. "Mind if I come in? It's a little soggy out here."

She looked as if she wanted to shut the door in his face but after a pause she held it open. Rain dripped from his coat onto the wood floor of the entry but she didn't offer to take it from him. Probably hoping he would catch the hint and leave soon, he thought.

He decided not to wait for permission she might not grant. He removed the coat and hung it on a gleaming brass rack by the door, earning a narrowed glance from her but nothing more.

"So why are you staying here instead of that dive of yours?" He shoved his hands in his pockets and tried to sound nonchalant, like her answer didn't matter to him.

She shrugged. "Not that it's any of your business, but my lease on the apartment was up and I… I didn't want to renew it. I didn't want to stay there anymore. Besides that, Beau is going to need somebody to look after him when he gets out of the hospital, at least for a little while."

"Does it have to be you?" he asked, then could have bitten his tongue off when she raised her eyebrows at him.

He raised his hands in a gesture of apology. "You're right. Sorry I asked. None of my business."

"What are you doing here, Jack?" she asked bluntly.

"I brought your things. Your suitcase is in the car. Oh, and Lily asked me to give you this."

He pulled the quilted square from the canvas bag where Lily had carefully stored it.

Grace felt her heart give a little flutter at the sight of the blue-and-white fabric in his fingers, those big, strong hands that could work such magic on her skin.

She had thought about the quilt many times in the last four days and had tried to figure out how she would possibly be able to retrieve it from his house without having to see any of the people who lived there. She finally decided she was going to have to see if Lily would mail it to her, but she hadn't yet summoned the courage to call her.

She still wanted to finish the thing, if only to prove to herself that she could, but the compulsion that had driven her to work on it so frenetically in Hawaii was gone.

Lily had been right. In some strange, mystical way she didn't fully understand, working on the quilt—creating something of beauty and worth to memorialize her daughter's life—had helped her work through her grief over Marisa's death.

But somewhere between their return from his Hawaii home and that terrible afternoon at GSI, she had come to a stunning realization.

Like the dolphins on the pattern—leaping in their eternal, joyous circle—her life had to go on.

She had spent the last year trapped in the icy world of her grief, but Jack and Emma had changed that. They had thawed all the frozen corners of her heart and now she had no choice.

She had to go on, even if it meant making a life for herself without the two people she had grown to love so dearly.

She pulled the quilted square from him and rubbed a thumb over the material, focusing on the raised pattern and the nubby ridge of the stitches instead of the sudden ache in her chest.

"The clothes and other things I didn't care about," she finally said. "But I... I'm glad you brought this. Thank you."

"You're welcome."

The silence stretched between them, taut and awkward. Again, she was the first to break it, willing him away before she gave in to the tears that had welled in her throat at just the sight of him, looking strong and vibrant and forever out of reach. "Was there something else you wanted?"

"Yeah. Yeah, there is." He shoved his hands in his pockets again. "I came to thank you for what you did the other day. For risking your life to save Em's—again. It was crazy and reckless and if I'd had the chance, I would have wrung your neck for it. But thank you."

She glanced away from him, suddenly fascinated with the diamond pattern on the area rug beneath her feet. She didn't want his gratitude. She hadn't wanted it before and she definitely didn't want it now.

Now she only wanted his love.

"Haven't we done this before?" she murmured.

"Yeah. I'm starting to lose track of all the times you've put your life on the line for my daughter's."

When she said nothing, he stepped forward and lifted her chin up so he could see her eyes. "Why, Grace? That's what I've spent the last four days trying my damnedest to figure out. Why did you do it?"

She hitched in a breath, praying he couldn't read the raw

emotion she knew must be shimmering in her eyes. "What do you mean?"

"I talked to Piper the other day. He told me that when he came to the house to get Emma, you insisted he take you along with him. He didn't want to, but you finally talked him into it."

"It didn't take much talking."

"But why would you even try to convince him at all? You knew what was going on, that Piper was involved in the smuggling and wanted to flee prosecution. You *had* to know. Yet you went with him willingly, knowing exactly what you were walking into."

She flushed. Why did he sound so angry with her? She jerked her chin away from him. "I'm trained to be a cop. To protect and serve. What else could I do?"

"I don't buy that. What kind of maniac cop chooses to turn herself into a hostage, then tries to draw the fire of a crazy woman with a gun?"

"This one, I guess."

"No, it was more than that. Don't try to deny it. Besides, you aren't a cop anymore."

"You're right. I was your employee, hired to protect your daughter."

"Come on, Grace. We both know the real reason you took the job and it had nothing whatsoever to do with protecting Emma. You took it because you wanted someone to pay for Marisa's death and you decided it would be me."

She opened her mouth to argue with him, then clamped it shut again and looked back at the floor. How could she argue with the truth? He was right. That was exactly why she took the job.

"Tell me," he pressed. "I'm trying to understand here. Why

would you flaunt death that way? Is it because you don't care what happens to you? Whether you live or die?"

She lifted wide, startled eyes to his and he watched emotions flash through their dark depths, one after another. First shock, then guilt, then shame, all in quick succession. Her gaze dropped and she twisted her fingers together tightly.

"I care," she said quietly. "I care very much."

"But that's the reason you risked your life the first time, wasn't it? Because you didn't give a damn what happened to you. That's the reason you don't like it when anyone calls you a hero for what you did for Emma."

Her fingers were clenched together so tightly they were beginning to turn white. "Yes. That's why. I was so overwhelmed with grief that night I wouldn't have cared if the car exploded, taking me along with it. I would have *welcomed* it then. I had nothing left to lose, nothing to keep me here."

"And what about the other day? Why did you risk your life, Grace?" He asked again, and he could hear his pulse pumping loudly in his ears, feel his breath catch in his lungs.

This was the true reason he had come looking for her, he realized. To hear her answer. He *needed* to hear it, with a fierce urgency that stunned him.

She was quiet for a long time and the only sound in the little house was the rain's soft drumming outside. He didn't think she would answer him, but she finally spoke in a low whisper, barely loud enough to be heard over the rain.

"That night on the highway I had nothing to lose." She paused, then lifted her gaze to his. "The other day, it was different. So different. I realized as I crouched over Emma with gunshots firing all around that this time I had *everything* to lose."

His heart did a long, slow roll in his chest. There were tears in her eyes, he realized with shock.

His strong, brave Grace was weeping those terrible silent tears.

"All I could think about was keeping her safe," she went on. "Keeping *you* safe. I realized I wouldn't survive if something happened to the two of you."

At her words, he surrendered to the aching need that had haunted him since she opened the door to him. He pulled her into his arms.

She came willingly with a breathy sigh. Her arms slipped around his waist, her cheek nestled into the thick cotton of his shirt. She was warm and soft and belonged exactly here.

And he was a thousand kinds of fool to have let her go.

"Ah, Grace," he murmured into her hair. "I love you so much I can't think straight."

She yanked her head away from his chest. Her mouth gaped open and she blinked at him. "What... What did you just say?"

"I said I love you," he repeated in a low, fervent voice. "With everything I have—with everything I am—I love you, Grace Solarez."

At his words, her lashes fluttered against her cheeks and her head swayed as if her neck couldn't support the weight of it for a moment.

When she opened her eyes, he hoped to see softness or tenderness or at least mild affection. Instead they crackled with righteous indignation. She stepped out of his arms just far enough to bring a fist up and pound hard on his chest.

"Hey!" He grabbed her fist. "What was that for?"

"For putting me through the misery of the last four days. For leaving me to think I would never see either one of you again. For making me so frightened I would have to live the rest of my life alone, without Emma's silly jokes or Lily's cooking or your sweet smile."

She paused and the indignation in her eyes softened. Everything he had hoped to see was there and more. So much more. "For making me so afraid I would have to live without ever being able to hold you again or kiss you or tell you what's in my heart."

Her mouth flattened into a tight line and she pounded his chest again for good measure. "What took you so long?"

Joy exploded within him like a Roman candle. It shot straight through his heart and burst through him with glittering, sparkling color.

He laughed and lifted her clenched fist to his mouth so he could press a gentle kiss to the skin of her knuckles. "I don't have your kind of courage, Grace. It took me a few days to work up to stripping my soul naked for you, especially when I didn't know how you feel." He frowned. "Although if we want to be technical here, I still don't know how you feel."

That trace of vulnerability in the eyes of the arrogant, beautiful Jack Dugan touched a deep, hidden place inside her. She smiled softly, then lifted her hands to caress his cheeks. With their gazes locked, she spoke solemnly, vehemently. "I love you, Jack. More than I ever dreamed possible."

"Do you love me enough for this?"

He reached into the pocket of his jeans and pulled out the small, square satiny box. He opened it, to reveal a gold ring with a circle of sparkling gems that perfectly matched his eyes. "I had this with me that day when I found you in my office. I knew you weren't ready for it then, but I hoped someday you would be."

Despite her words to him, for an instant, her heart clutched in panic as she looked at the ring. He was asking her for far more than just marriage. He was asking her to risk her heart, her soul, everything.

Could she do it? Knowing that on the other side of that love was the hell she had existed in for the last year? Giving her heart to Jack and Emma—tying her life to theirs—would make her vulnerable again to the kind of pain she was just barely climbing out of, and how could she survive it again?

As her silence dragged on, that edge of insecurity returned to his eyes. "You don't have to answer now. I swore to myself I wouldn't pressure you. I just wanted you to know where I stand. I want nothing more than to spend the rest of my life trying to make you smile, but I'll wait until you're ready. Forever, if I have to."

A sweet, pulsing warmth poured over her as she studied him, giving her all the courage she would ever need. Marrying him—becoming a mother to Emma, would mean risking great pain.

But the alternative—living without them—was much, much worse.

With tears coursing down her cheeks, she lifted her shoulders and faced him. "You said something before about the reason I don't like anyone praising me or thanking me for pulling Emma from that car," she said quietly. "The truth is, I didn't do anything."

He opened his mouth to argue but she held up a hand to stop him. "I didn't rescue Emma that night, Jack. She saved me. Both of you did. The two of you found me in that dark, terrible place where I lived, grabbed me by the hand and forced me out into a world of joy and light."

"Grace—"

"Yes, Jack. My answer is yes." A tremulous smile captured her mouth. "I love this world you've shown me and I don't ever want to go back."

Fierce emotion filled his green eyes, and then she was in his arms. As he bent his head to kiss her, she knew her heart had found peace at last.

★ ★ ★ ★ ★

Her Texas Rescue Doctor

CARO CARSON

This book is dedicated to my mother-in-law, Ilse, a woman who lives every day expecting happiness and good things. She deserves them.

CHAPTER ONE

"SOPHIA, YOU HAVE TO PUT DOWN YOUR PHONE."

"No."

Grace Jackson gritted her teeth and held out her hand. "Yes, Sophia. Let me have it."

Sophia tossed her blond hair, the perfect platinum blond that belonged to innocent young children, and jerked her phone out of Grace's reach.

Grace struggled for patience. They were in a parked van. How long did Sophia think she could play keep-away with the phone? Sophia had never been easy to deal with, but this phase was particularly trying. At least, Grace hoped it was a phase.

Please, let this be a phase. I can't survive this much longer.

"Look, Sophie. The firemen are waiting for us over there. They want to show you around."

"Don't care."

Grace felt a little desperate. She thought about grabbing the phone, but taking a hard line with Sophia always backfired. For the past year, she'd been able to manage Sophia by persuading her with rewards. *If you do this, you'll get that thing you want…* It was as simple as rewarding a toddler with a lollipop.

If only Sophia were a toddler.

Instead, Grace was trying to reason with a twenty-nine-year-old woman, a professional actress. After a decade of hard work, Sophia was now a genuine movie star. Grace had been her personal assistant through the hard times, the desperate times, the my-dream-will-never-come-true times. For the past two years, Grace had been with her for the even more stressful world of success, both critical and commercial. The world was Sophia's oyster. And now…

Grace glared at the top of Sophia's head, which was all she could see as Sophia sat on a bench opposite to her with her nose in her phone's screen.

And now, there was no way in the world that Grace was going to placidly stand by and watch Sophia destroy her own dreams.

Grace snatched the phone out of Sophia's hand.

"Hey!"

"I'll hold it for you. What's a personal assistant for?" She slid the phone into her tote bag. "The cameras are waiting. Photographers are everywhere out there. Smile."

Sophie bared her teeth at Grace despite her annoyance; years of habit were hard to break.

"No lipstick on your teeth. No spinach." Grace reached with two hands to fluff Sophia's shining waves and used her fingertips to arrange a few naturally wavy tendrils along Sophia's flawless cheekbones. "Perfect. I see a ton of teenage girls out there. Pose for some selfies with them, okay? A few minutes of smiles, and Sophia Jackson will start trending on Instagram and Twitter again."

But Sophia didn't want her lollipop anymore. She didn't want to be a respected actress with a loyal fan base, not since she'd fallen in with the bad boys of Hollywood. "Let's skip the squealing mass of girlies. What do I have to do before we can get the hell out of here?"

"Oh, Sophie." Grace's heart felt like a stone in her chest. It was a hard thing, very hard, to watch Sophia throw away everything for which she'd worked.

"Don't start with me. What am I required to do? Tell me the bare minimum. I'm so freaking tired."

Grace supposed clubbing all night could do that to a girl. Sophie coughed that annoying cough that had started shortly after dating Deezee Kalm, a DJ in Los Angeles. Grace always felt like she was choking on the secondhand smoke at his parties, when she was forced to go. Thankfully, Sophie hadn't been photographed with a cigarette in her hand yet. Accusations would fly that she was a bad role model. That would tarnish her good-girl image, the very image Grace was trying to save with this trip to Texas.

"This is a really good cause. Texas Rescue and Relief has done so much here in Austin after those terrible flash floods last summer. You're going to thank the firemen and the—the helicopter people, whatever they're called—and some doctors, and then you're going to cut the ribbon to reopen this health clinic."

"Good God, Grace. Could you have booked anything more stupid?"

The stone in Grace's chest wasn't hard enough to deflect that stab of a knife. *Don't confront her. Don't challenge her. Offer her a lollipop.*

"Your hero, Julia, did almost the exact same thing after California's forest fires. She trended on Twitter. Her visit was covered on all the celebrity gossip TV shows. Now her next movie is already getting award buzz, and it won't be released for months. Coincidence? No way."

Grace reached up to touch Sophia's hair again, a comforting gesture she'd been doing her whole life. After all, she wasn't just Sophia's personal assistant. She was her sister.

Grace would be the worst sister in the world if she stood by and watched her sister self-destruct.

"I've already got a Golden Globe," Sophia said.

"Julia's got two. And an Oscar." Grace nodded out the window toward the cluster of Texas Rescue personnel who were setting up the ribbon-cutting ceremony. "Go be Sophia Jackson, talented and gracious. You could jump in there and help set up right now. Everyone would talk about how down-to-earth you are, how you don't stand on ceremony."

But her superstar sister's cell phone chimed in the tote bag.

Sophia snapped her gum. "Or you could give me my phone so I'm not stuck in the middle of nowhere with nobody to talk to."

"Austin isn't nowhere."

And when did I become nobody?

Instead of defending herself, Grace defended their location. "Austin is a hot ticket in March, you know. It wasn't easy to get a hotel room because South by Southwest just started. The director of Texas Rescue had to call in some favors in town."

Sophia glared at her.

"You know South by Southwest. The fringe festival. Bands, indie movies, art—kind of edgy stuff. Why don't I get the hotel to extend our stay for the week? This is a really hip event. We could have fun."

"I know what the hell South by Southwest is. I just don't care."

Grace had always been the one who listened while Sophia brainstormed career goals. Grace tried to start a little session now. "Being seen here might add another dimension to your image. People might start thinking of you for projects that have more of an indie vibe, like a *Juno* or a *Fargo*."

"I am not sticking around here for a week of low-budget fringe films, and I'm not going out there to cut a stupid ribbon until I absolutely have to."

Grace knew better than to push the point. "Okay, we'll chill out here in their van until they're ready for you. Then you can go and shake hands like you're Kate Middleton. They'll love you, the studios will love you, and your agent will get you the best roles in the industry."

"Are little bluebirds going to start circling my head while I act like a princess? This is seriously stupid." Sophia gestured toward Grace's tote bag. "Check and see if that's Deezee on the phone. He wants me. Tonight."

"He wants you? You mean…like…a booty call? He actually calls you to tell you when he wants…" Grace couldn't finish the sentence.

"You are so last decade. *Booty* just means butt. By the way, Deezee says the bubble butt is last decade, so I'm not going to get the surgery now."

Grace felt ill. She didn't know Sophia had even considered having a plastic surgeon implant anything in her naturally perfect figure.

"He can tell if a girl's had implants during sex. He's so impressed that I haven't had any work done yet."

Grace wanted to stick her fingers in her ears and say *not listening*, just as she had when they were children and Sophia had explained the birds and bees to her. "I don't want to hear about his sexual turn-ons."

"Then stop being obsessed with my phone calls. Get your own sex life. When's the last time you got any?" She shoved Grace's tote bag with the toe of her spike-heeled sandal. "Back when people still used the term *booty call*, I guess."

Grace had to look away. Her sister, of all people, ought to know that she had no social life. Managing all the little daily details for Sophia was a never-ending job. Sophia's career dictated where they lived, who they saw, what they did—even what Grace wore. Her wardrobe consisted of dozens of outfits like the gray sweater and slacks she wore now. Years ago, she and her sister had figured out that wearing all black made Grace appear like a noticeable blot of darkness when she was caught in the background of a candid photo of Sophia, so Grace wore earth tones with a bit of heather, or sometimes gray with specks of beige and black. That was the best way to disappear into the background.

Not that Grace was complaining. She loved her sister. She only wished her sister would go back to being her normal self. When they were a sisterly duo, she hadn't minded living Sophia's life. This new phase was making her question everything.

She pretended the view outside the van was interesting, but the restored health clinic was only a normal-sized building in a normal suburb of a normal city. The ribbon-cutting ceremony was about to begin, so the men and women of Texas Rescue were taking their places.

She'd bet those people were married and had children and rewarding jobs. Grace and Sophia had once had that kind of normalcy, back when their parents were still alive. How could Sophia go from seeing their parents' loving marriage to jumping at the beck and call of a no-talent egomaniac like Deezee?

Of the two of them, Sophia had always been the bigger sucker for true love and weddings and happily-ever-after. She'd put all that on hold for her acting career, until this winter with Deezee. Maybe this phase meant Sophia was lonely. Maybe Grace could help her find a better man. A normal man.

Grace gestured out the window. "Check out these Texas Rescue guys. This looks like a casting call for an action movie—but they're real. I bet not one of those guys has chin implants or hair extensions. Real firemen and real doctors and paramedics and, um, police-looking guys. Rangers? What do you think that uniform is?"

"Like I care." Sophia sat up straighter, ready to talk business. "Listen, Deezee is opening a new club tonight. He needs me there to help him get more press."

Grace looked away from the handsome men of the real world. If Sophia wanted to talk business, they'd talk business. "Deezee could have his people contact me with a little more notice next time, and maybe we'll be able to schedule an appearance, if his career needs help."

Sophia's expressive blue eyes narrowed angrily, but a fresh round of her club cough kept her from saying whatever retort she'd been about to deliver.

Poor Sophia really did look tired. It was up to her personal assistant to help her look good for this photo op, so Grace dug in her tote bag and came up with her sister's very expensive, very red lipstick, the one Grace ordered for her and always kept on hand. "Here. And spit out your gum. It looks tacky when you speak."

Sophia's cough subsided. "Being with Deezee can do more for my career than this charity gig. Everyone will be in LA at the new club. No one is here. If you want me to stay visible in the industry, I need to be where everyone is. *Duh*." Sophia plucked the lipstick out of Grace's fingers.

Grace dropped her hand to her lap. Couldn't Sophia see that Deezee's club would attract the celebrities who were famous only for their ability to shock the public? Actresses would get out of their limos in a way that let the paparazzi document whether or not they wore underwear. Stars who were claiming sobriety would arrive drunk.

A man in a shirt and tie opened the door to the van. "Miss Jackson? Are you ready for your tour?"

Sophia ignored him as she gave Grace orders. "Book me a flight. Get me back to LA now. I'm going to cut this crap short."

Grace closed her eyes, but it didn't matter. She heard the man at the door suck in his breath.

Surprise. She's a little more crude in real life than she was in her award acceptance speech, isn't she?

Grace opened her eyes and looked at the man's face. Yep. They'd just alienated another fan.

For the past two years, Sophia had been so gracious in her interviews, so fun on her television appearances. She'd set a goal to be as well thought of as Audrey Hepburn someday, and she'd pursued her dream with unwavering perseverance until now. Audrey Hepburn wouldn't have told a Texas Rescue volunteer that she wanted to cut this crap short.

DJ Deezee Kalm would have, except he wouldn't have used the word *crap*.

Sophia replaced the cap on her lipstick and tossed it so that it landed on the bench seat next to Grace.

"Your gum," Grace reminded her gently, under her breath.

"Get me a limo to the airport. This van blows." Sophia tilted her head back, pursed her lips, and with a poof of air, spit her gum to land on the seat, as well.

She got out of the van. Grace watched out the window as Sophia shook back her hair in the Texas sunlight, looking like a million dollars in a classic coat dress that cost eight thousand. Grace had secured it at no cost. The publicity Sophia could bring a designer was worth more than the price of the dress. For now.

The adults applauded, the teenaged girls who crowded against the plastic barricades screamed and cheered, but Sophia didn't walk over to her waiting fans. Grace wished she hadn't suggested it. Maybe her sister would have done the obviously right thing if she hadn't felt like Grace was ordering her to do it.

Grace picked up the lipstick and returned it to the tote, then dug out a tissue and cleaned up the gum. *What's a personal assistant for, right?*

Not this. She'd been her sister's support, not her sister's servant. But her sister was no longer acting like her sister. Sophia was turning herself into something she was not, all in an attempt to make a man love her.

Deezee didn't love her—but Grace did. She'd dragged her from LA to Texas for her own good. Surely Sophia would come to her senses. Grace just had to find a way to keep her in Texas a little longer.

She sighed and looked out the window again, at the group of handsome men who were all shaking her sister's hand. What if, instead of a Hollywood bad boy, Sophia fell for one of these men? Maybe one of the doctors, someone who was caring by nature, someone whose profession meant he was successful and respected, independent of her sister's success. Wouldn't it be lovely if Sophia fell in love with a guy like that? It would cure all their ills.

A handsome man from Texas Rescue could be just what the doctor ordered.

"Hi, I'm Dr. Gregory."

Alex Gregory, MD, held his hand out to shake with the

young boy who'd come to his emergency room with a sports injury.

The child's father grabbed Alex's hand instead and squeezed. Hard. "What took you so long, Doc?"

"I'm sorry for your wait. Things are unpredictable around here." Alex extricated his hand from the bone-crushing grip. To restore some circulation, he made a fist and used one knuckle to push his glasses farther up the bridge of his nose. Then he spread his fingers out wide, and made a second attempt to engage his young patient.

"So, I'm Dr. Gregory, you're Justin, and I hear that you came in because you got hurt. Can you tell me where?"

"It's his leg, Doc. He's got a big game tomorrow. We need you to patch him up to get him through. Maybe a cortisone shot and a knee brace."

Alex kept his expression neutral for the sake of the little boy on the gurney. According to the chart, the child was eight years old. This parent was acting like his kid was an NFL superstar. "Justin, can you tell me where it hurts?"

The child looked up at him silently and pointed at his left leg.

"Okay, I'll check out your leg. Anywhere else I should look?"

"My chin hurts, too. I hit it right here, and—"

"Just tell him the important stuff, son. Shake off the little things, like a man."

Take it down a notch, Bubba. That was what Alex wanted to say. As Dr. Gregory, of course, he didn't. Part of every accident evaluation included screening for head trauma, particularly since this child had just reported that he'd sustained a hit to the chin. The screening could be as simple as listening to the child relate his injuries logically and with clear speech.

In other words, the father needed to shut up.

Alex crossed to the sink and washed his hands in preparation for an exam. His little patient was so miserable and tense, manipulating that injured leg was going to be an ordeal, unless he could get the child to relax at least a little bit. Confronting his father would only make the child more tense.

Alex began drying his hands on rough brown paper towels. "So, Justin, how'd you hurt your leg?"

"S-s-soccer."

"He was playing an aggressive forward position and he—"

Enough. Alex turned abruptly to face the father. In silence, he held the man's gaze. It helped that Alex was as tall as the father. He certainly lacked the beer belly, but he looked ol' Bubba in the eye. With his back to the boy, Alex let his expression show his disapproval as he dried his hands.

"—and he cut the ball back to this rookie, who…ah…." The father's monologue came to a confused halt under Alex's glare.

Alex crushed the paper towels into a ball and pitched them into the trash can. Deliberately, taking his time, Alex pointed at the chair in the corner. The father sank slowly into the empty chair.

Alex turned back to Justin. He started with the child's arm, knowing it was uninjured and wouldn't cause him any pain while he lifted it and bent the elbow, testing the range of motion, a way to let the child get familiar with the exam. "Do you play any other sports?"

The child darted a fearful glance at his father, making sure it was okay to talk. "Dad coaches me in basketball, too. Right, Dad?"

Dad hesitated and glanced at Alex before answering. "And baseball. We're doing baseball this year."

Justin looked from his father back to Alex. "And b-baseball."

"Wow, that's a lot of sports." Alex hadn't missed the child's fearful glance. He took his stethoscope off his neck. It gave him the perfect excuse to lift the boy's shirt to listen to his heart. He'd be looking for bruises, too. Usually, an overbearing soccer dad was just that, but sometimes that overbearing personality became violent, and children could be the victims.

"What sports do you do?" the boy asked.

Alex smiled a bit. Kids only knew their own worlds. If their world was an endless cycle of practices and games, they assumed everyone was involved in sports. Thankfully, little Justin had no bruises. His life with his dad centered on sports whether he liked it or not, but it appeared his life was free of physical violence. Not like Alex's had once been.

"I'm not on any teams like you are. I ride my bike a lot, though."

He could've felt the father's derision even if he hadn't heard the snort of disgust. Alex was used to it from a certain type of man. Alex had been raised in Europe, in the dangerous, crumbling Soviet Bloc. The best moments of his grim childhood had been seeing the professional cyclists in their brightly colored kits go whizzing through his town, training for the Tour de France. When Alex had escaped to America as a teen, he'd been shocked that his new schoolmates didn't know any pro cyclists by name.

"I can ride a two-wheeler," Justin said.

"Yeah? That's great." Alex started palpating the child's good leg, picking up the diminutive foot in his hand and rotating it to test the ankle. "Do you have a favorite movie?"

The kid lit up like a lightbulb. "I like *Star Wars*. Do you know that one? And I like *Guardians of the Galaxy*. And I like *Space Maze*."

"I'm going to bend your knee now." Alex wanted to keep Justin focused on something else. "Who's your favorite character out of the whole Maze world?"

"I like Eva. You know, Princess Picasso."

Dad snorted again. "A princess? Goya the Destroya, that was the best guy in the movie."

"But Dad, Goya was a bad guy. Eva was the good guy." Justin looked ready to cry, and Alex didn't think it was because his leg hurt him.

"So what? Goya kicked azzz…uh, butt."

Justin showed a little spark of defiance. "Eva had a cool laser gun. She kept it hidden in her boot."

Good for you, kid. You're going to need that stubbornness with a father like yours.

Alex had liked the Eva Picasso character, too. "She was really brave. She saved her people from the maze. I'm going to need you to be really brave for a minute. I'm going to move your knee as far as it will go." It was a matter of millimeters before Justin responded in pain and Alex stopped. He patted the kid on his good leg. "Do you remember what the princess kept in her other boot?"

Justin's grimace relaxed a bit. "Yeah, that really cool knife that could cut right through anything. Even metal."

"You're talking 'bout the chick who wore the boots?" His father sat back, sounding relieved. "She was hot. Sophia Jackson, that's the one. Okay, yeah, the boots chick was hot."

"And brave," Justin said.

"And brave," Alex agreed as he stood up. "I don't think the bone in your leg is broken, but I need to get an X-ray to be sure. It won't hurt. An X-ray is a special kind of camera."

"I know," Justin said. "It can take a picture right through your clothes. Princess Picasso could get one with her boots on."

Dear old Dad couldn't help himself. "I bet the doc would love to get a picture of Sophia Jackson right through her clothes. Who wouldn't? Am I right?"

Alex didn't reply. What he'd like to see was Princess Picasso giving this Neanderthal one of her go-to-hell looks.

A brave princess in his ER?

That would make his day.

CHAPTER TWO

GRACE WAS A COWARD. SHE DARTED A GLANCE around the van, petrified of getting caught.

Don't be such a scaredy-cat. All eyes are on Sophia, anyway.

Grace pulled her sister's phone out of her bag. What she was about to do was for Sophia's own good. When the lock screen lit up, she tapped in the four-digit access code.

It was rejected.

The code was supposed to be the year Grace had been born. Although it surprised the few people who learned of it, Grace was actually the baby sister, only twenty-five to Sophia's twenty-nine. Her big sister loved her. Her big sister used baby Grace's birth year as her code. Only it didn't work now.

How old was Deezee? Grace typed in his birth year. It worked.

The stab to her heart was starting to feel too familiar. With jaw clenched, Grace began deleting photos, horrible shots of her sister's bare breasts covered by Deezee's hands, shots that would never, ever end up on Instagram, not when she could prevent it.

Delete, delete, delete.

The van doors opened with a sudden rush of air. Grace dropped her sister's phone like a hot potato.

A woman about her own age poked her head in. "Hi. You're with Sophia Jackson, right?"

"Yes." She blinked in what she hoped was an innocent way.

"There's been an accident."

For one horrible moment, the world stopped.

An accident. Careers and reputations and idiot boyfriends evaporated before the image of a hurt Sophia.

"Oh, my God." The words were a whisper, but inside her head she was screaming. *My sister, my sister!* Their parents had been killed in a car accident. A stranger, a woman like this one, had come just this kindly to tell them there had been an accident. Grace had been fifteen. Sophia had been nineteen.

"It's nothing life threatening, I promise. We have so many Texas Rescue doctors and paramedics and firefighters here, she's being well taken care of, but they do think she should go to the hospital to have things checked out."

The only reason Grace had survived the loss of her parents was because Sophia had been by her side, taking on the role of parent, loving her with all she had. But now Sophia had been in an accident, hurt badly enough that she needed to go to the emergency room. *My sister, my sister!*

"Would you like to ride in the ambulance with her?"

Grace clutched her tote bag as she scrambled out of the van. The fans behind the barricade were silent, wide-eyed. The yellow ribbon had been cut. Its ends flapped in the light breeze as the ceremonial scissors leaned against the building, standing on their points, forgotten. All the men and women in suits and uniforms were now by the open doors to an ambulance. The kind woman escorted Grace right through the little cluster. A paramedic offered her a hand up, and there Sophia lay, looking miserable on a gurney. Miserable, but very much alive.

Grace threw herself onto her big sister for a hug. "Are you okay?"

Sophia put her hand on her shoulder—and gave her a shove. "Don't bump my leg. I'm going to sue somebody if this makes me miss Deezee's party. Give me my phone. I need to call him. He's going to freak when he sees this on Instagram."

Deezee was going to be worried? *What about me?*

While Sophia lapsed into another coughing fit, Grace sat on the metal bench that ran the length of the ambulance's interior. She slid her tote bag closer, slowly, buying herself time to get her emotions under control. For all of her life, she'd been the one whom Sophia had worried about. After their parents had died, they'd been afraid to be apart, afraid of the future—afraid they'd lose each other in a split second, the way they'd lost their parents. Sophia had let Grace crawl into her bed when she was afraid of the dark.

"You know, when they said you were in an accident just now, all I could think of was Mom and Dad…" The words hurt her throat.

Sophia went still and looked at her, really looked at her for the first time in ages. "Aw, Gracie." And then, also for the first time in ages, it was her sister who reached out to fix her hair, smoothing Grace's plain brown hair over her shoulder. It had once been blond like Sophia's but had darkened in adulthood.

A paramedic jumped into the bay with them, a man who could get work as a body double for Thor. Grace said hello; Sophia ignored him. Doors slammed shut, and the ambulance began moving.

The cell phone in her tote bag rang. Her sister practically

jackknifed into a sitting position on the gurney, which immediately made her yelp in pain and freeze in place. Still, she could give an order through clenched teeth. "Answer it. Hurry."

"It's mine." Grace dug in her bag and silenced the ring.

"Hand me mine. Maybe Deezee called."

Deezee never called. Sophia was to do the work. Sophia was to come and see him, at his convenience, without any notice. If Deezee saw a photo on Twitter or Instagram of Sophia being loaded into the back of an ambulance, he'd expect Sophia to call him and tell him the latest. Didn't she realize that?

Sophia held out her hand and made a little grabby motion. "He'll get pissed if I don't tell him what's going on. He'll want to know what hospital I'm at."

Or maybe Sophia did realize how little effort Deezee made, and she just didn't know that wasn't normal. Maybe she'd forgotten how Dad had treated Mom, once upon a time.

At any rate, Grace didn't have Sophia's phone. She'd tossed it aside in her haste to make sure Sophia wasn't dying. She couldn't say that, though. The phone should have been in her tote bag, not in her hand.

"It must have fallen out of my bag in the van."

"You *lost* my phone?"

The paramedic chose that moment to interrupt by wrapping the black Velcro of a blood pressure cuff around Sophia's upper arm. "Let's get your blood pressure."

Grace tried to reassure her sister. "I'm pretty sure I remember seeing it lying on the seat with your lipstick, actually."

Sophia laid back with a huff, her life so inconvenienced by a handsome paramedic who was taking care of her. She glared at Grace, looking pretty fearsome for someone who was hurt badly enough to be in the back of an ambulance at the moment.

"It'll be okay. We know it's in the van, and I'm sure the Texas Rescue people will find it and bring it back to the hospital."

"They'll look at my personal stuff. You're the one who is always so worried about what will get out on social media. You think those Texas Rescue people aren't going to pass around Sophia Jackson's personal phone for kicks and giggles?"

The paramedic didn't like that, Grace could tell from the way he clenched his jaw. Neither did she. She wouldn't lose her temper, though. Confronting Sophia never worked.

"They can't see what's in your phone." She spoke as sweetly as possible, but she knew it sounded fake. It was her sister who was the actress, after all. "You have your phone locked. Our special secret sister code is still protecting it, right?"

Sophia opened her mouth, then shut it again, and looked at her through narrowed eyes. "Of course."

The wall between them seemed just a little higher. Just a little harder to breach. It was a wall in the shape of a man. A stupid, worthless type of man, who was systematically pushing Grace out of her sister's life.

Grace couldn't imagine being so blind in love. If she were to fall in love, one thing was for certain: she would never, ever love a man who didn't also love her sister.

Alex Gregory hated Sophia Jackson.

It was a shame, because she'd been a good actress in some excellent films. He'd be blind not to think she was attractive, but it had taken less than two sentences to determine that the person behind the famous face was rude and shallow.

"Good afternoon. I'm Dr. Gregory."

"What took you so long?"

Rude.

But no more rude than young Justin's father. Alex had

pushed his glasses farther up his nose. "That seems to be a popular question this afternoon. We're a little busier than usual during South by Southwest. What's brought you in today?"

"Where the hell is my phone?"

And shallow.

Nothing during the exam was changing his first impression of her. While he examined her ankle, she complained about the facility. She'd been placed in the overflow area, an older part of the emergency department where the beds were separated by curtains rather than walls. This was, according to the not-so-noble woman who'd provided the noble face of Princess Eva Picasso, utterly unacceptable.

"It's also unavoidable," Alex said. "By definition, *overflow area* implies that all the other rooms are full."

"When my personal assistant gets back with my phone, she'll have me moved."

Alex raised an eyebrow on that one. Not many patients brought along a personal assistant, at least not this far from Hollywood. Still, a movie star's personal assistant had exactly zero influence on how the emergency department of West Central Texas Hospital ran. Alex took the stethoscope from around his neck and inserted the ear pieces.

"Oh, no, you don't. You don't get to slip your hand inside this dress. It's my ankle that hurts. Do you think I don't know that you're dying to tell everyone that you felt me up?" Her indignation dissolved into yet another coughing fit.

Sarcastic comments flashed through his mind. *You're right. The stethoscope works just fine if I stand three feet away and aim it at you. We doctors have been lying about that for centuries, but you're the one who figured it out.*

But he was here to provide medical care for a twenty-nine-year-old female patient, not to teach a lesson in sarcasm to a movie star. "I'll be able to hear your lungs through the material. Would you like for me to call in a nurse anyway?"

She crossed her arms over her chest, but leaned forward a few inches, granting him limited access. "You can listen to my back. Then go see if my assistant has found my phone yet. Your Texas Rescue people are probably hiding it from her."

Just provide medical care. Alex put the chest piece on her back, which felt like the back of any other human, whether male or female, attractive or ugly, famous or obscure. *Provide care, then get her out of here.*

He heard the crackles he'd expected to hear. He flipped the stethoscope to hang around the back of his neck again, then slid the curtains back on their metal rings. "We need to get some X-rays, but you won't have to move to a wheel-chair. An orderly will roll your gurney down to radiology. There's a bit of a wait right now, but the nurse will be in to check on you periodically."

"You're planning on wheeling me around the hospital in this bed? No, no, no. You need to bring an X-ray machine up here, right after you put me in my own room."

"That's not the way it works here."

"My privacy needs to be guaranteed. Be sure you send my assistant back as soon as you see her. She'll handle everything."

Alex left without another word, snapping the curtains shut behind him. If Sophia Jackson had that much faith in her assistant's ability to make a hospital bow to her whims, then that assistant must be even more of a harridan than Sophia herself. Dr. Gregory planned to steer clear of her. As the only doctor on duty, he didn't have time to spend deflating some puffed-up bit of Hollywood hot air.

His most senior nurse, Loretta, was coming on duty. He'd let Loretta handle Sophia Jackson's personal assistant.

Alex wanted nothing to do with her.

CHAPTER THREE

"DR. GREGORY, WE HAVE A PROBLEM."

Alex kept writing his notes on the patient in room three, but he nodded to his nurse to continue. Loretta had worked in the ER for so long that nothing shook her up. If Loretta was concerned, then Alex was concerned.

"Go ahead," he said, as he signed his name for the twentieth time today and tossed the paper into the in-box on the nurse's station.

"They just roomed another patient in the overflow area."

"That makes two. The overflow area holds eight."

"I know, but the beds are only separated by curtains in overflow." Loretta lowered her voice as if she were about to tell a secret. "Sophia Jackson is in one of those beds. We'd better do some rearranging. Her assistant is asking about HIPAA."

HIPAA, or *hippah*, as everyone called it, governed medical privacy. The harridan of a personal assistant had arrived, and now she wanted to threaten his ER with privacy regulations, did she?

"You know that the curtained area is considered HIPAA compliant."

"Yes, but Sophia Jackson is *famous.*"

Surely his best nurse didn't expect him to move a patient just to pander to someone famous. For the second time this shift, he felt as he had when he'd first come to America. The culture shock had been extreme. To survive the jungle that was the American high school, he'd quickly dumped his cycling stars and learned who the heroes of American football were. He'd killed all trace of his Russian accent. He'd worn blue jeans and Dallas Cowboy T-shirts, but all of that had been camouflage. Surface-level changes.

Deep down, he'd never quite caught that American mindset. To this day, he didn't understand the fascination with the famous. Of all the traits a person might have, fame was one of the most useless. In his old life, rank in the political hierarchy mattered. Wealth mattered, for money bought power, and both could assure safety. Smarts mattered—a smart man could be valuable to those who held rank. But fame? Fame didn't put bread in your belly when you were hiding from corrupt government officials. Fame didn't pay for passage on a rickety ship to a country that didn't want you.

"You know people will overhear you," Loretta said.

"Then I'll try not to call out her full name too loudly as I ask for her autograph."

"Be serious, Dr. Gregory."

He was always serious, even when the sarcasm slipped out. Sophia Jackson was famous and frivolous and nothing more. She'd be in no danger if her name slipped out, but she didn't need to worry: Alex was not a man who let names slip. He could remember a time when his mother's life had depended on his ability to keep her name a secret.

He paused, mentally closing the door on unwelcome memories. "Every room is full because you've got only one doctor on duty, so let me get back to work. Sophia Jackson will survive with curtains instead of walls. I've already examined her, so there's nothing medical for anyone to overhear, anyway. If she doesn't want anyone to overhear her other types of complaints, then she can stop complaining."

"Yes, Doctor."

"Loretta, one more thing. When the soccer kid in room three goes for his X-ray, make sure he doesn't cross paths with Sophia Jackson. He's a big fan of one of her movies, and I don't—"

"You wouldn't want him to bother Miss Jackson."

"Actually, I wouldn't want Miss Jackson to ruin his image of her."

"Understood. By the way, her personal assistant is going to want to know how we'll keep her identity a secret while we roll her gurney down to radiology."

"If Miss Jackson doesn't want to be seen, then perhaps her personal assistant would care to throw a blanket over her head."

"I don't get paid enough to deliver that message."

Alex sighed. "I'll talk to her assistant myself."

Grace was very aware that a new patient had been placed on the other side of the curtain, a woman who'd barely answered the nurse's questions with more than a syllable. There was a man with her, too, who'd loudly done most of the talking. Now that the nurse had left them alone, he was keeping his voice to a vicious whisper, but Grace could still hear him.

She wished she couldn't.

"You already know what I'll do to you, bitch. You want to see what I'll do to your kids?"

Grace looked at Sophia in a panic, but she was lying on her bed, twisted away from her, typing madly away on the precious phone Grace had retrieved.

The unseen man on the other side of the curtain was obviously trying to be quiet, but he wasn't quiet enough for Grace's ears. "You tell the doctor you fell down the stairs. Say it. Now."

"I f-fell down the stairs," the woman said. "But we don't have stairs."

"The effing doctor doesn't know that, you dumb-ass."

Grace was paralyzed in her vinyl chair. She'd be horrified if this were a movie scene, but this was even worse. This was real life, and she was no Sophia Jackson heroine. Grace didn't know what to do.

"Say it again, like you mean it."

"I fell down the stairs."

"Smile when you say it. You get me in trouble, I will hunt your kids. You send me to jail, and they're dead when I get out."

Grace couldn't move. Couldn't make a noise. The man clearly didn't know someone was sitting inches behind him on the other side of a cloth curtain. If she made a sound, he would.

What would he do? Would he hurt those children that were apparently waiting somewhere in a one-story house?

Frantically, she reached forward to tap the mattress of her sister's gurney, but her sister only hunched her shoulders and kept tapping away on her screen.

"Don't worry," the woman said, sounding so pitiful as she tried to soothe the man who had hurt her, who was threatening her still. "Everything will be okay. You can trust me, you know you can. I would never want you to get in trouble. I'll fix everything."

On her gurney, Sophia coughed.

Grace froze.

There was utter silence on the other side of the curtain, and then the curtain was pushed aside. "Who the hell are you?"

She had to do something. Her sister's back was to the angry man, so before Sophia could roll over and reveal her famous face, Grace jumped to her feet and faced him. "We'd like some privacy." She dared to grab the curtain and whisk it shut, right in the man's face.

The silence on the other side of the curtain was more frightening than the angry whispers had been. Her heart was already pounding out of her chest when she heard more curtains being pushed aside on their metal rings. Not hers—the ones next door.

"Good afternoon, I'm Dr. Gregory. What brings you in today?"

"I fell down the stairs."

Her sister chose that moment to emerge from her absorption in the phone. "How slow is this place? Didn't you tell them to bring the X-ray machine up here?"

Frantically, Grace put her finger against her lips to silence Sophia. *Shh, shh, shh...*

"What is wrong with you?"

"Nothing." Grace leaned in close to her sister's ear, so she could whisper. "I want to hear what they're saying next door."

"What for?"

She cringed. Every normally spoken word sounded like a trumpet blast to Grace. She could hear the man doing most of the talking next door. The woman's voice sounded so timid. The third person, the one who'd said he was Dr. Gregory, had a better voice. Calm and confident. He spoke with the good cheer of someone who didn't know his patient was in danger.

"We'll need a few X-rays because you might have one or more fractures. There's a bit of a wait for radiology right now."

Sophia spoke loudly. "This X-ray is taking forever."

Grace whirled around and pleaded for silence with her finger on her lips. It figured that Sophia had just now started paying attention.

Dr. Gregory kept talking. "While you're waiting, Mr. Burns, you can get the paperwork taken care of. You'll be able to leave sooner that way."

The curtain rings made their sliding sound again.

"Loretta, perfect timing. Could you show Mr. Burns to admin while we're waiting to take Mrs. Burns to X-ray? He needs to fill out the spousal consent forms."

"The spousal consent forms? If you'll just follow me, Mr. Burns."

After another swish of curtain rings, the violent Mr. Burns was gone with the nurse.

"We'll take care of you," Dr. Gregory said to the woman. "It might have sounded like I was rushing you out of here, but you can stay as long as you need to."

Grace held her breath, willing the woman to tell the doctor the truth while her attacker was gone. She heard only silence.

"I'll be back shortly." The doctor was leaving.

Grace needed to be brave. She should do something. Say something.

But she didn't. She was no superhero. Maybe she could write a note and pass it to a nurse or something...

Behind her, Sophia called out. "Dr. Gregory."

There was an audible sigh in the aisle. Then it was their curtain that was being pushed aside, and a man far younger than Grace had expected stepped into their little space. He was around thirty, bespectacled and bearded. Not the trendy kind of full beard that men in Hollywood were wearing this year, but the dark shadow of a man who'd perhaps worked a twenty-four-hour shift.

"Yes, Miss Jackson?" He sounded as tired as he looked.

Sophia began complaining. The doctor listened to her sister's demands without a flicker of emotion on his face, without so much as a blink of his eyes behind his brown plastic eyeglass frames. His white overcoat looked too big on him. He didn't look like a man, frankly, who could handle the vicious Mr. Burns, but—

But, actually, he did.

There was something very Clark Kent about him. Tall, dark and handsome could have described him if he were in Superman mode, but as Clark Kent, he was too unassuming to be eye-catching, not the way he stood with his hands stuffed in the square pockets of his lab coat. Still, although he might not have bothered to shave, his jawline was defined, and the blue of his eyes was only dimmed a little bit by the glare of the fluorescent lighting on his eyeglasses.

It was the look in those blue eyes that gave Grace hope. He saw right through her sister. He wasn't flustered by her beauty and he didn't look awed to have a movie star in his presence. In fact, he was looking at her with quiet disapproval. If he could see through the celebrity aura that surrounded Sophia Jackson, maybe he could see through Mr. Burns. Grace just needed to be brave enough to tell him what she'd heard.

"So, um, you're her doctor?" she began, forcing herself to smile when it was the last thing on earth she wanted to do at the moment.

He turned that blue gaze directly on her. A small eternity of silence followed.

"Of course he is," Sophia said, exasperated. "I told him

you'd fix everything when you got here. I need a private room. These curtains are so ghetto."

He didn't take his eyes off Grace, but he raised one dark brow behind the brown frames. "*You're* the personal assistant?"

Clearly, he wasn't impressed with her. She felt badly about that, another little dagger of hurt to push through. "Dr. Gregory, could I speak to you somewhere else? Somewhere private?"

"No."

Grace blinked. "I really need to speak to you alone."

"There are no other rooms available, and there is nothing you can say that will make radiology move more quickly. As soon as her X-rays are complete, you'll be discharged with treatment instructions, and you can seek out all the privacy you desire somewhere else."

He left.

Sophia's outrage drowned out Grace's disappointment. She yelled "Doctor" once more, but the doctor wasn't coming back.

Grace sank back into her chair, a failure.

"What do you think you're doing, Grace? Go after him." Sophia was loud for someone who prized her privacy. She gestured toward the ice packs on her leg. "I can't get up and walk out of here. You have to."

"He already said no."

"This whole trip was your idea. Go fix it. What's a personal assistant for, right?"

CHAPTER FOUR

ALEX HEADED STRAIGHT FOR THE STAFF'S KITCH-
enette. There were patients to be seen, lab results to read, decisions to be made, but he was only one man. He needed a
break—and coffee. Just three minutes, that was all he'd give
himself. Three minutes for a little caffeine and a chance to regain his emotional equilibrium after dealing with Mr. Burns,
the scum who'd beaten his wife.

Gut churning, Alex walked past the coffee to the cramped
locker room that was attached to the kitchen. The room barely
had enough space for a few metal lockers and a single cot,
but the door had a small sign which euphemistically declared
it to be the physician's lounge. He pushed a gym bag out of
the way with his foot on his way to the sink. The water ran
hot almost instantly.

The patient had not fallen down a flight of stairs, that much
was obvious from her bruising. Alex had needed to pretend
he believed her story, though. Abusers wouldn't stick around
after an accusation, and they often convinced their victims to

leave before they could be treated. Alex had started the hospital's official process, and he hoped the victim was ready to take advantage of the assistance the hospital could provide.

The system worked. He'd seen it work. But to use an American phrase, that first step was a doozy. The first step required Alex to smile and be cordial and shake hands with a man he was certain had beaten his own wife.

Alex scrubbed his hands in the sink. He was no actor, but he deserved an Academy Award for keeping up that facade of friendliness. To test his patience further, a real actor, Sophia Jackson, had decided to waste his time by chewing him out for problems that weren't even problems.

Alex scrubbed harder. Hot water, soap and vigorous friction could kill almost anything.

The woman on one side of the curtain had been a victim of a crime. Sophia Jackson, on the other side of the curtain, had been a victim of nothing more than her own stupidity and stubbornness. According to the Texas Rescue volunteers who'd brought her in, she'd decided to cut short a tour of the rebuilt clinic by storming off the path, stomping over the orange netting that marked off the rubble left behind by last year's floods. They'd called after her and warned her to stop, but the paramedic said she'd ignored everyone.

Alex could believe it. It seemed the movie star was nothing more than a miserable person who made everyone around her miserable, too. Her personal assistant looked to be the most unhappy person of them all.

He stopped scrubbing and let the tap water flow over his hands. The personal assistant hadn't been what he'd expected. Instead of a hard and edgy shark, she looked like an angel. The expression on her heart-shaped face was open and hopeful. Everything about her had seemed inviting. Her hair looked soft and touchable, a shade of gold so dark, it was nearly bronze. The overhead lighting had reflected off that gold, and Alex had been momentarily dazzled by her halo before he'd realized who she was. Only then had he noticed the subtle, anxious way she was twisting her fingers together.

Apparently, even an angel could be stressed out. It would take the patience of a saint to work for Sophia Jackson.

He used a paper towel to shut off the faucet. If the angelic woman was stressed out by the demands of Sophia Jackson, he couldn't help her. Since she was with the movie star, he could only assume that she enjoyed her job. Fame was alluring to most people, perhaps even more so to personal assistants. After all, they made a living by helping someone famous keep their famous life running smoothly. Princess Picasso's assistant was no exception.

He grabbed a coffee mug, feeling annoyed with himself for being annoyed at all. It shouldn't matter to him one bit that an angelic-looking woman who happened to pass through his ER was letting a movie star run her ragged. It was no business of his whether or not she thrived by facilitating someone's fame. Coffee was all he wanted.

The door opened after the most timid of knocks. "Excuse me, Dr. Gregory. I'm so sorry to bother you." The assistant stuck her angel face in the crack and smiled at him hopefully.

Speak of the devil.

"This area is employees only."

She bit her lower lip with perfect white teeth. "I know, I'm sorry."

He set down the empty mug. So, she was appealing. They had nothing in common and would never see each other again after another sixty minutes, give or take, so he called upon his medical experience to act dispassionately and moved to the door.

"I really need to talk to you," she said.

"There is nothing you can say that will change how this hospital operates."

You stay in your world, I'll stay in mine. He put his hand on the doorknob to shut it.

"Wait." The angel had more determination than he'd expected. She thrust her whole arm and shoulder in the door. "There are no stairs in her house."

He knew, instantly, that she was not telling him about Sophia Jackson's house. Surprise kept him silent.

"I heard her say so. I'm talking about the woman next to us. The man that was with her hurt her." She was breathless in her anxiety to tell him what she knew.

Alex opened the door and ushered her in with a gentle touch on her arm, a brief brush of her soft gray sweater under his hand. He shut the door in an automatic move to protect patient privacy. Still, it seemed intimate to be alone with this woman in this little bit of an inner sanctum. "I understand. That's why I arranged to have him removed from her treatment area."

She didn't seem reassured. "He's only filling out paperwork. Spousal consent forms."

She really had heard every word, then—and remembered them. "Spousal consent forms are a code in this ER. It means the spouse has to leave the treatment area. I've seen enough patients who have fallen down stairs to recognize the hallmarks of that type of injury."

"And she didn't have them?"

He shook his head silently. He was bound legally and ethically not to describe a patient's medical condition to a stranger. The assistant obviously knew some details already, but he couldn't tell her more.

"How long does it take for him to fill out the forms? He'll be back any minute."

"Security will explain that he can't reenter the treatment area. Doctor's orders. When the next room with walls and a door opens up, the patient will be moved there. I can't tell you more than that, but I assure you, she will have a chance to talk to me in private."

"She won't tell you anything."

Sadly, the assistant was quite possibly right. Victims of domestic violence were often silent in the hope that the situation would improve if they helped their abuser. "I hope you're wrong about that, but we'll give her every chance, every safety net we have available. You and I need to end this conversation now, because—"

Because of patient confidentiality, of course. But he didn't finish the sentence, because what had popped into his head was *because you're already too appealing*. Her compassion toward a stranger only increased his regard for her.

It didn't matter. He had no interest in pursuing a woman when no relationship was possible. Flirting was something else he'd never quite understood. It was a waste of time to indulge an attraction to a woman who lived in another state, let alone a woman who built her life on the shaky ground of fame.

The assistant furrowed her brow, determination stamped on her lovely face. "You can get her alone in a private room, but she won't tell you anything. She has children. He told her he would kill them if she talks."

The kitchenette door started to open beside them. He stopped it with the palm of his hand. "A moment, please." Without looking to see who it was, he pushed the door shut. All his attention was for the assistant. "You heard this? He actually said he'd kill her children?"

"He was inches away from me on the other side of that curtain. I heard every word. He said if he goes to jail, he'll kill the children as soon as he gets out."

She looked up at him with fear and worry—and something else. Hope. She was looking at him as if she hoped he would be able to fix this terrible situation. The desire to touch her again, to physically soothe her, was completely inappropriate. That wasn't how a doctor helped.

He crossed his arms over his chest. "Are you willing to relay this to the police?"

"I hadn't thought about police."

This protective streak was strong. He didn't want her involved in what could become a volatile situation. "The injuries are already enough to trigger social services, and that will include removing the children from his custody. I appreciate everything you've told me, but you don't have to do anything else."

"No, I'll talk to the police. That poor woman. I couldn't live with myself if I didn't try to help."

"Not everyone feels the same. You're very brave." He felt a little sloppy bit of tenderness toward her, despite the way he was standing with his arms crossed over his chest, scowling at her. He cleared his throat and tried for a more neutral expression. "What did you say your name was?"

"It's Grace."

"Grace." Of course it was. Grace was a blessing one did nothing to deserve, *milost'* in his mother's language. He'd done nothing to merit its presence in his emergency department today, but Grace was here, being an ally for a stranger in a dangerous situation.

She tugged the hem of her soft sweater an inch lower. "Well, thanks for your time."

A brave princess had shown up in his ER after all—just not the one he'd expected.

He liked this one much better. "Thank you for being so

persistent. I apologize for being so curt. I can tell you're worried, but you've done the right thing. I'll take it from here."

"What about the police?"

"If they need your statement, we'll do that with as much privacy as possible, I promise. I don't want you to risk anything if you don't have to."

"Thank you."

Grace left, slipping easily around the nurse who was waiting outside the door.

"Loretta asked me to tell you that we're taking Mrs. Burns down to X-ray now. Room three is ready to go, if you could discharge him. The social worker is on her way over."

Alex would have to get his coffee later. As he headed down the hall toward room three, Grace was about twenty feet ahead of him on her way back to the curtained area. Her plain clothing allowed him to enjoy the feminine shape of her. He knew firsthand that her sweater felt very soft, and her slacks were tailored over the curve of her backside.

The voice of Princess Picasso came shrieking down the hall. "You have got to be kidding me! Why is that woman getting an X-ray before me?"

Grace broke into a jog.

Alex shook his head as he entered room three. How could an angel who was so brave subject herself to a celebrity who was so selfish?

"Here's your macchiato." Grace hiked her tote bag a little higher on her shoulder and held up the cup of coffee she'd spent fifteen minutes locating, ordering, paying for and bringing to her sister.

Sophia was talking on her phone, and waved her into silence. The part-skim half-caff macchiato with the shot of regular caramel syrup and sugar-free vanilla syrup which she'd just *had* to have was not quite as important as her phone call, apparently.

Grace was tempted to place it on the bedside table and leave the table where it was, at the foot of the bed. Sophia would need her then. She'd have to interrupt her phone call with Deezee to ask Grace to roll the table closer.

Immediately, Grace admonished herself for being such a baby. What kind of sister would even think of placing something where a person with a broken leg couldn't reach it?

"You asked to see me?" Dr. Gregory entered their little curtained cubicle and stood at the foot of Sophia's gurney, next to Grace.

Grace put the coffee down. She wasn't normally klutzy, but she felt a little flutter now that Dr. Gregory was here, so it was better not to be holding a scalding-hot beverage.

Really, she needed to squelch this little Clark Kent crush. The man was on the job, caring for a battered woman somewhere else. Caring for her own injured sister, too, and who knew how many other people who were sick and in pain. Yet she felt a little buzz of excitement that he was here, despite knowing that her sister shouldn't have demanded to see him.

"The doctor decided to finally show up," Sophia said into her phone. "Yeah, tell me about it."

Grace stole a glance at Dr. Gregory. He pushed his glasses up with one knuckle. He had a perfectly neutral poker face in place, but Grace had the fanciful thought that the move meant he was ready for battle.

Sophia took the phone away from her ear and pointed it at the doctor accusingly. "I heard them talking next door. You know what they said?"

Grace held her breath. What had she missed while she'd been looking for gourmet coffee? The horrible Mr. Burns must have returned. Or perhaps Mrs. Burns had decided to unburden herself to a nurse, and Sophia had overheard everything.

"Your janitor told another janitor to take the patient's belongings to room three. That patient is getting a room? Seriously? When I've been waiting here with nothing but curtains all this time?"

Grace interceded before Sophia could make a fool of herself. "Sophia, it's okay."

"No, it is not. I was here first. She got taken for an X-ray before me, and now she gets a goddamned room before me."

"Sophie," Grace begged quietly. "The cursing."

"*Goddamn* won't even get you a PG-13 rating." Sophie pinned the doctor with her glare. Really, it was a sneer. Grace hated to see Sophie sneering like that. If she could take a photo, make Sophie see…

"I demand a private room, for obvious reasons."

"There are none available." Dr. Gregory didn't sound upset or intimidated by Sophia's behavior at all, not like Grace was.

Sophia must have heard that almost bored note in his voice, too, because she hesitated, just for a second, in the middle of ramping herself up for a good old-fashioned hissy fit. She gave it a go, anyway. "Even if I didn't need extra privacy, which you know I do, I should have been next. I've been waiting longer."

"That's not the way it works in a hospital. She needs the room more than you do, and there are patients who require my presence right now more than you do." He stepped back and grabbed the curtain, ready to leave. "Was there anything else?"

"More than I do?" Sophia's voice was getting high-pitched in her outrage. "I suppose you decide that?"

"I do."

Grace felt a little chill go down her spine at the quiet confidence in those words. She looked at Dr. Gregory again, at his calm profile, his unwavering gaze.

He can handle anything. He can handle Mr. Burns. He can handle my sister.

Then she realized he'd turned to her, locking gazes with her for the briefest of moments, just long enough for her to imagine he was silently asking her to keep Sophia under control.

I wish I could.

"You're just leaving?" Sophia sounded incredulous.

Grace wished she had as much control over her sister as Dr. Gregory seemed to think she had. She put a hand on her sister's good ankle and patted her reassuringly. "Thank you, Dr. Gregory. We'll stay right here, then, until a room opens up."

He nodded at her. "I'll be back."

Grace hoped he'd be quick. His hair was shaggy and he needed to shave—yesterday—and his glasses weren't chic geek, just geek. His white coat was two sizes too big, and yet he looked like a hero to her. Somehow, when Grace stood next to Dr. Gregory, Sophia seemed less intimidating, but he was gone with a slide of metal curtain rings, and Grace was left to manage her own personal movie star.

"Where the hell is that macchiato?"

Hurry back, Doctor. I need you.

CHAPTER FIVE

GRACE WANTED DR. GREGORY.

What she got was a frighteningly competent nurse named Loretta. The nurse seemed to be just as unimpressed with having a movie star for a patient as Dr. Gregory was, but still…

It would have been nicer to have Dr. Gregory by her side.

Sophia's ankle was not broken, the nurse reported, but she would need to wear a hard plastic medical boot for a week. The nurse removed the ice. She'd brought a few sizes of the plastic boot to try. By the time the correct boot was strapped around Sophia's lower leg, poor Sophia was clutching Grace's hand in real pain.

Nurse Loretta gave Sophia a pill for the pain, something Dr. Gregory had apparently foreseen the need to prescribe, then Grace and Sophia were alone again. This time, Grace perched on the edge of the bed, and they did yoga breaths together while they waited for the pain medicine to kick in.

"We could do 'breath of lion,'" Grace suggested.

"The dumb one where we stick out our tongues?" But Sophia made a funny face at Grace as she said it, one that always made Grace laugh. "Hope no one with a camera sees us."

The sarcasm, the cursing, the defiance had all disappeared in the last half hour. Grace stuck her tongue out and panted. Sophia did, too, but they couldn't keep panting with straight faces.

"Ohmigod, we look dorky," Sophia said, and the sound of her laughter was music to Grace's ears.

My sister is back.

Grace could have cried in relief. It was so good to be needed again—no, not needed. She was always needed. It was good to be wanted again. Sophia wanted her by her side.

Sophia's laugh turned into another round of coughing. Grace winced in sympathy; her sister's ribs had to hurt from the force of her cough. Sophia sank back into her pillow. She'd never looked more pitiful, not even on screen when she'd died as a pioneer woman to great critical acclaim.

Grace smoothed Sophie's hair over her shoulder. "Can I get you anything?"

She attempted another smile, a wobbly bit of bravery. "Just don't leave me again. I need you here."

"Of course."

I wish Dr. Gregory could see us now. He hadn't been very impressed with Sophia so far, that much was clear. When she'd complained about Mrs. Burns moving to a room, Dr. Gregory had thrown Grace that last look, the one that said *Can't you keep her in line?*

It nagged at Grace. Maybe the look had been more like *How do you put up with her?* Maybe the look had been simply disappointment with Grace. Or puzzlement. *Why do you help someone who is so rude?*

Because I love her. She's my sister. She's my whole family.

But, of course, Dr. Gregory didn't know that, just as Sophia didn't know anything about Mrs. Burns's dangerous situation. If she did, then of course she'd be content to wait a little longer. With a crinkle of the plastic-covered mattress under her, Grace scooted closer to her sister's side, ready to confide in her.

"Ouch! Don't bump me. Sit on that stool."

"Sorry." Grace slipped from the mattress onto the doctor's rolling stool, trying not to feel sad at how short-lived their shared laughter had been.

It wasn't Sophia's fault. She was still in pain, and the pain was making her irritable. Really, she was acting as normally as anyone would in her condition.

Grace leaned closer, too aware of the curtains, although no other patients were around now. "Listen, something kind of scary happened while you were on the phone with Deezee. The lady that was in the next bed—"

"The one who got treated better than I did?"

"I don't know about better. Maybe faster, but there was a good reason. Let me tell you what happened."

Mrs. Burns's sad tale had exactly the effect that Grace had known it would. Sophia was subdued, silent. Probably, like Grace, she was thinking how fortunate she was to have been born into a loving home, where the concept of Daddy hitting Mommy was unimaginable. This afternoon was a vivid reminder that other children were not so lucky.

"Then I'm glad they moved her," Sophia said.

"I know. Me, too."

"That would have been a mess, if the two of them had started fighting again. People would have come running, and these curtains wouldn't have kept us hidden. Hell, the guy could have thrown her right into our cubicle or something. I can't be involved in that kind of thing. Can you imagine

HER TEXAS RESCUE DOCTOR

the shock on everyone's faces if the curtain had come down and they'd seen Sophia Jackson lying here?"

Grace was silent. That wasn't exactly the empathy she'd expected.

"Martina is threatening to leave me if I'm involved in any fights," Sophia said. "She told Deezee the same thing."

Martina was a publicist, and one of the few people whom Sophia still seemed to listen to. Then again, Martina had been Deezee's publicist first. She'd introduced the two of them, actually. It was yet another reason that Grace doubted Deezee had any real affection for Sophia. She'd been awfully good for improving his damaged reputation. He'd had the opposite effect on hers—so now Martina was helping Sophia, too, for a hefty retainer fee.

Sophia let go of her hand and pushed herself into more of a sitting position. Her pain was clearly lessening. The medicine must be kicking in. "What time is our flight? I'm ready to get out of here."

I'm not.

Grace wanted to stay here, where Deezee and publicists had no importance. Here, someone else was in charge.

The curtain rings slid open, and Dr. Gregory walked in, laptop under his arm. Intelligent, empathetic, authoritative— Grace wanted to run to him and cling to his hand.

She stood up to let him have his rolling stool, but he waved her back down and took the straight chair on the opposite side of the bed. When he asked Sophia how her ankle was feeling in the boot, he seemed genuinely interested in what she had to say. His bedside manner, when he was literally bedside, was sympathetic and focused on the patient.

Then again, what man didn't focus on Sophia Jackson? The two of them looked quite striking together. Maybe not at a glance—Sophia had on that killer coat dress and her hair still looked fabulous after a couple of hours in a hospital bed, while Dr. Gregory was kind of lost under his baggy coat and shaggy hair—but they both had vividly blue eyes and really great bone structure. They'd make beautiful babies together. Beautiful, intelligent, talented babies.

Another stab to her chest caught her by surprise. Jealousy? She couldn't be jealous of the attention Sophia was paying to Dr. Gregory. The idea of Dr. Gregory and Sophia together ought to make her happy.

"The ankle will heal, as long as you don't push it too soon. That's the good news."

"There's bad news?" Sophia asked, half playful, half fearful. Clearly, she'd decided to try being charming and pleasant. She was succeeding.

Dr. Gregory opened his laptop. "Let's look at that chest X-ray."

Grace's heart squeezed again at the sight of their two heads leaning over the computer screen together. The good news? He'd make a wonderful brother-in-law. The bad news? Her sister was too shallow to look past the surface to see what a quality guy the doctor was.

I can see it.

Yes, but you aren't the one who needs to see it.

Grace snapped out of her conversation with herself. Chest X-ray? Sophia hadn't mentioned that she'd gotten her chest X-rayed along with her ankle.

"I have pneumonia?" Sophia sounded very skeptical, but she was looking at Dr. Gregory in a whole new way, like maybe he did know something she didn't know, after all.

Dr. Gregory smiled kindly at her, an appealing little crinkle of the corners of his eyes behind unattractive brown frames. "Walking pneumonia is the common term, because younger adults tend to get this particular kind, and they keep gutting it out and going to work despite feeling sick."

Oh, Sophia liked that implication that she was a trooper, Grace could tell. The show must go on, and all that jazz. Sophia relaxed back on her pillows a little bit.

"See this cloudy part of your lung? That's fluid accumulating in a place air should be. I could've diagnosed pneumonia on your lung sounds alone, to be honest, but since you were going into X-ray anyway, it was best to have your lungs checked out."

For weeks, Grace hadn't been able to persuade Sophia to take care of that cough, but Dr. Gregory had been able to do something about it. Still, Grace was astounded at the pneumonia diagnosis. She'd thought the cough was bad, but she hadn't expected it to be that bad.

"How long have you been coughing?" Dr. Gregory asked.

Sophia looked to Grace, the keeper of all mundane information. "How long? A couple weeks?"

Dr. Gregory looked at Grace, as well, waiting for her answer.

Grace felt that little flutter again that came with having his attention on her. "At least a month. It started shortly after… after we got back from Vegas." She'd been about to say *shortly after you and Deezee were caught in the police raid on that club*, but she didn't want to remind Sophia of something that would make her feel bad. Sophia had apologized for that already. Besides, she was finally showing her good side to Dr. Gregory, and Grace wanted him to see that her sister was a good person.

"I had pneumonia for a month and didn't know it?"

"I imagine you've felt worn-out every day," Dr. Gregory said, his attention back on Sophia.

Sophia nodded, managing to look like a martyr without looking overly dramatic at all. She was a great actress.

"But you've kept working anyway?" he asked.

Another nod.

Grace should have felt her usual amusement at how Sophia could have anyone eating out of her hand. Instead, she felt a little irritated. Sophia had been working only if one counted clubbing as work. The pile of scripts that represented future work kept stacking up, because Sophia had been too tired to evaluate new projects after running around with her boyfriend. Today's clinic opening had been the first actual work Sophia had done in weeks, and she'd tried to cut that short.

She had a good reason for that. She must have felt awful. She's really sick. What kind of sister am I to hold it against her?

Dr. Gregory nodded at Sophia in what surely looked like approval. "You need to take a break, starting today. Pneumonia won't go away by itself. I'm going to discharge you with some antibiotics. You'll want to see your own physician once you finish the medicine to be certain your lungs are clear, but in the meantime, you need to rest. Drink more fluids than you want to, and don't skip any pills, even once you start feeling better."

Discharge her? He was sending them away with some pills and a plastic boot? Grace felt a little panic. She didn't want to start negotiating an airport with a sick sister in a wheelchair. Her sister had laughed with her a few minutes ago. She was being positively pleasant to Dr. Gregory now. Texas was good for her. They needed to stay right here.

"You shouldn't fly again until we've had a chance to clear up some of this fluid in your lungs," Dr. Gregory said.

Yes! The man was a miracle. Forget clinging to his hand. Grace wanted to throw her arms around him.

Sophia's radiance dimmed. "I have to get back to LA right away."

"Even in a pressurized cabin on a commercial airliner, the

demand on the lungs increases. This fluid is making things difficult enough for you here on the ground. How did you feel on the flight here?"

"Ohmigod, I felt terrible, actually. I was so tired and I had such a headache. I thought it was just a crappy flight."

You thought it was all my fault, like I'd booked a flight just to torture you.

"You probably weren't getting enough oxygen." Dr. Gregory closed the laptop. "Low oxygen saturation can cause those symptoms and more. Irritability, confusion and eventually loss of consciousness."

"Irritability?" Grace repeated without thinking.

To Grace's surprise, Sophia held her hand out to her. "Oh, Grace, I really took it out on you during the flight, didn't I? I said some mean things. I'm sorry."

Grace took her hand. Squeezed. This was the second time she'd gotten to see the nice side of her sister again—and Dr. Gregory was here to see it, too. Maybe now he wouldn't give her that puzzled look. This was proof that she didn't work for an uncontrollable diva. The longer they stayed in Texas, the more like her old self her sister became.

"We didn't know I had pneumonia, though, did we? I'll make it up to you. I promise to be extra nice to you on the plane tonight. It won't happen again."

"No, it won't," Dr. Gregory said firmly. "You can't fly tonight. Your ankle injury is taxing your body more than you might think. Between that stress and the pneumonia, you'd almost certainly be oxygen deprived again."

Sophia blinked at him. "But you can give me something for that, can't you?"

"For oxygen deprivation?" One corner of Dr. Gregory's mouth quirked upward. "Sure. It's called oxygen. You carry a tank of it with you and stick tubes up your nostrils so you don't pass out at thirty thousand feet and force an emergency landing."

Sophia's hand slid out of Grace's to land on the blankets with a little plop. Grace looked closely at Dr. Gregory. His poker face was good, but Grace could have sworn he was getting some satisfaction out of setting Sophia straight.

He stood and tucked the laptop under his arm. "Carrying an oxygen tank aboard would require some planning with the airline in advance. It's only allowed when the patient absolutely must travel. I'm not going to authorize it. Your ankle needs to stay immobilized and elevated, as well. I'll write a medical excuse for you, so the airline won't charge you to reschedule today's flight."

Double yes. Grace wanted to pump a fist in the air in victory. He couldn't have been more crystal clear. They were grounded, stuck in Texas. Who needed Superman when Clark Kent was doing the job so perfectly? Oh, God—was she smiling?

Grace bit her lip. Karma was surely going to get her. She'd wanted to get away from LA and stay away, and now Sophia was both injured and ill—but neither too seriously. Perfect.

Yikes. She was such a bad sister. To assuage her guilt, she pulled out a notebook from her trusty tote bag and started a new list. Flights would have to be changed. The hotel would have to be extended. She'd ask the concierge at their Hollywood condominium to hold the mail, or possibly deliver it here, depending on the length of their stay.

She looked up from her notebook. "How long are we staying here, then?"

"You should give the antibiotics a week. When she's breathing easier and her cough is better, you can fly."

"A week?" Sophia closed her eyes and pressed her fingertips to her forehead, overplaying her role a bit, in Grace's opinion.

"It could take you a month or more to feel a hundred percent back to normal, so don't be surprised if the fatigue continues on well past a week."

"A month?" Grace couldn't keep the happy anticipation out of her voice as she flipped to a fresh page in her notebook. "Oh, Sophie. I'll find us a real house, a vacation rental for a month. I'll get our clothes sent here, and line up some grocery service, and—"

"No." Sophia opened her eyes and glared at her from under her fingers. "I already told you I didn't want to stay an extra day. I won't be able to stand a week. Don't make one of your damned lists for anything except getting me back to LA."

Grace pretended she couldn't feel the disapproval Dr. Gregory was sending her sister's way. "We don't have a choice, Sophie. It will be good for you. You've been burning the candle at both ends."

Sophia snapped her fingers. "Book Deezee a flight. He can come out here and keep me company."

No, no, no!

"There's plenty of room in our suite."

It would be a nightmare. There'd be bottles of tequila everywhere, a man who referred to women as his *bitches* ordering Grace to fetch food and find limos for the strangers he'd invite up to their suite. There'd be noise complaints and hotel security and charges assessed for property damage. Grace would be scrambling around the clock. She couldn't take it, she just couldn't do it.

Dr. Gregory, she realized, was watching her intently. Her hand was shaking. She pressed the pencil into the notebook to steady it, so it wouldn't give her away. If she got angry, if she said no, Sophia would be dead set on yes. She needed a new tactic. Quick.

The tip of the pencil broke, a little black scribble on her paper.

"Grace," the doctor said, "could I speak—"

"Isn't pneumonia contagious?" She tried not to sound desperate.

His easy bedside manner was gone, but his stilted answer was still courteous. "Pneumonia isn't contagious, but the bacterium that causes it is. Someone who comes in contact with her might develop any type of infection from it. Sinusitis, bronchitis. Those could lead to pneumonia."

"Are you kidding me?" But whatever else Sophia had been about to say was lost in a coughing jag.

Grace brushed the broken pencil lead off her notebook page. She could leverage this. She could tell Deezee that Sophia was contagious, although he was as bad as Sophia, doing the opposite of anything Grace suggested. She could tell their publicist. Sophia and Deezee both listened to Martina...

"Grace, could I speak to you for a minute?" Dr. Gregory asked.

She looked up at him. He was much taller than she was, so she'd been looking up at him all afternoon, but he seemed like a giant now as she sat in the chair. "Of course."

"What for?" Sophia croaked, not quite done with her cough.

"Alone?" he added.

Sophia grabbed Grace's arm, making the pencil drag across the page. "You said you wouldn't leave me again."

Sophia looked so genuinely distressed, Grace didn't have the heart to point out that she'd left her to fetch the cell phone and left to fetch the caramel non-van half-caff macchiato because Sophia had ordered her to. Right now, she looked like a little puppy that needed protecting.

Grace looked from her sister's blue eyes up to Dr. Gregory's.

He seemed so solid, so calm. He had the authority to deny air travel, to order medical tests, even to protect a woman from an abusive spouse.

He could help her.

She stood. "Don't worry, Sophie. I'll be back in a minute."

With a slide of metal curtain rings, she left with Dr. Gregory.

CHAPTER SIX

ALEX WAS DAZZLED BY THE SIGHT OF GRACE IN the bright Texas sun.

Being dazzled was, of course, the temporary effect of walking from the windowless emergency room into the bright sunlight of the ambulance bay. *Light adaptation* was the medical term. He watched Grace blink, a reflexive move to relieve the visual discomfort as the retinas chemically altered to favor cones over rods.

Or maybe she was just a pretty girl, shading her eyes on a sunny spring afternoon, and he was just a guy who wanted to get to know her better.

Life was only that simple in Hollywood movies.

Alex's life had never been charmed. He was starting to suspect this woman's life wasn't quite the American dream it appeared to be on the surface, either.

He couldn't grill her about her apparent anxiety when it came to Sophia Jackson. As he had with his young soccer-playing patient, he started with something that he knew wouldn't cause pain. "I wanted to let you know that Mrs. Burns has decided to use the services we offered her. She's got an advocate with her now who will escort her to a women's shelter when she's ready to leave."

"That's wonderful." Grace's smile dazzled him in a way that had nothing to do with the chemistry of the retinas. The fine tension she carried in her shoulders eased a fraction. With a firm touch, he could eliminate the rest, smoothing his thumbs from insertion to origin point on each tight muscle.

Alex put his hands in the pockets of his white coat.

"And the children?" Grace asked. "What happens to them?"

"They'll be picked up and brought to the safe house with their mother."

"That is really, really good news. Thank you so much for telling me."

"Of course."

He realized he was staring into her eyes—warm and brown and gold, like her hair—when she looked away. Just how long had that silent bit of gazing between them lasted?

She made a gesture, a small wave at nothing in particular. An equally delicate worry line appeared between her brows. "Are you going to get in trouble for breaking a privacy rule or something? Is that why you brought me outside?"

"No. You volunteered to be a witness if necessary. It's reasonable for me to let you know that the patient is speaking up for herself, so you don't have to."

Her compassion extended to him, then. She was kind to worry that he'd be in trouble. Maybe she was too compassionate, though. If she didn't guard her heart, she would always be worrying about others.

She smiled again, another bit of tension leaving her shoulders. "I'm so glad to hear that. Can you keep me updated? I want to know if everything turns out okay."

"That probably would be crossing a line when it comes to privacy laws. I doubt I'll ever get an update, either. I don't see most of my patients more than once."

That little frown of worry appeared again. "You don't get to find out how your patients are doing?"

"Not often. I do my best while they're here and discharge them with instructions and prescriptions and referrals. Whether they use them or not is up to them."

She touched him. There was no purpose to it, not like there was when he touched someone. She just laid her hand on his arm, not pressing, not squeezing, not demanding. "You must be a very special kind of person, then. I couldn't do your job. I'd go crazy wondering how everyone is."

He'd brought her out here because he was concerned about her anxiety, the hand wringing and the pencil breaking. If she worried for the whole world like this, then he supposed she must always need an outlet for her emotions. He hadn't meant to add himself to her list of people to worry about.

He'd been on his feet for hours, and he was ready for a break. The unexpected influx of afternoon patients was under control. He could take a few minutes now, with her. He nodded toward the empty metal bench that was usually occupied by a paramedic or firefighter whose emergency vehicle was parked outside the ER's portico.

The curved steel of the bench couldn't have felt better after hours of standing. The woman by his side couldn't have been more beautiful to look at. The sun was shining, the weather was perfect…

Life was never that simple. He'd brought her out here for a reason. Something about her relationship with Sophia Jackson was setting off his suspicions. *I'm sorry for being mean to you* her boss had said to her, but of course, Jackson had almost immediately excused her own bad behavior by bringing up the pneumonia. *It won't happen again. I'll make it up to you.* How many times had a woman with a black eye heard that from the man who'd hurt her?

He doubted Sophia Jackson physically hurt Grace, but she was still pulling some emotionally manipulative stunts. Why did Grace put up with it? There had to be other jobs, other people she could work for. He'd brought her outside because he was concerned about all these things, but now she was concerned for him.

"Don't all these people weigh on your mind? How do you handle the not knowing?"

Maybe she was hoping he'd give her some advice on controlling worry. He rubbed his jaw and looked past a red ambulance to focus on a green cypress tree. The solitary evergreen pillar thrived in its allotted space in a median strip, surrounded by the concrete of the hospital parking lot. "I've found it helps if you choose their fate. Use your imagination. I helped a little girl with significant respiratory distress yesterday. I did everything I could to educate her family about asthma triggers. Today, I wondered if that family filled their script for the asthma inhalers. Did they stop smoking for her sake?" He fell silent, knowing the odds that smokers faced. Nicotine was as addicting as narcotics.

Grace prompted him with her gentle voice. "And you decided yes, the parents must have done the right thing and given up smoking?"

"I'm not so vain to think I can convince people to give up a lifelong addiction with one conversation." He glanced at her face, at her hopeful expression. "But I decided I was good enough at my job to persuade that family to never again smoke while that child is in the car with them. That's something."

"You're an optimist, then. I wouldn't have guessed that was hidden behind your—those—ah, never mind."

"Behind my what?"

She was blushing and utterly charming to him. She made a little gesture toward his face and shrugged.

"Behind my glasses? Are you afraid I'm insulted by that? I know I have glasses on." He took off his glasses. "Contacts are tough when shifts run into the next day without warning."

He looked at her as he wiped the lenses with a corner of his white coat, and thought the softer focus suited her.

Grace blinked again. Adapting to what? Surely her chemistry had settled down.

She cleared her throat. "I was going to say I didn't think you were an optimist behind that poker face. You don't give much away when you're in there, being a doctor."

He put his glasses back on, sliding them into place with one knuckle. He hoped his poker face didn't slip. He wasn't an optimist at all, but he didn't want to add to Grace's apparent worries. He couldn't tell her about the patients whose fates he did learn, the little girls who returned to the ER with blue lips, gasping for air, smelling like the cigarettes their families still smoked around them, triggering their asthma attacks for which the inhaler prescription had never been filled. Reality was too often bitter. It made a man hard.

An optimist wouldn't meet a movie star and assume her personal assistant was somehow trapped by her.

"When I discharge Sophia Jackson, what kind of living situation will she be in?" It was a legitimate question, one he asked every patient to be sure they could follow their treatment plan. What he really wanted to know was Grace's living arrangements. He had no professional justification for investigating this. He was just…

Abusing my position to satisfy an unhealthy curiosity about this woman?

It didn't matter. He wanted to know that Grace was going to be okay when she walked out of the ER and out of his life. He wanted to be able to imagine a better fate for her than fetching and carrying for a diva, having her self-esteem chipped away with each selfish demand.

"Will you be with her, or will Miss Jackson be living alone?"

Grace seemed to sink a little bit, without slouching or changing her posture at all. "I'm her personal assistant. Where she goes, I go."

"Even at night? You live together?"

At Grace's nod, he felt a distinct disappointment. It was almost like finding out she belonged to another man. Spoken for. Unavailable.

Again, he was annoyed with himself. It was absurd to be disappointed that all her time was devoted to another person. It wasn't like he'd intended to ask her out for dinner.

He needed to behave like a doctor. "It's good that she won't be alone, because she's going to have a hard time getting around. Even with the hard boot, she won't be able to touch her foot to the ground without pain for at least twenty-four hours. She'll need assistance getting in and out of the shower, for example. Do you feel comfortable giving her that kind of aid? If not, I can write orders for a visiting nurse who can help her with personal care."

Grace turned her face away, looking as he had toward the distant cypress tree. "She taught me how to brush my teeth. We've been sharing a bathroom our whole lives. Sophia Jackson is my sister."

Family.

All the pieces fell into place. A bright angel, subjecting herself to servitude. A movie star, bossing around a valuable employee without fear that she'd quit. Sisters... Of course.

I really took it out on you. It won't happen again.

No one could hurt you like family could hurt you.

Papa. Mama.

He firmly pushed the memories back where they belonged.

There were no bruises on Grace. Her sister might be using the same soundtrack that most abusers used, but Grace wasn't *physically* scared of her sister. When it came to emotional manipulation, Alex was too pragmatic to believe he could help her unravel any knots of family power struggles, not during a five-minute break on a metal bench. His own family was so fractured, he had no advice to give.

As for his attraction to her, it was irrelevant. She lived in Hollywood; he lived in Texas. She chased fame; he helped the injured. There was no reason for him to invest energy and effort when there was no possibility of a lasting relationship.

But he wouldn't let his moment with Grace end yet. He needed to find out what she was going back to—what his patient was going back to, as well—what was behind the white lips and broken pencil when the name Deezee was mentioned. Sophia might not be hurting her sister, but someone named Deezee could be.

Who was he, and why was Grace scared of him?

Dr. Gregory had fallen silent next to her.

Grace had said she'd help her sister in and out of the shower, and now he had nothing to say. Perhaps he'd been struck speechless at the image of Sophia Jackson in the shower. That was pretty typical of most guys. He didn't have a smile on his face, though, not even the ghost of a smirk.

Grace had also told him she was Sophia's sister. She resigned herself to the more likely possibility that he was quiet while he, like everyone else, studied her face, looking for the resemblance. *Sisters? I never would have guessed.*

Being told she didn't look like her own sister was a fairly new phenomenon in the overall course of her life. As little girls, they'd worn matching dresses and been declared darling. Even during her first two years of high school, every time she'd had a teacher that Sophia had already had, Grace had been told how she looked so much like her sister. It was only the stardom of the last few years that had begun separating them.

Sophia had acquired the polish and appearance of a star, that indefinable something that made people do a double take. Some of it was professional makeup, professional hair, and hours and hours of professional fitness training. Yet even without those things, Sophia still had a wow factor that Grace just didn't have. Sophia had been born with that charisma. She'd also been in the drama club, taken theater classes in college and developed a stage presence, but some gifts couldn't be taught, and Grace had always been proud to have such a gifted sister.

She was still proud of Sophia. This was only a phase. Grace just had to get Deezee out of their lives. Would Sophia ever consider Clark Kent?

Maybe, if they stayed away from LA long enough. Maybe, but no one could fall in love with someone they only met once. Grace needed to arrange more time between Dr. Gregory and Sophia.

"We're at the Hotel Houston," she said, before she could chicken out. "In Austin. It's called Houston, but it's not far from here."

"I know it. Very nice. I'm sure the concierge will help you

get some chicken soup for your sister. Hot beverages and hot, steamy showers will help loosen up the debris in her lungs."

Back to the shower fantasy, then. Grace felt glum about that, although it boded well for the hope that he might become a future brother-in-law. But Sophia wouldn't give the doctor or anyone else a chance, not if Grace couldn't keep Deezee away. "And she's contagious, and definitely can't be around other people right now, right?"

"That's the second time you've asked that. Are you afraid you'll catch something, or are you afraid of someone else?"

A little shiver threatened to go down her spine. He was looking at her so intently as he asked.

"Afraid? I guess I should be. Sophia Jackson causing an epidemic would be a terrible headline to try to spin." Grace sighed, realizing her plan to replace Deezee with this serious man was a laughably long shot. She couldn't explain how her sister needed saving and then expect him to turn into Superman and sweep her away to safety. Grace couldn't dictate who Sophia fell in love with, and she couldn't prevent her from throwing her life away on a selfish jerk like Deezee.

Grace knew that. She did. She just wished...

She looked at the cypress tree again, a single, tall pillar of green in the middle of an acre of asphalt. A lonely pillar. "I wish I was as good as you are at imagining that everything will work out okay."

He turned toward her, laying his arm along the back of the bench. She was aware that his hand rested on the bench just behind her shoulder blades, right behind her spine, the very spine she needed to stiffen.

"Is everything not okay with you?" he asked.

She didn't want to have a spine of steel. She wanted to melt into his arms. "Isn't everything not okay with everyone? We all have our little troubles, right? Everyone's fighting their own battle."

She was babbling, fighting the desire to lean into him, into Alex Gregory, MD, according to the embroidery on his coat. *Can I call you Alex? Tell you all my worries?*

"Grace, you can talk to me."

Okay, that was a little scary. He was like the perfect guy.

But he was a doctor. He meant she could talk to him about medical things. "I don't think I've caught anything from her. I'm a generally healthy person."

He was studying her again. She didn't know when anyone else had ever looked at her so closely. She was only an assistant, for goodness' sake. Keeper of the lipstick and the schedule. What was there for him to see?

"I'm fine. Honest."

Alex Gregory, MD, began unbuttoning his white coat. He stood and shrugged out of it. The scrub pants she'd seen beneath his coat were matched by a loose green scrub shirt that had been pulled on over a long-sleeved white knit shirt.

"What are you doing?" she asked.

He sat back down, coat folded over his arm. "There. Now I'm not a doctor. Call me Alex. I'm not asking you about your health. You're not my patient. There are no legal obligations for me to report anything you want to tell me. Is there anyone you're scared of?"

"Listen, Dr. Gregory—"

"It's Alex."

His stethoscope was still hanging around his neck. She tried not to stare too long at the dusting of dark hair in the V-neck of his top. "You still look like a doctor."

He waited, silent.

"I'm sorry," Grace said. "It's not you. I just don't talk to anyone except Sophia. I can't. Everyone else, from the limo driver to a cashier at the grocery store, could make some money selling tales to tabloids, you know?"

"No, I don't know. I wouldn't know how to go about finding a tabloid to sell anything to."

"They'd find you."

"We're opposites, then. You can only talk to Sophia, and I can't talk about Sophia at all. Not legally. She's my patient, so the tabloids will be out of luck if they find me." He smiled at her a bit, a little crinkle at the corners of his eyes behind those frames. "I don't have any restrictions when it comes to you. Do you think the tabloids would offer me money to hear about you?"

"I'm nobody."

"Me, too. But I'd rather you called me Alex."

The little joke was pleasant, coming from such a serious man, but she couldn't find it in herself to return his smile. The desire to tell someone about her fears was painful. She looked over her shoulder out of habit. No one was in earshot, and Dr.—Alex—was sitting right here, all blue-eyed concern. God, she hadn't had a friend in a million years.

"Sophia's got herself mixed up with a terrible guy. A new boyfriend."

"Is that Deezee?"

"You've heard of him." She sat back, determined not to say anything else.

He tapped her back lightly with the hand that had been resting behind her shoulders. "I hadn't heard of him until ten minutes ago. You turned white when his name was mentioned."

"DJ Deezee Kalm? That doesn't ring any bells?"

He shook his head.

"He's the first guy she's been interested in for years, but I don't know why. He's awful for her. He's awful to her."

"This boyfriend is abusive?"

"Persuasive."

"Persuading her to do what, exactly?"

Grace wasn't sure how to answer that. Everything sounded melodramatic. Deezee was persuading her sister to throw away her career. Persuading her to destroy her own reputation. Persuading her to push away her own baby sister.

"Nothing that's really illegal." Even yelling at a police officer wasn't illegal. It was just horrible.

The thought of police made her think of the other patient Alex was dealing with this afternoon. "Oh—did you think he was like a Mr. Burns? Nothing like that. Deezee has just been persuading her to be mean to me. Not exactly a crime, is it?"

But how nice that Alex had been worried about her, like a big brother. She felt tears threatening. She started to get up, ready to go back inside.

He stopped her with a question. "How long has this been going on?"

She was startled into silence. He wanted to know more, even though she'd given him the easy out. Without physical abuse, it was hard to explain how poisonous Deezee was. A boyfriend was setting one sister against the other—no big deal, not enough to make an episode of reality television. Alex could easily dismiss her complaint as drama, but the way he'd said *How long has this been going on?* sounded like he thought *this* was significant. She could have kissed him for taking her seriously.

"They met at a thing in Telluride, three months ago. He's not as big a star as Sophia is, not nearly, but he hired a very well-known publicist. That's who introduced them. Sophia never would have met him, otherwise. She doesn't do the club scene, or at least she didn't do the club scene before Deezee. She doesn't know any of the D-list wannabes that he hangs out with, and—" She clapped her hand over her mouth, mortified. "That sounded so snobby."

Her parents had raised her better. Each kid at school was to be treated the same, whether one wore expensive sneakers or one didn't. Having money hadn't made kids superior then, and being more famous didn't make her sister superior now.

Except it did. Those things mattered in Hollywood.

"She *is* an A-list celebrity. She earned that. It's not a matter of being photogenic or even being a good actress. She never fails to make her call. She's always prepared. I know I sounded bad just now about the D-list, but Sophia isn't snobby like that. By the time she leaves a set, the entire crew is always in love with her because she's nice to everyone. It's kind of sad that saying hello to the other people on the set is enough to make you stand out, but that's Hollywood, I guess. Anyway, her good reputation makes people want her on their projects."

She knew she was babbling, but the floodgates were open. "It's also Hollywood to lose your A-list status in the blink of an eye. Right now, Deezee has her dancing to his tune. The best scripts in circulation are sent her to read, but she's blowing them off in order to party with him. Deezee says he needs her, and she goes running."

"It sounds like the D-list guy is hoping her A-list status will elevate him."

"Exactly. Yes, exactly." Grace realized she'd reached out and clutched his forearm for emphasis. Despite the lightly chilly Texas air, she could feel the heat of his skin through the white shirt. His arm was solid in her grip. She meant to let go, but instead she gave his arm a little shake in her frustration. "How can you see it so easily, and she can't see it at all? I've pointed it out to her, but it's like talking to a child who doesn't want to believe that eating a bucket of candy is the reason she's sick to her stomach. I'm the one that's getting sick of it. We spent ten years building up to where we are now, and she's managing to destroy it in three months."

Grace did let go of his arm then. "Everything is going downhill. She's starting to act like him, disrespectful in public. Worse, she's being disrespectful *to* the public. Invitations have dried up, because no one wants her to bring Deezee to their event. The job offers will dry up next. The money will dry up. He's hurt her reputation, her finances—heck, he's even given her pneumonia."

Alex raised a brow at that. "He had an upper respiratory tract infection?"

She shooed away an imaginary bug. "I'm on a roll. I'm blaming him for everything, okay?"

Alex made a little sound of amusement, and Grace found herself doing something she never thought she'd do: laughing at the situation. Chuckling, at least. For a moment, anyway.

Her smile faded. "It's embarrassing, the way she talks to me now. I'm not normally a pushover. You probably find that hard to believe."

"Not at all. You didn't let me push you around when I was being short with you. I'm sorry, again, for shutting you down when you first asked to speak to me alone."

"You didn't know what I wanted to speak to you about."

"You're letting me off the hook pretty easily. That makes you kind as well as brave." He moved his arm, a simple shifting along the back of the bench, but his fingertips grazed her shoulder as he did. Did he linger? Had he touched her on purpose?

Please. She wanted to be touched. *More.*

She had no one to talk to but Sophia, no one to even hug except Sophia. Alex was too tempting. He was sympathetic and interested and warm, physically warm. And tall. With amazing blue eyes.

He almost touched her. She saw his gaze drop to her shoulder, but he stopped himself and raised his eyes to hers instead. "You were brave enough to report a crime today. I'm sure you are brave enough to find yourself a new job. You should work for someone who appreciates you."

It was either the conviction in his words or the kindness in his eyes that just about undid her. Whichever it was, her throat felt suddenly tight with emotion, making her voice sound husky. "She's my sister. I have to keep trying. I can't just let her crash without trying to get her to put on the brakes, you know?"

He hesitated only a moment. He set his hand on her shoulder, and gave her a firm squeeze, solid and warm, a masculine touch.

"Family."

That was all he said. One word. It was the bottom line, she realized. It was her purpose in life, to take care of her family. Her only family.

It felt like finding an oasis in a desert. Someone understood.

But then Alex let go. He looked resigned even as he gave her a small smile. "I hear sirens coming. My break is going to be over whether I want it to be or not." He stood, so she stood with him. "Are you going to be able to handle Deezee when he arrives?"

"He won't arrive. He can't. Sophia's contagious. You said so."

"Yes, but only for about forty-eight hours. She shouldn't fly for a week, but she won't be contagious for long. Antibiotics are effective."

Her heart sank. "I thought I had a week, maybe a month. I need to keep her in Texas as long as possible. We've only been here a day, and already I've caught some glimpses of the real Sophia returning."

In silence, he began putting his coat back on.

"Couldn't you tell her she'll be contagious for a month?"

He pushed his glasses into place with his knuckle. "She's my patient. I won't lie to her."

Lying to celebrities was a given in Hollywood. *You don't have to wear anything you object to. There will be plenty of time to rehearse. This interview will only take five minutes, then we'll get you some lunch.* Telling Sophia she was contagious for a teensy bit longer than she really was barely counted as a fib in Hollywood. At least Grace's lie was for Sophia's own good.

"Um…could you not tell her how long she'll be contagious?"

He looked at her in silence, and she imagined all kinds of disapproval focused on her through those lenses. Clark Kent never told a lie, if Grace remembered her superheroes correctly. Her sister would like dating a man who didn't lie to her.

"I'm not asking you to lie, just not to mention it if she doesn't ask." The sirens were getting closer by the second, feeding some sense of urgency that Grace hadn't known was building. "The contagious thing is all I can think of to keep Deezee away from us."

Alex put his hands in his pockets. His poker face was back in place, but after a small eternity, he sighed. "I'm sure the nurse has given her the discharge orders by now. Unless she requests to see me specifically, she and I are done talking. Whether or not you choose to lie to your sister is something I can't control."

They were done. Alex was going to leave her. She'd be on her own with Sophia again, with no one else to talk to, no one who shared her concern. "When can we see you again? I mean, when does she follow up with you?"

"Unless she takes a sudden turn for the worse or spikes

a significant fever, she should finish her antibiotics, travel home when she feels well enough and see her regular physician for follow-up."

This was goodbye, then.

No, no, no. She needed to think of something, but with the sirens closing in and the clock running out, she could only fall back on what she knew. Sophia was a powerful draw for most men, and Grace had the valuable commodity of access. "I'm sure Sophia would like to thank you properly when she's feeling better. If you give me your number, I can call you and we could set up a time for coffee or something."

"That isn't entirely appropriate. I don't normally visit a patient in their home—or hotel room. It stretches the limits of the doctor–patient relationship."

Desperation made her bold. "Let me give you my number, in case you change your mind."

She didn't have her tote bag with her. She found one of Sophia's gum wrappers in her pocket, but she had nothing to write with. Alex had a couple of pens clipped onto the edge of his pocket. He made no move to hand her one.

The ambulance pulled under the portico with a deafening noise. Grace winced, but she only had seconds. She grabbed a pen, scribbled her number on the paper side of the foil wrapper, and shoved the pen and the little silver square into his pocket.

He only raised one brow at her.

"I'm not your patient," she shouted over the sirens, "so you can call me."

The sirens cut off. Doors started slamming and personnel ran to open the back of the ambulance. Still facing her, Alex took one step backward, then two. "Stay safe. Don't climb on any rubble like your sister, and don't take any garbage from Deezee. Goodbye, Grace."

Then he turned around and joined the paramedics as they all jogged back into the building, pushing a gurney between them, calling out numbers to one another. Alex gave orders in Latin. He was saving someone else.

Grace stayed, rooted in one spot, stuck in Sophia's world. *Come back, Alex. Save me.*

CHAPTER SEVEN

GRACE HAD NEVER BEEN KICKED OUT OF A
hotel before.

The South by Southwest festival had the entire city booked,
and someone else had already paid for the suite she was trying so desperately to keep.

The hotel's general manager had given up any pretense of
a friendly Texas drawl about twenty minutes ago. His words
were brisk and his manner was as cold as the marble floor
of the foyer. "The Presidential Suite was reserved a year in
advance. We must honor that reservation. The bellhops will
help you with your luggage, and the valets will call you a
cab downstairs."

"Yes, but to where should we take the cab?"

He pressed his lips together. Grace knew he wanted to tell
her to go to hell.

"You cannot stick Sophia Jackson in a cab and have her
drive in circles around Austin, for goodness' sake." She smiled
as she said it. *Wouldn't that just be so silly, Mr. Manager?*

"We did our best to find you another hotel room. I regret that South by Southwest has the city completely booked. Otherwise, we would have certainly extended Miss Jackson's stay." He raised his voice as he looked past Grace toward the suite's living room, where Sophia was doing a fine job of following Dr. Gregory's orders, reclining on the sofa while keeping her sprained ankle propped up on the armrest. "The cab could return you to the airport, perhaps. Your reservation was only for one night. We agreed to a late checkout, but it is nearly seven o'clock in the evening. You must leave."

Grace gritted her teeth. "Miss Jackson was in the hospital this afternoon. The doctor said she cannot fly today. I have a letter for the airlines explaining the medical necessity of changing her flight. That means it is a necessity for us to stay here, as well."

"Perhaps the hospital would care to provide you with a room, since they provided you with the letter."

Two bellhops stood like good soldiers, flanking the door. They had to be the two biggest bellhops on staff, hearty Texas boys who'd probably grown up eating steak on a cattle ranch. Despite their organ-grinder-monkey costumes, they were here to serve as bouncers, not bellhops. Sophia Jackson and her entourage, which consisted of one personal assistant, were being kicked out of this hotel. Deezee and his crew hadn't even had a chance to show up and trash it first.

Somehow, Grace kept her spine stiff with a dignity she didn't feel. "If you'll just give me a few more minutes, the director of Texas Rescue and Relief is going to call me momentarily. She's trying to find Sophia another place to stay."

"If there were another room available in the city, we would have secured it for you. The Hotel Houston prides itself on the highest level of guest care."

Oh, obviously. Grace nearly choked on the sarcastic reply.

Antagonizing the general manager of the hotel wouldn't help her right now.

Sophia began another coughing fit.

Grace grasped at her only straw. She raised her voice for the benefit of the bellhop bouncers as she spoke to the manager. "The doctor said she's highly contagious right now, but since her ankle is also broken," a slight exaggeration, hardly a fib, "one of your bellhops will need to carry her to the elevator. I hope your staff is up to date on their flu vaccines."

The bellhops looked at one another in gratifying concern as Sophia sounded like she was hacking up a lung.

"We have a wheelchair for emergencies." The general manager nodded at one of the bellhops, who left the suite immediately, no doubt as eager to get away from Sophia's germs as he was to locate a wheelchair.

Grace hoped it would take a long time to find it. She looked at the cell phone in her hand, but the screen was still dark. The director of Texas Rescue had rather coolly informed her that she would ask if any Texas Rescue personnel were willing to put up two adults for a week in their own house. Knowing one of those two adults was sick with pneumonia made it unlikely, as she was sure Grace understood, but if she was successful, she'd call Grace.

She hadn't called.

No one in Texas Rescue seemed very enchanted with Sophia Jackson after her grudging appearance at the ribbon cutting. Grace had seen the videos on social media during the cab ride back to the hotel. Her sister had clearly caused her own injury, stomping into an area marked with bright orange off-limits signs. Six-second Vines and little gifs with grammatically incorrect captions were now posted all over social media. Bloggers and meme makers had helpfully circled all the warning signs in bright colors. *When Princessezz No Read.*

Sophia Jackson, who three months ago was a smart actress who made smart movies, had become a joke.

Threatening to sue Texas Rescue hadn't been the way to make them open their guest bedrooms, either. Grace didn't know what to try next if no one in the organization took pity on them. She looked over her shoulder at Sophia. Yesterday's complimentary fruit platter, a gift from the hotel before the Jacksons had refused to leave on time, adorned the coffee table like a work of art. It was an easy reach from the couch. Sophia ate a strawberry.

Grace's stomach rumbled. Her phone stayed dark. The manager stared her down.

A knock at the door made everyone jump. The bellhop practically ran to the door, as if Grace might try to beat him to it. A police officer in a blue uniform, badge and gun on display, strode into the hotel room. His radio loudly sounded off with some official dispatcher talk.

"Seriously?" Sophia said, lifting her head and pitching her half-eaten strawberry onto the coffee table. "You called the goddamned cops on us?"

The manager was looking smug, but the cop was looking from the bellhop to the manager to Sophia, and the look on his face was definitely confused. Grace had barely had a second to wonder what the policeman had expected to see when Dr. Gregory walked in.

She would have been as surprised to see the president of the United States walk into the presidential suite. Alex was still wearing his green scrubs, but the stethoscope was missing and he'd pushed up the long sleeves of that white undershirt. His day's razor stubble was reaching beard status. He looked tired, but he was looking for her, because he stopped and nodded at her once he saw her.

Sophia commanded center stage from her sofa. "You know

what they say about men who have to compensate by calling in cops." She'd propped herself up on her elbows, taking in the scene. When all the men looked at her, she arched back a little bit and gave her blond hair a shake. The look she leveled on the manager conveyed both confidence in herself and derision toward him. "Were you afraid of me? Thought you needed a *bigger* man to back you up?"

The way she pronounced *up*, popping the *p* sound through her strawberry-stained lips, made Grace want to blush. She didn't dare make eye contact with Alex.

The manager snapped his fingers at the bellhop. "Charles, please go into the bedroom and get Miss Jackson's luggage for her."

"Don't you dare touch my stuff," Sophia said.

The bellhop froze in place, looking like he'd rather be anywhere else.

Grace smiled in vain. "You can't get our luggage, you see, because it isn't packed yet. It's just a big empty suitcase."

"I suggest you pack quickly," the manager said. "The police don't have all day. You can wait for your phone call in the lobby."

"We cannot wait in the lobby." Grace spoke through a clenched jaw, but she couldn't keep smiling and being deferential forever. "She's Sophia Jackson."

"I'm well aware of that."

"She was in *Space Maze*. That's a huge sci-fi hit, and the reason you're out of rooms is because South by Southwest is in full swing. Your hotel is full of *Space Maze* fans." It was another small lie. The indie music and film festival wasn't the same thing as a sci-fi movie convention, but accuracy didn't matter right now. "They'll mob her. Then you really will need the police, because she'll be in danger on your property." And that much was too true.

Alex stepped into the center of the room. The manager, bellhops, cop and movie star were arrayed all around him. He rested his hands on his hips and looked right at Grace. "I seem to have walked into the middle of something here."

She took a breath to explain, ready to plead her case one more time, but Alex slowly winked at her.

He didn't break his poker face, but that wink...

He'd walked into the middle...

Was he—was he making a *pun* while she was being kicked out into the street?

"And you are?" the manager intoned in what was now some kind of British butler's voice.

"Dr. Alexander Gregory. And you are?"

Grace bit her lip. Alex did a better man-in-charge voice than the manager, probably because he was used to being in charge in the emergency room, where things were a lot more important than who got two queens and a sleeper sofa.

The manager was only halfway through giving his official title when the police officer interrupted him. "I need to speak to Miss Jackson. It's time sensitive."

"Indeed. They were supposed to vacate the room by four o'clock—"

"He means there's a judge and a possible warrant waiting to be issued. We need to speak to Miss Jackson." Alex sounded calm, but there was something in his voice, a little impatience, perhaps.

"Ohmigod. What did I do?" Sophia definitely sounded less than calm. "I didn't do anything."

Alex actually rolled his eyes before turning toward the couch. "Everything's not always about you, Sophia. We need to talk to Grace."

Sophia didn't have a chance to recover from her momentary shock at being dismissed by Alex, because the bellhop arrived with the wheelchair. Alex and the police officer exchanged a look.

The officer held out his arms and made a general shooing motion toward the door with the clipboard in his hand. "Everybody out. I'm conducting an interview."

The manager thought about objecting, Grace could tell, but the officer didn't look like he was open to discussion. The manager followed his bellhops out the door.

The officer hesitated before shutting the door, looking from Sophia's cast boot to the wheelchair, but Alex shook his head. "That's her sister."

"Ah." The officer was subtle about it, but now he looked between bombshell Sophia and gray-clad Grace.

Yeah, I know. Never would have guessed, would you?

"If you'd rather speak in private, your sister could move into the bedroom," he said.

Sophia rolled her booted foot from side to side. "Only if you carry me, big guy. My little tootsies can't touch the floor."

Grace tried to ignore her sister and focus on Alex. "I thought you didn't want to visit a patient in her hotel room."

A ghost of a smile briefly touched his lips. "I discharged her this afternoon. Technically, she's no longer my patient, but I didn't come to see her, anyway."

"I thought maybe Texas Rescue had sent you over, but the policeman gave it away. You must have an update for me on Mrs. Burns, after all." Oh, but wouldn't it have been nice if Alex had been the person from Texas Rescue to offer her shelter from the angry hotel staff? It was a selfish wish. The officer's uniform, with its holster and handcuffs, was a vivid reminder that no matter how frustrating her situation was, another woman in Austin was in far worse straits. "Isn't that why you're here?"

The officer spoke. "I'd like to ask you a few questions. You aren't obligated to answer, but I'm hoping you can help us."

"Yes, of course."

She followed the officer to sit at the dining room table. Alex sat in the chair next to hers, resting his forearms on the table. With his sleeves pushed up, she could see his arms were tan. A real tan, not a Hollywood spray tan. She already knew his skin was warm...

He caught her staring.

She was hungry, she was about to be homeless, but she forced herself to focus. He hadn't answered her question. "Why are *you* here with the police officer?"

"Because I knew you would say 'yes, of course' without stopping to think of yourself." He phrased it like a criticism, but the warmth in his ice-blue eyes made her feel like she'd been complimented. "I made you a promise back in the ER that I'd personally make sure any interview with the police was private."

"I wouldn't have interviewed her on a street corner with a megaphone," the officer said with some amusement in his voice.

Alex ignored him. "I also told you not to worry, that I'd handle the situation. If I gave your location to the police and went home while you got a surprise visit from law enforcement, I wouldn't be a man of my word."

A man of his word. She hoped Sophia had heard that. Her sister was the one who needed a kinder, better man. But honestly, if Sophia couldn't appreciate a man like Alex, then Grace was tempted to...well...tempt the man herself. If she could remember how.

What kind of sister am I? Alex is just what Sophia needs.

The police officer silenced his radio. "Shall we begin?"

CHAPTER EIGHT

SO THIS IS WHAT AN EXHAUSTED ANGEL LOOKS like.

Alex was tired, but he was accustomed to functioning while he was tired. It was part of being a doctor, something he'd been doing since his first year of medical school. Even earlier—he'd studied until dawn to pass organic chemistry and the other undergrad courses required to be accepted to med school.

Grace hadn't had his training. She looked more than sleep deprived; she was under significant stress. She looked fragile. Alex was glad he'd come.

The officer on duty was Kent Grayson, a longtime acquaintance through Texas Rescue. He'd come into the ER just as Alex was leaving, looking for a woman who'd encountered Mr. Burns earlier in the day, according to the wife's account. Alex had known with a sinking feeling that the woman must be Grace Jackson. He'd flipped the gum wrapper with her phone number through his fingers for a few seconds, then decided to hell with it: if Kent was going to the Hotel Houston to see Grace, so was he. He'd put the wrapper back in his pocket and grabbed the key to his truck.

"If Mrs. Burns is safe at the women's shelter now, then where do I fit in?" Grace asked Kent, but the possibility obviously hit her before she finished her own question. "The children. Did he hurt the children?"

"We don't want to give him the chance. He's being processed at the jail now, so Mrs. Burns and her advocate went to pick up the children to take them to the women's shelter. Unfortunately, the children are with a relative of the husband's, and she's refusing to let Child Services take them."

"The police can't take them?"

"If someone's in immediate danger, I don't need permission to go in and save them, but otherwise, I need a warrant. Since the husband's sister isn't actually harming the kids, we need a warrant to enter the home."

"So that's why there's a judge waiting. You need me to explain that I overheard him say he'd kill the kids? Let me get a pen."

She jumped up to help, but Alex stopped her with a hand on her upper arm, her soft sweater sliding over toned muscle beneath. "You didn't tell me that you and Mr. Burns spoke face-to-face."

"He just opened the curtains and said, 'Who are you?' and then I said we needed privacy and shut them. It was nothing, really. It took maybe two seconds."

"He saw you, and if you volunteer to give this statement, your name will be in court documents."

"I see where you're going with this." She sank back down to her chair. "That could be bad for Sophia's career."

"Grace, look at me. It could be bad for *you*, not Sophia. This man has a violent arrest history. He could decide to come after you for testifying against him. I wanted to be sure you know this is optional. You don't have to put yourself in harm's way."

"Her name will be redacted from her statement, actually." Kent took a blank form off his clipboard and slid it across the table to Grace.

Alex slapped his hand on it, stopping the motion. "Her name won't stay hidden if the case goes to trial and she faces him from the witness stand. Grace, it isn't mandatory for you to write a statement. We had a long discussion about this with the shelter's administrator before we came."

"Let me do my job here," Kent said.

"Grace can't make an informed decision if you don't give her all the information."

"I can't give her all the information if you do all the talking."

"Good one," Sophia called from her sofa. No longer lounging horizontally, she'd sat up and propped her booted ankle on the coffee table, next to what Alex assumed was an obscenely expensive fruit arrangement. "Point for the hot cop. This could be so much more entertaining, though. When a cop and a doctor walk into my hotel room in their Village People costumes, I expect them to start stripping."

A stupid grin broke Kent's serious cop expression, but Grace looked mortified.

Alex wanted to get this over with. Grace wasn't enjoying any of it. "Most states require medical personnel to report suspected child abuse, but Texas law requires all citizens to report what they know."

"I did report it," Grace said. "To you."

Kent stopped grinning and returned to cop mode. "Specifically, Texas law requires a report to either law enforcement or Child Protective Services. Doctors, school teachers and the like aren't considered the proper authorities."

Alex was impatient. "The shelter staff believes that you haven't broken any law. You aren't legally required to report anything in this case."

Grace was sitting with her hands on the table, her fingers interlocked, her knuckles white.

Kent took over. "The consensus is that there was no way for you to determine if you overheard a credible threat. You don't know the couple involved, you don't even know if they have children and so on. 'I'll kill you if you do this or that' is a pretty common threat that people make in the heat of the moment, and it usually means nothing. There's practically no chance that you'd be charged with failure to report child abuse. You still should be made aware of the law, though, and be given the opportunity. You never know if a judge might interpret the law differently in any particular instance."

To Alex's surprise, Sophia spoke up from her sofa. "Passive aggressive much? You tell her she doesn't have to write a report, then you threaten her that if she doesn't write the report, there's a chance a judge could interpret the law differently than your posse does. Then you tell her it's totally up to her to decide whether or not to take that risk. Thanks for coming here to jerk my sister around."

So, the movie star had some family loyalty, after all. Alex was glad, for Grace's sake.

"I think you've done nothing wrong and everything right, Miss Jackson." Kent leaned to one side to glare across the room at Sophia. "*Grace* Jackson."

Grace smoothed over her sister's interruption. "So what do you need from me, Officer Grayson? I'm worried about those children. I never doubted they existed."

Alex felt that sloppy bit of tenderness for her again. She was brave, she was selfless, and her spirit fit that angelic appearance, but he'd wanted to be here to make sure she was down-to-earth. Good people got caught in bad situations even when they were only trying to help.

"Alex gave the judge all he needs to issue a warrant," Kent said. "When he told the hotel staff the judge was waiting, he exaggerated. We'll have those kids safe with their mother before Burns can ask for bail, but as a police officer, it's my job to talk to every possible witness, even if I'm ninety-nine percent certain a prosecutor won't need the testimony."

Alex watched Grace. "It's that one percent chance I wanted to make sure you're aware of."

She twisted her fingers one more time, then lifted her chin and looked him in the eye—not Kent, but him. "This afternoon you thought I was brave. Now you don't want me to make a statement?"

"If this was the only way to help those children, it would be worth the risk. Sometimes, doing the right thing is dangerous."

He was hit by an old memory—*his mother unlocking her office late at night, too afraid to turn on the lights. She'd been a structural engineer, wanting the town to know their factory was not safe. She was betting her life that glasnost had weakened the old Soviet regime enough so that the factory workers would strike once they knew the danger, but the remnants of the Communist Party had suppressed her report.* Doing the right thing can be risky, *she'd told him. She wanted to make copies of the report that would circulate from house to house, even if she was jailed. Her hand had trembled as she'd pressed the green button on the battered Xerox machine.*

Grace's clenched hands trembled.

Alex placed one hand over hers. "But those kids are going to get picked up even if you don't agree to be a witness. To put yourself at personal risk for no reason is a waste. I don't want you to have even a one percent chance you'll get hurt."

There it was. Something about Grace spoke to his soul.

Whether he ought to care or not, whether he *wanted* to care or not, didn't matter. He didn't want to see Grace Jackson hurt.

Sophia's voice jarred him back to reality. "Is this Burns guy rich?"

Grace and Kent and Alex all looked at one another around the table. The question seemed irrelevant, but Kent answered her. "Their address isn't in a very affluent part of town."

"Ours is." She popped another strawberry in her mouth and kept talking around the fruit. "This loser isn't going to buy a plane ticket to come out to California, anyway, but if he did, he'd have to get past walls and gates and security guards. Hell, the paparazzi would make him the best photographed criminal you ever tried to ID. If you want to do this, Grace, then do it."

Surprise, surprise. In her own obnoxious way, Sophia was supportive of her sister. Alex grudgingly revised his opinion of her up one notch.

Grace began to write. Her penmanship was neat, her movements quick and certain despite the fine tremor in her hand. In the end, it took less time for her to write the statement than it had taken for them to decide she should write it.

Kent filled out the rest of the form. Name, address, phone number, all asked with a smile, all given the same way. Alex wished he hadn't been such an ass when she'd tried to give him her phone number. What had he been afraid of? Violating patient privacy rules?

I'm not your patient. You can call me.

It had been hard to force that out of his mind while he'd dealt with the ambulance arrival.

"Thank you again for your help." Kent was leaving, all smiles, his mission accomplished. Alex watched Grace smile, too, as she shook hands and wished Kent luck.

Hot cop, Sophia had called Kent.

Alex rubbed his jaw, the scratch of his beard not helping his mood. Kent nodded a goodbye to him, looking like some kind of poster boy for the All-American clean-cut look. Alex looked like...

Aw, hell.

He looked like hell, and he knew it.

The door closed after Kent. Grace turned to Alex and held out her hand to shake his, too. "Thanks again for coming."

Things felt stilted between them, as if they weren't on the same side. The whole reason he'd come tonight was to be sure she had someone on her side.

He didn't let go of her hand. "For what it's worth, I think you did the right thing."

"Thank you." Her polite smile relaxed into something more genuine; he felt rewarded. "You were playing devil's advocate for me."

They let go of one another.

"So, is this goodbye again," she said, "or am I going to see you in a couple of hours?"

"This is goodbye." But he didn't like that feeling, either.

"Better start packing, Gracie." Sophia tucked her hands behind her head and settled back, putting her good leg up on the coffee table, too. "That manager is going to be back the second he sees that cop leave."

A knock on the door was immediately followed by the sound of a card unlocking it. In walked the same bellhops that had been here when he'd first arrived.

"Told you," Sophia said. "Losers."

The hotel had no respect for privacy. Alex waited, ready to chew out the manager, but the manager didn't walk in next. Instead, three maids pushed in a cleaning cart. Ignoring both him and Grace, the bellhop spoke to Sophia. "I'm sorry, Miss Jackson, but we got a call that the next guest has landed at the Austin airport, so we're to get the room ready immediately, and, uh…if you could…you know…"

Two maids disappeared into the bedroom, as the third maid began pushing in the dining room chairs they'd used. The sound of the shower being turned on in the bathroom jerked Sophia out of her lazy pose.

"Grace! Our stuff is in there."

"Okay, okay." Grace pressed her hands to her temples. Her fingers still had that fine tremor. "Let me think. I'll think of something. I just—maybe—maybe we could head out of town and start trying different exits. Once we are out of Austin, one of those interstate hotels is bound to have a room, right?"

"Go get our stuff."

"Right. I need to call the front desk."

"Go to the bedroom. Our stuff isn't at the front desk, Grace. Jeez."

But Grace was almost talking to herself now, moving to the old-fashioned house phone beside the couch. "We can't use an app to get a lift if we can't type an address in first. No cab is going to want to go on a wild-goose chase out of town. We'll rent a car. I'll drive a car. It's been months, but— Hello?"

He swore he could hear a tremor in her voice as delicate as the one in her hands, but then a maid fired up a vacuum sweeper.

Grace turned to him suddenly, phone pressed to one ear, and raised her voice over the vacuum. "The main highway is I-35, right? I can't remember."

It hit him that more than stress could make a person's hand tremble. For a doctor, he'd been slow to notice the signs. Shakiness, confusion—she was on the verge of a breakdown, tears welling up in her eyes.

"Grace, when's the last time you had something to eat?"

She held up a trembling finger, asking for one minute while

she listened to someone on the other end of the line, then covered her ear with her hand. The maids were all making clatter of one type or another. A second later, she turned away from him, and he knew from the movement of her hand that she was dashing a tear from one eye.

"Yes, I know, I know. I'm calling to ask if you could arrange a car? Not a limo. I need a car that I could drive myself."

"Grace." He walked closer and took the phone away from her ear. She let it go without a fight. "When is the last time you had something to eat?"

"I'm sorry. Did you need me to order some dinner?"

He hung up the phone.

Despite her sudden frown, tears started to fall. *Emotional lability, secondary to hypoglycemia.* He should have seen it sooner.

"It's going to be okay." Damn it, but he couldn't cross his arms over his chest or stick his hands in his pockets one more time. She swayed into him, and he put an arm around her. She felt soft and warm and real, but a hug was not what she needed right now. He turned her toward the empty couch that ran parallel to her sister's. "Sit."

He held out his hand toward Sophia, who'd just helped herself to some kind of apple carved into a flower. "Toss it here."

She was surprised enough that she obeyed him.

"Eat this, Grace. I promise, we'll have you feeling better in a few minutes if you do as I say. I don't suppose there's a minibar in here?"

Sophia jerked her chin toward a corner of the living room. "To hell with mini, they gave us a whole liquor store. I'm presidential, baby."

Alex pushed aside the bottles of top-shelf liquor in the brass and lacquered bar area. He didn't want the alcohol; he needed the mixers. He found a small bartender's can of orange juice, shook it, then poured it into a crystal highball glass. The maid chewed him out in a foreign language—not Russian—and stopped vacuuming in order to pluck the empty can off the shelving and wipe away an imaginary ring.

Fine. She had her job to do, he had his.

His new patient was as uncooperative as the maid thought he was being. Grace stood and managed two stumbling steps toward the bedroom before Alex got in front of her and physically blocked her way.

"It sounds like they're breaking all of our stuff," she said.

"You're not going anywhere until you take care of yourself first."

She tripped on her next step, but he steadied her with one hand and managed not to slosh the orange juice out of the glass at the same time. "Drink this."

She placed two palms on his chest for balance. Her fingers curled into his scrub shirt. Tears were welling in those brown eyes again. Knowing they were nothing more than a physical result of exhaustion and low blood sugar did nothing to lessen the tug he felt in response.

"I'm sorry," she whispered.

"There's nothing to be sorry for." His voice sounded gruff, and he knew it. He wasn't angry at her. He just resented that tug of sympathy. He hated having no control over his reactions to her. She made him feel... God, she made him *feel*.

She kept one hand on his chest for balance as she took the glass and downed the orange juice. It wasn't her fault he found her so damned appealing. He shouldn't have such a hard time treating an angel with some basic friendliness.

"All right, let's go pack your stuff together." He forced himself to smile at a perfectly lovely woman whose blood sugar had crashed. This was simple attraction, nothing more, nothing less. He could deal with it. "I'm going to keep an eye on you until you feel better."

Her answering slow smile reminded him less of a noble angel and more of a woman who'd had one drink too many. "Promise?"

"Sure."

"Good, because you're a man of your word."

He had a feeling the light-headedness from hypoglycemia mimicked the light-headedness she'd get from being intoxicated. The impression was helped by the highball glass in her hand.

She poked him in the chest with it now. "You're a really nice guy, even though you are hard to read. You have such a good poker face."

"And you have none," he murmured.

"I don't? Can you tell what I'm thinking?" She leaned in one inch closer to whisper to him. "I'm thinking that I'm glad I met you today."

"Thank you." He looked over her head to Sophia. "Does she always get like this when her blood sugar is low?"

"Nope. Usually, she gets all weepy."

He hadn't meant it as a trick question, but Sophia's answer made him angry. "Usually? So you knew that she was prone to low blood sugar, and you didn't remind her to eat something today?"

"I've been just a little bit sick myself, you know. Emergency room. Pneumonia. Any of that ring a bell?" But her uncaring, tough-girl defense didn't quite ring true. The way she looked at her sister confirmed it. Sophia the Diva felt some guilt. "She'll be fine in, like, ten minutes. You should give her another glass of juice."

He was a doctor. He knew how hypoglycemia worked, but instead of aiming a sarcastic comment at Sophia, he pushed Grace onto the couch to sit right next to her. He got another can of orange juice and tossed it at Sophia. "Pour it for her. Don't let her get up again. I'll go pack your suitcases."

She caught the can. "You'd better arrange that rental car first. I really can't sit in the lobby, hoping someone will find us a place to stay. It'll turn into a big mess. Grace wasn't exaggerating."

He kept walking toward the bedroom. "I'm not sticking her behind the wheel of a rental car ten minutes after a hypoglycemic episode."

"She'll be fine." He heard the pop of the can being opened, the pouring of the liquid into the crystal glass. "She'll perk right up in a second."

"I already feel better," Grace said, sounding anxious.

He stopped then and turned to assess her appearance.

"I'm so sorry, Sophie, I'll fix everything. I should've eaten something, but I just got busy. My bad."

"No." His voice sounded harsh.

Both women looked at him.

No, you will not keep trying to make Sophia happy. You won't apologize for things that aren't your fault. You won't shoulder every single responsibility alone.

"Drink that juice. Forget the rental car and the roadside motel hunt. You can stay with me."

Damn it, he sounded angry again. He shouldn't be. He was doing the right thing, and he knew it. It was just that sometimes doing the right thing was risky.

He left the two women on the couch and walked into the bedroom, where two maids had beaten him to the packing. An unzipped suitcase lay on the foot of the bed. One maid tossed a stack of folded clothes into the suitcase.

He leaned against the doorjamb and brooded about his unexpected houseguests.

What, exactly, was the risk here? What was he so damned afraid of?

That he'd catch pneumonia from a movie star? Not likely. He had the constitution of an ox after years as a doctor.

That he'd have his routine disturbed, that he'd have to share his living room and relinquish control of the TV? He spent most of his nights reading, anyway.

That he'd have to listen to Sophia complain and Grace apologize for a couple of days?

Ah, that was getting closer.

Grace Jackson. That was the risk. He could feel himself getting involved, actually starting to care about a woman who would disappear within the week.

The maid he could see through the bathroom door let loose with a string of foreign words that were surely curses. The maid was apparently repulsed by the number of cosmetic bottles and jars she was tossing into a plastic bag that bore the hotel's logo. Her cursing fit his mood, too.

Grace Jackson had been stirring up his emotions all day. He ought to be glad that she was destined to return into the world of California celebrities within a week. After all, everyone disappeared sooner or later, whether he cared about them or not. His ER patients tended to disappear the same day. His family had taken longer, but he'd literally watched his father disappear on a seashore, growing smaller and smaller as the boat he and his mother had crowded onto sailed farther and farther out to sea, until finally the shore itself had disappeared.

His mother had disappeared, shoved into a car with black-tinted windows, gotten out of the Russian jail, disappeared again. Even now, as a successful professor, she still left Texas for long stretches of time, always on the go to a developing nation to set up another school. He wouldn't be surprised if he got a call that she'd disappeared in a third-world nation, taken hostage or caught in a rebel war. Even his coworkers disappeared without warning, called up by Texas Rescue to work at the sites of natural disasters.

Aleksander Gregorivich hadn't been able to control his life, but Alexander Gregory could. He'd chosen one city he liked and settled there. He worked at one hospital. His role with Texas Rescue was to be the physician who stayed to man the home front, pulling extra shifts, covering for those who disappeared when the mobile hospital was needed. He was anchored firmly to one place. He knew better than to get involved with anyone who might leave.

He was involved with Grace Jackson, though.

She would leave.

Still, helping her out was the right thing to do. For a week, he'd help a woman who was being overwhelmed, and he wouldn't be shocked when she left. There'd be no tearing of his soul, no broken heart like there'd been when his father had refused to board the boat or when his mother had been handcuffed by the secret police of a crumbling government.

The bathroom maid spotted him before she could sling the bag of cosmetics into the suitcase. He waited until she'd placed the plastic bag in the suitcase with exaggerated carefulness, then zipped up the suitcase. He hefted it off the bed, amazed at what was considered an overnight bag for a movie star and her assistant, and turned to leave.

Grace was standing there, soft sweater on her body, golden highlights in her hair. She'd recovered. He could tell by her alert expression and the faint blush of pink on her cheeks as she thanked him for the juice.

"And thank you for letting us stay at your place. I'm sorry to keep bothering you."

"You're no bother at all."

In this moment, Alex was glad that when she left the hotel, she'd be leaving with him.

He could regret taking the risk later.

CHAPTER NINE

ALEX GREGORY WAS A MAN WHO KEPT HIS WORD.

Squashed up against him in the cab of his pickup truck, Grace could also tell he was a man who kept in shape.

It seemed that half the vehicles on Austin's roads were pickup trucks. Luckily, Alex's truck had a bench seat that could hold three people. Since it had been hardest for Sophia to get in the cab with her injured ankle and clunky cast boot, she had, reasonably enough, demanded the seat closest to the passenger door. Grace had to sit in the middle, and since Sophia kept complaining about how uncomfortable she was, wiggling to sit at an angle to stretch out her leg, Grace was quite firmly pushed up against Alex.

He moved his arm to hit the turn signal and flexed his thigh to apply the brakes. Under those shapeless scrubs, she felt some totally masculine musculature in motion. Grace studiously kept her gaze on the traffic light out the windshield, trying to look like she wasn't aware of the hard body that was making her feel so very feminine in contrast.

"Move over," Sophia demanded.

Grace didn't mind that demand at all.

Alex didn't seem to mind much, either. He actually had a bit of a smile playing around his lips. Grace wasn't certain what had happened up in the presidential suite to change his opinion, but Alex seemed less disapproving of Sophia. Slightly less, but it was a start.

Grace knew she didn't have the power to make two people fall in love, but if she could get Sophia to see what it was like to spend a little time with a man who treated her well, maybe she'd snap out of this phase. After a week with Alex, maybe she'd be able to see Deezee in a new light.

If I don't steal Alex first.

She twisted her fingers together in her lap. When had she started having such awful thoughts? She'd never been jealous of Sophia in her life. Men wanted Sophia. They always had; they always would.

But Alex...

Grace had assumed he'd come to the hotel tonight as an excuse to see Sophia, but he'd spent all his time sitting next to *her*, Grace, and talking to her. In fact, the only discussion he'd had with Sophia had been about her, about when she'd last eaten and whether or not she should drive.

Her cheek brushed against his shoulder as he turned the truck away from the city lights. Yep, there was solid muscle under those scrubs.

Was it really stealing a man if he preferred her to begin with? There was something about the way he'd offered his truck and his home that implied they were for Grace. *I've got a spare bedroom for you. We'll find something for your sister to sleep on, too.* It was as if Sophia was the afterthought. Grace noticed it, because for her entire adult life, she'd only gone to places that tolerated her because she was part of Sophia's entourage. Tonight, she couldn't help but think that, despite the way Sophia was hogging more than half the bench seat, Sophia was only being included because she was tagging along with Grace.

Alex liked *her*. Grace. She was almost certain of it, although she hadn't done anything differently to catch his attention. She'd just been herself, and Dr. Alex Gregory had noticed her. To please Deezee, Sophia had changed her nightlife, her friends, her clothes, even her way of talking.

See, Sophia? You don't have to compromise to make a man love you. And you don't have to be with a man who hates your sister, either.

Sophia made a sarcastic comment about something on the side of the road, and Alex actually laughed.

Grace had hoped Sophia would dump Deezee if she was attracted to a normal guy here in Texas. But as Alex's body brushed hers as he pulled into his driveway, she reevaluated that. Wouldn't it be just as effective if Sophia saw Grace fall for a normal guy? If Grace let herself be treated right by, say, a handsome doctor from Texas Rescue, wouldn't Sophia see that Deezee didn't treat her as well as her sister's boyfriend treated her?

Talk about indulging in a fantasy scenario—but as Alex walked around the hood of the truck to get the door for Sophia, it actually seemed possible.

Sophia was hesitant to jump down from the high cab. Alex, being so wonderfully tall, was able to slide an arm behind Sophia's back, scoop another under her knees and simply lift her out of the truck.

He set her gently on the ground. "You should be able to walk in that boot. Try it and see."

At the hotel, Sophia had hopped on one bare foot to the wheelchair, and then Grace had put her spike-heeled sandal on her good foot for her, to keep her as elegant-looking as possible for the fans with cell phones who would see them leave the hotel.

Now, Sophia stood up straight on her high-heel-wearing good leg, which meant the flat boot didn't even touch the ground. Everyone laughed. Grace scooted to the edge of the bench seat, ready to hop down herself, but Sophia didn't move. Instead, Alex took a knee in front of Sophia. She leaned against the door jamb as she gingerly put her weight on her boot.

Alex unbuckled her sandal for her. He was smiling, his shaggy hair falling over his forehead in an appealing way as he looked up at her sister. "I don't know how women wear these things even when they aren't injured."

Sophia's hand rested on his shoulder for balance as she lifted her foot. In her coat dress, she could be a modern-day princess, bestowing knighthood on a man at her feet. Or he could be on bended knee, ready to give her a diamond ring.

Grace swallowed. They did look good together.

"Heels make our legs look great, don't you think?" Sophia asked Alex.

"I understand *why* women wear them." He slipped off her sandal. He stood again, bringing his face level with Grace's as she sat in the truck cab, but he was laughing down at her sister. "I'm just glad I don't have to wear anything like that."

Sophia actually smiled, not an actress's smile, and Grace watched the two of them talking, blue eyes matching bespectacled blue eyes.

They surveyed the walkway to the door. The porch lights shone off a sea of river rocks. Stepping stones were spaced to create a path. Grace craned her neck a bit to look past Sophia's head. Sophia would have to treat the stepping stones like lily pads, hopping from one to another, if she couldn't put her foot down yet. The house was a 1930s Craftsman-style home, complete with concrete stairs leading up to its square-pillared entrance. It made a pretty intimidating obstacle course for someone on only one foot.

"Oh, boy..." Sophia wrinkled her nose and looked up at Alex once more. "Could you have just provided burning coals for me to cross?"

"It looks impossible, doesn't it?" Alex picked her up again, carrying her like she was a bride. Sophia actually looked grateful. She wrapped her arms around his neck, her sandal dangling from one finger.

Grace half slid off the bench seat, falling the last few inches to the ground to land squarely on her own feet. She didn't need a man to lift her or carry her or ease her pain.

Sophia did. Grace should let Sophia have what she needed. Sophia had raised her after their parents had died. She'd tried to cook their mother's recipes. She'd made Grace do her homework. She'd dropped out of college for her, and she'd kept her by her side ever since.

Grace would walk over hot coals for her sister. The least she could do, now that Sophia was noticing Alex, was to stop selfishly wishing she could keep Alex for herself.

She'd fix this. She wouldn't allow herself to fall for Alex— or, at least, not fall any farther than she already had.

The little stab to her chest was her own fault. She shouldn't have started the truck ride by letting herself fantasize about the man her sister needed.

I'm sorry, Sophia. I'll be good from now on.

Personal assistant. Sister. Grace couldn't even imagine herself as a competitor, not with the charismatic Sophia Jackson, not even for a man like Alex Gregory.

There was a beautiful woman in Alex's bed.

Too bad he was stretched out on his couch.

Technically, there were women in his beds, plural. His

house had two bedrooms, and each bed held a sleeping woman, but thoughts about only one of those women kept him awake. Grace Jackson, whom he'd thought he'd never see again at five o'clock this evening, was now sleeping on his pillow. The knowledge kept his body taut and his adrenaline too elevated for sleep.

Otherwise, his couch would work fine as a bed. One reason he'd bought the modern black couch was because it was extra long, an excellent trait in a piece of furniture when one fell asleep on the first available horizontal surface after the odd twenty-four hour shift. But he didn't think it was good enough for Grace. He'd insisted she take his bed.

Grace had resisted, of course. There'd been no question that Sophia would help herself to the guest room. She'd taken off her cast boot and hit the mattress, completely unconcerned about her sister, leaving Grace and Alex to work out the rest.

I'll share the guest room bed with her. It'll be like the old days.

The old days, like when we had the Plague? She's contagious. Take my bed.

He'd pulled out a change of sheets from his hall closet, and they'd made up his bed together, a strangely intimate chore he'd never done with any other woman. If he and Grace had come here for sex, they could have fallen into bed together. But since they weren't intimate and she was his houseguest, he'd pulled out a fresh set of sheets like a good host. And yet, plumping pillows, stretching sheets taut—it had felt like foreplay to him.

She probably thought he was a germaphobe. If she was generous, she might think he was a geeky doctor who cracked lame jokes about plagues and worried about upper respiratory tract infections in bed. Hell, he'd even reminded Sophia to wash her hands more often than usual until the antibiotics kicked in.

He shifted on the couch and scrubbed his hand over his face, feeling the heavy stubble again. He didn't look like a neat-freak germaphobe. He probably looked like a hippie who'd been lost in the wilderness for a week, scrounging in the woods for food.

In other words, Grace had no reason to lie awake on fresh sheets, obsessing about him.

He could not stop thinking about her.

In the light of day, he'd spent his time wondering why she was under sister's thumb. He understood a little better now that he'd seen some flashes of loyalty from Sophia. She'd backed up Grace when it came to the domestic violence case, a point that had softened his attitude toward Sophia just a bit.

But he knew the patterns and habits of domestic violence. He couldn't help but recognize the parallels in the way Sophia treated her own sister. Her own bad behavior was excusable—*I had pneumonia*—but Grace's failures were not—*You need to fix it, you need to move over, you need to find us a place to stay*—an unreasonable demand during South by Southwest. He'd dealt with enough domestic violence to see the one-sided relationship. Could Grace see it? Could he help Grace see it in the short time she'd be in his life?

Those were the thoughts that had consumed him while he and Grace were fully dressed and on their feet. Now, in the still of the night, his thoughts were considerably less philosophical. He was horizontal and half naked, wearing only plaid pajama pants. Grace was horizontal. Was she half-naked? Did she wear pajamas, comfortable and worn? Did she wear a nightgown, silky and new? Did she wear anything at all?

The possibility that Grace was sleeping nude between his sheets was the reason he was still awake. *Use your imagination*, he'd told Grace earlier, when they'd taken a break on the bench. He'd never expected to use his imagination tonight in quite this way, but it was easy to picture her. Grace was beautiful. Nothing like her sister, thank God. Sophia's sort of professional beauty was an achievement, a victory over nature. Grace's beauty was touchable, soft, genuine.

He'd had a great chance to check out her curves when she was pressed up against him in the truck. For once, he'd found Sophia's bossy routine amusing. Every time she'd barked *move over*, he'd wanted to say *thank you*.

He was paying for that pleasure now. The curve of Grace's shoulder, the way her hair felt as it swept over his own skin— he could imagine the angel in his bed all too vividly. His muscles were taut, demanding that he go to her. Muscle couldn't distinguish between the fantasy of what he'd like to do and the reality of what was acceptable. Sexually, he felt thick and full and aching for more.

He sat up, determined to get control so he could get some sleep. He headed for the kitchen and a midnight glass of milk.

The reality was, sharing a bed with Grace was off the table this week. She'd be heading back to California and a life that kept her tied to someone else, twenty-four hours a day. He yanked open the fridge door and blinked into the sudden light, deliberately obliterating the images he'd drawn in the dark. Cold air cooled the bare skin of his chest. Women who disappeared held no appeal for him.

Liar. She's got more appeal than you know what to do with.

He took the milk out of the fridge. In order to shut the door, he took a half step back, and backed right into Grace herself. He hadn't heard her come in to the narrow galley kitchen. She looked warm and rumpled and delicious in the appliance light.

Pajamas. The answer to his earlier question was pajamas. They weren't worn and comfortable, but satin. The material flowed over her body, white satin conforming to the shape of her breasts like liquid. His reaction to the sight of her couldn't be denied. He slammed the fridge door shut, plunging them both into blinding darkness. Retinal chemistry bought him time to fight another type of chemistry.

"I couldn't sleep," she said, her voice as appealing at midnight in his kitchen as it was at noon in the ER. Her feet were bare, which was probably why he hadn't heard her.

"Want a glass of milk?" His voice sounded stilted, stiff.

"Does milk really make you sleepy? Scientifically speaking?"

A medical question. How could she ask it in such a bedroom voice?

It was hard to not touch her, even if she thought of him as more of a doctor than a man. In one hand, he clutched the milk carton. He set his free hand on his hip rather than hers.

"It's a myth, but if it makes you feel better, have a glass. You could use the calories after forgetting to eat all day."

"I made up for it with the pizza tonight. Thank you for ordering that."

"You already thanked me."

She lapsed into silence. Had he been rude? His eyes were rapidly adjusting to the dark. There was a sheen to her pajama top in the small light from the microwave's clock. The aroused peak of her breast was not a trick of the light.

He tore his attention away from her body. If her vision was adjusting as fast as his, he didn't want to be caught staring at what he was craving.

"Sorry," she breathed quietly. "I'm in your way, aren't I?"

But she didn't move.

He realized she wasn't looking at his face at all. Her gaze was on his biceps, flexed as he held the milk carton. Her chest rose and fell with a quickening breath as her gaze moved across his body to his chest.

I can see you staring at me.

She moistened her lips, her eyes traveling lower, following a center line down his body, lingering in the area of his abs—his navel?—then lower.

You want me.

The knowledge changed the game. He knew what a woman wanted when her eyes went all heavy-lidded and her attention was all on his body. Grace's awareness redoubled his.

He wanted her, too. He'd wanted her all day.

She was going to leave, permanently. He even knew when she'd leave, but at this moment on this night, it didn't matter. Desire was obliterating his ability to think in the long term.

He watched her tentative fingertips reach for his body. The pad of her thumb brushed the bare skin of his waist as her fingertips trailed over the loose elastic of his flannel pants. He tossed the carton of milk onto the counter, startling her, so he used his now-empty hand to soothe her with a stroke down the soft length of her hair. He scooped a handful into his palm, all its golden highlights hiding in the dark. They were safe and alone at midnight, he and she.

"Grace." Her name sounded so much like a prayer, a husky benediction, a gift.

"I can't."

She stepped back, her hair sliding over his palm until it was gone. He let his hand drop to his side.

He wouldn't ask why not. He'd only met her today. Her sister had been brought in to the ER sometime after lunch; it was only midnight now. Less than twelve hours he'd known her, and in those twelve hours she'd been through stress of every kind.

All the more reason to hold her, his mind whispered. *Touch her, soothe her, make her worries disappear for a while.*

"I just can't," she whispered. She turned on her heel and disappeared.

That old feeling of abandonment was fleeting, because she hadn't truly disappeared. He knew where she was: in his bedroom, under his covers. Lying there, wanting him.

He almost gulped the ice-cold milk straight from the carton, but he had guests. He poured the milk into a glass and downed it in strong swallows, feeling the drink cool his mouth and throat. It didn't wash away the image of Grace on his pillow, in his room, *wanting him*.

He shook his head at his own intensity. They felt the same way about one another. If it was too soon tonight, there was still tomorrow. She wasn't leaving for a week. There were more midnights to be had. Time stretched before him, his ally.

He headed back to his couch to try again to sleep. The anticipation of spending tomorrow with Grace was a pleasure so sharp, it was nearly a pain in itself.

Wasn't that how life always worked? Pleasure followed by pain. Since childhood, he'd known that happy moments were followed by grief. A trip to the beach with Mama and Papa was followed by a raid on his home. Receiving a loaf of bread at a refugee camp was followed by a fistfight to defend it. He'd spent many years avoiding pain, which meant he'd spent many years avoiding pleasure.

But tomorrow...

He'd forgotten how intense the pleasure could be. The brush of a woman's fingertips and the softness of her long hair, the knowledge that she found him as desirable as he found her—those were things that could make joy explode in a man's chest.

He wanted to savor the joy.

He could deal with the carnage from the explosion later.

CHAPTER TEN

ALEX WOKE TO SUN SHINING THROUGH HIS patio door. The plants on his back porch were soaking it up, just as he'd calculated they would when he'd designed his landscape. Sun in the morning, shade in the afternoon, cactus flowers that bloomed at night.

Last night…

He was only slightly stiff from sleeping on the couch. It wasn't the first time he'd fallen asleep here, but it was the best reason he'd had for spending the night in his living room. He hadn't succumbed to exhaustion after hours in the ER. Instead, he'd slept on the couch in order to give Grace Jackson his bed—but at midnight, she'd been in his kitchen, letting her fingertips graze over his skin.

Today was going to be a good day. Dappled sun reflected off the racing bikes he kept mounted on the wall when he wasn't riding them. The polished concrete floor of his living room shone like clean glass. All was right with the world.

He had the day off work. He had a beautiful woman to get to know better. And then tonight...

He shouldn't get ahead of himself. It was only morning. Pancakes seemed like a good way to start a good day. Fortunately, he hadn't drunk all the milk last night—

A woman's sudden cry had him rolling to his feet on full alert.

"He can't! He couldn't!"

Princess Eva Picasso stumbled into his living room, blond and bare-footed, hopping and hissing in pain every other step, eyes glued to the phone in her hand.

Not a princess. This was no movie scene. Sophia was a real person, Grace's sister, and she had a look of absolute horror on her face. Alex instinctively took a step toward her, ready to help.

She looked up from her phone and seemed shocked to see him. "Where's Grace?"

"She slept in my room."

Abruptly, Sophia turned and headed down the hallway. Her first step made her yelp in pain, but she kept going around the corner. "Grace—oh, Grace. He's such a cheating bastard."

Alex heard his bedroom door open and slam shut.

He walked into the hallway and listened for a moment. He heard women's voices, one hysterical, one soothing. His idyllic day with Grace, he realized, had depended on Sophia staying in bed and sleeping through her pneumonia. Damn it. He'd been awake maybe sixty seconds, and his plans were already shot.

Sophia's presence jolted him back to reality. What had seemed possible in the dark looked unlikely now. Whatever the problem was, it hadn't been medical, but Sophia's dramatic reaction made it medical now. She'd undoubtedly bought herself another day or two in the cast boot by running through the house without wearing it.

Instead of whipping up pancake batter, he went into the kitchen and started putting ice in a plastic bag. Medical care was the only kind of help he had to offer. This emotional crisis was beyond his expertise.

He'd studied emotions from a medical standpoint, of course. Research had proven that unrelenting stress had health consequences. His childhood had been full of crises, which made it all the more important for him to keep his adulthood under control. The only stressor allowed in his life was his job.

That was enough. An emergency doctor's routine was never routine, although the chronic frustrations that were punctuated by high-adrenaline moments of trauma were predictable, in their way.

To balance his on-duty stress, he kept his off-duty life calm. His home was clean and uncluttered, his cycling events were planned and trained for months in advance, his diet was healthy. With a lifestyle built on that solid base, he didn't fear being derailed by an occasional indulgence: a beer with co-workers, a late night of billiards, pancakes with white flour and sugar.

A week with Grace Jackson.

He should be fine with a short-term fling, but as he sealed the plastic bag of ice, it didn't feel so simple. Which was he was afraid of—that the week wouldn't happen, or that it would?

Or that she could be the one indulgence that derails my life?

Impossible.

It'll happen when a goat eats a wolf, his mother's favorite phrase. He nodded to himself. A week with a woman, no matter how appealing she was, couldn't change his calm and orderly world.

Or could it? Yesterday, he'd spent his only break talking

with her on a bench. After work, he'd gone to her hotel to sit in on a police interview. He'd brought her into his home. He was tolerating the presence of a diva with pneumonia for her sake.

It's been less than twenty-four hours since you laid eyes on her. What do you think a week will do to you?

He threw the bag of ice onto the concrete floor, shattering the cubes.

He was in control. The crushed ice would conform to the ankle, reducing inflammation more efficiently. He bent down to scoop up the plastic bag, shook it out, and placed it flat in the freezer, ready for his patient when she emerged from the bedroom.

With her sister, of course. Grace would emerge after soothing Sophia and fetching her cast boot, at a minimum. She'd lose any trace of the early-morning sleepy look before he had a chance to savor it.

Poor Grace.

She didn't need a fling with him. She needed a new career, if not a new sister. Any kind of decent man would focus not on sleeping with her, but on helping her. That was the important matter. That was why he'd offered to take her in. To help her.

Alex pulled out an iron skillet and set it on the stove. He might as well make the pancakes. It was still his day off work. It was painfully obvious that Grace never had a day off work, but she could eat the pancakes, anyway. They'd be something comforting to balance the chaos of her life.

It was a shame she'd never know they'd been meant for seduction.

Grace ate her pancakes on the back porch, alone.

She had her reasons. For one, the backyard was a landscaping work of art, incorporating rocks and cactus and shade trees that she was certain would exceed any Californian's eco-friendly, water-conserving, xeriscaping standard. She needed the soothing surroundings because of reason number two: Sophia was being nice to Alex.

This morning, Alex had been concerned about Sophia, icing her ankle and bringing her pancakes after pouring exactly as much syrup as she'd requested. Thank goodness Grace hadn't done anything too stupid last night. He must not have been thinking sensual thoughts about her in the dark after all. It was obvious this morning that he cared for Sophia.

Incredibly, the odds of Sophia falling for Alex were much higher today because of reason number three: Deezee had cheated on Sophia. Photos of Deezee with some girl he'd met at a bar were all over the internet this morning.

The Deezee phase was abruptly over. Her sister was furious, and rightfully so, but Grace felt like the weight of the world had been lifted from her shoulders. She was afraid she'd burst into a round of the "Hallelujah Chorus," or at least smile, so she'd taken her plate of pancakes and headed outside. What kind of sister would she be if she was caught smiling at those incriminating photos?

In several of them, Deezee had been talking to an unidentified woman in a club, which wouldn't have been so damning if his hips hadn't been pressing her up against a wall as they talked. One showed them holding hands as they waited at a valet stand. Somehow, the hand-holding one looked more intimate to Grace than the wall one. In a final blow, someone had snapped him disappearing into a hotel room with his arm around the same girl, who barely looked old enough to be legal despite her very adult dress.

The dress was revealing and cheap, a knit with crooked seams being worn a size too small, something which Sophia had actually noticed. *She's got no class, no style, no money. She's not even a celebrity. What was he thinking? She can't be any help to him at all.*

Grace had refrained from hazarding a few guesses about what Deezee had been thinking. It seemed pretty obvious what kind of help Deezee expected the girl to be.

Grace ran the pad of her thumb along the rim of her plate. As tempting as it was to throw stones at Deezee, she felt terribly exposed in her own glass house. Last night, she'd been thinking about the same thing. Deezee had been dating one woman, but touched another. Not so different from Grace, who'd chosen one man for Sophia, but wanted to touch him for herself.

Wanted to? She *had* touched Alex. Very briefly, but the sensation was burned into her fingertips. Grace had fallen asleep believing he wanted her, too. He'd touched her hair, hadn't he?

Her hair. In the morning sunshine, she felt like an idiot. When a man desired a woman, really burned for her with passion, the only time he touched her hair was in some kind of a historical film, set in an era when a woman's hair was the only part of her body not covered in an acre of cloth. Grace had read way too much into it. He'd just brushed his hand down her hair the same way one might soothe a dog or cat.

Thank goodness she'd chickened out and run away. No harm done. He'd been able to serve her pancakes today with a friendly smile.

She should have been able to take the plate from him the same way, with no embarrassment at all, but no. She'd babbled something about how Austin had such mild weather and then she'd run outside.

Talk about a temporary solution. She couldn't stay out here

for a week. She couldn't even stay for half an hour. Her sister needed her.

She peeked over her shoulder into the house. Through the sliding glass door, she could see her sister sitting on the couch, her head bowed with grief. Alex hadn't stayed to eat with her, after all. Grace felt guilty for leaving her alone. She should be there, helping her pick up the pieces. At least she and her sister wouldn't constantly be at odds anymore, now that the Deezee phase was over. It was time to go back inside.

Sophia didn't look up as Grace shut the sliding glass door behind herself. Her posture was so abject, Grace's guilt doubled. "How are you doing, Sophie?"

Sophia shrugged.

Grace came closer and saw the phone in Sophia's hand. Irritation warred with guilt. Alex probably would have sat with her while they ate, if only Sophia had been polite enough to make conversation with a human.

"Ready for more pancakes?" Alex called from the kitchen.

Sophia ignored Alex totally. Not wanting to be rude, Grace pretended she had an appetite. "That would be great, thank you."

She carried her plate into the kitchen. Alex was eating as he leaned against the counter, plate in one hand, fork in the other, finishing off a short stack. He smiled at her. "Eat them while they're hot, right?"

Something was hot, all right. She'd changed into jeans and a beige blouse, but Alex was still wearing the loose-fitting plaid pants from last night, the same eyeglasses from the day before. He'd added a blue T-shirt that hugged his body. His hair and beard might be scruffy, but that body was tight.

She'd dreamed about that body. What a surprise for her senses last night had been, walking into the kitchen to find him bare-chested in the light of the refrigerator. She'd already guessed in the truck that there was more muscle under those scrubs than met the eye, but she hadn't been prepared for quite *that* athletic of a physique. Clearly, when a doctor's white coat had to be big enough to fit a large chest size, the manufacturer assumed the coat needed to fit an even larger waist. He'd been hidden by an extra yard of white material yesterday. Not now.

He popped the last forkful in his mouth, set down his plate and pushed away from the counter. "The pan's already hot. They'll be ready in just a minute."

There was definitely no flab on that waist. She'd touched those six-pack abs.

"I like a girl with an appetite," he said, and she forced herself to stop ogling his body and look at his face instead. He was smiling.

What did he like? Oh—a girl with an appetite. She set her plate on the counter next to his. "I'll go ask Sophia how many more she wants, then."

His smile dimmed and he turned back to his frying pan. "She'll have to wait for the next batch. These are yours."

Once he shook them out of the pan and onto her plate, the weight of the iron skillet causing his biceps to flex in a rounded bulge, he didn't pour any more batter. He set the pan down, pushed his glasses up with one knuckle and walked the few steps to the entrance to the living room.

"Sophia, do you want any more pancakes?"

No answer.

"Sophia." Alex sounded more like a father speaking to a child than a man wooing a woman.

Grace hurried to smooth things over. "She probably didn't hear you."

Alex shot her a look that made her feel how weak her excuse was for her sister's rudeness. What had happened? Sophia had started the morning being nice to Alex while he'd iced her ankle. Usually, when her mood soured this suddenly, it meant she'd just gotten off the phone with Deezee. Surely, she hadn't been texting Deezee just now.

Sophia tossed her phone aside. "That screen is too small. Go get my iPad."

"Okay," Grace said. She started to duck around Alex, but he stopped her with a hand on her arm.

"Eat your pancakes first. They'll get cold."

"Oh." She looked from him to Sophia, not sure which one to listen to, but she'd been obeying Sophia far longer. "I know right where it is. Be back in one second."

She felt his disapproval when she returned with the iPad and handed it to her sister. She wished he hadn't seen Sophia's bossy side. Or maybe, she wished he hadn't seen her being so…subservient. She was just being a good assistant, making sure her boss had her devices when she needed them and where she needed them. Honestly, she was only practicing common decency, doing a small favor for someone with a badly sprained ankle. It was no big deal, any way one looked at it.

Then why did she feel like she'd been taken advantage of?

Alex came into the living room and handed her the plate. She gave him a lukewarm smile and ate some equally lukewarm pancakes.

Sophia could have phrased her request a little differently. *Hey, Gracie, when you're done eating, could you do me a favor and bring me my iPad?* Grace probably still would've gotten her the iPad immediately, but at least she wouldn't have looked like she was…inferior.

Subservient. Inferior.

She couldn't eat another bite.

"Martina will be here in a minute," Sophia said without taking her eyes off her screen. "Do we have any vodka?"

That snapped Grace out of her funk. She pulled her phone out of the back pocket of her jeans to check for messages from the publicist. "Martina's in town? She didn't call me to set up a meeting. What's this about?"

"Deezee. She'll make him straighten up."

Grace was stunned into silence. The publicist could spin a lot of mistakes, but not this. Deezee had been caught in a hotel with another woman. The damage had been done.

Grace knelt down to her sister's level. "Why?"

"She's coming because I called her."

Sophia had to know that wasn't what she'd been asking, but Grace didn't know how to start a real conversation with her anymore. At any rate, it would be wise to have Martina write some kind of statement for the press announcing that Sophia and Deezee were no longer a couple. But...

"Did Martina know he was going to be caught? Did she arrange it?"

"Are you crazy? This makes Deezee look bad. This makes me look bad."

"How else could she get here so soon from California?"

"She's in town for that South-by thing. There's a lot of people here."

Grace knew that *people* meant people who had power in the entertainment industry. *I told you it was a big event, but you didn't believe me.*

"So do we have vodka or what?"

Grace didn't look at Alex. She knew her cheeks were hot with embarrassment. "I don't know, Sophia. This isn't our house. Don't you think we ought to meet Martina at a restaurant or something?"

"No." Sophia was indignant, but at least she looked up from

her screen. "For the amount of money we're paying her, she ought to come to me."

"Yes, but you can't host someone in a house that doesn't belong to you. Alex might want to use his own house for something this morning. We might be in his way."

"I've got a cast on, for God's sake. I'm not going anywhere. I don't want to be photographed like this." She looked up from her phone to fix teary eyes on Grace. "Besides, it really hurts to walk, even with the boot on."

It was no use. Sophia had too many points to back up her obstinacy, and it was Grace who had to be flexible. She turned to Alex, forced to apologize for Sophia. "I'm so sorry about this. It's just one woman coming to talk business with Sophia, and she's already on her way. We'll try to keep it short. I didn't mean to invade your house on your day off."

Alex looked at her with those blue eyes for a long moment. "I know you didn't."

"Vodka," Sophia said.

I cannot believe I'm having to ask this.

"And do you happen to have any vodka on hand?"

Alex walked right past her and stood over Sophia. "I'm not serving you vodka. You're on pain medicine and antibiotics. Neither one goes well with alcohol."

Sophia tossed her hair back and looked up at him. "It's not for me. It's for my publicist. That's her trademark. She always has a vodka and tonic when she takes a meeting. And yes, before you say it, I know it's only nine in the morning. That's what makes it a memorable trademark."

Alex ran his hand over his bearded jaw in a move that looked like he was trying to restrain himself. Grace held her breath, afraid of the showdown that was surely coming.

Sophia capitulated. "You know what? We're not in public, so it's not like anyone will see her. Don't worry about the vodka."

"Thanks."

Grace could taste the sarcasm dripping from that one word. Alex turned his back on Sophia. Grace thought he was headed for her, but he only passed her on the way to the master bedroom.

"I'll be in the shower," he muttered.

The bedroom door slammed before she could offer to clear her things out of his way. Quickly, she pictured how she'd left the bedroom. She'd left it neat enough, only her white pajamas lying across the bed. That shouldn't aggravate him any more than he already was.

Her tote bag was under the coffee table. She retrieved her notepad just as the doorbell rang.

"Get that."

Grace straightened abruptly. *Did you think I expected you to jump off the couch and hobble over there yourself?*

But she swallowed the sarcastic question. Maybe Alex could get away with it, but she never could. There was no sense in confronting Sophia, anyway. Once the Deezee effect wore off, her sister would stop being so rude and bossy.

The phase was over. It just didn't feel like it yet. But if Sophia didn't change her attitude soon, there would no longer be a question of whether or not Alex had a chance with her. Judging by this morning's exchange, it was Sophia who wouldn't have a chance with Alex.

What kind of sister would feel so hopeful about that?

CHAPTER ELEVEN

"WHAT DO YOU MEAN, HE ISN'T GOING TO APOL-ogize? He has to apologize."

Sophia's tantrum was directed at her publicist, but it was loud enough that Grace feared Alex could hear it through the walls and over the sound of running water in his shower.

"Don't yell at Martina." The words were out before Grace thought. Of course, Sophia would now do the opposite. It was rapidly becoming clear that Sophia was acting more like Deezee than ever, now that he'd cheated on her. Grace was baffled.

On cue, Sophia shouted, "I'll speak however I goddamned please."

Martina pointed at Sophia with her stylus. "Not when you are anywhere that anyone could possibly hit the record button on their cell phone. Your boyfriend could never get that through his thick head, and I'm washing my hands of him. You, I expect more from."

"You're firing Deezee?" Sophia was so aghast, she only seemed to have enough air to whisper.

"I fired him this morning. I don't keep clients that refuse my advice."

Sophia sat up a little straighter and set her phone aside.

Grace tried to keep a neutral expression on her face, a poker face like Alex, hoping no one could see how irritated she was with Martina's tactics. The publicist's ability to intimidate Sophia was useful, in its way. She'd kept Sophia from completely committing career suicide several times during the past three months, but Grace still didn't trust Martina.

Martina was the reason that Sophia had met Deezee this winter. Sophia and Grace had taken a week off in Telluride, a ski resort centered on a tiny Colorado mining town that was a haven for billionaires and A-list celebrities, one of whom had hired DJ Deezee Kalm to set up a rave in an old warehouse. Grace hadn't been enthralled by the neon lights and electronic dance music, so she'd stayed off the dance floor. So had Martina.

Within half an hour, Martina had found out for whom Grace was a personal assistant. The rest was history. Martina had introduced Sophia to the DJ that night, while he was in all his glory, standing on a stage and controlling a crowd with music. Martina had arranged for them to have an intimate lunch for two the next day in an excruciatingly expensive man-made snow cave. It had been money well spent. Now Martina was Sophia Jackson's publicist, as well.

That was Hollywood. Considering the way Grace had been befriended for an introduction and Deezee had practically been prostituted in order to achieve that goal, being Hollywood was awfully close to being Machiavellian.

"Couldn't you have released his apology before you fired him?" Sophia asked.

"Darling, when I fire a man, I refuse to spend another moment on him."

Grace wanted to set the record straight. As his publicist, Martina couldn't have fired Deezee: she was his employee. Martina might have decided not to work for him anymore, but that was *quitting*, and she'd quit when her client needed her most.

The *firing* verbiage worked on Sophia, though. She was blinded by the way Martina conducted herself, unable to see that it was Sophia's money, therefore it was Sophia's power. That was Hollywood, too.

"So what are we going to do?" When she didn't know she was the boss, Sophia pouted and whined like a child to get her way. "I don't wanna look like a loser. Everyone is laughing at me."

Thank goodness Alex wasn't in the room to hear this. Whiney Sophia wasn't necessarily preferable to Bossy Sophia.

"We will do nothing," Martina said. "Rumors die more quickly when you don't respond."

"I have to say nothing?" Sophia sounded like a kid saying *I have to eat broccoli?* "It's not a rumor when there are photos."

The sound of water running in the shower stopped. If they didn't get a plan together and conclude this meeting, Alex was going to witness everything. Despite the modern feel of his house, the 1930s floor plan had been preserved, and houses hadn't been built very large in the 1930s. The kitchen was separated from them by a wall, but there was a pass-through to the little dining area, which connected to this living room. He'd have to share this space with them, unless he stayed in the bathroom for a very, very long while.

Sophia took up the entire couch to keep her cast boot elevated, of course. Martina had enthroned herself in the large armchair. That left Grace to use one of the little dinette chairs. She'd carried it over to the couch, so she could sit next to Sophia. She ought to bring one over for Alex soon. She didn't think he was a man who'd hide in his own bedroom.

"We have to come up with something for me to say," Sophia said. "Have you read the comments on the photos? Everyone is wondering how bad I must be in bed if Deezee would cheat on someone who looks like me with someone who looks like her. Fix this."

Martina, her dark red lips forming a displeased line at receiving an order, clipped her stylus to her tablet.

Sophia froze, not even daring to cough, clearly afraid Martina was about to fire her. Grace held her breath, too, but she felt something closer to hope than fear. Sophia didn't seem to be actually sad about losing Deezee, and if they could lose Martina, as well...

"After all, you're the best publicist in the industry." Sophia spoke the hyperbole meekly, then lapsed into her anxious silence.

With her audience suitably subdued, Martina spoke. "We can release a statement. You'll say that of course you've seen the photos, but they don't concern you. It was never serious between you and Deezee."

Grace's patience ran out. She didn't want to be abusing Alex's hospitality with this meeting. She didn't want Alex to hear her sister whining. Most of all, she didn't want to stay silent while Martina gave her sister bad advice in return for good money.

"No one will believe it was never serious," Grace said. "Sophia and Deezee were photographed kissing at the beach the day before yesterday. You made sure of it."

Sophia looked at her like she was a table lamp that had suddenly offered an opinion.

Remember when you used to ask my opinion on everything, Sophia?

Sophia reached for Grace's arm. "Remind me. Which outlets showed those beach photos?"

Grace kept a list on her own tablet device, of course, along with screen shots whenever she spotted her sister on gossip blogs and entertainment media. With Martina glaring daggers at her, Grace dropped her gaze to her tote bag, which was still sitting under the coffee table. She'd have to literally bow down before Sophia and Martina to reach it and retrieve her tablet.

She heard the bedroom door open. Alex would walk in as she was crawling. *Subservient. Inferior.*

She made no move toward her tote bag. Instead, she looked back at Martina, and hoped her poker face wasn't as nonexistent as Alex had said it was. "Let's look at your list of the media outlets you were successful with."

After a long moment, Martina unclipped her stylus once more. "Of course. This is what I'm here for."

This is what we pay you for.

Sophia gave Grace a little pat, then slowly rolled her booted foot from left to right as she listened to Martina's list. Grace watched the motion with pleasure; that pat had felt like sisterly approval.

Alex must have passed behind her on his way to the kitchen, for she heard the sound of a drawer opening, the rattle of silverware. She guessed he was putting away the breakfast dishes.

"Obviously, then, everyone knows we were serious. Pretending we weren't won't fix this." Sophia sounded more like the pre-Deezee version of herself. No whining, thank goodness.

"I'll come up with a way for you to get the most mileage out of this bad publicity." Martina tapped her stylus on her tablet at the same rapid pace that she tapped her spiked heel on the polished concrete floor.

We didn't need anyone to handle bad publicity until you brought bad publicity into our lives.

The kitchen sounds had stopped. Grace peeked over her shoulder. Alex was sitting down at the dinette table with his back to them, intent on a newspaper. He was being so polite, giving them a sense of privacy, but he had to be able to hear every word.

Martina's stylus and her heel both went still. "The mystery is this trip to Texas. You're dropping out of the public eye for a week. Why? We can spin it so that you left Hollywood to visit a hot new lover in Texas. You abandoned Deezee, you see. You left first. If you'd already found another man *before* last night, then this girl becomes nothing more than his rebound girl. She's a consolation prize, or a woman Deezee was only using to assuage the pain of *his* broken heart."

"And she's so hideous, the fact that he went from someone like me to someone like her will make him look desperate."

Grace cringed. When she and Alex had talked on that bench yesterday, she'd bragged about her sister's lack of snobbery.

"What do you think, Grace?"

Her sister was actually asking for her input. It felt like it had been years instead of months since she'd been treated like a part of her sister's team instead of her sister's errand girl.

Martina steamrolled over Grace's chance to offer her opinion. "It's the best option. You stay hidden, and I'll let it be known that you are not to be expected to attend any South-by events, because you're on something of a honeymoon with your new man."

Grace glanced at Alex's back again. Had he heard Sophia ask for her advice? She wanted him to believe what she'd told him yesterday, that her sister was a good person and a hard worker who deserved her success—and who deserved Grace's loyalty.

"I think a fake boyfriend is a dangerous idea." Grace scooted her chair so that she was facing Sophia more squarely. "You know what they say. If there's no photo, it didn't happen. Eventually, when no photos of a mystery man in Texas surface, you'll end up looking desperate, so desperate that you made up a fake boyfriend. Don't risk it. Your reputation always was that you're smart and mature."

"Was?" Only Sophia could put so many nuances of emotion in that one syllable.

"That's why it caused a sensation when you started dating Deezee. He wasn't the kind of guy people expected Sophia Jackson to date."

"It was a brilliant move," Martina said. "It got you tons of exposure."

It was time for Grace to do some steamrolling herself. "Dating him changed your public image, but not for the better. If the industry is already less confident that you are the smart and mature actress they thought you were, then imagine what will happen to you if word gets out that you made up a whole fake boyfriend scenario. Professionally, it could be a disaster."

Sophia looked from her to Martina. "Grace is right."

Grace is right.

Grace's hands were shaking again. Thanks to Alex's pancakes, she knew it wasn't low blood sugar. It was sheer relief. She'd just fought for her sister's career against an experienced publicist, and she'd won. She sat back, sagging in relief as much as she could in a hard chair.

Martina stood and began pacing. "Then we need to arrange for you to be seen. That hideous boot comes off in a week, correct?"

"I'll still have to wear an ankle wrap." Sophia shot a look at Alex's back. "And the doctor says no high heels for two more weeks after that."

Martina checked her tablet without slowing her steps. "There's a black-tie event put on by a few oh-so-worthy causes toward the end of South-by. A charity gala. Tell your stylist you need one of those hems that puddles on the ground, so no one will see you're wearing flats."

Grace picked up her trusty notebook. It was time to make a list and get this meeting adjourned, so Alex wouldn't have to politely ignore people in his own house any longer.

"I'll contact the stylist," she said. "The messaging is everything. We need a gown that a smart and mature woman would wear who wasn't pining after a cheating boyfriend. It shouldn't look desperate, like she's trying too hard. Something that says she's confident being out in public alone."

"Alone?" Sophia and Martina both looked at her like she was a bizarre talking table lamp again.

"She needs to be seen with a new man, so it's not just a rumor," Martina said. "She'll be a surprise celebrity at the event, and she'll have a surprise boyfriend on her arm. This will solve the mystery of why she's disappeared in Texas. The press will eat it up."

"What man do you have in mind?" Sophia asked. "Is there anyone still in the closet who'd like to appear devoted to me?"

Grace didn't dare turn around to see Alex's reaction to that. She spoke as quietly as she could to her sister. "I thought you said I was right about avoiding the fake boyfriend?"

"You were right that rumors about a fake boyfriend weren't enough. We need an actual man for photos, someone who is here in Texas to justify why I flew down in the first place, *before* Deezee cheated on me."

Martina gestured toward the flat-screen television, as if she could bring its black, powered-off screen to life with a dramatic flourish of her hands. "I can see the gossip shows now. 'Sophia Jackson has a secret rendezvous in Austin.' A classy gown, a handsome mystery man. It will sink Deezee and his tawdry hotel girl. Sink him."

She was totally focused on defeating the man who'd once been her most famous client. He'd only been a stepping stone to Sophia.

Grace gave up trying to look bold. "Deezee is going to be angry. He's unpredictable when he's angry."

Sophia dropped her head back on the couch, looking tired. "Well, then, we need someone brave enough to weather his crap. Better yet, we need someone who won't care if Deezee goes on a rant about him."

Grace doodled in a corner of her notebook. "Someone with no reputation left to save? I don't think you should be paired with another loose cannon."

Martina stopped next to Grace. "Sophia means someone who isn't in the industry at all. Deezee couldn't hurt someone who didn't need to impress the press."

And you wouldn't have to deal with another celebrity's angry publicist, would you?

Sophia had her eyes closed now, pneumonia wiping her out. "It's hard to find someone who isn't in the industry. Grace had a point about reviving that smart and mature approach, although *mature* is the absolutely wrong word to use."

"Let's say *down-to-earth*, shall we?" Martina said. "We need someone normal. An everyday man, making Sophia Jackson seem approachable, someone women identify with. Someone men think they might actually stand a chance with."

Sophia opened one eye. "But Mr. Normal Guy will have to be attractive. Hard body. Not old."

Grace glanced over her shoulder. Alex was still sitting with his back to them. His hair was damp from his shower, almost black against the nape of his neck, longer than it had looked at the hospital. He wore a red T-shirt that was so worn, it had faded to a pinkish mud color. He looked down-to-earth to her. Not old. And last night, in the light of the refrigerator, he'd definitely had a hard body.

Martina kept talking. "So, we need a man who is respectably employed but not tycoon-wealthy who lives here in Texas who is the right age and who is straight and single and willing to pretend he's dating Sophia Jackson. And we need to find him today, tomorrow at the latest."

A moment of silence followed that.

This is my sister. I have to try one more time.

Grace clenched her notepad in her hands. "Or we could try the truth. Deezee was a lousy boyfriend, which you found out when you flew down for the Texas Rescue grand-opening ceremony."

No one answered her. Behind her, she heard Alex shove his chair away from the table.

Martina was glued to her tablet screen now, as obsessed as Sophia usually was with her phone. "This black-tie event benefits several causes, including Texas Rescue. Absolutely perfect. Your trip begins and ends with a Texas Rescue event, and you'll have a secret getaway with a hot guy in the middle."

Grace felt Alex's presence behind her. Martina did a little double take when she looked from her tablet to the man standing behind Grace's chair.

"Alex," he said over Grace's head, the briefest of introductions. "I live here. If you're referring to next week's Black and White Ball, it's sold out."

"They won't turn Sophia Jackson away."

He addressed her sister directly. "You can have my ticket if you need it. West Central is one of the beneficiaries, as well. Part of the proceeds are going to help replace those curtains in the ER with walls. I'm sure you'll want to help make it a success."

Sophia opened both eyes then. "Like I care. I'm never going to be your patient again."

"Glad to hear it."

Grace wasn't sure how to interpret that. Maybe he meant that he was glad Sophia wasn't his patient, because he couldn't date a patient.

Martina dismissed Alex with a flick of her fingers. "There is no question that she can go to the ball. Now we just have to pick out which guy she should take." She sat down on the armrest of the couch, nestling right next to Sophia, like they were sisters about to share a Netflix marathon on her tablet.

Grace had to scoot her chair closer to the sofa to be able to see the screen, as well. Alex was behind her still. It would take more than Martina's finger flick to make him move if he didn't feel like it.

Martina ignored them, cozy with her client. "The only positive photos of you on social media for the past three months were taken with Texas Rescue yesterday."

I arranged that photo op.

No one thanked her.

"Let's review that ribbon-cutting group photo." Martina pointed at the screen. "How about him?"

Of course, she'd pointed at the most obviously handsome guy. Grace shook her head. "Thor? He's not interested in Sophia."

Sophia roused herself, offended. "Says who?"

"You didn't like him, either. He's the paramedic that actually rode with you in the back of the ambulance."

"Oh, him. I'm an actress. I can pretend I like him."

Martina had already moved on. "There are three firefighters. This one is too young."

Grace felt Alex step closer behind her. On top of everything else, she now had to suffer while he listened to her sister sort through all his friends like they were her personal shopping catalog. This wasn't going to put Sophia in her best light.

"This one's too old," Sophia announced.

Charming, Sis. Just charming.

Martina tilted her head and considered the photo. "But very distinguished. A little Clooney gray at the temples. He could add some gravitas to your reputation."

"Too old." Sophia tapped the last fireman with her fingernail. "This one's just right. Looks about thirty. Confident. Photographs well."

Alex bent so close, Grace could feel the rumble of his deep voice as he spoke over her shoulder. "That's Luke. He's married to the director of Texas Rescue."

"Buzz kill," Sophia muttered, as if Alex had arranged for this Luke to be married just to spoil her day.

"How about one of the doctors?" Martina asked. "They get instant respect as soon as you say their name. Imagine yourself saying 'I'm here with Dr. John Doe from Texas Rescue.' This one looks perfect."

"All those guys are married and happy about it. Some of the women in that photo are single, though." Alex sounded a little sarcastic to Grace's ear.

Martina set the tablet in her lap. "Here's a story. 'Sophia Jackson has a female fling, a girlfriend with benefits, taking a break after all the drama of dating men, most recently DJ Deezee Kalm.' We could work that angle."

Alex stood up straight again, leaving Grace's shoulder feeling cold. "You don't decide to change your sexual orientation for a week. That's not how it works."

"It's called experimentation," Martina said, sounding condescending. "Very Bohemian and naughty in my day, but now it's almost *de rigueur*. Still, if any of these women were inclined…"

Grace hated her blush, but she hated even more that Alex was witnessing this. They were in his house, though. She couldn't ask him to leave his own living room.

"I want to be seen with a man," Sophia said. "Thirty-ish. A doctor would work."

They were describing Alex. He was standing right here. It wasn't like either woman to beat around the bush, but maybe they were hoping he'd volunteer.

"It sounds like you're talking about Alex," she said, wanting to get this over with. "Dr. Alex Gregory."

Sophia dismissed her with a wave of her hand. "The man has to be drop-dead gorgeous to make it believable that I'd leave Deezee for him."

Grace felt all the pain of that insult, but more, the unfairness of it. She dared to turn her head far enough to see how Alex was taking it. He was really very handsome underneath all that scruffy…

Oh, my.

All that scruffiness was gone. Alex had shaved. His hair, still wet from the shower, was slicked back. With those dark-framed glasses…

Martina had twisted around, too, and was openly studying Alex. "Actually, he's got a very Clark Kent vibe going."

Grace's breath caught—it was what she'd thought from the first.

Martina tapped her stylus. "Which means we could turn him into Superman."

Sophia slid farther down the couch, settling in for a nap. "Be serious."

"I am," Martina said, her voice as sharp as the points of her designer pumps. "Open your eyes, Sophia."

She obeyed, craning her neck to check out her host. "Oh."

"*Oh*, indeed. Clark turned into Superman in seconds, but thankfully, we've got a whole week." Martina stood and tossed her tablet on the couch. "Well, I'm positively parched. Someone get me a vodka tonic."

No one moved.

Grace couldn't stop staring at clean-shaven Alex, but his neutral expression was impossible to read.

"He hasn't agreed to anything, Martina," she said.

Martina only laughed. "Well, Dr. Gregory, are you ready to become the most interesting man in Texas?"

CHAPTER TWELVE

"NO."

Alex crossed his arms over his chest, refusing to cower or cringe as three women evaluated him solely on his looks. He knew how to act like he didn't care: tall kids who wore glasses and spoke with Russian accents had to learn quickly in high school.

"That's all you have to say?" The woman named Martina looked exactly as he expected a behind-the-scenes show business shark to look. She was what he'd expected Sophia's assistant to be. "I'm offering you the chance to walk the red carpet with one of America's hottest stars, and all you can say is no?"

"No, thank you."

"Very funny."

At least Martina got his sarcasm.

He looked at Grace, the voice of reason in this group. Her knuckles were nearly white as she clutched her notebook. He hated to see her so anxious. She'd done such a good job defending her sister and taking on Martina, even if she'd lost the battle over this publicity stunt.

"Do you have someone in your life, then?" Martina persisted. "Someone you're afraid to make jealous?"

"No."

"You'll be compensated for your time away from work, of course. I hear those med-school student loans are such a burden. Young doctors are drowning in debt, they say."

The loans weren't fun, certainly, but a substantial portion of his medical school had been covered by scholarships. As Chief Resident during his last year, he'd earned a higher salary than the other young doctors-in-training. His house was the right size for a bachelor. He had one high-end pickup truck and two carbon-fiber road bikes. He was doing just fine.

Ms. Hollywood Shark was taking the wrong path to persuade him. The day he paid off a med-school loan by dressing up as a starlet's boy toy was the day he needed to turn in his man card.

Grace was looking at him with that same look she'd had in the ER's kitchen. Fear, worry—and hope. She was facing a mess, and she hoped he'd be able to help her fix it.

Of course, anything that hurt Sophia's acting career would hurt Grace, too. That was unfortunate, but still not a reason to make him play their game. This entire conversation had only driven home the point that an actress's life was inherently self-absorbed. He didn't feel obligated to support that.

"Grace will arrange your clothing," Martina decreed. "I don't know how much a personal trainer can do in a week, but try."

He had a landscape project to finish this week. The only thing he could use a personal trainer for was as an extra set of hands to haul wheelbarrows of gravel.

"A haircut. A facial. Spray tan. I expect him to be able to

dance," Sophia said between coughs that sounded fractionally better than yesterday's.

Grace spoke to her sister. "You don't sound like you'll be dancing a week from today." Then she looked to him, trusting him to have the answers. "Will she?"

"It's possible, at least for a song or two, if she doesn't do anything crazy. Shortness of breath or pain in the ankle are pretty obvious signs it's time to stop."

"I'll be ready. Get him dance lessons. Be sure the photographers are told ahead of time to expect me to dance. It's the easiest way to make a couple look more romantically involved than they are."

Grace opened her notebook and started writing.

Something inside him snapped. Grace was Sophia's personal assistant, and that meant she'd execute this fake boyfriend plan to the best of her ability, whether she agreed with it or not. Whether Sophia appreciated her hard work or not.

Whether he was the fake boyfriend or not.

He'd advised her to find a new job, but she'd explained that her boss was her sister, as if that made it okay for her to put up with being treated badly. *Family.* Sometimes, a family member could calm a frightened patient, but it was just as likely that the family member made the problem worse, like a father who pushed his son to play soccer the day after an injury. *Family* made people stay in bad situations, even when it was a family member who hurt them and caused them pain. People like Mrs. Burns.

His mother.

Grace.

He walked around the couch and looked out the sliding glass doors, letting his focus settle on the shapes of the cactus he'd protected throughout a freezing winter. Behind him, Martina took a phone call as Sophia continued to dictate the list of her wants and needs. He stared at his cactus and tuned them out.

He wasn't being logical about this. He couldn't equate Grace's situation with women who'd been physically hurt by the family members who supposedly loved them. There was no assault and battery. Grace was in no physical danger here.

He turned around to watch her writing with her white-knuckled grip on her pen, hunched in her hard chair while the others lounged on upholstery, and he felt a quiet fury all the same. Of all the people in this room, only one was anxious and stressed and unhappy. The one who wanted the best for someone who didn't care how she felt in return. The one who was expected to do the most work and sit in the least comfortable chair.

That one was Grace. There was no violence, but Alex recognized other similarities. She was kept in line with scraps of attention. She was ignored until any reasonable person would leave, and then thrown an almost-apology. *I really took it out on you—we didn't know I had pneumonia, though, did we?* She was condescendingly allowed to have made a good point. *Grace had a point—although* mature *is the absolutely wrong word to use.* It was just enough to keep Grace hoping that if she stayed a little longer, her sister would treat her better. *It won't happen again.*

How could he make Grace see how warped that pattern was? Her job and her family were making her miserable. She ought to be doing something she found more rewarding, whatever that might be. As it was, she was so busy running and fetching that he doubted she'd had the chance to be alone with her own thoughts. She needed time to evaluate where she was and where she wanted to be.

He could give that to her.

He spoke to the group as a whole. "I haven't agreed to escort Sophia to the Black and White Ball."

Sophia stopped whining. Martina stopped texting.

Alex spoke evenly, without emotion, as he'd been doing since childhood. "As you said, my time is valuable."

"Which is why we'll pay you," Martina replied. "You'll be allowed to keep the clothing, as well. Any jewelry will have to returned, of course."

"I have commitments during my days off work which I can't ignore. If I have to spend time preparing for your project, then I'll need someone to spend time on my projects in return. I want to be paid for my time by being given time."

"You want me to visit the hospital, whoop-de-doo." Sophia managed to sound both vain and world-weary at the same time.

"I want Grace's time in return for my own."

"Grace's?" Sophia tipped over, going from sitting to horizontal on the couch. "Okay, fine. I don't care. It's a deal."

"It isn't your deal to make, Sophia. If Grace agrees, then you and I need to clarify that if Grace is working with me, then she won't be around to fetch and carry for you. I don't want her to work any more hours than she already does. Once she puts in eight or nine hours in a day, whether it's with me or with you, she's done."

"Whatever. I'm so effing tired, I just want to sleep."

He walked around the couch to stand before Grace and held out his hand for a formal shake. "I'm willing to give you my time if you're willing to give me yours. Do we have an agreement?"

It was a simple deal. Sophia would get what she wanted. Martina would get what she wanted. There was no risk that anything would happen to him other than getting a haircut and a tuxedo. Simple.

Hope returned to Grace's angelic face, and she placed her hand in his, confident that he'd solved all her problems, unaware that he had ulterior motives. He intended to help Grace change her life.

Alex felt a twinge of guilt. A woman who lived in Hollywood ought to know that life was only this simple in the movies.

Grace was simply delighted.

Everything was going according to plan. It seemed like it had been ages since she'd looked out a van window and wished her sister would fall in love with a nice, normal guy from Texas Rescue.

As if she'd been granted three wishes, everything was coming true. Overnight, Deezee had been eliminated from their lives. Alex had volunteered to date her sister. And Sophia—

Well, Sophia wasn't showing much interest in Alex yet. Martina had actually taken more notice of him. *And I can't stop staring at him.*

She wouldn't dwell on that. This was about saving Sophia. Her sister had only cried over Deezee for a short time before fury had set in, but her heart couldn't have hardened between eating pancakes and having a meeting with Martina. When Deezee realized how much he'd lost, he might come crawling back. Sophia might still want him, and they'd be right back where they'd started.

Grace couldn't let that happen. Alex was the key. If Sophia fell for Alex, then Deezee couldn't suck her sister back into his dysfunctional world. Grace had one week to turn Alex into the perfect man for her sister.

At least she didn't have to try to turn Sophia into the perfect woman for Alex. All morning, Grace had been worried that Alex would be totally turned off by the calculations and machinations that were necessary to keep Sophia's career and reputation intact, but apparently, Alex had overlooked it. He'd volunteered to be her fake boyfriend, despite it all.

He agreed to help Sophia by spending time with me.

It would be foolish to feel flattered. She was Grace the Assistant. Grace the Sister.

"Grace?"

"Yes?"

"I'm taking another meeting." Martina headed for the door, moving fast on those stilettos.

"Wait—we need to work out the details."

But Martina didn't slow down, so Grace jumped up to follow her, notebook at the ready. "You'll get the tickets to the ball, right?"

Martina flicked her fingers. "You handle this, Grace. I'm the idea man. You're the one who makes it happen. *Ciao.*"

Grace clenched her notebook as Martina slammed the door.

"Is it safe?" Alex murmured behind her. "Is she gone?"

Grace turned around, feeling foolish for running after Martina.

Alex didn't step back. "You know, Martina was exactly what I expected you to be. Before you got to the ER, your sister had been threatening me with her fearsome assistant. She said you were going to straighten everything out."

Grace couldn't remember ever being told that Sophia had talked about her when she wasn't around. What an odd thing for Sophia to have done, threatening a doctor with her.

"I can't imagine why she thought I'd be able to get her the hospital room she wanted."

"You help her get everything she wants."

Grace hesitated. Had that been a compliment, or a criticism?

"That's my job," she said, watching him closely for a response.

He studied her in return. "That is your job, isn't it?"

Grace looked toward the couch. She was pretty sure Sophia was sleeping through this conversation. Well, her sister had pneumonia. She was supposed to be sleeping right now; that was her job. Sophia had to look smart and mature—no, down-to-earth—and unaffected by the antics of an LA disc jockey when she appeared at the Texas Rescue benefit in one week. In order to pull that off, she needed to get healthy. And she needed Alex.

Which meant Grace had a job to do.

It was time to turn Alex into the perfect man for her sister.

CHAPTER THIRTEEN

GRACE HAD NEVER FELT LESS MOTIVATED TO do her job in her entire life.

Her three wishes had been granted, and the rest was up to her. She'd wished they could stay in Texas. She'd wished for Deezee to disappear from their lives. But that third wish...

She's wished for a good man for Sophia. He was standing right here, and it was up to Grace to bring them together.

"Sophia's asleep. Let's get a cup of coffee and go on the porch." Alex was already halfway in the kitchen as he spoke. "You take it black, right?"

He remembered.

She shouldn't be so surprised. After all, they'd just had breakfast an hour ago. But he'd paid attention to a little detail about her, and it gave her a thrill to know she'd been noticed.

Being in the tight confines of the galley kitchen with him brought up memories of midnight. She had to squash them down; this was her sister's new fake boyfriend, and if wishes came true, he'd become a real boyfriend.

She took her coffee and skirted around the couch to the sliding glass door. Alex stayed right behind her, reaching around her, opening the door. As she stepped onto the patio, her long hair caught on his hand, producing the gentlest tug behind her ear.

She might as well be that woman in a historical movie, she felt so very *aware*. Had her hair brushed him accidentally, or had he touched her on purpose?

If she could have a fourth wish...

Oh, that would be so easy. She'd wish that Alex was hers. She'd stop pretending she didn't notice him. No more tentative touches. She'd turn and bury her hand in the thick, dark hair at the nape of his neck and pull him close.

Why not?

Alex set his coffee on the patio table. "I'll be right back."

He went into the living room, took a folded blanket from a shelf and shook it out, blue-and-silver sports team colors looking bright in the sun that poured in the window. As she watched, he lifted it above the couch and let it fall softly, naturally, over her sleeping sister.

Sitting in the warm sunshine, with her hands wrapped around a mug of hot coffee, Grace felt her heart freeze.

She hadn't seen anyone take care of her sister like that, not in ten years. Not since they'd lost their parents in one horrible blow, forcing Sophia to be the oldest, the breadwinner, the decision-maker. Sure, Grace might fetch her coffee, but only when Sophia told her to. Hair and makeup artists might fuss over her, but Sophia paid them. The studios, the agents, the publicist—they all wanted something from the bankable commodity that was Sophia Jackson.

Only Alex, wonderful Alex, was tall and strong and confident enough to treat Sophia like a person, not like a money-making celebrity. He was nice to her, despite having seen her at her worst. Because he wasn't in awe of Sophia, because he didn't depend on Sophia, he was just what Sophia needed.

That's why not.

Grace sat at the table and took a deep breath, forcing the air past the stone in her chest, expanding her ribs despite that sharp pain of jealousy. She'd wished for this. She'd wished that her sister could meet a man like Alex, and she had.

She would pull off this transformation, and Sophia would notice Alex. More than that, she'd make sure Alex knew how great Sophia was, too.

Alex sat down on her side of the patio table. Their chairs were side by side, so close that she could feel his body heat. Her heart began to thaw.

I wish I didn't want you so much.

Pen poised over the blank paper, she waited until she was sure her breathing was steady. Then she looked up at Alex. "What traits do you look for in a woman?"

He raised a brow. "That's your first question? I thought you might ask me what jacket size I need for the tuxedo. I've already rented one, by the way."

She forced a smile and turned the page, titling it *Clothes*. "If you tell me where you rented it, I'll cancel it. The maker of Sophia's gown will probably have an agreement with a menswear designer. They'll send a tailor to fit you."

"You're not my secretary. I'll cancel it myself if I have to. Let's wait and see if it's really necessary."

"It will be. If Sophia wears Lauren, for example, then you'll be expected to wear a Lauren tux, as well. It's all contractual." She felt steadier on this familiar ground, speaking about the workings of her Hollywood life. Her heart could remain cold, indifferent.

Alex took off his glasses and set them on the table, then kicked back in his chair and contemplated the porch ceiling for a moment. "How about your gown? Will you coordinate with Sophia, or do you get to choose your own color and style?" He turned blue eyes on her.

Oh, so blue—vivid and naked, with no glasses adding a layer of safety. Grace swallowed hard. "I'm not on the red carpet, so I don't need a gown. Um—do you have to wear your glasses? Do you have contacts?"

One eyebrow rose again. "Do my glasses have to be a particular designer when I stand next to your sister?"

"We'll get you new frames. But if you can get by without the glasses at all… Sometimes the cameras catch a reflection, and then people wouldn't get to see your—" She was blushing, darn it. Warm cheeks, cold heart. "You and Sophia would look striking together. You both have such blue eyes."

She couldn't quite look into his. She dropped her gaze. Under that loose, faded shirt, his biceps were tight and tan. Her heart didn't feel so frozen.

Alex was quiet, so she peeked up at him.

"You're not afraid Sophia and I will look too much like brother and sister with our matching eye color? That's not a turnoff?"

"Blue eyes are never a turnoff."

"I'm glad to hear that."

Had he meant that he was glad *she* wasn't turned off?

As if.

She felt antsy, edgy. If he and Sophia actually got married, he'd be her brother. She didn't want such a hot brother. The Thor paramedic guy would've been fine, but Alex? No way.

She needed to stay focused on the task at hand. That was what her lists were for. She jotted *cancel tux* and *eyeglass frames*, then turned back to the previous blank page. "Let's get back to the first question. What do you look for in the ideal woman?"

"I'm taking Sophia to this event whether she's my ideal woman or not."

Grace needed to know, anyway. If there was some trait that Alex liked and Sophia already had, then Grace intended to emphasize it. If there was anything she could do to make Sophia more appealing to Alex, she'd do it. Her cold heart would let her be ruthless. Someone like him wasn't going to cross their paths again.

"You can just smile and pose for photos as you enter the venue, but there will be press asking you questions all night. You have to remember that when you are part of a celebrity's life, you are on the record every single second, with every single person, not just reporters. You have to be very careful about talking to people."

"I'm not going to talk about Sophia with strangers. We'll be sitting with people I know from Texas Rescue."

"You still have to guard what you say. My dry cleaner has been asked by a blogger if I told him anything new about Sophia. The clerk at the deli counter has been asked which sandwich I ordered for myself, so he could figure out that the other one was for Sophia. She likes turkey, dry, on whole wheat with sprouts, by the way."

He'd started frowning. When it was just the two of them, she realized, he didn't keep that poker face in place. "I think the guys in Texas Rescue are going to be a little more loyal to me than a deli counter clerk is to you."

"They can be your loyal friends, but they'll still be grilled. You can't slip when you talk to them, so they won't slip if they talk to a reporter. We have to prepare. It's like that movie *Green Card*. Do you know it?"

"I can't imagine how my life is like a movie."

"It's one of the standards in the industry, a marriage-of-convenience story that came out twenty-five years ago. Gérard Depardieu, Andie MacDowell. It was a rom-com—that means romantic comedy—but it still got an Academy Award nomination, which is unusual."

"And this has to do with my ideal woman?"

"It has to do with telling me your preferences. In the movie, the marriage began as a sham to get him a green card, but then the man and woman had to get to know one another in order to pass government interviews, sort of like how you'll have to pass reporters' interviews. They memorized each other's wants and likes to make their fake relationship seem real. And, of course, once they got to know each other, they ended up really falling in love."

Love. The word seemed to linger in the air, suspended between the warm coffee and his blue eyes.

He looked away first. "You know your movies."

She shrugged, just one shoulder. "I guess you could say it's part of my job. I'm in the industry, sort of."

The frown deepened. "You are definitely in the industry. Sophia Jackson wouldn't be the success she is without you."

"You don't know her very well yet. She's driven. She's the one who won't waste her time reading a rom-com script unless someone says it's *Green Card* caliber. The last few months with Deezee were really an aberration. She's normally very focused."

"She can focus on her career because you save her so much time and distraction. This morning, from what I heard, you know the industry as well as she does. That's why she asks for your advice."

He'd noticed. Grace had hoped it would make her look better in his eyes, but that was before she'd seen how tender he was toward her sister.

Had she misread that? As the blanket had floated down over her sister, Alex had looked...not exactly tender, actually. Perhaps he'd looked sort of matter-of-fact about it all. There was a person with pneumonia who might feel chilled while she slept, so he put a blanket on her. That didn't mean he was falling in love, did it?

It would by the time she was through with it. Alex was about to learn everything good there was to know about Sophia.

"She could hire a hundred different people to be her assistant, but you couldn't hire anyone to be Sophia Jackson. I only know the year *Green Card* was released because it was the same year I was born."

"So you're twenty-five."

"Yes." Her pen hovered over the paper. "How old are you?"

"Thirty-one."

"Perfect. Sophia is twenty-nine."

"You're writing down my age?"

"I'll make a list of things Sophia should know about you. She'll memorize it. She has an amazing memory. When she's filming, she memorizes pages of script every night. Sometimes, the writers will change the dialog and hand her new pages in the morning, and she'll know them by her first call. You'll see. I'll type up the notes I take this morning, and she'll know you inside and out by tomorrow."

"Or, she and I could have a normal conversation on the way to the ball."

"I wouldn't be a very good personal assistant if I let you two get into the limo unprepared."

"The limo? I take it I'm not driving." He held up a hand to forestall her. "I'm sure there's a good reason for that. What else do you want to know?"

He rested his forearms on the table, leaning toward the serenity garden that was his backyard, but he didn't look at the cactus and fruit trees. Instead, he looked at her. It was amazing what a difference a shave made. A few good photos of those sky blue eyes, and the public would have no doubts that Sophia Jackson had spent the week in Texas *not* being heartbroken over DJ Deezee Kalm. Anyone who pitied Sophia this morning would envy her once she made her appearance with Alex.

Grace wrote *Preferences* at the top of her page.

"I don't have a list," Alex said. "How can I order up a human being to my specifications?"

"You could start with the basics, like blue eyes and blond hair."

"I've never had a thing for any particular coloring." He let his gaze roam over her, as if he was seriously considering her coloring.

Beige, boring, blushing...

His voice grew quieter. "But I'm definitely not immune to beauty. When a woman is really beautiful, it doesn't matter if she's dressed up or dressed down or...wearing her pajamas."

That was Sophia. No plastic surgery, no Botox, no fillers. Thank goodness Deezee had self-destructed before he could convince her to change anything.

"I'll tell you something else I notice," Alex said. "I admire a woman who isn't afraid to stand up for what is right. Loyalty to her friends and family is very appealing."

He was describing Sophia perfectly. Grace jotted down *loyalty, ethics, beauty.*

"It's too bad we can't use the whole story when you're asked how you two met. If you could tell everyone how you were impressed with her loyalty yesterday, that would be something unique."

"When was this?" He sounded genuinely curious.

"At the hotel, when she encouraged me to talk to the police. She knew that writing that witness statement was the right thing to do. It seemed to me that you liked her a little more after that."

He sat back, which made his shoulder brush hers. "It was nice to see that you were getting some support from her. *You* were the one doing the right thing."

Grace angled her chair toward him. It allowed her to face him more fully. It also kept their shoulders from touching. "You two have so much in common, see? You came to the hotel to support me, too. You both want to see justice served."

"That's one way to look at it."

Grace counted it as a small victory.

Alex seemed impatient. "We can't bring police statements into this. Everything with Mrs. Burns is confidential. We should stick to our initial contact. It's simple and it's true. I met Sophia when she came into the emergency room with a suspected fracture."

"And what was your first impression?"

"An X-ray would be necessary."

Grace stared at him for a second.

He hadn't made a joke, so she tried not to laugh, but a little snort of amusement bubbled out of her, anyway. "You can't be such a doctor with the press, okay? When someone asks you what your first impression of Sophia was—" She couldn't finish her sentence because she was trying too hard not to laugh. "I'm sorry. I just—it's just—that is the least romantic answer a man has ever given."

This time, his raised brow was accompanied by a little duck of his chin. The calm and confident Dr. Gregory looked a little sheepish. And adorable.

Was it okay to think of a brother as adorable?

Grace got her giggles under control. "We've got a lot of work to do. Don't worry, I won't let you down."

"I'm sure you won't let anyone down. I think you're almost too good at your job. Don't let anyone treat you like you're easy to replace."

The last of Grace's laughter died. Easy to replace? Had Martina said that? Sophia?

Alex put his glasses back on. "I'm so confident that you'll get your job done that I think we can stop here and move on to my project."

When he stood and held out his hand for hers, she was curious enough to forget that touching him was off-limits. She placed her hand in his, and he pulled her to her feet.

"You never told me what your project was," she said.

"Come for a ride with me and find out."

CHAPTER FOURTEEN

ALEX THOUGHT HE WAS A GOOD DOCTOR. HE
was a strong cyclist. He was proud of the way he designed
landscapes with geometric precision. But there was one thing
he couldn't seem to be able to do: he could not get Grace
Jackson to talk about herself.

Every question which he hoped would reveal a little bit
about the woman sharing the bench seat of his pickup truck
turned into a dissertation on her sister.

Have you ever been to Texas before?

The first word of her answer had been her sister's name.
*Sophia's last movie was filmed just outside of Austin. We were here
for almost three weeks of shooting last September. The flood damage
was still really noticeable. I knew she'd agree to come this week for
Texas Rescue because the destruction upset her at the time. I knew
she'd like to help.*

His concern for Grace grew with every mile.

Last night, when all he'd been able to think about was this
beautiful woman in his bed, he'd wanted to believe that he'd

jumped to the wrong conclusions about her relationship with her sister. He'd heard a few manipulative comments, seen a few anxious hand gestures, but really, nothing extraordinary. Having just handled the Burns couple, he might have too easily assumed Sophia and Grace were in a dysfunctional relationship, as well.

Midnight was a convenient time to decide that he'd been wrong. If Grace wasn't really in trouble, then he could focus on her as a potential date—or to be brutally honest with himself, as a lover—rather than as someone who needed saving.

That had changed over pancakes. Listening to this morning's meeting with the publicist had been as sobering as a cold shower. Grace was clearly in a dysfunctional relationship with her sister. Still, he had been impressed with how she'd handled herself. She'd been outnumbered by the publicist and her sister. She didn't agree with their decisions and she'd seemed embarrassed by some of the discussion, but she'd handled herself with poise.

He would be able to help her this week. Grace wouldn't be one of those women who refused assistance. She wouldn't be like his mother, sticking with a family member who made her miserable for far too long. Grace was surely more like Mrs. Burns, ready to get out of a bad situation and move on with her life.

But that had been twenty-five miles ago. Twenty-five long miles during which only one subject had been covered: Sophia the Great.

"What did you study in college?" he asked, a direct question to Grace, about Grace.

"I didn't go to college. I was lucky to be able to work for Sophia right after high school. She had a scholarship to study theater at UCLA. She'd finished two years there when our parents died. She dropped out and came home just so I could finish high school in our hometown. She did a lot of local modeling and some local TV commercials. After that, we headed back to LA, but by then she felt the window of opportunity for her to get her degree had passed. Actresses need to work while they're young."

Incredible. Every single answer led back to Sophia.

He shouldn't be so surprised. Victims of domestic abuse could lose their own sense of self. He knew that, yet he'd truly thought Grace was more independent than this. She'd been assertive enough to come and find him in the ER's kitchen. She'd argued with hotel managers and publicists and him. Hell, she'd even had a face-to-face moment with an angry Mr. Burns. But now, she was all about Sophia, every second, every word. It was unhealthy.

He could see a traffic light ahead. It was time to make a judgment call. His plan had been to take her to his latest landscaping project, an outdoor space for a nursing home located in an Austin suburb. He'd thought she could decompress in a Zen-like contemplation of nature while he took some measurements and did some maintenance. After this nonstop Sophia-centric conversation, though, he wasn't sure that was a good idea. What would Grace think about, if he arranged time for her to have no other obligations? Sophia. That was the only thing on her mind.

Grace checked her cell phone. "She must not be awake yet. She hasn't texted me like I asked her to. Usually, she's really good about keeping in touch with people she cares about. She's not an inaccessible celebrity once you are part of her inner circle."

Weird. Just a weird thing to say. Was she trying to reassure herself that she was part of her own sister's inner circle?

Alex fell silent. Every attempt at conversation had been futile, anyway.

The silence didn't last long. "Where did you go to college?" Grace asked. It was the first question she'd initiated during the entire drive.

"Rice University for undergrad. Baylor for med school." He glanced over.

She was writing in her notebook. "When I type this up for Sophia, I could type up a list of identical facts for you. Baylor versus UCLA, that kind of thing. Sophia's really good at memorizing things that way, but I don't—"

"Grace." The traffic light up ahead turned yellow, then red. He stopped the truck gently when he wanted to slam on the brakes. "I know she has a good memory. You told me that. Three times."

"Oh." She scratched something out. "I won't type that in your notes, then."

His notes?

"Were all these Sophia stories supposed to be trivia I was memorizing about her?"

"Of course."

Jeez. Twenty-five miles of this. The conversation was still weird, but at least it made a little sense, in a Hollywood kind of way. If Grace had been writing things down, he would have realized what was going on sooner. He supposed she didn't take notes when she was the one doing the talking.

Her pencil was poised over her page now. "Our project this morning was to prepare you for the media scrutiny. Don't you feel like you know Sophia better now?"

"I've had more than enough of Sophia Jackson."

Grace's answering silence made him feel like a jerk. She was emotionally fragile. He should handle her with care.

Grace yanked open the tote bag at her feet and dropped her notebook in it. It wasn't a very fragile move. "You're the one who kept asking me questions about her."

The light turned green. Alex turned in the opposite direction of the nursing home.

"I asked you about you," he said. "Where did *you* go to school? Where did *you* grow up?"

"I'm well aware that what people want to know is *where did the two of you grow up?* Why would anyone want to know those things about me?"

He pulled off the road and parked next to a building that was half gas station, half barbecue joint. It was early for lunch, but if they did the landscaping first, lunch would be late. He didn't want to risk Grace getting hypoglycemic again. She was in a delicate state already.

Grace kept staring straight ahead, even after he killed the engine. She didn't look delicate; she looked angry. He'd been afraid that she was obsessed with her sister, but now he suspected she was obsessed with her job. That seemed marginally more normal, but it still indicated that she lacked balance in her life.

He strove for balance in his. He made sure his emotions were in check before he spoke. "I didn't realize we were cramming for an exam about your sister's life. The last half hour would have made more sense, then."

She sighed in defeat. "It's okay. I'll put everything I told you in writing."

"Don't. You have enough work to do. I may not have memorized a new scene after having the screenwriter read it out loud to me once, just once, while I was having my hair and makeup done on site in a remote part of Tunisia, before running to a hilltop and nailing the scene in one take, getting every word right and catching the light as the sun rose, thus saving the cast and crew and production company from having to strike the set and repeat the entire process the next day at great cost, but I do have a decent memory."

She stared at him, mouth open in surprise. He gently used one finger under her chin to close it, smiling to soften his sarcasm. "Don't be so shocked. Doctors have to memorize a lot of stuff, too. I'm officially declaring a lunch break. No notebooks, no phones. Just brisket."

Grace frowned down at the phone in her hand. "I think we should have a working lunch. We don't have a lot of time."

"We have a week until this ball. Sophia is living in my house. I'm going to get to know her whether I want to or not."

Grace looked at him then, her special blend of hope and worry in her eyes. "But you do want to get to know her, don't you?"

That made him pause. "This is supposed to be about photos. What's really going on here?"

"You're supposed to be her boyfriend. You're supposed to be the reason she's no longer interested in Deezee. We're establishing a better life for her."

"You can't establish a better life for someone. They have to choose it. As for the boyfriend thing, the term was *fake* boyfriend, if my memory serves—which I'm certain it does. However, since I'm not an actor, I'm not going to try to fake that I like her. It's fortunate that I don't need to fake anything."

"Oh, good."

She said it with such relief, it silenced him. Did she want him to be her sister's real boyfriend?

"You and Sophia are perfect for one another."

When a goat eats a wolf.

Grace had to feel the chemistry toward him that he felt toward her. He hadn't imagined those fingertips trailing along his waist last night. Her arousal had been revealed by her clinging white pajamas and her quickened breaths. How could she want him to want someone else instead?

"Let me be clear. I mean that I don't need to fake anything in order to pull off a photo op at this ball. I'm not going to fake that I have more of a relationship with Sophia than I do. I'm not going to worry about who is a reporter and who isn't, because I'm only going to tell the truth. I met her when she came into the emergency room with a suspected fracture. I offered her a place to stay because she couldn't make her flight. Because I'm bringing her to the ball as my date, good manners and common courtesy require me to do my best to make sure she has a pleasant evening. We'll sit together for dinner, we'll dance if her ankle allows, we'll talk. If the public wants to jump to conclusions, that's not in my control."

"Martina will control it. She'll make sure everyone jumps to conclusions. She'll imply you knew each other before the ER visit. So will Sophia." Grace turned those beautiful brown-gold eyes away from him. "So will I."

"Is that what you want?" He touched her again, his fingertips light against her jaw as he turned her face toward him.

She kept her eyes downcast. "It's my job."

"I don't have to do any of this," he said. "Neither do you."

He had a long moment to study the feathering of her lashes, dark against her skin, until she opened her eyes and looked at him, startlingly direct. "You said you would. You're supposed to be a man of your word." She jerked her chin free.

Rejection. Abandonment. He let go of her instantly. If she didn't want him, then he didn't want her, either.

A part of him knew that wasn't true. The angry self-defense was an old reflex, born from the need to protect himself from all the miseries of a violent parent. *I don't care about you, either, Papa.*

He'd spent his adult life mastering that negative emotion.

He didn't have to react defensively to Grace's rejection, but control required consciousness. Introspection. Focus.

They were on their way to build a garden to give other people a place to focus their thoughts, but right now, with the feel of Grace's skin still fresh on his fingertips, he was having a hard time keeping his own wants and needs straight. Rejection had a way of screwing with a man's mind.

He got out of the truck and shoved the key in the front pocket of his jeans. The feel of the packed dirt under his work boots and the smell of the barbecue's wood smoke centered him. He walked around the front of the truck and opened Grace's door with equanimity.

Because he was calm, he could see that she was not. She'd put her tote bag in her lap, and her knuckles were white as she clenched the handles in her fists. He noticed the tension in the way she held her neck and remembered his desire yesterday to smooth his hands over her shoulders to release all that tightness. That desire was stronger, now that he knew her better. The truth was, he wanted Grace, even if she did not want him.

"I'm sorry," she said, not quite meeting his eyes. "I shouldn't have said that about keeping your word. You've done so much for us, and I keep asking you to do more."

It didn't matter what her job was or who she was related to. It didn't even matter that he knew in advance she'd disappear from his life. Something inside him responded to everything about her. He wanted to be her lover, but she needed a friend—and he wanted to be what she needed.

"I offered you a place to stay. I offered to take your sister to the ball. You don't need to say 'I'm sorry' just because you said yes."

He offered her his hand. She pushed the tote bag onto the

seat and took his hand, then jumped gracefully from the high cab to the ground. Neither of them let go.

Be her friend. She needs a friend.

Standing a little too close to her, their hands linked by their thighs, he spoke quietly. "Everything I offered was to help you, Grace Jackson. I'm giving you my word that I'm on your side. You said this morning you thought Sophia should tell the truth. You thought Sophia should go to the ball alone. If you still want to go that route, I'll back you up."

"Thank you." She sounded breathless. She sounded like she had at midnight.

He wanted to kiss her. He did not.

"But she's not just my sister, she's my boss. She usually has good instincts. I think I should do my job."

"Then I'll support you on that, too."

"Which means you'll take her to the ball." But her gaze had dropped to his mouth.

"Of course." He waited, every muscle aching to reach for her, the woman who needed a friend.

She still didn't let go of his hand, but with a sigh that sounded like defeat, Grace reached up to the bench seat with her other hand to grab her tote bag.

He stopped her by placing his hand over hers. "Sometimes a job is nothing but a job. Why don't you leave that here? I meant what I said about taking a lunch break. No work."

They stood in the shelter of the truck's open door, each with an arm resting on the seat, hands touching, their bodies open to one another, only inches of air keeping her chest from his. He took a deliberate, calm breath. This wasn't the time to give in to that physical awareness.

Under his palm, Grace's hand formed a fist around the bag's strap. "We could work on your project over lunch instead. Plan our schedules for the week, for the times we'll be…together."

"Leave it." *And don't look at me like that.*

That inch of air between them was full of heat and electricity.

She let her gaze drop to his chest, then lower, the same as she had at midnight. Any sane man would move away at this moment, but the torture was too addictive.

She's leaving at the end of the week. The truth of that should kill his desire.

It didn't. He watched her breasts rise as she took her own deep breath before she let go of the bag's strap, her fingers uncurling under his hand.

"Then what will we talk about?" she asked.

"We'll get to know one another, like any man and woman do. There's nothing to memorize. We can say anything."

"I don't think I've been in that position before. Not since I was a teenager."

He saw her mouth form the words, but he barely heard them over the hum of arousal in his brain. His own voice was low. "You and I aren't famous. No one will care what happens between us. Except us."

And then there was no air between them. Bodies touched, shirt brushing blouse, mouth on soft mouth. The kiss they should have had at midnight was too intense at noon, but they were swept into it together, mouths open and tasting and taking. When she made a little sound of greed, he let go of her hands and pulled her into his arms, a feeling of *yes, this* and *finally* as he molded her pliant body to his.

When her hand slid up his back pocket to cling to his leather belt, when her fingers dug into the hair at the nape of his neck, the sound of greed came from him. They made love with their mouths, hot and moist. Intimate. Jeans became the worst possible piece of clothing. His were tight and restrictive, hers were a coarse barrier to the soft curves he wanted to feel, and—

And there was nothing he could do about it. They were in a parking lot, about to be surrounded by a lunch crowd.

It didn't matter. He didn't want to give up any taste of Grace he could have.

The frustration was exquisite, but it was building too hot, too fast, so he forced himself to end the kiss. Kissed her once more. Ended that, but didn't move away from her. After a moment of listening to her pant for breath, he kissed the soft skin of her cheek, but his control was a flimsy thing. He needed to put space between them. He placed his palm on the metal of the truck, breathed in Grace one more time, and pushed himself away.

"Wow," she whispered.

He nodded, trying not to think, not to feel.

A work truck parked beside them. Grace moved out of the way, so Alex could shut his truck door and let the other driver open his. He kept his back to Grace, standing between her and the driver. He didn't want another man seeing her sexy, just-kissed look. Behind him, he heard Grace's breathy, bedroom voice.

"Wow," she repeated. "That was a huge mistake."

CHAPTER FIFTEEN

GRACE KNEW SHE WAS A GOOD PERSONAL AS-sistant. She never missed a detail or dropped an assignment. She knew how to handle celebrities. She could hold her own against a publicist. But there was one thing she couldn't do: she couldn't make Alex Gregory tell a lie.

So she skipped that part.

"I won't ask you to lie, but could you at least not mention that you kissed her sister?" That didn't sound fair. It wasn't as if the kiss had been all one-sided. "Or that her sister kissed you?"

"You don't need anyone's permission to kiss anyone you want."

"I know that." She kept her eyes on the picnic table. A huge chunk of beef brisket sat on white butcher paper, look-ing like a pot roast for the two of them to share, along with breaded and fried jalapeño peppers and two plastic bowls of banana pudding. It might be typically Texan, but it was the strangest array of food she'd ever seen at a lunch, working or not. It added to her feeling of disorientation.

She should be consulting stylists and lining up fittings for her sister, or making lists of local press and arranging transportation. Instead, she was eating at a table outside of a restaurant that had gas pumps, as if the cars and trucks needed to be fed, too, while she sat across from a man that she so desperately, physically craved. She didn't want to eat. All she wanted to do was plaster herself against his shockingly strong, deliciously warm body and kiss him until her brain dissolved. That way, she wouldn't have to think about the mess she'd just created.

Her hands were tempted to reach over the table to brush his hair back from his forehead. She interlocked her fingers tightly, just to sit still. "We're supposed to be making you into the perfect man for her. I don't think the perfect boyfriend would kiss her sister."

"Fake boyfriend. For one date."

"I know that." She clenched her hands tighter. If she'd been holding a pencil, it would have snapped by now.

"For what it's worth, I have no intention of telling Sophia I kissed you when we get back to the house."

She winced and leaned forward to whisper. "Don't use her name outside of your house, okay?"

He shook his head slowly. There was no mistaking that sad downturn to his kissable mouth, that wrinkle of worry on his brow. He pitied her.

"I'm not being paranoid," she said.

"I mean this as kindly as possible, but yes, you are being paranoid. Look around you. This isn't LA. This isn't even Austin."

Obediently, Grace looked to the nearest patron, who sat at least six feet away at another picnic table. He was tearing the meat off some ribs with his teeth, elbows on the table, ball cap on his head. He said something to his table partner, a similarly attired man, as he chewed. All Grace could pick out from their conversation were a few numbers. She looked back to Alex.

"They're talking about tractor tires," he said.

"It's still a good habit to get into, not saying names. You'll need that this week."

"I'm not going to tell *her* about kissing you because it's none of her business. I absolutely have no obligation to report to her what I was doing and with whom I was doing it. I'm very sorry that you think you do."

Did she? Grace hadn't really thought it through, this instinctive need for secrecy. "It's not like I have to tell her, but…"

She fell silent. Did it matter now if her sister found out Grace had a thing for Alex?

The damage was done.

She'd had a whole week, a golden opportunity to give her sister the experience of being with a man who didn't treat her like she was lucky to get his time. A chance to remind Sophia that there were men out there who liked women as people, not as accessories. A chance for Sophia to live in a real house and be treated like a real person instead of a celebrity. A chance to take care of Sophia in return for the years she'd taken care of Grace. One week—and Grace had ruined her big chance to change her sister's life on the first day.

As she stared into Alex's sky blue eyes and struggled for something to say, it hit her: she wouldn't have missed that kiss for the world. Not even for the sister who'd been her world. Having been held and kissed and wanted by Alex, there was no way she could possibly encourage Alex to hold and kiss and want anyone else.

What kind of sister am I?

Grace put her hands over her face, and tried not to cry.

* * *

Alex should have seen this coming. For a doctor who'd treated dozens of victims of domestic violence, for a son who'd lived through his mother's multiple attempts to leave his abusive father, he should have known it would be hard on Grace to do anything independently of her sister. *You knew she needed a friend, not a lover. You couldn't just be content being her friend, though, could you?*

He rounded the edge of the table to go to Grace's side. The men at the next table had noticed that a pretty woman was sniffing back tears and hiding her face, of course, and they were doing their best not to stare. Alex straddled the plank seat, facing Grace and keeping his back to the men to give her some illusion of privacy.

Their kiss had triggered these tears, somehow. He remembered the kitchen at midnight, the way she'd whispered *I can't.* He hesitated now to hold her again. Falling back on his experience as a doctor, he tried to maintain a caring objectivity. He reached for the roll of paper towels on the table and tore off a sheet and held it out to her, but with her hands hiding her face, she didn't see it.

"Grace," he said, feeling like a physician, "it's going to be okay."

She burst into tears in earnest.

To hell with it. He pulled her closer, so her body was in the V of his legs, and wrapped one arm around her to anchor her to him. With his hand, he pressed her tearful face into his shoulder.

"I don't want you to be scared of Sophia."

"I'm not scared of Sophia."

"Then what are you scared of? What terrible thing will happen if she finds out we like one another?"

"I...never mind. I can't explain. It's so embarrassing."

She pressed her forehead into his shoulder, hiding. He remembered seeing his mother looking into the mirror, the bruise on her cheek darkening by the moment. The way she'd spotted him and covered her cheek with her hand and turned her face away, embarrassed. *Oh, my little bear. I can't explain anything right now. You don't worry about Mama, okay?*

He'd never asked his mother to explain it, not even when he was a teenager and it was just the two of them, learning a new life in the land of cowboys and cattle. They'd once been so close. Even as a very young child, he'd witnessed everything she did to expose the dangerous factory. Then later, he'd been old enough to help hide money, hide identification cards, hide food. They'd survived together, then eventually thrived together. They should be close now, or close still, but there was a wall between them, built of the things they did not discuss.

Walls were too sturdy. He didn't want to begin building one here, with this woman. He laid his cheek against her hair. "Can you explain to me why that kiss was a mistake?"

"First, you have to promise not to laugh at me for being stupid."

"I promise." What an easy promise to make. He'd just shared the best kiss of his life with a woman who was crying. He'd never felt further from laughing.

"The thing is…" She lifted her head enough to peek around them to ensure that the other outdoor diners were still at distant tables. "I'm afraid Deezee will try to win her back at some point. It's possible Martina will advise him to. I thought if you and my sister were into each other, then she might not fall back into Deezee's trap. You're nice to her. You bring her ice and pancakes and you covered her with a blanket. You can't imagine how long it's been since she's had

411

someone other than me be nice to her. I wanted her to be with a good man, but now I've stolen you away."

It was a good thing she couldn't see his face, because he had to smile into her hair, a little moment of pleasure. She'd stolen him, had she?

"You didn't deprive your sister of anything."

"I disagree. I think you're something very special."

The pleasure, so mixed with the pain...

Her tears were very real. She carried a terrible guilt. It was as if she didn't think she had a right to anything she wanted or needed. Only Sophia's needs mattered.

"I meant that your sister didn't lose out on a relationship with me, because she never had a chance. It's been you from the moment I first laid eyes on you."

Grace went very still in his arms.

He was being too intense, talking like a lover. She needed a friend.

He let go of her and sat back a few inches. With the paper towel, he dried the cheek he'd so recently kissed in the parking lot. "When I walked through that curtain and first saw you, I must have looked like an idiot. You knocked the words right out of my head. I just stared at you."

"I thought you were disappointed in me. You said, 'You're the assistant?' like you couldn't believe it."

"I was expecting someone like Martina. I saw an angel. The only reason I agreed to take Sophia to the ball was so that you wouldn't spend this week helping some other man get ready. I wanted you to myself. Pretty devious of me, if you think about it."

He smiled at her; tears welled in her eyes.

"I'm no angel. I'm a terrible sister. Do you remember when I said I couldn't stand by and watch Sophia crash? I didn't tell you the whole truth. I'd decided this week would be her last chance." She waved those words away quickly with her hand, and started over. "I mean, this week was *my* last chance to see if I could save her from herself. And if I couldn't, if she continued to follow Deezee's lead in everything, I was ready to move out."

Words spoken on that metal bench burst from his memory. *I'm the one that's getting sick of it.* If she'd already decided to leave, then he wouldn't have to help her make those decisions. He wouldn't have to wait while she worked through those issues. The physical desire he'd been trying to tame roared back to life. Friends could become lovers. They could take that kiss as far as they wanted it to go.

"I've got a list." She fiercely dashed her cheek on her sleeve. "It's in my tote bag. Just some different options and th-things I'd have to take care of if I decided to move out on my own."

Yeah, he was a hell of a friend, all right. His mind was skipping ahead to taking her to bed, to losing himself in all the shades of gold that made up Grace Jackson, while she was worrying about her future. He handed her the paper towel and eased himself back a little farther.

She mopped up the last of her own tears. "But Deezee made that decision for Sophia, didn't he? He left her high and dry, so I guess that's that. I'm staying now."

To his surprise, she plunged her hands through her own hair, squeezing her skull. "Why am I not happy about this?"

Because you don't really want to go back to the way things were.

"I'm glad Deezee's gone," she said. "But Sophia didn't make any decisions. I wanted her to choose."

Alex stayed quiet and listened, feeling humbled. He'd thought he'd be the one to lead Grace to all these revelations this week. He was so accustomed as an emergency physician to being the one who stated the problem out loud and offered the solution. *I don't think you fell down a staircase. There is legal and financial help available today. You don't have to leave with the man who hurt you.*

But Grace was not a patient. She was already aware and ready to change her life. Listening to her was a revelation. Some victims found their own way out. He knew that; he just never witnessed it. He only saw the women in his ER who were still trapped.

My mother got out.

Another revelation. He'd never thought of it that way. Officially, they'd escaped from the political corruption that had followed the collapse of the Soviet government. His mother had exposed the factory conditions, putting a political target on her back—for which his father had shaken her, the back of her head smacking into a picture frame, shattering the glass, the blood matting her hair. *How could you bring this down on us?*

It was the first time his father had hurt his mother. She'd later been jailed by the people his father had been trying to curry favor with. *I was going to be made a Party member. You've ruined my life.*

She'd dared to seek asylum in a foreign land, but Alex realized now she'd escaped from an abusive husband at the same time. Papa had stayed on shore as their unauthorized boat had ventured into deep waters. They'd sailed from Russia to Turkey, their identities a life-or-death secret. Then they'd walked from embassy to embassy, using their real names, hoping his mother's reputation as an engineer would be their saving grace. It had been. They'd been flown to Houston, Texas, where she could teach at Rice University. His mother had been victorious.

Why was it more comfortable to remember her as a victim?

"I wanted Sophie to decide if she still wanted her career

and everything that goes with it. There's a lot of sacrifice involved. She can't even go to a grocery store. I thought maybe she was done with it all, and that was why she was self-destructing." Grace let her hands fall into her lap. "I'll never know now. Sophie will make this Texas Rescue appearance a triumph. She wants Deezee to regret what he's done, and she'll do that by being more successful than ever."

"Good for Sophie. What about Grace? What will you do after this week?"

"I guess we keep going, the same as we have for years."

Selfishly, he wanted her to let Sophia return to LA without her. A week would not be enough time with Grace. He slid the butcher paper closer and pulled two battered metal forks out of a tin pail that held table settings, buying himself time to be sure he would speak from a neutral position, as a friend.

He handed her a fork. "Deezee didn't take away your options. If anything on your list is more appealing to you than continuing on that same path, then it doesn't matter what Deezee does. You get to choose your own path."

"I hadn't thought of it like that." She bit her lower lip, as she had yesterday.

He only had to bend his head, and her lips would be soft beneath his. He so badly wanted to kiss her. He held himself still.

Customers had begun spilling out of the indoor area, taking up more picnic tables as the lunch hour reached its peak. Grace slid a quick glance at each new table, calculating how freely she could speak. It was one of those sacrifices that went with the American obsession with fame, one he'd never taken seriously before. He did now.

"I can take you somewhere quiet," he began, but the rest of his thought about his volunteer project was completely swamped by the image of taking Grace somewhere quiet, just the two of them. If they had privacy, they wouldn't use it to think.

He was surely reading too much into her expression, a little surprised, a little…hopeful? She lowered her gaze, waiting for the rest of his invitation, and damn it, he wanted to kiss her again.

The last kiss had left her weeping.

He grabbed his fork and returned to the other side of the table, taking himself firmly into the friend zone, where she needed him to be. "I'm redoing a meditation garden at a nursing home. That's my project. I've got some repairs to make on a wall."

Two men sat heavily at the other end of their picnic table. He exchanged a courtesy nod with them. Strangers shared the long tables at places like this. Paper towels, utensils and condiments were all in the middle for anyone to grab.

Grace sat up a little straighter. "You make gardens for nursing homes?"

She might have been turning the conversation to something less personal for her, but it stayed personal for him. The gardens were his private outlet. "Nursing homes, rehab facilities. Wherever I happen to hear someone has the space for me to build something."

"Is this garden going to be like your backyard? I think that look is really beautiful."

Ah, the pleasure of a sincere compliment. "I'm glad you like it. This project has a long way to go, but it would give you some uninterrupted time to think about what you want. Anything you want."

One of the men at their table reached for a squeeze bottle of barbecue sauce, and Grace pushed it his way without waiting for him to ask. That was Grace. Always on high alert, always looking to make things easier for everyone else.

"That sounds nice," she said, "but we're supposed to be working together."

"I'm just going to pick up a load of gravel and deliver it to the site. Letting you have a chance to unwind after the stress you've been through is the least I can do."

She seemed to be back in control of herself, and he didn't want to upset her equilibrium again. He chose his words with care. "I'm sorry I added to that stress. I won't make the same mistake twice. Anything you don't want to happen, won't happen."

He raised his cup of banana pudding to her as if he were proposing a toast. "Eat up. We need to go buy some rocks."

I won't make the same mistake twice.

Grace had the peaceful surroundings of a rock garden under construction in which to stew over that particular statement. She was the one who'd said that incredible kiss was a mistake, and now Alex was sorry for it. She'd never had a man apologize for kissing her.

It sucked.

She wanted to make that same mistake again. She was supposed to be contemplating her future, but all she could contemplate was Alex's body. Under that faded red T-shirt, there were serious muscles at work as he hauled wheelbarrows full of gravel to bare spots in the garden. With a shovel first, and then a rake, he smoothed everything into place around the pillars of cypress trees. From her little perch on top of a limestone wall, she watched.

She was terrible at meditation. The only thing she seemed to be able to contemplate was how much warmer it would have to get before Alex would remove his shirt. The sun was plenty warm on her shoulders, and she wasn't doing anything physical like he was. More than once, he'd grabbed the bottom edge of his shirt as if he were going to pull it off over his head.

Yes, please.

But he'd glanced her way, and left the shirt on.

She gave up on meditation and opened her notebook, ready to brainstorm her options and then make a list of pros and cons for each possible choice. Instead, she drew little squiggly shapes in the margins, and turned his words over in her mind. *Anything you don't want to happen, won't happen.* What about the things she did want to happen? If she wanted another kiss that drove every thought out of her mind, was he up for that?

Apparently not. She couldn't be too shocked if a boy wasn't turned on by a girl who cried hard enough to soak a paper towel after being kissed. No wonder he was giving her space.

Alex tossed the shovel and rake into the empty wheelbarrow, then lifted the edge of his shirt high, using the bottom hem to wipe his forehead. His bare torso was tan all over, as if he usually worked without a shirt, and every muscle in his chest and abs was defined. The man had to be zero-percent body fat.

Let's make another mistake. Heck, let's screw up everything completely.

He dropped his shirt back in place, picked up the handles of his empty wheelbarrow, and headed for the truck that was parked off to her left. She heard the scrape of the shovel and the tumbling of rocks into the wheelbarrow. In an effort to look busy herself, she flipped from her *Options* page to the list Sophia had dictated earlier. *Spray tan* got a black line through it. So did *personal trainer*.

She closed her notebook and went back to contemplating

the beauty of nature—if a man's sculpted body counted as a natural wonder.

If the man was Alex Gregory, it did.

CHAPTER SIXTEEN

ALEX HAD TO WORK AT THE ER THE NEXT FEW days. The routine allowed them to settle into a sort of domestic tranquility.

He'd come home from the hospital, endure some sweet torture in the close proximity of the kitchen as he helped Grace finish cooking whatever she'd decided to experiment with that day for dinner, and then the three of them would crash in the living room. Grace would stay busy on her laptop, assuring him she wasn't working. Her sister was usually on her phone, but when she put a movie on, as she did every evening, Alex noticed she gave it her full attention. Her occasional commentary was usually snarky, and usually directed at something he hadn't even noticed, like a change in a scene's lighting. He sat in the armchair, flipping through medical journals, and tried not to be too obvious as he admired Grace's bare legs as she curled up in a corner of his couch wearing khaki shorts. Between those bare legs and the memory of the taste of her mouth…

He stretched out on that couch every night and waited, eyes well-adjusted to the dark, for the sight of Grace slipping into the kitchen for a midnight glass of milk. Every night, he was disappointed.

But every day, he saw signs that made him glad he'd opened his house to Grace Jackson. Despite the fact that Deezee was no longer in the picture, there were no indications that Sophia was becoming the paragon of a sister that Grace claimed she'd once been, but he could definitely see that Grace was done waiting for that miracle transformation.

His own surface transformation was nearly complete. Grace had arranged for an optical technician to bring designer frames and a large mirror into the ER's kitchen, and new frames for his existing prescription had been ordered with astounding ease. The hair stylist had arrived at his home one evening, all scissors and sass with a Malibu tan. She'd flown in from California for other South-by celebrities and would be returning the day of the ball to make up Sophia. She'd left his hair on the long side, cutting and trimming infinitesimal amounts of hair until every time she asked him to shake his head, his hair would fall into place to her satisfaction.

The end result had drawn an alarming amount of attention to him at work today. As far as he could tell, his brown frames had been replaced by black ones that were, granted, a little more sleek and touched with silver on the edges, and his hair had gone from being unintentionally shaggy to deliberately tousled, but neither change had been very significant. An absurd quantity of women at West Central Texas Hospital seemed to disagree. His eyes were suddenly a noticeable shade of blue. His hair had to be admired from every angle. It had been a relief to come home to the quiet of Grace and her sister.

He flipped the pages of his medical journal to a new study

on blood thinners. Sophia turned off the movie she'd started twenty minutes earlier, but stayed languidly draped over the couch. "I can't believe that excuse for a film made it onto a single screen. Get me my tablet, Grace."

Grace stopped typing on her laptop instantly, but she didn't jump to do her sister's bidding as she had over pancakes on that first morning. "You know, you could ask that a little more nicely."

Alex looked up from his magazine.

"Get my tablet, *please*." The way Sophia drew out the word *please* was plainly obnoxious.

"No, thank you," Grace said with equally insincere politeness.

"What?"

Alex turned the page, although he hadn't read a word.

"If you want your tablet, it's charging in the bedroom, in the same place I've been putting it all week."

"You have to get it for me." Sophia jerked herself a little more upright. "I'm in a *cast*."

"It's a walking boot. You're supposed to be walking in it."

"I can't."

Alex turned another page, and tried to sound more bored than amused. "And yet, you must have made it to the kitchen today to get yourself a sandwich while we were scouting out the venue for the ball. You left the mayonnaise on the counter."

He hid a smile at Princess Picasso's go-to-hell look.

"Which reminds me," Sophia said to Grace, not deigning to respond to Alex, "have the grocery service send in that ancient-grain bread. I had to use mayonnaise today because there isn't any gochujang here." She snapped her fingers. "Oh—we need ube chips."

Grace shut the lid on her laptop and left, heading for the guest bedroom. Sophia shot him a look of triumph when

Grace returned with the tablet, but as she held up one hand regally to receive it, Grace started tapping its screen.

"Stop that." Sophia lifted her head. Frowned. Pushed herself up to a sitting position. "Are you getting into my stuff? How are you getting into my stuff?"

"Deezee's birthday. Why is that still your password?"

"Give it here. What are you doing?"

"I'm giving you something to think about besides purple yam chips. I'm side-loading a script you were supposed to have read two weeks ago. They expected to hear from you yesterday. It's a very hot property, and your time is running out before they offer it to someone else."

"Whatever."

"It's Quentin. That Quentin."

Alex raised an eyebrow. The director's movies were critical successes, box office smashes—and famously violent.

"Great." Sophia made it sound like it was anything but. "They probably want me to go down in a blaze of gunfire."

"If they do, you can bank on it being very well choreographed, very big box office, very *Quentin* gunfire," Grace said.

Sophia pouted. "It's like my specialty now. I die in all these movies. Kill off the Jackson character, so we can watch her die in close-up. It's so stupid."

Grace stopped in mid-swipe. "You used to say it was storytelling. Do you want to read this?"

Sophia yawned. Alex knew her well enough now to suspect that she might have faked that perfectly timed yawn. It was hard to tell with an actress.

"I don't feel like it right now," Sophia said. "Maybe next week."

"Not giving them an answer is an answer."

Sophia didn't answer.

Alex watched, waiting, ready to help Grace in any way.

Grace held up the tablet, deadly serious. "This is it, then. You've come to a point in your life where you want to turn down a script from one of the directors you've dreamed of working with, without reading it or explaining why. You have that option, but be certain it's what you want. You can't rebound from this by posting a few clever quips on social media or finding a handsome man with blue eyes to help you save your pride. Make sure you're ready for your life to go in a different direction."

Silence stretched. Alex had been ready to rescue Grace for nearly a week, ever since the moment he'd seen her anxiety in the emergency room. He should have realized Grace could save herself.

"Give me my tablet." Sophia held up her hand, every bit as firm in her expression as Grace.

Grace gave it to her. At the tap of Sophia's finger, the recognizable color scheme of a social media site appeared. She settled back into her languid, lazy position, rocking her booted foot slowly from side to side.

Grace bowed her head, but Alex didn't think it was in defeat. She was only acknowledging the decision made. He felt the gravity of the moment, the end of a career, the wasting of a talent.

"I'm going to get some ice water," Grace said. She hadn't gone three steps toward the kitchen when Sophia stopped her with a tone of voice that Alex hadn't heard her use before.

"Gracie?" She sounded a little panicky. "Did you delete that script? I can't find it."

Grace froze, her back to her sister. "It's under the e-reader function."

"I don't know what *side-loading* means. I only know the social media apps." The sound of Sophia swallowing her pride was practically audible. "Would you please show me?"

Alex understood Grace's look of relief. She'd finally forced Sophia to make a choice, and Sophia had made the smart choice. Their lives would keep going as they were. Alex had to agree that was a better option than self-destructing for the love of the unfaithful boyfriend, but their lives would take them right back to LA.

He stared at the medical journal, open now to the wrong page.

I knew Grace would disappear. I knew which day she'd go. I kissed her only once. Once cannot change my life.

Sophia planted her boot on the ground and stood up. "I'll bring it to you. I'm thirsty, too." She thumped across his polished concrete floor, put her arm around Grace and disappeared into his kitchen, taking away the woman who no longer needed him to save her.

Alex got up, too, and went outside. In the dark, the inanimate rocks that made up his garden were precisely as he'd arranged them. Next week, when Grace and her sister were back in LA, he would take some satisfaction in imagining the women living well, just as he imagined for the patients he helped for a brief time in his emergency room.

I'd go crazy wondering how everyone is. How do you handle the not knowing?

He'd have more than his imagination in this case, actually. He'd be able to see Sophia's success, and he'd know for certain that Grace was doing well then, too. It would be more than he ever had with his patients, closer to what he had with his mother. He didn't have to imagine that his mother was doing well. He knew for certain she was chairing the university's engineering department and traveling on her personal quest for better education around the world.

His mother, his emergency patients and Grace Jackson. He helped them, then they left. He wished them well.

He put his foot on a low limestone wall, so like the one he and Grace had worked on at the nursing home this week. When Grace left, he'd carry on exactly as he had before he'd ever seen her brown-gold eyes looking at him like she hoped he could save her. His well-balanced life would be unchanged. This week had not derailed his life.

Perhaps nothing could.

He shoved at the wall with his foot, a sudden burst of frustration that accomplished nothing. The wall did not budge. What had he expected? The pattern was set.

I could change it.

To what? He had no other pattern to follow. He helped people in need, and then he moved on. Next patient. Next garden.

But there'd never be another Grace.

It was only one kiss.

He kicked the wall once more, and headed back into the house.

Alex knew Grace needed his help with one last thing: the Black and White Ball.

More accurately, her sister needed his help, but Grace and her sister were inextricably linked. What helped Sophia, helped Grace. And so, on one of the last days Alex would have Grace in his life, his house was invaded by a team of stylists and seamstresses.

They rearranged his furniture and brought in entire clothing racks of evening gowns and tuxedos, all carefully wrapped in plain cloth bags in case there were paparazzi hiding in his bushes, trying to get a scoop on what Sophia Jackson might wear to this gala. The secrecy wasn't necessary. No one had thought to look for a movie star in the home of an ER doctor, and surely no one would care whether that doctor wore Armani or Tom Ford or Calvin Klein.

These people cared, though. It could not possibly matter in the grand scheme of life whether his pockets were slit or had flaps, whether his coat had one button or two, whether the satin of the lapel would reflect well in photographs. It could not matter, but the stylists were deadly serious about every detail, Sophia almost as committed. Grace, ever supportive of her sister, offered thoughtful opinions.

She'd done the same for him, this week in the garden. Did it really matter if he trimmed back an overgrown peach tree by two feet or three? And yet, Grace had stood patiently on the ground, pointing out each branch that needed to be evened up, so that he didn't have to keep climbing down to judge for himself.

His sense of fairness demanded that he treat this project with the same respect. When they asked for his opinion, he gave it: he'd wear the Armani.

Once that was decided, he was expected to stay and give an opinion on the gowns. On colors and hems and accessories—good God. It was beyond frivolous.

Sophia was spending her first day out of the boot, adjusting to the ankle wrap. She didn't want to put her ankle through the standing and sitting and stepping in and out of multiple gowns. Grace was acting as her double. To him, the sisters were so different, with Grace's warm gold so much more appealing than her sister's platinum, that he hadn't realized they were nearly the same build and exactly the same height.

With Grace as the model, the succession of gowns became an excuse to openly admire the woman he should have kissed a thousand times this week.

Too late.

The only purpose he served was to stand by in his tuxedo. He wasn't treating illness and injury. He wasn't clearing a garden path so a wheelchair could fit easily. He wasn't even reading clinical studies on trauma methodology. Instead, when a gown received general approval from the team, he stood next to Grace so everyone could evaluate how their clothing would photograph together.

"Now put your arm around her. Hmm... I see the problem, the skirt gets pushed off center if she gets close to him." The stylist walked to the other side of the room. "Especially noticeable from this angle. Grace, move a little bit to your left."

Sophia scrutinized them. "But I'm going to need to stand very close to him. Put your arm around his waist, Grace. Let me see what that does to the silhouette of the gown."

The feast for his eyes became a feast for his senses every time he touched Grace. The scent of her each time she cuddled into his side was like rain in the desert that had been his week in the friend zone. Every gown left her shoulders and arms bare, and the feel of her skin whetted his appetite for more.

More what? A one-night stand with a woman you know will disappear the next day?

It would be a novel twist in the pattern of his life, at least.

The next gown had plenty of *more*. The skirt was full and fit for a princess, but the plunging neckline was scandalous, revealing Grace's body all the way to her navel. The V was too wide just as it was too deep. Instead of revealing her cleavage, the dress exposed the full curve of each perfect breast, modesty only barely maintained by the fabric strapping that covered the center of each breast.

Alex said nothing. He could hardly think straight. Mere

mortals didn't wear gowns like that in the real world. She looked like a movie star.

He was aware, suddenly, that Grace was looking right at him, her unique blend of worry and hope bright in her eyes. What reaction was she looking for?

"That's the one," Sophia declared.

Alex bit out the phrase the stylist had been using all morning to dismiss Grace from the room. "You can change now."

Sophia laughed. "No, she can't. I want to take a picture of you two together first. I need to see how this one photographs."

"You're not wearing that tomorrow, Sophia."

"Oh, yes I am. Every man who sees me will have the same reaction as you. You can't take your eyes off her."

He tore his gaze from Grace and rounded on her sister. "If you wear that, the deal is off. This is real life. My real life. I'm not going to introduce you to my coworkers and have them not know where to look while they're trying to eat a damned dinner with their wives."

"This is about making a statement. And that dress makes exactly the statement I want to make."

Alex knew what message that dress sent to men, because he was hearing it loud and clear. Grace looked deliberately provocative, yet she looked like a woman who was all the more powerful because she could send men's thoughts in the direction she chose—as if he needed to be provoked to want to take Grace to bed.

He gritted his teeth. "Not tomorrow. That dress says—"

"It says Oscars," Grace interrupted. "Maybe even Met Gala. But for this week, it's too much, Sophie. You're reestablishing your reputation as a smart, mature—"

"Would you quit using that word? Yo, Alex." Sophia

bumped him with her shoulder. "Stop drooling on the Armani. That's my baby sister you're staring at."

The stylist thrust a metallic silver gown between them. "I was saving the best for last, but maybe we should try it on now."

Alex and Sophia waited in frosty silence.

Grace returned to the living room in a column of silver. It covered her from a simple circle at the base of her throat to the tips of her polished toes, skimming over her body without clinging. There was something innocent about it—short sleeves, Alex realized, almost a schoolgirl look. Although the sleeves and the neckline appeared demure at first glance, they were made of silver netting that allowed the warmth of her skin to show through. She didn't look like a sexual fantasy and she didn't look like an untouchable movie star. She looked like an incredibly lovely Grace Jackson.

"That's the one," Alex said. When he felt Sophia's stare, he realized he'd said it almost reverently. He ignored Sophia.

"Isn't it perfect?" the stylist asked. "An echo of that Audrey Hepburn spirit we captured during last year's award season, but the column dress says modern and smart."

Alex didn't wait for a request to stand next to Grace. He walked up to her, tuning out the cluster of people who'd invaded his house. "You look very, very beautiful."

"Thank you."

Princess Picasso gave an order. "You two should dance. I need to see if I'll be able to move in it. What kind of music are they going to be playing, anyway?"

Grace didn't look away, so neither did he, but she answered her sister. "Some country-western bands. Pretty big names. We have a dance lesson scheduled later today."

"I know how to waltz and two-step." Alex stepped closer and picked up her hand. "Do you?"

"I waltz." They assumed the traditional position of a man and a woman in a ballroom dance, and Alex took the first step.

Grace's voice was as lovely as everything else about her. She counted to three over and over in a little nonsense melody, smiling at him, his beautiful golden girl, silver in his arms, glowing with happiness.

He realized he was smiling back.

So this is happiness. He recognized it, although it had been a very long time since he'd felt it. It was not equilibrium. There was no balance. He was absolutely at the far end of a scale, a feeling of pure pleasure unadulterated by pain—yet.

There was always pain. He knew that, but at this moment, he couldn't imagine ever feeling pain again, not with Grace in his arms.

"One, two, three. One, two, three."

"You look wonderful," the stylist said, clapping. "Sophia, what do you think?"

He and Grace had to stop, or risk looking like fools. She gave his hand a friendly squeeze as she stepped out of his arms. A *friendly* squeeze. Friends. There was pain in being friends with someone he desired so keenly.

"Two things," Sophia announced. "First, you can cancel the dance lesson. He'll do. Second, as pretty as that dress is, I don't think it's for me. Grace should wear it."

For once, Alex thought Sophia was absolutely right.

Grace was less sure. "Me? I couldn't. It's too…gorgeous."

Sophia rolled her eyes impatiently. "Do you have a dress in the suitcase for the ball? No, you do not."

"But I'm not doing the red carpet. I never do."

"That doesn't mean you can wear slacks and a beige sweater. Just take that one. It's pretty, but it's not my style. I'm getting too old for that innocent look. You want me to be more mature, remember?"

The stylist protested. "But the designer provided it for So-phia Jackson. It's a courtesy loan with the understanding it would gain some exposure."

"Tell the designer I'll owe him one next season. Let her wear the dress."

CHAPTER SEVENTEEN

THE DRESS SHONE ON ITS HANGER, WAITING
for tomorrow.

Tomorrow.

Time was running out. Tomorrow would be her last day
with Alex. He'd traded in this morning's tuxedo for green
scrubs and left for the hospital. He was covering someone's
half shift in order to have tomorrow off for the Black and
White Ball. She could tell he was nonplussed at the concept
that it might take an entire day to prepare for five minutes of
photographs, but to humor her, he'd traded shifts.

He'd left; Martina had arrived. By the time Martina and
the rest of the team had left, Alex's vodka had been poured,
declared to be an authentically Russian brand and poured
again, and the decision had been made: Sophia and Grace
would catch a red-eye back to Los Angeles after the ball.
The plan was simple: the press began covering the red carpet at six. Sophia would arrive at seven. The dinner would
be served at eight. Sophia would dance with Alex just after

nine and then the job was finished. They could strike the set, pack up and go home. *End scene.*

"Wouldn't it be easier to come back to the house and spend one more night?" Grace had asked, feeling that stone in her chest once more.

But the stylists volunteered to pick up their suitcases tomorrow after they stitched her and her sister into their dresses. It was no problem at all for them to take back the gowns and give them their suitcases and send the limo to the airport in plenty of time for a late night flight to the West Coast.

Sophia had pulled her aside and given her the real reason for the rush. "Martina says Deezee is flying in to catch the rest of South by Southwest. I'm not going to be here when he arrives. Haven't you been following his Instagram the last couple of days?"

Grace had not. She'd been out in the sun and fresh air, working shoulder to shoulder with Alex on his days off, trimming peach trees and lemons and figs. She'd worn new garden gloves to handle the cactus, and taken them off to return hugs from great-grandmas at the nursing home. After work, she'd loved watching Alex's hands as he'd whipped up omelets with the same easy dexterity that he must use to tie off a stitch at the hospital.

But they hadn't kissed.

It hadn't been for lack of desire. How many times had their laughter faded away as his gaze fell to her lips? In the silence, she would hold her breath, but he'd turn away. Every time, so far.

If they had more time…but Sophia had decided their time was up.

Grace held her phone and flipped through Deezee's public photos, full of exaggerated pouting expressions and his hands making the shape of a heart over his chest, and she'd understood the red-eye flight. They were running. Whether her sister was running from the possibility of more bad publicity or running away from temptation, Grace wasn't sure.

She only knew one thing for certain: she didn't want to go.

A pane of glass stood between Grace and the man she wanted.

It might as well have been a stone wall.

Alex had returned home from the hospital as darkness fell. Sophia had looked up from her movie and made what was, from her, a friendly overture. "You're going to gag when you hear this medical dialog. Even I can tell it's fake."

Alex had nodded, walked right past her, and headed for the shower.

For half an hour now, he'd been sitting outside in the dark, his hair shower-damp on an evening that was probably a degree too cold for it. Grace thought about bringing him a jacket, but that might make her seem too motherly. She could offer him a cup of hot coffee, but she didn't want to seem like a waitress—or even a personal assistant. She didn't want him to keep seeing her as a friend.

Grace watched him through the sliding glass door, studying the set of his shoulders. He wasn't sitting at the table, but on the edge of the patio, where it dropped off a couple of feet to the garden beyond. His dark hair almost blended into the night.

"You need to fix that."

Grace hadn't realized Sophia was next to her. Now that her sister wasn't wearing the plastic boot, she was as quiet as a cat.

"Fix what?" Grace asked.

"He needs to look like the happiest man in the world when he stands next to me in less than twenty-four hours, and he's no actor. Go find out what's bugging him. Cheer him up."

"I think we've invaded his personal space enough this week."

In the glass, she watched the reflection of Sophia as she shook her head. "Grace, you're no actress, either. You're dying to go to him. So go."

Grace knew herself. She was going to need a prop to get through this scene. She turned around to pick up her laptop from the couch. "I did make him a little going-away present. Since this is the last time we'll have any peace and quiet, I could show it to him now."

"You're going to go out in the dark to see a man and you're bringing your laptop? What did you make for him? A collage of you in that plunging dress, I hope." Sophia laughed at Grace's scowl. "Take your laptop and do your thing, sis. But trust me—whatever you've got on there isn't what that man really wants. I'm going to bed. See you in the morning."

With her laptop in one hand, Grace slid open the door with her other. Alex turned his head immediately, his profile highlighted by the light that spilled onto the patio from the living room, the handsome angles of his face defined against the black night beyond.

What a pleasure it had been this week to be able to look at him whenever she pleased. Twenty-four hours from now, she might never have that privilege again.

No, no, no…

She set the laptop on the table with a new feeling of determination. She'd give him her gift, and if it worked, she'd have a connection to him, a reason to contact him after she returned to LA.

"Do you mind if I join you?" She rubbed her arms as she strolled over to where he sat on the edge of the patio. Her gray cardigan and blue jeans were warm enough for now, but he'd been outside for a long while. "I could run back inside and grab a jacket for you."

That sounded just as motherly as she'd been afraid it would, the impression made worse by the way she was standing over him. He stopped watching her and turned back to his view of the night.

"Or I could bring you a cup of coffee?" There was the waitress vibe.

Alex gave her some kind of negative-sounding syllable.

She might as well go for broke and add *wife* to the mix. "How was your day at work?"

He stood abruptly and walked a pace into the dark.

She twisted her fingers a bit as she remained on the edge of the patio, watching him. "That bad, huh?"

He turned to look up at her. The soft light illuminated his harsh expression. "I can't talk about specific patients."

"Did somebody die, maybe?"

He shook his head, but it had to have been something almost as bad. The worst thing she'd witnessed in the emergency room had been the violent threats from Mr. Burns to his wife.

That's it. She'd seen Alex with this sharp edge to him once before, in the kitchen in the ER.

"You had to treat another woman like Mrs. Burns," she said quietly.

Alex didn't shake his head.

She passionately hated all the misery domestic violence caused. The horror was the worst for the victim, of course, but the effect rippled outward, affecting children and extended family—and the medical personnel who had to deal with the aftermath.

"I'm so sorry. I know you're imagining the best outcome for your patient." Grace felt a hot anger that Alex had to endure that emotional wringer. "At least we'll get that for real with Mr. Burns. I'm telling you, I hope he doesn't take a plea deal. I want to go to his trial. I can't wait to get called to the witness stand."

"No." In one stride, Alex came to stand below her, so intense that he grabbed her hips, his fingers firm through the denim. "I don't want you anywhere near that son of a bitch. If you get called to testify, you tell me. Immediately. Do you understand?"

"Alex." Her heart beat hard at how fiercely protective he was being. He must care for her. He must.

"Burns won't touch you. Not you." His face was inches from her stomach, his hands gripping her hips firmly, and she felt the tension in his every muscle as she set her hands on his shoulders.

She had a second moment of intuition. "It was actually Mrs. Burns again, wasn't it?"

Alex bowed his head. He pressed his forehead to her middle, a moment of intimacy that made her catch her breath. He breathed, too, one strong, swift breath, then another.

Grace clutched his shoulders, then jumped off the ledge to land in the darkness with him. She wanted to be the one to soothe him, but it was he who held her protectively, tucking her head against his shoulder, setting his cheek on her hair—and then, he very gently opened his arms, and stepped away.

She felt a little cold, a little confused. "I'm sorry the happy ending you imagined for her didn't come true."

Alex tucked his hands in the back pockets of his jeans and took another step away from the house. "Everything may still turn out okay for her. It's not that unusual to get pulled back in. Some women get away the second time. Or the third. But they still get away."

"I told you when I first met you that you were an optimist, do you remember?"

He spared her a small smile. He didn't believe her.

Grace tried again. "I'll bet Mrs. Burns was glad you were the doctor on duty. She didn't have to explain anything or try to find a way to speak to someone alone."

"One of us is an optimist, Grace. I think it's you." He kept his hands in his pockets when she wished he would hold her again.

"You don't think she was relieved you were her doctor again?"

There was a beat of silence, barely enough to make her wonder if he was going to answer her.

But he did. "I think she was embarrassed. I know my mother was, when she had to get stitches. Strong women think it shouldn't happen to them, perhaps." He shrugged, as if he hadn't just told her something momentous.

"Your mother? You lived through that as a child?" She'd thought she'd gotten all the important facts during their little interviews. He had no siblings. His parents were divorced. He and his mother had moved from Russia to America when he was fourteen.

None of that was important.

"It only turned physical that last year. There were a few years of tension before that. When the Soviet Union fell apart, so did my parents' marriage. There was an opportunity for the average person to have more say in government, but it was risky. My mother thought it was worth the risk. My father didn't. The arguments escalated every time my mother was jailed. The government was more of a threat to my mother than my father was, but looking back, I think we were escaping both."

When Grace had written down the facts of his youth in her

notebook, she'd admired his ability to complete high school in the usual four years despite knowing almost no English the first year.

She'd admired the wrong thing.

"Clark Kent." She sighed the words into the night.

He automatically moved to push up his glasses, but he wasn't wearing them, so he dropped his hand and frowned at her instead.

"It was what I thought when I first saw you. You weren't in awe of my sister. You weren't afraid of Mr. Burns. You even came to the hotel so I wouldn't be intimidated by the police into…into taking an unnecessary risk. Oh, Alex. Thank you."

She took a step toward him. She was dying to touch him. He'd just held her so protectively, but now he seemed so far away.

"Clark Kent isn't far off, is it? You step in to help a lot of people. I am sorry that you're so good at identifying spouse abuse because you witnessed it, though."

"All ER doctors are trained to look for the signs." He put his boot on the ledge and stepped back up to the patio. He turned and offered her his hand to give her a boost up, as well, then smoothly slipped his hand free of hers.

"It must bring up bad memories."

He was silent.

"What do you usually do, when you're home alone after a bad shift?"

"Brood for a little longer, maybe. You snapped me out of it sooner. Thanks."

Something was off here. He was too calm. Too fully recovered when she could still feel where his fingers had dug into the denim waistband of her jeans.

He nodded toward her laptop. "Did you come out here to work?"

She had little choice but to go along with the change of subject. Her crutch had become his. She couldn't drag him back out into the dark.

"It's sort of a thank-you gift for this week." She opened the computer's lid and waited as the screen, too bright in the dark, displayed the first page of her project. "Do you remember that first day when we bought the rocks?"

The day you kissed me like I was the oxygen you needed to breathe?

But there was no sign of that emotion now. No more fierce protectiveness, either. Just...friendliness. Didn't Superman always turn a car right-side up and then fly off alone?

"The manager gave you a couple of extra bags of gravel when he found out what they were for. It started me thinking. If you set up a nonprofit for your landscaping projects, you'd make it easier for a business like that to donate supplies. This is just some brainstorming, but I looked into it, and setting up a nonprofit wouldn't be that complicated."

"Just brainstorming?" He sank into the chair, eyes on the screen as she scrolled down to the table of contents.

"There are grants you'd be eligible for, too. I listed some of them here."

He took over, paging through the mission statement she'd composed, the links to the legal requirements, the proposals she'd written for initial and future workflow. He said nothing until he'd scrolled all the way to the appendix, where she'd created sample spreadsheets he could use for tracking finances and labor.

"This was all inspired by a free bag of rocks?"

"The manager really liked what you were doing. So did I."

Alex nodded, but that harshness had returned to his expression—something about the set of his jaw. "This is what you were doing all those evenings you supposedly weren't working. This is an entire business plan, Grace. We pay people at the hospital to put together grant proposals that aren't as complete as this."

"It's not a big deal," she said, although she wasn't sure why she felt defensive. "I've never had so much free time. You made sure I didn't work more than nine hours a day, and Sophia stayed in one place for an entire week. This wasn't hard to do."

He shut the lid to the laptop and stood, his physical presence both familiar and intimidating at once. "This takes skill. Don't devalue yourself. Ever."

She fought a shiver. "You keep saying things like that. Like I'm not easily replaced, and I shouldn't let anyone tell me I am. Who said that? Sophia? Martina?"

"You did."

She froze.

Then his calm words started an avalanche of words in her mind. *I'm just doing my job. Why would anyone want to know about me? She could hire a hundred different people to be her assistant.*

Grace felt as light-headed as she did when she skipped a meal. He touched her as he had in the hotel, a firm hand on her upper arm, lending her balance, the touch of a doctor.

His voice was more intimate. "If you could see what I see when I look at you… I want you to believe in yourself. I want to be able to imagine you confident. Please. Be happy."

The unspoken words were loud enough: *when you're gone.* She felt another chill that had nothing to do with the cool night. *I want to imagine you confident when you're gone. Be happy when you're gone.*

He couldn't let her go, never to be seen again. Ten minutes ago, he'd pressed his face into her middle, swearing no harm would come to her. He cared about her.

"I don't want you to imagine me at all. I'm not your patient. We can stay in touch." Grace was no heroine in a movie, but she'd learned this week that she was more courageous than she'd given herself credit for. She dared to touch him, placing one palm on his hard chest, not caring if he could feel the tremor in her hand.

"How long before you go?" The bass in his voice resonated through the palm of her hand.

"We leave for the airport right after you dance with Sophia."

He winced. For one second, one precious second, she saw that the loss of her meant so much to him that it caused him pain. The next second, his expression was polite, controlled. That poker face was in place, the one he hadn't been using when it was just the two of them.

"The problem is Deezee," she said. "He's coming to Austin, so Sophia is getting out. She's scared to run into him."

His eyes narrowed. "Are you?"

She knew with certainty that if she said *yes*, he would keep her by his side until she felt safe, but she couldn't lie. "Not anymore. There's nothing Deezee can do to hurt me."

"He could come between you and your sister again."

"He can only do that if Sophia lets him. And if she does, I'll be okay without her. I'll still love her, even if she makes a dumb choice."

His scrutiny gave way to a ghost of a smile. "I hope it never comes to that. You and your sister belong together." He let go of her arm and turned toward the house.

He was leaving. She'd just told him this was their last night together, and he was leaving. They were friends, nothing more. Maybe not even that much.

"Wait." Beating down a sense of panic, she scrambled to remember her plan. Her prop. Her crutch—the nonprofit information—she opened the laptop again. "I need your email address. I'll send the business plan to you. And then…

and then you could appoint me to the board. There only needs to be three of us. I'll be your secretary. Between the phone and email, it would be no problem at all for me to do the bookkeeping and get grant applications ready, even when I'm out of state."

And I'll have an excuse to call you when I want to hear your voice.

"No."

She felt all the air go out of her chest. Out of her world.

"I'm sorry, Grace, but no. I don't want to continue on that way. Not being together, but not falling completely out of touch, just in case our paths cross again."

Tears stung her eyes and clogged her throat. He didn't want to stay in touch with her, not at all. They weren't really friends.

"It's what you were thinking, wasn't it? Maybe you'll be back next year for South-by. Maybe your sister will come back to film a sequel to whatever she filmed here last September. Maybe..." He set his hands on his hips and looked out at the dark garden, shaking that perfectly cut hair back from his perfectly blue eyes. "Maybe Burns will go to trial, and we'll catch dinner while you're in town. I don't do that, Grace. I can't be on call for you. I'm not that man."

"Then what man are you?"

"Not the kind that dates the personal assistant of a movie star."

That sounded so final. She *was* the sister of a movie star. She couldn't change that. "I thought you and Sophia were teasing each other, mostly. Do you really not like her?"

Do you hate my sister the way Deezee hates me?

She had his attention, at least. He looked from the dark back to her, mildly surprised. "I've got a newfound respect for her this week, actually. She's chosen a difficult career, but she's loyal to you. That's the most important thing."

Wrong. Having more time with you is the most important thing.
But she wasn't quite enough of a superhero to say such a thing.

"So if it's not the movie star, then it's me. The girl with
no friends. The girl who's afraid to say her sister's name in
public. I know that's not normal."

But he was shaking his head. "I'm no judge of normal.
You and your sister were together during the toughest time
of your life, and now you're never apart. My mother and I
were together during the toughest time of our lives, and we
hardly see each other. Which of us is normal, Grace? You
get your stability from another human being, at least. I spend
my time with rocks."

"You spend your time making beautiful gardens for people."

"Ah, Grace. *Milost'*."

He touched her, smoothing his hand over her hair. She
couldn't mock herself for being so hyperaware as he touched
her hair, for she felt it as acutely as if he'd slid his hand over
her breast.

He's going to kiss me.

His gaze moved from her hair to her mouth, but he didn't
lean in, didn't give in, to what she knew he wanted. She
waited, anticipating, but his look of want was replaced by
that poker face once more.

"We should get some sleep," he said, dropping his hand
to his side, all business now. "What time in the morning are
the first people—"

She silenced him with her kiss, her mouth, desperate to
erase that neutral expression and snap that calm control. His
lips were warm and surprisingly soft and seriously strong. It
was so wonderful, such a relief to be kissing the man she'd
been so attuned to all week, that it took her long, blissful
moments before she realized that while he was kissing her
back, he wasn't taking over. He wasn't letting the kiss take

over, either. He allowed nothing to burn out of control—it was nothing like that kiss by the truck.

She became aware of this as she became aware that she was nearly on her toes, pressed against him, her soft chest against his harder one, her hands once more clutching his shoulders.

His hands weren't on her.

She ended the kiss and stood solidly on her feet once more.

"I thought… I thought I meant more to you." Grace knew, somewhere in her objective mind, that she ought to feel embarrassed. But Alex was so calm, so unaffected, that she felt a little bitter. "You said everything you did this week was to help me. You said you had my back."

"I'm still backing you up. I'll be spending all day tomorrow backing you up."

"Until I get on that plane. Then that's it, isn't it?"

Her heart broke as he nodded.

The bitterness became huge. "I didn't realize your friendship had an expiration date."

"I always knew you were leaving in a week. You knew it, too, Grace. That's why we never let anything go too far."

"We didn't? *We?* Did you really think I didn't want to kiss you every single day?" Tears stung her eyes, born of embarrassment that he hadn't been swept away by her kiss—or perhaps the tears were simply because it hurt to hear him say he'd never planned to see her after this week. Or perhaps it was worse than that.

Perhaps she was in love.

Tears fell. The man she loved was going to walk out of her life.

How puny all her wishes this week had been, wasted on wanting to stay away from LA, wasted on wanting a dumb DJ to leave her alone, as if geography and her sister's affairs mattered as much as Alex. She loved him, but he was leaving her.

I wish you loved me, too.

Alex pushed her hair away from her face, his warm hand lingering on her cheek. "You started this week by saying it was a mistake when we kissed. I thought you were being smart. We won't miss what we've never had."

"But we don't have to miss each other. I can visit you here. You can fly out to California."

"For what? To spend a day or two together?" His hand stayed gentle but the look in his eyes turned almost angry. "Some sex, a few dinners. A long weekend here, a holiday there. It's not enough, Grace. It's going to be hell watching you disappear tomorrow. Don't ask me to live through a dozen more disappearances in the future. I meant it when I said I'm not that man."

"Then I don't know what to do," she said, closing her eyes against the intensity in his, "because you're the only man for me."

The silence was electric, then his hand on her cheek was cupping the back of her head instead, pulling her close as he kissed her, hungry this time. Starving. His arm came around her as he opened her mouth with his own, and the slide of his tongue made her whimper with pleasure. He was delicious. He kissed her as if *she* were delicious, and she felt herself melting with each slow, strong taste. She held on to his arms, felt his muscles bunching as he slid his hand over her backside, lifting her higher against his hard body. The intimacy of their kiss, the sure touch of his hands—everything between them was so gloriously hot in the cold night.

Then he tore his mouth away, and she was left dizzy and disoriented once more, clinging to his arms. He was breathing as hard as she was, uneven, uncontrolled. Still hungry.

"That was not a mistake," she panted.

"It was for me."

Alex let her go, and disappeared into his own house.

CHAPTER EIGHTEEN

ALEX LAY ON HIS COUCH, STARING INTO THE dark, obsessed with the woman in his bed.

He should never have kissed Grace. She felt like forever in his arms; she was leaving. In hours.

Some last scrap of self-preservation had kicked in, and he'd broken off that kiss before it had turned into more. He'd headed straight for his bedroom—alone—to pitch his jeans and shirt into the laundry basket and pull on a pair of loose track pants, and to hell with a shirt. Then he'd settled in for one last night on this couch as if he weren't aware that Grace Jackson was still on his back porch, staring at her laptop with a look of misery on her beautiful face.

It was cold out there. He'd been just about to throw off his blanket and bring it out to her when she'd come in and headed straight for the bedroom herself.

The house was silent now. Dark. It was impossible not to relive the kiss that had guaranteed that this last night would be just like the first: sleepless and full of sexual frustration.

He threw off the blanket and headed for the kitchen. The refrigerator light blinded him. The cold milk chilled him to the bone, but he drank it anyway, all of it, straight from the carton, wishing it would numb his brain.

Grace Jackson. One week with her and his life would never be the same. And what did she want from him? To be her pen pal. They'd play at setting up a nonprofit and send each other e-mails.

He tossed the carton onto the counter in disgust.

"I can't sleep, either."

Grace's voice was gentle behind him. He knew how she'd look if he turned around. Barefooted. White pajamas. Irresistible.

He turned around, anyway.

You look very, very beautiful.

The thick satin wasn't as modest as she probably thought it was. It was not sheer, but it molded every curve, from the roundness of her shoulder to the peak of her breast. The impact she had on him was so much more than body parts. She was a complete person, not merely luscious but full of life. She was anxious only in her desire to help others, generous with her time and determined to be optimistic, with hope in her brown eyes and a halo when light touched her hair. She was Grace—and he knew, in the low glow of the kitchen clock, he was in love with her.

She opened her palm and offered him a USB flash drive. "It's got the business plan on it. Even if I'm not part of the project, you still might want to use it."

He didn't move. He couldn't, because the only move possible was to crush her in his arms, to claim her as his own, as if tomorrow wouldn't come and she wouldn't fly a thousand miles away.

His eyes were too well adjusted. He could see the hurt on her face when he didn't reach for the small stick.

She closed her fist around it—and stepped closer to him.

"That first kiss, at the barbecue place, that was the best kiss of my life. When you never kissed me again, I thought it must not have been that amazing to you. Maybe you just weren't that into me. But then tonight…" She let her fingers trail along his waistband as she had that first night, her touch less tentative now. "Out there on the patio, you didn't kiss me like a man who's not that into me."

His stomach contracted, his arousal hardened, and he fought to remember that the woman he loved was only passing through. She'd be gone tomorrow.

I can't. She'd said that the first night. *I can't, I can't.* Then she'd run away. Tonight, she smoothed her empty hand up his chest.

He had nowhere to run.

"While I was packing, I told myself maybe tonight was only physical. Maybe you and I just happen to be physically compatible. You kissed me tonight like you wanted to take me to bed. A lot of guys would take what a willing woman offered."

While she was packing. She'd thought through these possibilities while she was packing. To leave him.

Grace slid her hand over his shoulder, then erased the last of the distance between them by putting both arms around his neck. The move was as confident as a siren's, but the look in her eyes was too vulnerable, as if she thought he might possibly be able to resist the dark and the satin and the sincerity.

He could not. His hands circled her waist, sliding the satin up so his palms warmed her skin. No more, just that.

She shook back her dark gold hair. "If you only wanted

sex, you could have taken me to bed every night this week. You know I would have gone willingly."

Never had he been so tempted in his life. He pushed himself away and turned his back on her, then drove a hand through his own hair.

"But you didn't." She sounded sad, like a woman who'd been rejected. Damn it, he felt guilty for not scooping her up and throwing her on his bed.

It's not you, it's me.

"So I think you aren't that kind of guy. I think you want an emotional connection before you take a woman to bed. But you know what? We do have an emotional connection. So there I was, folding my clothes and putting them in my suitcase, and I thought about Mrs. Burns."

Surprised, he turned around.

"You told me you rarely see the same patient twice. Until tonight, I hadn't realized that was a good thing for you. No one goes to the ER because they are well and happy. If you see them again, it's bad. Like Mrs. Burns. Of course you never want to see people again. It's so much better to assume they are doing fine without you. It gives you peace of mind when they don't return."

She paused to take a breath. He was already holding his.

"That's your life, isn't it? People come in. You help them. They leave."

He exhaled, a sharp hiss of a sound because she'd cut right down to the problem with surgical precision.

"And now I'm leaving tomorrow, too." She took his hand and pressed the plastic stick into his palm. "My phone number is on that flash drive. Call me."

Not pen pals, then, but phone-a-friends. He would still be burning for her, while she would still be living her sister's life in LA or New York or Tunisia or any of the places she'd told him about this week.

When he didn't close his fist around the stick, she closed his fingers over it herself. She had tears in her eyes.

Alex hated being the one who'd put those tears in her eyes. The sooner he could make her understand, the sooner she would resume her life without him. "You'll be fine without me. I thought you needed me to slay a few dragons for you this week. You didn't. You've got everything it takes to slay those dragons yourself. You always did."

"What dragons?"

He had to shake his head at his own mistaken assumptions. "Your sister seemed manipulative. You were so anxious to avoid going back to California. I jumped to conclusions, but now I've seen how you can hold your own. More than that. You are very good at your job. You never needed me."

"I did need you. I needed a friend desperately. I still do."

"You need a man who doesn't give a damn about some idiot DJ in Los Angeles to wear a tux tomorrow. When you leave, you're going to be fine. You're a very strong person."

"You're determined to imagine me living a good life without you, aren't you?" She gripped his fist in both of her hands. "Don't you dare imagine that."

There was nothing fragile or delicate in her touch. It was as if his compliments had made her furious.

"It won't be true. I'm going to be missing you, Alex, every day. That's not a pleasant way to live. I'm going to be imagining you building gardens all alone, and I'm going to wonder if you wished you had my help. But the worst thing of all, the thing that's really going to leave me gutted, is that I'm going to wonder if each day was the day that you saw Mrs. Burns a third time. I'm going to wonder if you are sitting alone on your patio with no one to talk to."

Her anger didn't stop her tears from falling. Each one hurt as if it were his own. He'd messed everything up so badly, falling hard for a woman who hadn't had the good sense to see that he wasn't the right man for her.

"I'm sorry," she said, subdued. "It's not normal to never see people again, and it breaks my heart to know you've trained yourself to live as though it is. If a long-distance lover is too unstable for you, I could still be your friend. I want you to see what it's like to have someone you can call. So call me."

She squeezed his fist once more, pressing the hard stick more deeply into his palm, and then she let go and began backing away. "Just call me, if you can. If you want to. I want you to. Good night."

She disappeared down the hall, an angel gone in a flash of white.

No.

He couldn't let it end this way. She was leaving—didn't the pain always come?—but she wasn't going to disappear entirely. She understood him and the reasons he craved stability, and she was offering him as much as she thought he could handle. Having a friend to call after a hard, painful day would be a new experience for him. Yes, she was leaving, but she was throwing him this one thread, this one connection. It would be a giant step outside his comfort zone, but she thought he could do it.

No, she *needed* him to do it. If he didn't call her, she'd be unhappy. He was that important to her. He mattered to her, and the sweetness of it pierced his heart. It would hurt him to hear her voice and have nothing else, but if it would hurt her more not to have any connection, then he'd do it. For her, he could do anything, because he loved her.

He strode into his own bedroom. She was standing by the bed, her open suitcase an ominous sight on the comforter.

"Grace." He captured her face in his hands. "Yes, I will call you. Every damned day that you're gone, I'll call you."

"Every day?" He'd startled her, but the hope was clear in her eyes.

"I don't know how to do this, but I'll find a way."

"How to talk every day? I'll do all the talking, if you don't know what to say. I would love to talk to you every day."

"If we can only be friends on the phone, then I'll take it, but Grace, I am in love with you. I have been since you shoved your arm in that kitchen door, I think, so determined to make me listen. I don't know how to live with part of you, when what I want is all of you, but I'll figure it out."

Because he was in love with her, he had to kiss her, a hard kiss—a swift kiss, because more words needed to be said as he kept her precious face in his hands. "You were right then, and you were right tonight. I let go of too many people, my patients, my friends, even my mother, when they didn't need me. You may not need me, Grace, but I need you. It's going to hurt like hell when we're apart, but for once in my life, I'm keeping someone I love."

"I don't want to settle for friends on the phone, either. I love you, too, Alex."

There were tears in her eyes again, but this time, his heart didn't hurt when they fell. He wiped them away with his thumbs.

"I have to leave tomorrow, but I'll come back. As soon as I possibly can, I'll be back, Alex. I promise."

God, she loved him. He wanted to hear her say it again, but she was kissing him, and it felt too perfect to stop. Her touch at his waist was bold. She slid her hand into his waistband and used it to pull him with her as she lowered herself onto the bed, stretching out sideways beside the hated suit-case. He followed, sheer desire threatening to obliterate every other thought. Her hair, her skin, her hands on his body—the effort it took to get back up from the bed was monstrous.

Grace sat up, confused. "You don't want…"

Alex almost laughed. "I've never wanted anything more." He picked up her suitcase and set it on the floor, went to the bedroom door and shut it firmly. Then he stood over Grace a moment, taking in her beauty.

He scooped his arms around her and moved her with him to the center of the bed. "Come here, beautiful."

"Oh," Grace said, a little sound of relief as she slid one satin-clad leg over his. "You said it was hard to miss what you'd never had, so I thought for a moment that maybe you didn't want to have this, so you wouldn't miss it tomorrow."

It was their first time to be horizontal together, the first time she could nuzzle her face into the side of his neck.

"I'm going to miss you, anyway," he said, his voice rough with the truth of it. Their clothes allowed him to keep some shred of control as he rolled onto his back and lifted her to lie atop him. Her knees slid to either side of his hips, the first time of countless times to come. He gritted his teeth against the sharp spike of desire, and ignored the looming pain of tomorrow.

The first time of countless times. He'd find a way to make that true.

Grace sat up, straddling him, unbuttoning the first white button. "Then I guess we should find out exactly what we'll be missing."

The chauffeur opened the limousine door.

Grace stayed on the bench seat, out of the way of the open door and the paparazzi's cameras. Alex stepped out, looking less like Clark Kent and more like James Bond as he popped his cuffs and buttoned his jacket. Then he reached a hand into the limousine to assist Sophia Jackson onto the red carpet.

Her sister had decided to wear white at the last minute. Grace leaned forward to give the train of the gown a flip as Sophia exited the limo, so she and Alex looked perfect as they walked up the first shallow steps to the photographer's area.

The chauffeur handed Grace out. She carried her purse and Sophia's, and walked quietly along the edge of the carpet, the silent signal to the organizers that she was an assistant, not to be photographed or fussed over despite her silver designer dress and her obviously professional hair and makeup.

Sophia said something to Alex, then started walking toward Grace. Grace actually turned to see who might be behind her. "What are you doing, Sophie?"

"We've never done pictures as sisters. Don't protest. That silver dress is the bomb."

For the first time, Grace found herself arm in arm with her sister, strolling to the center of the red carpet, smiling at the barrage of camera flashes. The rhythm of it came naturally after watching Sophia do it for years—look left, center, right, pausing for just enough seconds that it felt awkward—then they turned toward the stairs, and Alex escorted them with one sister on each arm.

That hadn't been the plan. Grace hoped Sophia knew what she was doing. This little threesome would only raise speculation. Which sister was Alex escorting?

Their happy family group turned back into a twosome as Alex and Sophia took their places at a reserved table at the front of the ballroom. Grace, like the good personal assistant she was, slipped a white purse to her sister. "Your cell phone and lipstick are in there, safety pins and bobby pins."

As she turned to leave, Sophia caught her hand. "Thanks, Grace. You really are the best."

Well, okay. That seemed a little intense for a few pins, but Grace smiled and then concentrated on winding her way to the very back of the ballroom. Her dress was too valuable to let it get caught or stepped on, so she was absorbed in avoiding chairs, sidestepping waiters with their heavy trays, turning sideways to pass other women in gowns, and dodging Deezee Kalm as he came barreling past her, running toward the front of the room.

Deezee Kalm!

Grace whirled around and started fighting her way back to her sister's table. The going was harder, because everyone was pushing back their chairs and standing to see what was happening. Deezee made it easier for them by leaping onto the center of her sister's dinner table, planting his high-top sneakers right where the salads and rolls sat, a filthy, asinine, attention-getting move.

"Excuse me," Grace said over and over, pushing her way to her sister. Her dress would have to survive the crush. "Excuse me."

Grace broke through the crowd as Deezee dropped dramatically to one knee. Since he was on the table, he was still above Sophia, not exactly the humble pose of a man about to propose. Alex had Sophia tucked behind his back protectively, but Sophia looked ecstatic, positively glowing with excitement.

"Run away with me." Deezee held out his hand, more of a demand than a plea. "Right now, baby. Let's go. I've got a private jet waiting. Just you and me on a tropical island, away from all this crap."

Sophia sidestepped Alex and placed her hand in Deezee's. "You want to marry me right now?"

"Sure, girl. Let's go crazy."

"That was crazy." Grace looked out the limousine window at the Austin city lights.

Alex held her hand. "Are you okay?"

"I suppose so. I'm not really hurt. Sophie just wants to be happy. I'm just afraid that Deezee isn't the man who is really going to make her happy."

"We could be wrong."

Grace put her head on Alex's shoulder. "Martina set it up yesterday. I should have known there was a reason Sophie switched to that white gown. I know this isn't important, but I always assumed I'd be her maid of honor. I guess that's not going to happen."

Alex dropped a kiss on her very fancy hair. "Maybe that's why she wanted those photos with you tonight. She knew she was in her wedding gown."

"And this is my bridesmaid's dress?" Grace sat up and turned to face Alex. "If you're trying to make me feel better, you're succeeding."

She wanted to talk to him about everything, but the limousine was moving toward the airport, and her time was short. She took her cell phone out of her silver purse, her prop for this talk. "I have something to show you. It's Sophia's boarding pass to get on the plane tonight."

Alex watched her as she swiped her finger over the screen.

"But here's mine. It's cancelled. I'm not going to back to LA tonight."

Alex looked truly stunned.

"Some woman named Jackson was supposed to spend a week making love to her new man in Texas, so I thought it might as well be me. I told Sophia today I was taking some long overdue vacation days."

Alex started to laugh as he reached into his inner jacket pocket and pulled out his cell phone. "Let me show you something. This is my boarding pass. I decided if I couldn't stand to be apart from you, then I ought to stay with you. I was going to be on your flight to LA tonight. I arranged with the other doctors to take my long overdue vacation."

"Oh, my gosh. What should we do?"

Alex raised one eyebrow at her. "We should take a vacation."

Grace wanted to cuddle that digital boarding pass on his cell phone to her chest like the treasure it was. It gave her courage. "I've been thinking more long-term. When Sophia gets back from her trip, I told her I'd help her interview new assistants. I'm ready to live my own life."

Alex said nothing.

Grace held on to her courage. "Conventional wisdom says I should take some time to adjust. I should get a job and think only about myself for a while."

"You're probably right about that."

It was a terribly neutral answer, but Alex was watching her closely, intently listening to every word she had to say. He wasn't neutral at all when it came to her.

There was no time like the present—no time like a private limo ride in a silver gown to proposition a man in a tuxedo.

"But here's what I really want to do, in my heart. I'm good at being a couple. I like living with someone else. It's too much, too soon, everyone will say, but I'm afraid I'm going to miss seeing your face. I love being around you. I love having you for a friend. I don't want to be clingy or dependent, but I want to live with you." She came to a stop, choked up by emotion and afraid she was babbling.

Alex looked so terribly serious as he picked up her hand.

"When it comes to living together, I'm afraid that all I can do is offer you all or nothing."

"Oh." Grace could feel her heart pounding hard. She didn't know quite what he meant.

"I can love you like that, but it would have to be for keeps. I couldn't handle living together for a few weeks or a few months or a few years, only to have you disappear. It would have to be forever, Grace."

"I can do forever." But she looked at him cautiously, unsure of his mood. He was so very grave.

"Good, because that's the kind of man I am." Then he reached in the pocket of his jacket once more, and her heart tripped in a seriously happy dance of anticipation. "I bought something today. I was prepared to carry it with me until you were sure of what you wanted, no matter how long that took. I should have known you already had a plan. The best plan. The only plan for us."

"Oh, Alex. Are we really going to do this?"

He pulled out a diamond ring and smiled at her, the most intimate, perfect smile a man has ever given a woman.

"Yes, Grace. We're really going to do this. Together. Forever."

★ ★ ★ ★ ★

HARLEQUIN®

SPECIAL EDITION

Life, Love & Family

Save **$1.00**

on the purchase of ANY
Harlequin® Special Edition book.

Redeemable at participating Walmart
outlets in the U.S. and Canada only.

Save $1.00

on the purchase of any Harlequin® Special Edition book.

Coupon valid until May 31, 2018.
Redeemable at participating Walmart outlets in the U.S. and Canada only.
Limit one coupon per customer.

52615577

5 65373 00076 2 **(8100)0 12348**